# CHICKEN 65

## HUGH O'NEIL
## GALLAGHER

ISBN: 978-0-9964625-1-8

Art direction by Hugh O'Neil Gallagher

Design by May Phan

www.chicken65book.com

For DM

bros before prose

Is he not sacred, even to the gods,
the wandering man...

Homer

**The more I lounge around South East Asia I think I get where the Buddhists are coming from.** There's something about the mud, heat, rain and rivers here. It all wallows together, swallowing plans like some lumbering animal. Slim percentages of what you want done here will ever happen as planned. The jungle has something to do with it, all those branches and roots and moist deadly soil, monsoon muds and rains, the slumbering growth of slowly ferocious bush thwarting all linear motion. What the jungle doesn't take is slayed by heat. It's hard to imagine until you're set loose in it, trying to do things and get places, while dazzling sun slams down like a trashcan lid in the face. The heavy viscous syrup of heat here presses down on you, dissolving days into sleep until you wake up wondering where it all went to find the first whiskeys being poured and there goes the night.

They say life is cheap here, but I think it's just taken in bulk, so there's massive discounts. People just drop. Smashed up in bus wrecks, swallowed by sink holes, lost in collapsing third rate architecture, invaded silently by the wretched plethora of diseases swirling through soil, water, sea and air or claimed by a staggering rate of suicide. That happens so much amidst the foreign population that there's entire web sites like *www.flatinpattaya.com*, tracking their leaps from high rise condos that line the beach. But it's not just forlorn foreigners. Death in Thailand flickers everywhere, the native departed honored in candle laden spirit houses that dot the landscape. Shrines in Thai bars show photos of former workers and patrons. Honored daily, loaded with food offerings and fresh incense at the opening of business, the spirits of the dead are never far. Life is lighter here because of it, reminding us that we won't be around forever.

Then there's the karma thing. Back home the system is more solid, linking cause to effect pretty apparently. Out here things just happen. Or maybe it's just that cause and effects get all jungled up and melted in heat, splayed out in patterns nobody ever really unravels. Life only makes sense by being Buddhist about it all, mumbling something about karma while kids are born with half a spine and a spinning motorcycle wheel from a traffic wreck flies half a block to smash your date dead while walking out of dinner. People don't look for reasons (Like more comprehensive rural hospital systems or inspection regulations on all motorcycle taxis) because that would take lots of work. And lots of work in Thailand is hard to do. Part of that is the heat. Don't forget the heat. The other is the inertia of corruption that any major effort in this part of the world slimes into. What's more is that Thais really don't want to be bothered with that shit. They're pretty good with things working kind of alright most of the time. Karma helps them shrug shit off instead of lean into it. From high tragedy to slightly skewed weekend plans, it's always just karma. Obscure numbers being called in by ever revolving interdimensional orbs of debt and payback, spinning through endless deaths and rebirths.

Supposedly, one day enlightenment will dawn and we'll cross "get born" off the To Do list. Till then, solace as we swirl through these parts chased by past life karma comes from Buddhism. I don't claim to be a scholar. My understanding of the religion boils down to highly ritualistic IDGAF with deep historical roots, run by bald guys who don't wear shoes. But even that's enough. If you let their world view rub off on you, life is better out here. Buddhists reminds you not to get too attached to anything—not your plans, your dreams, even your life, and definitely not the girl in your lap drinking tequila shots at Crazy Place at three in the morning.

*"I like girls who leave the price tag on the sole!"*

My friend shouted over blasting music, that soul bludgeoning digital stuff America produces like war. His grin flashed through strobe lights. Beard, stomach, and beer: that is Monteblan. He pointed out a slim thing on stage. She had a price sticker for her shoes still stuck on the bottom. I didn't see it for a moment and thought Monteblan liked the ones that left a price tag on your soul. Which is pretty much all of them in Crazy Place. The name fits. Lots of spots in Bangkok have titles that don't match what happens inside. I've been to The Swan several times but haven't seen a bird. Never found a cactus in the Cactus Bar, Country Road is in the middle of the city and Heaven is far from it. But Crazy Place is pretty much just that.

Thai girls are dancing totally naked, or walking around equally nude in your midst. Lights are flashing, mirrors are shining, music roars and liquor runs silly. The floor is sticky and there's two of them. Stairs are shaky but the elevator is solid. Time it right and you'll ride up packed in with five naked Thai girls. One slipped into Monteblan's lap now for an overpriced shot. Ferociously gorgeous. Real air bender. Slamming tequila in the nude, she slipped away laughing. Monteblan picked up the bill. The shift changed and new girls materialized on stage. My friend sat back laughing at it all.

"Dude, come on! You really want to leave all this?"

I sipped my beer, reflecting on the year. My plans of starting a design career in Bangkok had met with the fate of most plans in Thailand. This lead to that, that lead to nowhere, then something lead to someone which all added up to whatever. Sprinkled with a liberal layer of pointlessly fantastic sex, the year wasn't a total loss. And I had taken the thing half seriously from the jump. Most of my life has been in Manhattan. But years back, I had traded New York City for Portland lured by some obscure value called "quality of life." According to every arts and leisure section across the nation, Portland has lot of it. With that comes lots of rain. Portland leads the world in downpour. Plus no sun. Then more rain. It's not bad at first, but one day you're crying and smearing shit on the wall and you don't know why.

Two years in I was done. Set the controls for the heart of the sun. Found a cut rate flight leaving LA for Bangkok and pounced on it. Packing my laptop, I put a few freelance clients in my back pocket and flew. My plan was travelling through fascinating, exotic lands and experiencing a vast potpourri of cultural offerings. If my plane hadn't landed in Bangkok, that might have happened. Instead, I drank and screwed for a year.

Bangkok swallowed me whole. Party town like you wouldn't believe. Chicks flying around on motorcycles, bars in the streets, drinking till dawn, dance clubs everywhere, pools halls in between, and a trippy sing-song language tying it all together. Quality of Life here was debatable, but Quantity of Life was through the roof. Never had I seen a place with so much happening from so many different directions. Starved for city living after my rainy residence in pleasant Portland, I threw down. Landing a condo with a pool at half the price I'd pay for a room in New York, I plugged in the laptop and picked up with my US clients.

For a lovely minute I found heaven. What stalled this personal renaissance was the fact that every woman in the Western Hemisphere hates guys who live in Thailand. Lots of them were client account directors. They didn't like where I landed, and made that fact plain, in passive aggressive corporate underhanded ways. At first, phone meetings started with: "So... Rich is on the line, he's working with us from, uh, *Thailand*". This was pronounced with a slight pause and dubious intonation that did the same as saying "So... Rich is on the line, he's working for us from under a dirty pile of third world prostitutes."

The tone must have spread to men in the department, who distanced themselves from "Thailand guy" to stay on the good side of femme heavy HR. Within three months those annoying phone meeting introduction had finished. That's because the phone meetings had finished. LA, Chicago, and NYC clients who didn't think twice of me working remotely from the gloom of Portland had quietly faded away. I looked into Thai work, but there's a tricky dance of visa laws that pretty much make it impossible unless you launch a business. I'm no CEO, so at years end I was wrapping up. Folding my dream of being a dashing expatriate designer, I was looking through flight prices home when Monteblan showed up out of nowhere.

That's how my friend always shows up. He emerges from some mystifying place I have named "The Mists of Monteblan." This distant realm is impossible to penetrate. For months on end, they claim him entirely. Emails are unanswered, phone calls are pointless, and you almost forget he's your friend until a large man with a beard suddenly appears, ready to party. With him I've partied lots. Up and down Manhattan too much to recall, briefly in Portland (which Monteblan didn't like much) and in our younger, flowing bro years, annual trips all over the map. Honduras, Panama, Venezuela, Berlin, Vegas and Greece had all yielded epic levels of debauch, dismay, and recovery. We had never hit Asia, but apparently that was happening now. My friend had a wedding in Tokyo and pulled three days from his layover to party with me in Bangkok. This was announced via text message sent at Don Mueang airport, followed by another from a taxi flying down a Bangkok expressway. Which is how the Mists of Monteblan part: suddenly, revealing man with beer in striking clarity. On the back end of a bust ass year, half way around the planet from anybody I used to bullshit with, Monteblan's arrival was a thrilling development for yours truly. We started drinking upon his arrival, and ended up at Crazy Place.

Monteblan just had that chick on his lap for laughs. He was the happiest almost married man I have met in my life. I was solid being single, so we balanced out well. Leaving the girls, we turned left and walked up the road to one of those British pubs you find out here all red carpet and hunting horns on the wall, playing Bee Gees and pouring cold, blessed beers to beat the streets of slaying heat.

We slid into a booth, ordering beers and Monteblan asked for a menu. His slow brown eyes were already working the room looking for specials and deals. But in a British pub it's best to keep things simple. Bring on some bangers and mash. Past that you're pushing luck. These people are perfectly capable of conquering the world, but really never conquered the kitchen. They probably took on the planet looking for decent take out. I took this up with Monteblan.

"I listened to a lecture once by a drunk Jamaican in a Hell's Kitchen bar. He thought the whole history of civilization was people who didn't have flavor conquering people who did."

Lost in his menu, Monteblan merely nodded as the owner approached us. Gold frame glasses, eyes owl large, the elderly British gentleman smiled politely for our order.

"How's the chicken?" Monteblan asked.

Two rough looking, tattooed Brits drinking at the table nearby went silent. Pudgy patrons at the bar turned slowly, looking at us. Aside from the Bee Gees asking how deep somebody's love was, the pub went quiet.

"Oh." The owner looked at us, surprised. "You're here for the chicken?"

One of the rough Brits glared at us. "They ain't with the chicken."

"Well if they ask they are," the elderly bartender said nervously. "You know the rule, lads."

The rough Brit was incensed. Black eyes blazed. Tattooed arms flexed from his tank top. I thought he would throw his table at us.

The owner turned cleared his throat nervously, confirming our order. "You're here for the chicken, then?"

A drinker at the bar shouted angrily. "Jayzuz, George! Look at 'em! They ain't here for the chicken!"

"Right," Monteblan mumbled. "Brisket will do."

"Top choice. *Excellent.*" Our bar man sighed with relief. "Brisket is spot on, gentlemen. Lager as well?"

We nodded for brews, settling back as bar chat slowly resumed. Drinkers looked away from us, muttering. Brits beside us shook their heads, repositioning burly bodies to shut us out.

"What the hell was that all about?" I whispered to Monteblan.

"How should I know?"

Monteblan didn't look too deeply into much of what happened on the planet. This was his beauty; beer belly Zen. Food was on the way, Bee Gees were singing, and life beyond that was details. Listening to the music, my friend nodded pensively.

"I've heard this song forever. Thought it through. I'm gonna say six feet is ideal."

"For what?"

Beers arrived. We toasted cheers and drank. Monteblan continued.

"For love. Love should be six feet deep. That works."

"Dude what are you talking about?!" I leaned in. "Love is bottomless. You can't measure that shit."

"Six feet is perfect," Monteblan sipped his beer. "You can jump in and swim around, but you won't drown."

"No way." I leaned back, crossing my arms. "Love has to be deep. So you can dive in head first. That's how to do the big things in life."

"Like flying to Bangkok with a laptop and no ticket back?" my friend said. "You still aren't off that acid, are you?"

Monteblan had received a call from me a month back, after I had been microdosed by a potential business partner. Shit like that happens in Bangkok. I remember leaving the meeting feeling funny. Then suddenly understanding everything. Calling Monteblan in maniacal capitalism, I roamed foreign streets ranting about hexagons being the ultimate pattern for business plans. Backing that up with frantically emailed pictures of giraffe fur, soccer balls, and for some reason, the Washington Monument, I thought I had mastered reality. When I came down, I realized doing business with people who drug you probably doesn't lead to flourishing future potentials. Leaving the partnership before it started, I chalked up one more BKK business collapse.

"At least I got a psychedelic massage out of it," I said, shrugging.

"Wait. The guy dosed you then rubbed you down?" His eyebrows raised. "Now *that's* sophisticated."

"Please. No. After calling you I found a massage place and got an oil massage while rolling on a quarter hit of very clear, very clean LSD." I raised my glass. "There are oil massages. And there are oil massages in Bangkok. And *then*, there are oil massages in Bangkok on acid. I felt like a seal being stroked by Proteus."

The Brisket arrived and Monteblan dug in. I had another beer, tipping back in my chair, wondering how the hell I would get out of Bangkok, or if I really even wanted to. For three weeks I had debated this, wandering the greasy streets of the Big Mango while burning through savings. Logically, there was no future here. But the city had grabbed my heart, the same way New York had taken me as a teenager. And how could I go back home after the prolific, public announcements I had made following the last Presidential election? Proclaiming with bold finality that America was doomed, I had gone global with theatrical resolve.

"All who wander are not lost," I sighed.

"What's that?" Monteblan said. "The 'Just Do It' for every fuck up in the world?"

"Nah, saw it on some refrigerator magnet." I drained my beer. "And I'm not a fuck up."

"Not saying you are. But all the stories you tell about business here are. Although I have to say Bangkok rocks. Titties in your face then brisket? Come on, man. What's better than that? Be a fuck up to walk away from here."

I didn't bother replying to Bangkok's central dilemma. The place was heaven on earth but hell to survive in. Our meal went by, we paid our bill and jumped into a tuk-tuk. Upon arrival, Monteblan became instantly addicted to these three wheeled motorcycles. Sputtering in smoke through traffic, the blasting machine shot us past a jumbled panoply of cluttered streets, jammed traffic and scattered street bars. While barely dodging collisions, I pointed out the Buddhist pictures on the tuk-tuk roof, along with protection prayers scribbled in squiggling Thai symbols.

"Don't worry!" I shouted while blasting around another perilous turn. "Om is on our side!"

Through the grace of higher traffic powers, we landed unscathed in Silom. Walking past blaring, grinding go-go bars, we glanced at girls dressed like cowgirls, school girls, or just plain sluts. Outside were folding tables selling brass knuckles, porn DVDs, dildos, pellet guns, body armor, mace, binoculars and Viagra. Navigating the vice maze, Monteblan picked the bar at random; a shadowed doorway set back from the sidewalk. Heading towards the dark wooden door, I realized he was bringing us to one of the few remaining old school Bangkok haunts. How my friend had found it was miraculous. Void of signs, layered with decades of street soot, the place itself slouched like a lifetime drunk. But one with local graces. Out front, chipped statues of wood carved Thai women welcomed us with artfully poised hands. Passing them, my friend's hand pushed on the door.

When he did, the hand of Fate pulled us into something I'm still trying to understand, and probably will be, for life.

**The door closed behind us, shutting out the world beyond.** Time here had frozen. Seventies tunes played in darkness where lit pictures and mementos of Thailand's past glowed softly. Thai Royals, American GI's, traditional portraits and ancient whiskey ads. We found our way through dusty design elements, floating past wagon wheels, sea turtles, old rotary telephones and an ornately carved abacus. Finding a thick wooden table in the back, we slid into booth seats beneath a TV playing badminton matches.

The place was packed. Girls in tight black dresses were draped over foreigners all around. Some wore rumpled oxfords and business dress, riding out an epic evening stretching from happy hour. All were drunk and laughing, calling for drinks brought forth in frosty bottles and ice jangling glasses. Whispering, caressing women struck deals, drifting out the door or disappearing upstairs to the rooms where beds waited for drunken sex bought by the hour. Grinning in the action, alive with illicit thrill, Monteblan and I took it all in.

Then before our eyes, the whole place flipped. Seventies songs were traded for traditional upcountry Thai pop. Twangy guitars and rocking rhythms ripped through the speakers and every working girl yelled in delight. Scattered through the bar, they leapt into Thai traditional dance. Arms outstretched with wavy, curving hand motions, their heads angled this way, then that. Long black hair framing glowing smiles, all of them moving in ancient, memorized moves. Men watched, entranced by the shared language of female bodies, still languid even through the liquor. Shining like soul sisters in the rough world of night, moving in rhythms passed through time, the women were everything beautiful about Bangkok. Random and traditional, laughing and sexy, captivating actions I would never truly understand.

Then it was done. The room lurched back into old seventies hits. Women melted back to their men, playing their marks. The night partied on. Monteblan and I joined the happy masses shouting over music and laughing in the crowd. But in a shifting movement of bodies, a distant table was revealed. Squinting through the bar glow, I saw an old man. In the bar but apart from us, a slumped soul over whiskey, I watched him drain a few rounds. None were paid for, and the bartender's hovering attention implied special privilege. Wondering what such a forlorn, faded soul had done to elicit celebrity treatment, I leaned into the Thai manning the bar.

"Hey!" I shouted over 70's pop. "Why does that old guy back there drink for free?"

The Thai's eyes narrowed in suspicion a moment. Without answering me, he turned his back.

"Maybe that's our cue to bounce!" Monteblan slurred loudly. "Any other time warp Bangkok spots you know?"

While bodies pressed in, I called out over the din. "There's this place called the Check Inn, been in Bangkok since the 60's! It's here or the Check Inn."

*"What?!"*

Drunk, tired of the noise, I shouted: *"HERE! OR! THE CHECK INN!"*

Before us, the bartender froze. Thai girls narrowed their black mascara eyes, then slipped away, pulling their men into the gloom. Monteblan and I were suddenly alone at the bar. Stunned at how fast it had happened, I watched the bartender lean in. Glancing quickly around, his voice was barely a whisper.

"You're here for the chicken?"

A lot seemed to be hinging on this question; metric tons of very serious shit which I sensed, but didn't understand. My reflex reaction was to walk away. But Monteblan answered before I could.

"Yeah, we're here for the chicken."

Then I remembered that pub. The Brits. The way it had all gone quiet when we ordered the chicken. I shot a questioning look to my friend. Monteblan smiled wide, loving this. Cryptic moments in forgotten bars on the far side of the planet were my portly friend's stock in trade. His vacation had just been made. He didn't know enough about Bangkok to note a crucial danger sign. The whores had vanished. That was something like horses feeling impending earthquakes and bolting the barn. When I noticed whose presence was revealed through the shadows, my foreboding deepened. The mournful old white man drinking alone was staring at the Thai bartender. Through the gloom, their eyes were locked in silent battle. The bartender shook his head *no*. The old man shrugged a fatalistic *what can we do?* Finally, the bartender looked back at us, jerking his head towards the drooping alcoholic's lonely table.

I walked to him on shaky legs. It wasn't the liquor. The mood that had descended on the bar was part reverent, part dangerous, and all weird. I glanced at my friend and saw that Monteblan was oblivious to it, still smiling, casually spilling whiskey from his tilted glass. Sitting down next to me at the heavy wooden table, we joined the ancient stranger.

Up close, he smelled of liquor, old laundry, and a lifetime of cigarettes. Definitely European, there was something not only old world, but otherworldly about him. Glowing pale in bar lights, he regarded us both with sad, watery eyes. When he finally spoke, it was more like a sigh.

"So you're here for the Chicken."

"That's why we're in Bangkok." Monteblan replied, patting my shoulder too hard. "Nothing but the chicken."

The foreign stranger slowly drummed his pale fingers on the table. There was something he didn't want to tell us. I could feel that. But I could also tell that something was making him. Strange, arcane rules and obscure requirements were playing out. With them I felt Fate. In this old, dark bar of shadowed secrets, far from everybody I knew and everything I had ever done, a sure and solid feeling shifted silently. Something irreversible was in motion. My life would change entirely, utterly, and inexorably after hearing his next words. In those final, stretched moments before I heard them, I nearly leapt up to silence the man. But frozen by powers I did not understand, I merely listened as he spoke in heavily accented English.

"It is a brotherhood and a way of life. Are you prepared for this?"

"For what?" Monteblan asked. "A Chicken?"

"Chicken 65," the stranger said gravely. "You have been called. You have been chosen."

Monteblan and I turned to look at each other, then back to the old man.

"This is what it does, the Chicken." His watery eyes looked beyond us, into worlds unknown. "The lucky ones are merely chosen. Others are entirely taken. It's the Chicken don't you see? That's what brought you here. The Bird."

He shuddered with his last word, then gulped down his glass of whiskey. Thai hands immediately refilled it, bartender disappearing. The faded, foreign man stared at nothing, light from neon beer signs shining softly in his eyes.

"I was once a successful man in Denmark. I had an enviable position in the civil service. The love of a beautiful woman from a prominent family. My future was secured. Then, the Chicken took me. All my plans, my career…finished." He shook his head, slow and deep. "Here I sit and shall sit for life. But it is not too late for you. Don't let it take you. Leave Chicken 65 before it begins."

On the old stereo system, a song about broken wings played. His eyes held mine in the gloom, their defeat timeless and grave.

"But what is it?" I asked.

"That depends on what you bring with you." he replied.

"Is it fun?" Monteblan asked.

"Fun? Yes, more than you will ever have again. That is the problem. After the Chicken, life is just a shadow. Chicken 65 is a dream and when you are in it you are more alive, more *a man* than you will ever be."

Staring at his whiskey glass, the stranger turned it in slow circles.

"You will see the worst of what man is. You will see his best. You will laugh as you have never laughed before and so shall you weep. And when it is finished, in hospital or in prison, mad by the side of the road or crashed into temple walls, whether chased by Thai mafia or drinking whiskey in your hotel suite, you will think of only one thing."

"Chicken?" Monteblan said.

"*Returning*," the old man sighed. "Because life is never enough after Chicken 65. You'll come back again. And again. And *again*. Fighting, cheating, weeping, all to win the Chicken. Please, I beg you, turn back. Do not ask me to tell you more."

Monteblan and I were enraptured. In the halo of bar lights, the old man had transformed from slouching tragedy into glowing holy man. A hush had descended in the dark corner where we sat with him. I heard my voice without realizing I had spoken.

"We want in."

"Everyone wants in." Smiling wistfully, the old man regarded us with watery eyes. "Then all they want is out. But once you are in, this is final. If I tell you the address, there is no turning back. So please, think deeply about the consequences of—"

"Bro." Monteblan burped. "Totally appreciate the Ancient Mariner rap, but it's late. How about that address?"

The man regarded us with gentle pity, then laughed softly to himself. "Yes, of course. You are young and have no time for foolish talk from a lonely old man. Others will tell you more. Tomorrow, 5 PM. The Miami Hotel on Phetchaburi Road. Do not be late."

A long moment passed, all of us looking at each other.

"Thanks," I finally said. "I think."

"I am wondering if you will still thank me when you finish." The elderly European smiled. "*If* you finish."

Monteblan and I looked at each other. Then we laughed.

But if we had known what was ahead of us, we would have cried.

**Bangkok's skyline was a brilliant glittering line beyond the infinity pool.** Sun shone down as we lounged through the day, sipping drinks on Monteblan's hotel roof. Just below were the lush green trees of Lumpini Park, where monitor lizards had once roamed free. Ambling with flicking tongues, low to the ground, slipping into water or crossing jogging paths, the gentle monsters had made too many tourists jump in fright. Recently rounded up at the bequest of the new Thai Prime Minister, the three foot long reptiles were replaced with cats and kittens. No protest was made, the lizards probably ended up as belts, and Thailand took one more step towards homogenizing.

The whole year I had been here, sanitizing moves like this had been happening incrementally. Street bars closed, legit bars shuttered early, dance clubs raided, brothels stormed, street food banned, visas tightened and formerly chaotic street bazaars suddenly regulated. Such moves illustrated an uneasy shifting of government dynasties, initiated just after I arrived. People don't talk politics publically in Thailand, and it was hard to follow the drift. But pieces I put together suggested some long, simmering feud between the rural north and rich Bangkok south.

The latter was standardizing the city for more corporate investment, with regulations threatening the simple way Northern Thais survived while slaving as unskilled labor in Bangkok. The dents kicked in their lifestyle was echoing through the old school foreign population, too. As their whore bars were shuttered and street tables taken away, visa regulations changed and nightlife curfewed, leathery old sex pats were disappearing like lizards from the park. Their rambunctious, fuck-happy ways were ceding to the new breed of expats. Starting internet companies and working out, launching lifestyle blogs from cafes, they had changed the city's flavor considerably. Or eliminated it totally, depending on who you asked. And now my friend, lazing in the blazing sun, asked what I thought about last night.

"So what do you think?" Monteblan splashed pool water with his foot. "We going to rock out Chicken 78?"

"Chicken 65," I corrected. "If we want to get to Phetchaburi Road by five, we should leave soon. Might offer an interesting side trip, too. All the soapies are out there."

Monteblan squinted in the sun. "What are soapies?"

"Massage parlors. Like really insane ones. Five floors with restaurants, cigar lounges, saunas. It's like a resort for your penis. Girls sit behind glass. You pick one out and she gives you a bath, then soaps up and rubs all over you."

"Nice," Monteblan said. "I'll pass on the ass but I'm good with a cigar and the tuk-tuk ride over. Probably the best way to arrive at Chicken 65. We'd take a tuk-tuk, right?"

I didn't reply. And part of me didn't want to go to Phetchaburi Road. Sitting in the sunlight, last night's surreal conversation played like a foreboding dream. But another part of me was drawn to whatever mystery waited. Our cryptic foreign friend had roamed Thailand when lizards still slithered through the park. Whatever remained of that world was fast vanishing. Up here on the roof, new Thailand was invading. My glance lingered on the lounge chairs before me, filled with fashionable, phone tapping Euro bros and a pair of American girls. The former was lost in pristine, digital worlds. The latter was laughing in the flat, hard flurry of "likes", "ums" and "yeahs" customary to my countrymen. Far away from Americans for so long, now suddenly among them, I understood the ire we inspired. The polite ones call us optimistic and open. The rest call us dumb. The French don't call us at all.

"Dude, being honest?" Monteblan shrugged. "Last night it sounded funny. But right now, I don't know. Found a killer monkey beach online, just outside of Bangkok. What if we just do that instead? I have to see monkeys on the beach before I leave."

"Right. The Monkey beach."

The more we had drank last night, the more Monteblan had mentioned monkey beaches. Oblivious to gyrating go-go girls, he had scrolled through endless monkey beach listings on his phone, showing me different photos and clocking their time from Bangkok. The more liquor was poured, the more obsessed my friend became. At one point he was lobbying for a taxi to monkey beach that night. I was hoping he had forgotten about them today. He hadn't.

"That all said..." Monteblan debated out loud. "This is Thailand, and Chicken 65 could be anything. Can a girl pull 65 chickens out of her vagina? They do shit like that here. Probably had a show at the bar we missed."

I shut my eyes to remember last night's shadowed world of dancing Thai women and cryptic Europeans. Odd mementos from whatever vanishing dimension had produced it floated in my mind. Dashing royals and adding machines, traditional statues and monsters from the sea, old rotary phones and pop stars in army fatigues... Mysterious and cool, shadowed and obscure, that world held poetry I wanted to explore. In contract, the world I opened my eyes to glared harshly. Brilliant skyscrapers and glossy trip hop, phone addiction and Bellini swirling Americans.

"We should go," I decided. "Probably it's bullshit, but what if it isn't? Maybe there's a buffet with sixty five chickens or something."

The mention of food made Monteblan's eyebrows raise with interest.

"Monkey beach can wait," my overweight friend decided. "I've waited long enough for it, anyway. Let's do some Chicken 68."

"65," I corrected. "And good call. We already broke into the brotherhood. Wouldn't want to walk away and ruin our karma."

We stood, stretched, and moved through the lounge chair jungle, picking our way away from the pool.

"I don't think Karma exists," Monteblan yawned, stepping into the elevator. "Dick heads just do whatever. That's life."

My friend binged a button. Doors slid shut and the brilliant rooftop vanished. Our elevator descended, heading someplace darker. A place where Karma, I would learn, definitely worked. A place that was designed, perhaps, to show two fools what terrible forces balanced the weights. But all that was unknown as we glided down from our rooftop oasis, bossa nova Muzak playing.

"You're sure we can get a tuk-tuk?" Monteblan confirmed as the doors slid open.

"There are three things that are very easy to get in Thailand," I told my friend, leading him through the lobby. "Herpes, a drinking problem, and tuk-tuks."

**The Miami hotel smelled like a million cigarettes, with an infinity of fucks seeped into the walls.** Everything that wasn't linoleum was cement. The buzzing wall clock ticked. A broken jukebox showed old records layered with dust. Dust layered everything in that old hotel lobby on Phetchaburi Road. Even the people who worked there. The ancient Thai man manning the warped desk sported a Colonel Sanders bolo tie. He probably had been since '65. Behind him, bloated paperbacks slumped on shelves. Beyond him, a window showed cracked cement courtyard. A raised swimming pool sat on cinderblocks. The splintered Hotel Miami sign loomed over it, painted pink. Nothing else here remotely evoked Florida. It could have been the Hotel Detroit, the Hotel Estonia, or the Hotel Cement Hole of Woe. Walking to the desk as the old man stared at us, I cleared my throat.

"Hi, we're here for the Ch—"

The clerk held up his hand, stopping me from speaking. Motioning us closer, leaning forward over the lobby desk, he whispered.

"Why you here?"

"We're here for *the Chicken.*" Monteblan whispered back.

The Thai man frowned, regarding us like we didn't belong.

"65," I added, just as softly. "Chicken 65."

The lobby man smiled, then rubbed his thumb and forefingers together in the universal symbol for money.

"Oh," I said. "How much?"

"Up to you," the clerk shrugged.

I pulled back to regroup with Monteblan and explain.

"Thais do this," I whispered. "Whores usually, but I guess Chicken 65 desk attendants, too. Make you guess. I hate it."

"Well, what do you think?"

"I think I didn't go to the ATM. So I think it's up to you."

"I don't even know what this money means," Monteblan said, fishing through his wallet. "What's five bucks? Ten maybe?"

I looked around at the shabby dim surroundings, wondering if anything positive would emerge from this run down hotel of the Vietnam War era, set along a forlorn road of soapy massage parlors near a highway overpass.

"Maybe we should leave," I suggested. "Maybe this whole thing's a scam."

"No way bro. That traffic was ass and I'm not doing it again. We're here and it's ten bucks. That's like… two of these, right?"

Monteblan held two red bills together, holding them up. The old Thai man cleared his throat, wincing painfully through his smile. Thais smile at everything. They call their country The Land of Smiles. After a year in their midst, I was starting to tell the difference between grins. There was the *Hello This Is My Store* smile, the *Hi I Like You* smile, the *I Am Poor And Having Sex With You For Money* smile, the *I Want To Punch You In The Face But Won't* smile, and many more. Right now, the old desk attendant was giving us the *You Are Cheap* smile. Reaching into my practically empty wallet, I added another few hundred baht. The old Thai's smile shifted slightly into the *Right Idea But You Are Unfortunately Still Too Cheap* smile. Monteblan added another few bills to the pile. The old man's thin grin morphed into the *I'll Let You Slide*

*Because You Clearly Don't Know What The Hell You Are Doing Here And It Will Get You Out of My Face* smile. While he tucked the cash into a drawer, a woman appeared from the doorway behind him.

Thai and tired, she looked like she had been working there forty years, smoking through every minute of it. A cigarette smoldered in her fingers now, smoke curling before hard dark eyes and a perma-frown. Sallow and hostile, taking us in, the Thai woman reflected what was becoming a familiar look of suspicion from all we encountered in the Chicken 65 universe. *Who the hell are you two clowns?* practically hung over her head in cartoon balloon. Shrugging it off with a slight shake of her head, she turned and motioned us with a waving hand, not bothering to see if we joined her.

Down a dim hall we followed. She wore a pants suit. Her butt was shapely and had somehow survived the hammer of time. Although who knew how many layers of hose, tights, pads, and extra strength *mama san* panties pulled that off. Aging women have lots of tricks. Men just get fat and lose hair. Her black lacquered slides clacked on the green and grey linoleum tiles, leading us past walls of old pictures. Polaroid collages were a *de rigueur* feature of old school, expat spots in Thailand. Marking party moments from the past, they created unique local his-tories instead of ubiquitous social media pages. Passing through the hall, my eyes roved through Miami Hotel shots of Americans and Europeans partying through the 1980s and 90s. Flush in a time when the economy still worked, the guys glowed like the world was theirs. Beers in hand, faces bright, they had arms around pretty Thai girls.

The women from their era looked less jaded. None had tattoos. Most wore dresses instead of crotch clinging short shorts. Their pretty faces and open smiles were worlds away from the calculated stares of inked up, pudgy hustlers I saw in Bangkok's red light district today. Was it possible that something so dirty as prostitution had a touch more charm back then? The happy, party faces from the vanished 80s suggested such notions might be true. Regretting the end of whatever world I was glimpsing now, I reached the end of the hall.

A closed door was waiting. Our guide stopped before it. She looked us over with that fast, practiced prostitute glance which sums up respective net worth precisely. Then she held out her hand. Monteblan groaned lightly, shaking his head. But he pressed the right amount of money into her hand. The miserable old woman opened the door, then turned and vanished down the hall of parties past.

**It was a small, dingy conference room, the type for hotel convention meetings.** The ceiling was Styrofoam with panels of weak fluorescent light. There were no windows. An old, decrepit air conditioner rattled. Round tables were spaced out on a ratty carpet. Forty or so men were gathered, most of them 40 plus. In a collective movement, all of them turned their heads to look at us. Some were smoking, most were drinking, and none of them really liked what they saw. Noticing frowns of doubt, eyes narrowing with questions, I pulled my friend quickly from the spotlight of our entrance to an empty back table by the wall.

Turning away, the strangers forgot us. But they weren't strangers. This was something like a reunion. Men made their way from table to table, saying hellos, waving from across the room, laughing and jovial over frosty beers. Two glasses appeared before us, served by a silent Thai waiter who hadn't arrived so much as materialized. I was halfway through my brew when I noticed something odd about this room. Struggling to put my finger on it, Monteblan leaned in with the answer.

"Weird," he whispered, "Nobody's on their phone."

As if on cue, someone stood and looked directly at us. The guy's gaze was intense. He worked out a lot. A light skinned, cappuccino colored black American guy, he wore pressed cargo shorts and a

Peter Tosh T-shirt. Putting his fingers by his head like an imaginary phone, he slowly shook his head. Moving through the room, the man walked towards us. Everybody knew him. Nodding hello to a couple of blonde Germans in steel aviator glasses, he gave passing high fives to a sunken eyed, smoking pair that was unmistakably French. Passing two Japanese, he said something quickly in their language. The men laughed, raising their beers. All here were in pairs, I realized, like Monteblan and I. Some looked old enough to have been in the photos lining the Miami Hotel hall. In a far corner, I recognized the Brits from the pub last night. People here were from all over the world.

The muscular black man approaching us looked mixed race; probably half Asian. His large, nimble body passed the only person there sitting alone: a dashing blonde man, looking immaculate in a pressed linen suit, complete with boutonniere. He cheerfully raised a glass of champagne in greeting to the man lumbering past, getting only a grumble of gruff acknowledgement. A moment later, the large American was towering before us, holding out a strong, square hand.

"Phones."

He possessed such instant authority and natural command that Monteblan and I handed our machines right over.

"When do we get them back?" I asked.

"After the race."

"Race?" Monteblan was confused. "Chicken 65 is a race?"

The man's brow furrowed, eyes narrowing. There was a simple rawhide band around his large neck. Hanging from it was the longest looking bullet I had ever seen. Dangling on either side of the bullet were two Buddhist monk pendants that traditional Thais wore. He crossed his arms, showing massive biceps with a *Semper Fi* marines tattoo. Suspicious now, his low voice was a growl.

"Who sent you?"

"I'm sorry," I said nervously. "This is—"

*All some terrible mistake*, I was about to tell him. But before I could, the lights flicked on and off. Hesitating one last moment, eyeing us both, the man just shook his head.

"This is Chicken 65," he said. "And if you're here, you in it."

Leaving with our phones, he headed towards a shelf in the back of the room, piled high with other devices. A slim Thai in white oxford and black slacks was waiting there. Taking our phones, he put a sticker on each and then marked a clipboard. The lights flicked off and on once more, as room conversations trailed into murmurs.

Up front, a man took the floor. Instant hush descended. He slowly swept his gaze over the room. I placed him at early sixties, lean and fit, with a full head of crisply parted blond hair. The bifocals on his face were the only betrayal of age or weakness on his body. Hands on hips, perfectly postured in shorts and a polo shirt, he smiled.

"Gentlemen," he called out, voice loud and strong. "Welcome to Chicken 65."

There were cheers and hollers from the room, as everybody lifted their glass. The man who had taken our phones banged the table before him, leading a raucous chant.

*"Chicken!*

*Chicken!*

*Chicken!"*

The room repeated the word, whistling, pounding their tables until glasses were dancing and spilling. Louder it grew, thunder in our ears until finally the crisp man addressing the room held out his hands. Voices trailed off into laughs, then quieted completely, as men settled back into their chairs.

"Like every year," the crisp American said. "Let's start this Chicken with a moment of silence. All rise in respect for our founder, Somchai Kitapoon."

Lights went dark. Someone's laptop projected the face of a Thai man on the wall. Simple and strong, his eyes stared from a black and white photo taken long ago. All around us, men stood, heads down. Monteblan and I did the same, standing with the others in silence. The moment passed, photo clicked away, but the room stayed dark. Men took their seats as the commanding American stepped into the spotlight from the laptop projector.

"On to business." He picked up his notes, glancing at pages through his bifocals. "Our usual bribes were paid for the parade. Departure won't be a problem, but escalating tensions in Bangkok, I have been told, may perchance impact your return."

Men turned to each other in the gloom, murmuring. Words and phrases floated over the rattling air conditioner: *coup*, prime minister, north, royal military… Then bubbling voices were silenced by the speakers strong, loud tone.

"That situation is impossible to determine at this time, but we will return to it. Right now let's move onto standard procedures. From here on, no phones. Nobody online. Maybe you think you can get around that. So did the 28 people who have been bounced since '99 for going online during Chicken 65. We have our ways, we have our tech, and eyes are everywhere. With this much money at stake, nobody gets a pass."

"How much this year, General?" someone shouted.

"In US Dollars…" He peered through bifocals while paging through notes. "Just over three million."

A low whistle went out through the room.

"Lot of money," The General said. "And that's just through our channels. What's being handled by Thai bookies may well double that. Just about every Bangkok neighborhood pools up for The Bird. Racers can't bet, aside from The Splits. Other rules are simple. Chicken Promise is a Chicken Promise. Make one, keep it. Flying is outlawed.

Don't leave the ground. Psychological tactics are highly encouraged, physical violence or vehicular sabotage are entirely forbidden. But anything goes on Phetchaburi Road. And most importantly, Chicken 65 finishes."

He paused here, staring out over his bifocals to the hushed room.

"Chicken 65 finishes, gentlemen. We've been running since 1965 on pay offs, friendships, favors, and many a blind eye. We make people money and we make people mad. Some who would love to see this all stop. Like most of you know, we have a deal with such parties. If The Bird doesn't make it back to The Miami one year, we walk. Our presence in the region is abandoned, our activities cease, and Chicken 65 is no more. So it's on you, gentlemen. Our tradition is in your hands. Finish Chicken 65, or Chicken 65 is finished."

Murmurs and nods went around the room.

"Map." The General stepped aside as a map of the region flashed up the wall. "Chicken 65 will start at oh six hundred, tomorrow, from Democracy Monument. From there, you are all welcome to my traditional grill party in Changers."

He pointed out Chang Mai on the map, in northern Thailand.

"From there we're into The Splits. That's as nasty as it ever is. Especially here."

The slide shifted, a closer view of Laos, and The General walked to it, tapping a red highlighted area.

"The hill tribe situation outside of Vang is deteriorating rapidly. Look out for snipers. They're popping tourist busses, mostly. Intel suggests you drive by night. Keep your head down and keep it moving. Nobody's been crazy enough to run The Splits for years, now you have another reason not to. Nothing's changed in Vang. Shifty as always. More 65ers get locked up in Laos than anywhere else. Every year, I say the same thing. Every year, you numb nuts party."

Knowing laughter spread through the room. The General shook his head, continuing.

"Watch those roads in Laos, not many of them, so if one goes out you got a whole lot of backtracking to do. That's miles on your vehicle and time off your race."

"Dude, we're in a race?" Monteblan whispered. "We don't have a car."

I was too busy listening to comment, trying to take it all in, feeling lost like I was in some strange dream.

"The bird will be in 'Nam," the crisp, commanding man continued. "Sabon Sai like every year. Payments are in the process of making their way north and you'll get the proverbial blind eye, like every year. But damn if that village don't charge one hell of a lot for the privilege. Take Cambodia how you like, but watch out for mines and steer clear of temples. Five years back that clown from Finland ripped through Angor Wat. Still in jail today. Don't be him. From there it's back to Thailand and remember gentlemen, your passports will be checked so get those border stamps. Live Chicken wins the race. Bring it back to Bangkok still flapping. I'll be waiting for it here at the Miami. We do have it blood tested, so no switching birds. Next."

The slide showed a detailed map of Bangkok, with one highlighted road leading to a Miami Hotel icon.

"It's always easier leaving Bangkok then returning. This year especially, since the new PM took control. There have been rumors of a *coup*."

"Every year!" One of the dark eyed French men called out. "Every year I have been running zee Chickeen, every year, zee rumors of zee *coup*!"

People in the room nodded their heads in agreement.

"Be that as it may," the fit, elderly man up front replied. "We have intel suggesting a strong rise of Northerners in Bangkok. That might just be more construction jobs and a whole lotta whores…"

The room laughed.

"Or it might be something else. We really don't have the assets to determine. My opinion—and this is only an opinion—is that rumors of a *coup* are unfounded. Thais with money aren't leaving town and they'd be the first to go if trouble was brewing. But all that is immaterial. Because Chicken 65 finishes."

Stepping into the light, The General's face was dramatically lit in the darkness of the room.

"Since 1965 this race has been run through bullets, bombs, tsunamis and the goddamn Khmer Rouge. If Bangkok is burning you damn well drive right through it. Because you're Chicken. And Chicken 65 finishes. Lot of history wrapped up in this thing. Lots of money down on it. Finish the race. Deliver The Bird. Which gentlemen, brings us to our final reminder."

The room went quiet. The General took a breath, looking round the room with a level, penetrating gaze. When he spoke, his voice was low.

"Anything goes on Phetchaburi Road."

The room was dead silent. I felt a chill ripple through me. Uneasy glances shot through the room. The General clapped his hands sharply. Slides went down and lights went up.

"Let's get that bird. See you all at oh six hundred, tomorrow. Those of you who haven't signed the Chicken Ledger, step to the front."

A sharp whistle cut through the milling, murmuring men. I looked up. The marine who had taken our phones was staring at us. He pointed to the black ledger on the table in the front of the room.

"Y'all want to sign that book."

**"Hi... um, Hello?"**

The General had been sorting through papers on the table, organizing them neatly in a plain manila folder. He looked up over his bifocals as we approached. He didn't think much of what he saw. The instant assessment was almost visible. Like everybody else in the weird world of Chicken 65, the man didn't think we belonged. But rising up, smiling with crisp cordiality, The General shook both our hands.

"First Chicken?"

"Yes," I said.

Monteblan nodded, just staring at the floor.

"You two legacy?" He thought for a minute, squinting with guesses. "Georgie Macalister's boy? Larry Crenshaw out of New Hampshire?"

"We heard about it," Monteblan mumbled.

"Heard about it." The General confirmed flatly. "You just *heard* about Chicken 65."

There was tense silence in the empty room.

"No," I told him, recalling last night's tangle of rules and rituals from the bar. "We didn't just hear about it. We asked about it. So now we're in it."

A slow smile spread on his face. "You might have some Chicken in you yet."

"So we're in?"

"You're in," He agreed. "But I don't think you two know what you're in for."

From just beside the neat stack of papers, The General produced the old ledger, black and worn with age. There was no title on the front, just the ghostly smudges of a thousand finger prints. He spun the book facing us, cracking it open. The smell of old paper, dust and history floated towards me. Flipping through the pages, The General passed name after name scrawled in black pen. Faded with age at first, the signatures appeared less ancient as they progressed, ending with the clearly written name of a racer from the previous year.

*Smiler Grogan, Chicken 2019*

The General tapped the page right after it.

"Sign here and you're Chicken. During the race, you will abide by all rules."

"Yeah…" Monteblan said, scrawling his name with the low, mushed letters of his signature. "What are all those rules?"

"Gentlemen, I just don't have the time. There are payoffs to make, bets to secure, and women to be…" He winked here. "Pursued and appreciated. This *is* Thailand, after all. Enjoy it. And have a damn fine Chicken. Ask around, the fellas will set you straight."

Squinting at my writing as I signed, the General read my signature aloud.

"Asser?"

"Archer," I corrected. "Rich Archer."

"No son. I know a Chicken Name when I see it. You're Asser now." Smiling, he shut the book and tucked it under his arm. "I'll tell the boys."

"I'm… *Asser?*"

"Indeed." Marching smartly towards the door, The General winked. "And Asser, if you'd like to fully appreciate the long line of bullshit you have just stepped into, find Mississippi Charlie. He'll be more than happy to show you the Bible."

"Asser?" I echoed dumbly.

"Who's Mississippi Charlie?" Monteblan asked.

Leaving the room, The General called back over his shoulder.

"The one who looks like he's been drinking for fifty years."

**We stepped outside, down the hall, passing old photos.** Some went back to Vietnam. Faded GIs chugged beer from their combat boots. Others cheered them on. Passing in a daze, I fumbled to grasp the size and shape of Chicken 65. Although precise contours remained vague, the rough outline of the thing suggested a sprawling reality, potentially lethal, and definitely not the terrain for a freelance graphic designer. I thought of how we might drop out, wondering what The General meant about 'eyes everywhere.' Did that mean airports? Train stations? Were all avenues of escape blocked? Were we *trapped* in Chicken 65? I glanced nervously at my friend. Monteblan didn't seem to mind any of this. Very few things bothered my friend. Even the promise of a deadly car race through foreign lands littered with land mines wasn't much to work him up.

"Let's grab beers," Monteblan said placidly. "Looks like they're serving outside."

The Miami lobby was empty, but groups of men were in the decrepit courtyard, drinking beers. Following my friend, we joined them on the cracked white pavement. Shielding my eyes from the late afternoon sun, I surveyed the area. Hotel wrapped around the courtyard; two floors of it. A balcony of blue doors showed a dozen rooms overlooking the cement. Nearby, two short French men were talking to a lanky German who towered above them both. Across the courtyard, the dapper English man was smoking a cigarette. Blowing smoke theatrically from the side of his mouth, he pontificated to a nodding Japanese man in tailored khakis. By the pool, I heard the loud flat laughter of Americans. The one who had taken our phones was listening to an animated, paunchy man whose red face and booze battered nose made him the most likely candidate for Mississippi Charlie. Moving towards him through the crowd, his friendly Southern drawl grew louder.

"Back in the war they'd just roll them jeeps right up. See those holes in the wall there?" He pointed to small circles with rusty ringed edges, showing where nails had been. "That was where the curtains were. Fellas just rolled up in the jeep with their girl, pulled the curtains, and it was boom-boom time. Half the price of a short time room. Oh it was wild, boy, wild. Howdy."

With this last word he turned to us, tipping a beer can in salute. The nose, up close, looked almost like a special effects team had placed it there. Smashed to pulmonary hell by a lifetime of drinking, it sat like a battered squash on his red face. His flowered shirt was bright, but still looked pale compared to the bright pink of his visage. Blonde hair made for strange contrast, like a tomato with straw on it. The eyes were blue and friendly, if a little sad, and the paunch looked comfortably accepted. Mississippi Charlie was a man who enjoyed the pleasures of life, and had been, for many a long year.

"Hi," I said. "We're um... well... new."

"Oh, you don't have to tell us that. You boys never done this shit or nothing like it in your life. It's all over your face." He pointed a friendly finger right at me. "*You* look like you want to jump a flight to Brazil. Oh Sweet Lord!"

Charlie busted out laughing, then lowered his head towards me with a wink.

"Not like the good Lord Jesus gonna help you here. Best get good with Buddha in these parts. Like my man here."

He reached over to the Marine who had taken our phone. Picking up one of the Buddhist medallions from the large span of his chest, Charlie angled it towards us in the sun.

"This right here is pure gold. Blessed by the village monk. Right there at the wat. We are *covered*. And this one…" He reached to the other gold amulet, sealed in a small plastic bubble. "Specially made for drivers. You'll see them on the cabbies in Bangkok and truckers up North."

"How do you know all that?" I asked.

"I don't. He does. Reggie here is half Thai." Charlie winked. "Half crazy too."

"Full on crazy when I have to," the half black, half Thai man added. He extended a firm hand.

"Reggie, and this old windbag here is Mississippi Charlie. We run together."

We shook their hands.

"I'm Rich."

"Not what I heard, Asser." Charlie winked. "Already got your Chicken name."

"When do I get mine?" Monteblan asked.

"Oh, it'll happen out there on the road. Lots does."

Reggie nodded in agreement, looked at both of us in turn. "Which one of you drives?"

"Um. Well…" Monteblan shifted the bulk of his weight on his boater shoes. "We didn't really know we had to have a… uh… car?"

He finished it like a question, realizing half way through the statement that both Reggie and Charlie were looking at him, eyes wide, unbelieving. Glancing at the bullet around this buff marine's neck, I guessed the best thing to do was be honest.

"Look, here's what happened. We were in Silom at this bar. We asked about the chicken. This old guy told us to leave and we didn't. So he gave us this address. So here we are. We signed the book and now we're in."

"Well I'll be." Mississippi Charlie shook his head in disbelief. "I believe you two here might be the first fools who ever just stumbled in on Chicken 65. Reggie? What you think?"

Reggie shook his head. "Never heard it happen before."

I was confused. "How does everybody know about it then?"

Charlie took a swing from his beer. "Their daddies, friends, family mostly. People they served with. Or people they worked during the war years. Engineers, merchant marines, SAS. Then they all have buddies, people they do business with. Sons, nephews. Happens like that. They get asked in. But only after it's clear they're Chicken material."

Those last two words hung uncomfortably between us for a long moment.

"Well, I'm not really sure if we're, you know, Chicken material," Monteblan finally said.

"That's right," I agreed. "I was actually thinking that maybe we could, let's say, *leave?*"

"Oh hell no," Mississippi Charlie said. "You in it. That's done. Those are rules. Try to walk now you'll get bounced."

"Bounced?" Monteblan repeated.

"Eliminated from the region," Reggie said. "Break Chicken law, they'll pack your bags for you. Drive you to the airport. Seen it happen."

"Yup," Charlie confirmed. "When you been bounced you don't come back. This part of the world is *allllll* about connections. And Chicken 65 connections go back to the war, then over the river and through the woods to Washington DC. Four Star Generals, Naval Intel commanders, hell, there's a damn Secretary of Defense ran this thing back in his 'Nam days. And once you're Chicken 65, you're *always* Chicken 65."

Reggie spoke up, spelling it out. "Somebody gets Bounced, people hear about it. Powerful people. Ain't real difficult for them to make damn sure the offending party doesn't find his way back to this part of the world. Ever. Passport rejections, back taxes, no fly lists, shit like that."

"Other shit, too," Charlie added. "Takes all kinds to run Chicken 65, and some of them ain't real kind. Not the people you want on your six, as The General says."

"So." Monteblan made a thoughtful face. He stared at the ground, then looked at the pool. "If we don't want a world of military strength shit in our face, we race."

Both men nodded affirmatively. Reggie poked Monteblan in the chest.

"And if you don't want that same shit on you when you finish—if you finish—you don't talk about Chicken 65."

"Like a secret society?" I said.

"Society?" Charlie laughed. "Half the fools here damn fell out of society. Why we want to start a secret one? Hell, this just a bunch a fellas get all fired up and drive."

"Dude, I didn't even know we had to have a car."

"Well *duuuuuuuude*," Charlie said, playfully imitating Monteblan. "You best get hold of one. I might even have some help for you..."

Pulling out a fat, battered wallet, Charlie fished and rifled through a mess of bills, receipts, and papers. Finally producing a ripped old business card, he held it up with a smile.

Monteblan took it from him, reading out loud. "Mr. Boom."

"Runs the finest Chicken garage in Bangkok. Brother-in-law is up in Vang. Between them two, you'll be well served. Boom will have a whole mess of cars to choose from. All of them Chicken ready."

Monteblan looked up from the card. "What's Chicken ready?"

"No computers, no GPS, none of that digital shit," Reggie filled in. "We had some electromagnetic sabotage one year. Since then, everybody runs old school."

"And speaking of school," Charlie smiled. "You two need yourself a Chicken education. Let me fetch that Chicken Bible."

Hauling himself away, Mississippi Charlie wound around the pool towards the hotel rooms. That left Reggie looking at us. He didn't say anything. Just looked directly in my eyes, then Monteblan's.

"This is probably a mistake," I finally said, when I couldn't take the silent stare anymore.

Reggie shook his head. "No mistakes in Chicken 65. What happens here is meant to be. You agreed to this."

"What? How?"

"You agreed to this," Reggie repeated, holding me with his eyes.

"Look man," I told him. "I didn't know what Chicken 65 *was* before that slideshow in there. This is an accident. I wouldn't agree to join a road race through mine fields, where some Navy Seal team throws The Pentagon at me if I talk about it. Believe me."

"You agreed," Reggie repeated.

"Or you were called," Charlie suggested, reappearing with a book under his arm. "The Chicken calls to people, see. And I believe…"

He paused for a moment, squinting his eyes, taking us in, then slowly nodding. When he continued, his voice was softer, reverent even.

"I believe you boys been brought into this thing by the mysterious and powerful forces of Chicken 65. Forces I will try my best to elucidate and historically extrapolate…" He held up the battered book. "Over cool beverage in yonder lobby."

With a nod of his head showing the way, Mississippi Charlie walked ahead. Monteblan followed while I walked slightly behind with Reggie. The Marine's flip flops scuffed along the pavement.

"Reggie?" I asked. "What are we in for?"

"Can't know that till you're in it. Like your first piece of pussy. Just got to be in it." The big man laughed. "Then after you're out, all you'll want to be is back in it. Again and again. For life."

We walked the last few steps in silence over the cracked concrete courtyard. The bullet on his neck swayed gently, brushing up against his amulets.

"For life," Reggie repeated, almost to himself as we walked into the old lobby. "That's what you're in for. Life."

**The battered, dog eared Chicken Bible was self-published and falling apart.** Ruptures in the binding made sections of it hang like papers in a folder. The cover lamination was bubbling in places or worn off entirely. The back had a black tar streak that looked a lot like a…

"Tire tread," Charlie laughed, tapping the black jagged mark with his finger. "Reggie ran it over last year in Battambang."

"After you dropped it out the window," Reggie said.

"I did not *drop* the Chicken Bible," Charlie said. "It fell from the car as I was sliding inside for our getaway after you drove that motorbike into the lake."

"'Member that shit?!" Reggie lit up in laughter. "Motherfucker run outside yelling, he ain't even have pants on! We just roared the hell out and Charlie say: 'Hold up Reg, we ran over something.' I look back it's the damn Chicken Bible!"

"Sweet Lord. *That* was good Chicken."

Shaking his head in remembrance, Charlie reached for the book. Flipping it over, he paged through the dog eared pages of cheaply printed text and photos.

"Chicken goes back to 'Nam, but this here Bible started twenty years back. I got all the dirt. Hell you should see my place back in Biloxi. Boxes full of Chicken history and mystery. Chicken Bible II and III just waiting to be made."

"You should get a new binding for it," I said. "I know a place over in—"

"Oh no," Charlie said. "This is not information for public consumption. Lot of people don't even want my bible around. Think it'll get in the wrong hands and lead to trouble. Want the damn thing burned. Probably best to start with the history. Here…"

Turning a few pages in, Charlie pointed out a section with a jaundiced looking finger, blonde hair curling on the knuckles. I took the book from him. Tapping Reggie on the shoulder, Charlie started towards the courtyard.

"C'mon Reg. Let's get the bar-b-q sorted with Hans."

Both men left the dingy lobby, rejoining the others outside. Monteblan trailed after them.

"Gonna grab a beer,"

I nodded. Left alone in the dusty lobby, with nothing but the sound of the old clock ticking, I walked over to a sunken, ancient, aqua colored pleather sofa and read.

## *THE LEGEND OF CHICKEN 65*

Thai national Somchai Kitapoon was a US military asset, trained by the Green Berets for deep cover operations and activated in 1965. Inserted deep within Northern Vietnam, Somchai married a local woman and posed as a farmer. Officially unacknowledged, working alone under threat of imminent death, Somchai developed a vast and penetrating intelligence network. Winning critical assets that illuminated the murky dawn of US involvement, Somchai's highly cultivated channels were credited with saving more US lives than any other network in country. But the Thai agent's activities aroused suspicion which peaked in 1965. Through his operatives, Somchai received word that a particularly brutal and infamous brigade officer- the notorious Quan Loc- had discerned the simple farmer's true identity. Hastily packing wife and daughter under cover of night, Somchai narrowly escaped with his life, mere hours before Quan Loc raided his village.

Evading the gauntlet cast by the furious brigade officer, Somchai spirited his family out of Northern Vietnam, through Laos, and into Thailand, where he was debriefed in Bangkok.

Recently declassified documents relate these recorded sessions, held in a nondescript "short time" hotel on Phetchaburi Road. The hotel stands today, as does Somchai's reputation as perhaps the most brilliant Thai operative to serve within the South East Asian theatre. His official story ends there. But the legend of Somchai Kitapoon was born shortly after his US military files were sealed and classified. It started early on a January morning, 1965, when the 32 year old father once again awoke to the sound of his only daughter crying.

Since arriving in Bangkok, his daughter's tears had been incessant. First attributed to the trauma of refugee flight, the five year old's wailing lament was later clarified as devastation by chicken. Or rather, lack of one. In the urgent flight from Vietnam, Somchai had forgot to pack his five year old daughter's favorite pet: the family fowl. Now inconsolable with grief, she cried for the lost bird throughout the days and nights. Both civilian and Army doctors prescribed a battery of sedatives. Pills did nothing. Her grief deepened. Days passed in bleak parade. Local elders began whispering of possession and malevolent spirits. Somchai loudly cursed them, while silently recognizing the nearly supernatural lament which gripped his daughter. When the girl's tears dried into leaden, life threatening depression, a desperate Somchai finally summoned the local monk. In hushed ceremonies of smoke and prayer, the sage elder determined that deep karmic bonds bound daughter and chicken. This vital relationship, established in other planes of time, had been tragically ruptured in flight from war. Because the bond was broken, Somchai's daughter would surely die. The only solution was both Herculean and absurd. To save his daughter, Somchai was tasked with a return to Vietnam, and retrieval of the family chicken.

Whether the bird had survived the mounting inferno of war

was in doubt. But debate was immaterial regarding Quan Loc, the homicidal brigade officer who had narrowly missed apprehending Somchai's fleeing family. His position was making border penetration both increasingly impossible and patently suicidal. In addition to these damning details was Somchai's recent discharge. Debriefed and decommissioned, the former operative had no capacity for summoning official support. What made matters more pressing was a recent boon that now seemed the stuff of tragic farce. To reward his intelligence services, Somchai's handling officer in the US Military had bestowed the exceedingly rare gift of American citizenship on the Thai national and his family. But having never officially existed within the US Military, this transfer of nationality would occur in the vague landscape of plausible deniability. Rare and precisely ticking favors would begin in three weeks' time, when Somchai and his family were scheduled to arrive in America, then be quietly ushered through a momentary opening into full citizenship. Failure to grasp the rare instance meant missing it forever. This was not an option for Somchai. He had seen the rising wave of chaos set to engulf the region, and had determined that his family would live in peace. They would be on that plane, with that chicken, in three weeks' time.

At 7 minutes past midnight on February 11th, 1965, Somchai Kitapoon roared out of Bangkok in a powder blue Pontiac Tempest, on loan from his Special Forces commander. Blazing through Northern Thailand, lighting through Laos, the former intelligence operative was met by former comrades near the enemy border. The small band of elite S.O.G. soldiers specialized in long range patrols, deep behind enemy lines. More than one of them owed his life to intelligence Somchai had furnished while active in Northern Vietnam, and were happy to unofficially return the favor. None questioned his mission objectives. All joined to help him find the chicken. Stashing his Pontiac Tempest, the hardened band lead the Thai father through the war zone by less conspicuous means. A night drop by silenced helicopter was followed by a five day trek by foot through heavy jungle, dodging enemy patrols. Advantage was found in the absurdity of their mission: a small dispatch of soldiers with no artillery backing, this far behind enemy lines, was so unlikely it hardly deserved consideration. Like wraiths in the jungle, Somchai's chicken mission evaded enemy camps and patrols, arriving finally at his former village, shortly before supper time. The hour was propitious, as his mother in law was just then sharpening her knife for a chicken dinner- the very karmic fowl that bound his daughter's fate.

Rescuing the chicken, Somchai and his men waited for cover of darkness. They then retraced their route back to the powder blue Pontiac, hidden in deep camouflage near the Laos border. But half way along their chosen path, the group was halted by their point patrol scout, who had looped back swiftly to share grim intel. Quan Loc, through his own vast intelligence network, had learned of Somchai's inexplicable return to the war zone. Waiting in ambush, the North Vietnamese nemesis had closed off the path back to Laos. A hasty and daring plan was quickly devised: the mobile and highly agile US troops would lead Quan Loc on a roundabout diversion bearing north, while Somchai broke South with the chicken. Upon reaching Saigon, Air America cronies would then return him to Bangkok. With this new objective set, Somchai vowed brotherhood. Marking the mission and the year, he spoke the immortal words that would live forever amidst our brethren. "Chicken 65", the Thai whispered, slipping with his bird into the jungle.

Mere hours later, he stumbled upon a lone VC scout caught literally with his pants down, mid squat in defecation. Neutralizing this propitious target, stealing his uniform and later hijacking a Viet Cong jeep, Somchai drove the chicken on a nerve racking journey down the coast of Vietnam, bluffing and dodging his way through enemy territory. Meanwhile, the ruse laid by S.O.G. soldiers in the North finally wore thin when Quan Loc received intelligence of Somchai sightings along the coast. The brigade officer left in furious pursuit, mobilizing forces that trapped Somchai just short of the DMZ. Jeep lost to tank fire, pinned down by mortars as his enemy closed in, Somchai and chicken prepared for death. But old friends and favors go far in a place like Vietnam. And although Air America could not officially sanction the rescue of Somchai due to diplomatic constraints, they were approved to air drop the powder blue Pontiac Tempest via Huey helicopter into the combat zone.

With ticket to ride and chicken in hand, Somchai narrowly escaped Quan Loc, on what is perhaps the only muscle car race through heavy combat in the history of warfare. Piloting the Pontiac in and out of mine fields, mortar batteries, napalm drops, and hand to hand combat zones, Somchai pressed forward with his daughter's karmic chicken flapping in the back seat and a maniacal Quan Loc in fast pursuit. The Viet Cong brigade officer had radioed command to close all border entries to the South, making flight from Saigon impossible. Thus trapped, the fearless father veered out of Vietnam in an elusive and highly dangerous maneuver through bomb drenched Cambodia. His decision proved life-saving. While Somchai and chicken miraculously dodged through carpet bombing ballistics from droning US B-52s, Quan Loc was not so fortunate. Obliterated in a direct hit just outside Battambang, Somchai's arch nemesis was finally dispatched permanently.

Thus surviving the war zones- having traversed Thailand, Laos, Vietnam, Cambodia, and Thailand once more- Somchai barely beat Monday morning Bangkok traffic to meet his family's US bound Jet. Roaring onto the tarmac, screeching to a halt, the exhausted father finished his odyssey in a breathless chicken clutching sprint towards the departing jet. Pulled in by frantic family, Somchai just managed to board before the screaming engines blazed to life and shot his plane down the runway. Upon reunion with her karmic chicken, Somchai's daughter instantly recovered, emerging totally from fatal, funereal gloom.

As the plane moved upward into bright blue sky, Somchai bid good bye to his war torn lands. Obtaining full citizenship and settling in San Diego, the former intelligence operative prospered in pleasant obscurity. Once retired, his daughter maintained the family business: the only Thai restaurant in California that doesn't serve Chicken.

**"Something, inn't it?"**

I looked up from the book to see Mississippi Charlie smiling down over a freshly opened beer. Though I thought I had been over the initial shock, his nose startled me anew. Open pores and veins big as rivers, it was a bulbous, ruined mash. I remembered a board game from my youth, played out over a cartoonish man with a red light bulb nose. Part of me wondered if Mississippi's might glow like that, lit up in the dark.

"So that guy we met at the bar won Chicken 65?" I asked.

"Sure did. You boys met yourself a Chicken legend. Pass that Bible here."

Handing the worn old book to Charlie, I watched him flip through pages, muttering to himself, finally finding what he wanted.

"Right here: Brain The Dane, Chicken 2000."

He tilted the book towards me. I leaned in to see better in the fluorescent light of the ancient lobby. The face in the faintly reproduced photo looked much brighter, happier, and younger than the drooping, forlorn figure we had left in Silom. Trim and bright, almost glowing, the man in The Bible was holding a chicken. Behind him, just visible over his shoulder, I could make out the Miami Hotel courtyard. Leaning in, I read the text.

56

## BRAIN THE DANE

## Chicken 2000

Burgmond "Brain The Dane" Shloos took home the Chicken in what has been called the smartest race ever won. Using surveying skills and ground measurement tools from his work with the Danish Interior, he recorded road conditions and ground temperatures all along the race path and determined with fantastic precision the exact points where tires might blow out. Drawing on his facility for language and diplomatic skills, Brain travelled and made vital friendships in Laos, Vietnam, throughout Cambodia and Thailand. Stashing tires up and down S.E. Asia with people paid for their silence, Brain The Dane set himself up for the perfect Chicken. His precise measurements and estimations had him pulling in to change his tires at all the right moments, making his Chicken the smoothest ever. With no time lost for emergency tire changes or bent rims, he remains the only racer in the history of Chicken 65 to navigate the entire race without changing a wheel roadside.

His plan was five years in the making, with costs he refuses to disclose, to this day. But the fact that his house in Denmark was sold, and a marriage into one of Denmark's most prominent families was broken off just before Chicken 2000 is some indication of the investment. Thoughtful, measured and precise, the unique victory earned this Chicken 65er his name. Why it's Brain The Dane, instead of Dane The Brain or The Dane Brain, nobody really knows. But like most things in Chicken 65, the reasons can probably be traced to way too much drinking, by all involved.

I looked up from the page, trying hard to match the faded, slumping old man in Silom with this trim, grinning figure proudly holding a chicken.

"And he's been drinking for free in Bangkok ever since?" I asked.

"Them's the rules," Charlie nodded.

"Right. I need to learn the rules."

"You do. But I'm due for some shut eye. We'll fill you in at The General's BBQ in Chang Mai. Be sure to get yourself a suit. That's real important for you two. Don't show up in anything less than tailored duds. I'll take that, please?"

Mississippi Charlie reached out for the Chicken Bible. I didn't want to let it go. The legends, faces, recounted races, feuds, tragedies, and fatalities all listed within this dilapidated book were extraordinary. Chicken 65 wasn't just a race. It was something much more. I wanted to spend my entire night with The Bible trying to find out what.

Charlie recognized my hesitation and shook his head. "Chicken got you bad."

Smiling, he gently removed the book from my hand and walked away.

**Mr. Boom's Chicken garage was hidden deep in a Bangkok 'hood.**
We found it that night, winding down tight streets thick with traffic
smoke and the pale slash of headlights. Set behind an open air restaurant where greasy vats bubbled with slabs of roiling meats, the tire
strewn warehouse was grease slicked and silent. Cars in parts and
various pieces of assemblage were leaning or raised, lowered or abandoned. A 70s Datsun had jumped out at my friend: black with mags,
red lines on the trim. Inside, dials from the dash had been pried up and
placed on top of it. Racing style, Monteblan explained, so the driver
didn't have to glance down.

My friend, I was learning, knew something about cars. After
inspecting the rims, testing the metal by pressing his keys in and
scratching hard, he looked satisfied. Further encouraged by a spare tire
that was part of the deal, Monteblan popped the hood. Leaning over
the engine, glancing, examining, pulling on connections and testing,
my friend had nodded. Leaving his passport and myself as collater-
al, he backed slowly out into the street, testing clutch, brake and gas.
Disappearing for a few moments heading one way, my friend pulled
back into the garage the other, gunning the engine with large, powerful blasts that echoed through the dim garage. Monteblan emerged
from the test drive with concerns about the clutch. Mr. Boom threw
in an 8 Track from another car to get him off the fence. It came with

a greasy old box of ancient tapes. Monteblan nodded ascent and the funds were sorted out between us.

Leaving The Datsun with Mr. Boom for a final tune up, we headed downtown for supplies. Monteblan was quiet as we pushed through Bangkok's steamy throng. There was more to this race, I realized, than my friend was telling me. Something had imposed a type of gravitas upon my portly compadre which was rare. This change in nature was unsettling, and I tried to shake him out of it as we stocked up on strange items coughed up by Bangkok streets. Pellet guns, mace, body armor, binoculars, bootleg valium ("Velium") army helmets and knives were all arrayed in criminal smorgasbord on tables just outside the red light district bars.

"Hey, check this out." Holding up a samurai sword, I shifted it from hand to hand as Monteblan ambled over.

"Crazy story about one of these," I told him while go-go girls waved. "We were out one night down here in Patpong. Gets hectic real late. All those ping pong shows upstairs, ladyboys getting aggro since they haven't scored. Shady characters all around, plus you're ripped by that point, right?"

Monteblan nodded, picking up a Rambo knife and testing the weight in his hand. The neon beer light from a bar that featured post-operative transsexuals glinted on the blade. Japanese mostly fill such places, routinely fascinated with some element of manmade vaginas.

"So there's this guy I ran into one night down here. Met him in my condo. Independently wealthy, 30 something, money to burn and he was out there torching it like mad. Canadian, fun guy, always went black out drunk though. Always. But fun to drink with because you know what they say."

"What do they say?" Monteblan replied, placing down the knife and moving down the table towards some marital aids.

"A fool and his money are fun to go out with."

Monteblan nodded picking up something shrink wrapped that turned on, designed for insertion into whatever orifice might respond to such technology.

"So we go to this bank machine at like three, he's pulling out more money for more beers and I'm wandering down the street window shopping at the go-go bars. I turn back too late. Two Thai guys are standing ganged up on my guy at the ATM. I watch him put the money into their hands. They walk away laughing at him, and have the balls to just disappear into one of those Thai places where the girls go to drink after their shift."

"Sucks," Monteblan said, putting down sex toys and picking up weapons. "Hope you have my back better than that when we hit the road."

"I will. I was a rookie back then. I get back to my guy, and he's just *pissed*. Can't fight Thai guys out here. They don't fight fair. Or their version of fair is different from ours. If a white guy fights a Thai, they all jump in. They don't even care what about. It's like some bat signal goes out all over the city, and they just appear—like ten of them, and everybody jumps in, stomping the foreign motherfucker's ass. First thing you learn out here is never, *never*, get in a fight with a Thai. Practically pass out pamphlets about it at the airport. Thai guys are brutally pragmatic. The point is to win the fight. Ten guys will do that better than one. So that's how they do. Anyway..."

Monteblan and I moved through the tables, finding BB guns that looked like nine millimeter police issue pistols, rifle scopes, and body armor. My friend started gathering items in a pile while I continued.

"My guy. He's furious. He's drunk. He's out ten thousand *baht*. Just pacing there, on the slick scummy Pat Pong streets, seeing red. Then he sees one of these...." I nodded towards the weapon laden tables all around. "He mumbles: 'Be ready to run.' I watch him buy a samurai sword. He walks to the bar with it. He was *brandishing* the thing. Like in a movie. Have you ever seen someone brandish a samurai sword?

It's one thing to hold it, brandishing is a whole other level. That's where he is. Kicks through the door like Toshiro Mifune and the place swallowed him up. I'm standing there like: *what?*"

Monteblan held up a pair of binoculars, zooming in long distance on some go-go booty. Nodding satisfied, he checked the price while I continued.

"3 AM, Patpong, my guy just walked into a bar with a samurai sword. I'm lost. Drunk. Trying to process how to respond to the situation when the door kicks open and he comes running out, hands full of cash, samurai sword shining, running for the taxis. Suddenly it dawns on me that I'm the only other white guy around. Not the color to be at that particular moment and place in time. I break the other way and by some miracle of God catch a motorbike all the way to Huay Kwang. Quite a haul when you're drunk on the back of a motorcycle. Whoa. Excuse me?"

I was jostled aside by a laughing pack of Arabs. Recovering my footing in their cologne clouded wake, I continued.

"So a few days later at my place, I hit the pool on the roof. My guy's there lounging with one of his girls. Had great taste in women-slim things. Isaan spinners to die for. I sit down next to them. Casually steer the conversation towards the night he brandished a samurai sword in the middle of Bangkok. Start with some joke: 'So dude, what happened to that sword?'

He squints a second, looking at me in the sun, like he didn't hear me right. 'Sword?' He says. 'What are you talking about?'

I reminded him about the other night, when we ran into each other and he ran out of the bar like the last samurai. He leans back in his chair and shakes his head.

'Shit,' he says. "Did I go to Patpong again?'

Didn't remember it. No recollection *at all* of drinking with me for three hours. He had blacked out before I even showed up. I had no idea. We had argued about baseball—he was giving shit to me about the 90s' Yankees. Saying they were shit compared to the 80's Mets. Then movies! He knew *Zardoz*! Only person in Bangkok probably! Detailed discussion about film and he was black out drunk the whole time. Good lord that's a drinking problem. And we're not even getting to the samurai sword issues. I mean, I get it. This is Thailand. People party. I'm one of them. I drink too much, I put my penis in someone I hardly know, then float in pools of regret the following day. That's Bangkok. But *that*? Highly animated sports discussion followed by classic cinema debate, topped off by a samurai sword raid in Patpong he didn't even remember? *That* is a drinking problem."

Shaking my head at the memory, placing down the weapon, I watched Monteblan pile up on combat contraband. Looping back to the marital aid table, he looked twice at a huge pink dildo.

"Great name." He picked it up, tilting the label towards me. "Check this out."

I ambled over to examine the plastic encased dildo. The packaging card sealed between sheets of pressed plastic showed an American flag with neatly typed title: *American Strong*.

"Who names dildos?" I wondered out loud.

"Who names them American Strong?" my friend added. "I want an address. They need fan mail."

I hefted the dildo momentarily, nodding as the name resonated.

"Well, that's pretty much what we are: a large blunt instrument fucking the world."

Dropping the marital aid, I surveyed our gathered items. Ballistic booty implied very weird adventures ahead. Pellet guns, army helmet, flak jacket, a few bottles of whiskey, six packs of beer, Velium, retracting billy club, zippo lighters and Rambo Knife added up to suggest quite a night. Although probably routine, given Bangkok standards. Monteblan paid for the bulging sack of mayhem while I dashed into a souvenir store for maps. The Indian shop owner was surrounded by bootleg headphones, designer luggage, cologne and carved elephants.

Monteblan wondered in with weapons and whiskey while the old man was ringing up the maps. He frowned, wondering if he should take my money or turn me in.

"Road trip," I assured him, as if that made our purchases any less likely to produce prison terms.

Leaving, we elbowed and pushed our way through throngs and settled at a sidewalk restaurant. Noodles roiled in vats while pork was hacked to bits on a grease slicked chopping block by a Thai wearing an *I Love Croatia* shirt. Unfolding maps, I pinned them down with beers. Abstractions of the region in pastel colors mystified my American eyes.

"Geography," I muttered. "I've heard of that somewhere…"

Eyes running over the countries of our intended mission, I familiarized myself with the terrain while rotating lights from street bars strobed on latitude and longitude lines.

"What do you know," I recognized. "I'm poring over a map. I've never done that before, but it's in every cheap thriller I've read in my life. People always pore over maps."

"Pour me a beer bro," Monteblan said, reaching for the bottle. "And make sure you mark Chicken Town. You find our way. I get us there. Deal?"

"That's how it's done," I agreed.

Map use had been my saving skill in online video games. I showed up mostly as target practice for 12 year olds. Live chat didn't help. Hearing prepubescent virtual murderers calling me *butt wipe* and *dick breath* while plasma blasts dashed my avatars had eventually chased me from the genre in bitter frustration. Since then, it had been GPS all the way. Years had passed since I had to map things out. Now I struggled to marry our actual location with the abstraction of Bangkok before me, taking on the daunting task of tracing potential routes. First was our path through the city towards our starting point at Democracy Monument in the morning. Finding a reasonable route, I had traced it out in pencil then made other probable paths through Laos and Vietnam in another bar. Last stop was a return to Mr. Boom's. We were on the way when I remembered Mississippi Charlie's wardrobe requirements.

It wasn't hard to find a tailor. Well buzzed, we stumbled into the first place showing suits in the window. Pounced upon by a bespoke Indian hustler who grinned broadly at our arrival, we drunkenly ordered a pair of tailored suits like late night pizza. I pulled a black fabric with herring bone inset cut 44 long. Monteblan ignored all warnings and went white on white, then scribbled his hotel address down for the delivery. Assured our suits would arrive by midnight, we made our way back to Mr. Boom's.

The Datsun was tuned and ready. Eight track loaded, we blasted soft rock and rolled. Finding my friend's hotel, exhausted from preparations, we found our suits waiting at the desk. Hanging them on the wall in the room, we showered, crashed in twin beds and turned out the lights. I stared at the ceiling, wondering how Monteblan's girlfriend was taking the news of our adventure.

"What'd you tell Rayne?" I asked my friend.

"Not that I bought a Datsun with an eight track. Shit. She'd break it off for playing Gordon Lightfoot."

"So what'd you say?"

"That I was having a blast out here and was partying for another week."

"What'd she say?"

"You know Rayne." Monteblan turned over on his bed. "Told me to have fun."

I laid there for a while, listening to the humming air conditioner,

"Do you think we will?" Staring into darkness, my foreboding from The Miami returned. "Have fun I mean?"

My friend didn't answer. The air conditioner rattled. Shivering slightly in the cold, I finally closed my eyes and fell to sleep.

**We left at dawn in a black car filled with weapons and whiskey.** Our bucket seats were blood red leather and the engine roared. Monteblan gunned it repeatedly as we wound through Bangkok streets. Shouting over engine thunder and 70s pop from the eight track, I called out our turns. Most of me wondered if I any of them were right. When we finally emerged on the open boulevards of Old City, I was thrilled and relieved. Looking up from the map that morning, struck with the magic of reality actually meeting my projection of it on the map, I shouted in triumph.

"Dude, it's there!"

Pointing down the spanning European style boulevard in Bangkok's old town, I directed Monteblan towards the rising form of Democracy Monument at dawn. Golden sun was bathing the towering metal form. Surrounding it were Chicken racers, speeding and flowing together, circling the roundabout. Monteblan didn't respond, just pressed the gas. Speed was immediate and the feeling was exhilarating. Bangkok opened up like a woman in love, trading the restraint of narrow side streets for a rushing plunge down wide open avenue. Dials on the dash leapt right, pinned and quivering in the red and suddenly we were in.

"This is it," I said, staring out our window at the cavalcade of circling drivers. "This is Chicken 65."

I looked at my friend and he nodded slowly, biting his lip while weaving past a boxy blue hatchback. I turned in my seat, eyes scanning through the floating sea of familiar faces, framed now behind windshields of Chevys, Mustangs, Corvettes, tricked out Impalas, low and ominous Lincolns, a few buzzing Citroens, one ponderous Land Rover, and a cherry red T-Bird Camaro.

I was stunned at how it had all happened. Life was the race now. I had been preparing myself all night, but had still expected speeches or something, maybe breakfast. Instead we were instantly blended into the impending mayhem, circling with Chicken 65ers in what appeared to be some sort of promenade. Monteblan shifted his foot on the clutch and moved with things expertly. Over his shoulder, distant buildings caught the first light of rising sun. Crowds had gathered all around. Thais lined the roundabout or stood on top of taxis and trucks beyond, all of them eyeing vehicles, pointing out cars, flashing hand signs to bookies. We whizzed past one draped in Buddhist medallions, multitasking the action furiously. The old Thai man had two cell phones in each hand, rubber bands holding them back to back. Flipping between both, carrying on four different conversations at once while simultaneously flashing hand sign confirmations, he made book on different racers.

"They're betting!" I shouted to Monteblan.

Smiling behind shades, sunk down in his red bucket seat, Monteblan was enjoying the ride. Familiar with the vehicle now, Monteblan moved through the competition effortlessly. He had worn the army helmet, matched it with the flak jacket, and had half a breakfast beer lodged snug in the crotch of his madras shorts. Just as he was piloting another graceful, curving arc around the roundabout, the gunshot exploded behind us.

Monteblan just knew what to do. Every driver did. From all around they leapt into high speed. The race was on. With sudden acceleration, like a hand pushing from behind, we shot past The General as he

holstered the revolver that had started Chicken 65. Across the roundabout, cars were roaring out into the city at high velocity and with
considerable head start. Lowering his chin, Monteblan pressed down
on the accelerator, slipping us between a blue Citroen and a matte
black Chevy, then sliding past an Impala with breathtaking fluidity.

"Chicken 65…" my friend said, slow and cool.

His adept moves caught the surprised looks of Thai gamblers, many
of whom stared in surprised appreciation. We were the dark horse, I
imagined, the rubes who had stumbled into this thing. But these rubes
could drive. Monteblan was moving magic and I was amazed at the
revelation. Through hours and untold nights we had spent bullshit-
ting about every aspect of life, he had never mentioned cars. But now
he looked like he had been born in one. Pressing effortlessly into the
last turn, he tapped the clutch, flipped the stick, pressed brake then
poured on gas. It was done like the snapping of fingers, rapidly fast, the
combination shooting us between two speeding vehicles and out of the
roundabout full speed.

Holding the ceiling to keep me straight as we swerved, I let out a
yell of surprise that sounded like laughter. It had all happened so fast, so
unexpectedly and instantly, that I was in shock. Now I held tight as we
screeched down narrow roads, all of them cleared of traffic by untold
bribes. Thais lined these streets, street vendors with fruit carts, parked
taxi drivers, young kids and old people too, some of them standing on
their fenders, others atop taxi roofs, more leaning from dark windows
in cement block buildings with air dirty conditioning units and dangling wires. How I saw this all I still don't know. We were moving so
fast it was like a blur. My eyes were picking out people like snapshots
as we shot through: toothless old man, a grinning child, fat beefy Thai
drinking whiskey… All of them a blurring, ambient, gambling wave
of appreciation and speculation. Shooting through their midst I felt a
dawning awe. Block by Thai lined block, I finally understood the size

of this thing, the money involved, the avalanche of odds solidifying now into mighty piles of bets.

"Shit, hang on buddy!"

Roaring full speed forward, Monteblan winced while looking ahead and I followed the line of his gaze. One hundred meters distant, some suddenly arching asphalt jumped up like an oversized speed bump; bridge across one of the myriad filthy canals that ran through Bangkok like the dirtied veins of a lifetime chain-smoking drunk.

Before I could protest, my friend's hands and feet shifted in another dance of motions as we hit the rise, his large body leaning forward in the seat as if willing the car into place. Full speed we smashed right into the rising road and momentarily left the planet.

In that half blink moment when we lifted from the streets, Monteblan looked at me, grinning. I'll never understand how I saw so much in that moment. The entire landscape of our potential demise was illustrated instantly. While airborne wheels spun silently beneath us, the world around rotated, my friend's smile the pinning hub. Beyond and below us the klong sparkled in dawn's grey lights. A lumbering commuter boat chugged up the dirty river, past the shanty houses where laundry hung outside. The boat driver looked up at us, mouth agape, understanding what would happen when we touched down on the tight road. Nothing but the most perfect of landings would prevent us from flip flopping onto his chugging, commuter packed craft. Grasping this, passengers watched us in slowly dawning horror. Around us, Thai faces lining the road spread from smiles to dread, eyes widening while the '79 Datsun flew over the grease slicked road towards highly probable, deeply lethal tragedy. Beyond all transfixed gazes was a golden temple atop a hill. I'll swear I heard a gong sound in low, sonorous bloom. Then in flashed telepathic understanding, I understood why Monteblan was looking at me.

We were going to die.

My friend wanted me to understand this. The race had hardly started and here we were already done. I nodded to him in wordless acceptance, strangely unfazed. This moment suspended in air was our last. So be it. But just as I was closing my eyes to die, Monteblan snapped back to the wheel.

Everything sped up and roared. Our car's front end banged down strong, whipping us like puppets pulled by a furious child. Almost magically my friend understood what would happen upon hitting earth. Stick blurred. Clutch brake gas. His flicker of instincts combined to keep us from careening into klong water. Monteblan had anticipated every element of road response and married it masterfully with car reaction. Positioned perfectly, we did a breathtaking stretch on our two front tires. Angled absurdly with front fender scraping, throwing up sparks, we slid past the chugging boat, mere meters in water below. Then thumping back down hard, the car grabbed road with all four wheels. Roaring through throngs of cheering Thais, one last turn took us away, flying into the city beyond.

Monteblan turned to me.

"This car will do good Chicken."

Before me on the dashboard I saw all needles agreeing, pinned in accord, engine purring as if nothing had happened. But it had. We had almost died. My exhilaration and adrenaline were chased by dread as the chemicals in my mind finally caught up with what had happened in the car. Beside me, Monteblan was ice cold. Pressing the accelerator, we raced down a narrow tree lined street where doors were thrown open, showing wood-working masters busy at their trade. Most carved Buddhas. The last shop was the exception. Flashing by, I saw coffins stacked and polished, carved ornately with burnished curves. The old master making them paused as we passed, hammer and lathe in his hand, sawdust at his feet, staring as two potential customers flew recklessly past.

A small whiplash turn took us skidding out into a wider city street where the slowly churning mass of early commuter cars, taxis and busses formed an impassable jack straw scatter beneath the echo chamber of an expressway overpass. Through it all, Monteblan found possibility. I watched, stunned, as my friend sped forward infused with an artistry on par with the wood workers we had just left behind. With intrinsic understanding of what each driver would do, Monteblan anticipated everything. He left lanes just as they closed, raced towards others before they opened, and in one instance of beautifully drifting sideways slide, captured an impossible diagonal entry between barriers of cement divide. Shooting us exultantly up onto the ramp, we were out on the expressway. It all had happened so fast that my mouth was still open to suggest we slow down. But there was no slowing down. Monteblan could drive. Flying under the radiant morning sun, sailing gloriously towards Chang Mai in Chicken 65, the eight track grooved. I looked down at the tape title written in faded letters, worn away by more than a quarter of a century.

"Pablo Cruise!" I shouted over wind, reading the band's name aloud. "That's this car's name! This is Pablo Cruise!"

Touching the dashboard reverently, as if bequeathing or christening it, I felt myself both chilled and calm.

We had almost died.

But we didn't.

*Monteblan could drive.*

**Up ahead, the way was open.** Most people at this hour were heading into the city for a day's work. Skyscrapers loomed like upright tombs, waiting to embrace them in benumbed, embalming routine. Wildly alive, Monteblan pushed us into the open expressway, catching up with a pack of Chicken drivers. This was pure speed. Brought forward by hurtling forces we raced. Glancing down at my seatbelt, it struck me as silly and ridiculous. That such a small and tiny strap would possess the power to stop total, maiming destruction was patently absurd. I didn't care. This was a race and we were in it. Laughing out loud I rolled down my window. Wind whipped in, hitting plastic bags in the back that rippled hissing like snakes. Floating into the roving band of racers, we pulled up beside the last vehicle in formation.

The white Range Rover was thrumming grandly over the pavement, high above the others. The dapper blonde Brit was driving, lording over the road. Looking down at me, he laughed in pleasant surprise, raising a champagne glass. The window slid down and house music blasted free, mixing with roaring winds and thrumming tires. Shouting with glee through the melee as rippling wind tousled his blonde hair, his British accent was sharp.

"Well done! You've caught the pack!" Smiling grandly, he raised his glass of champagne. "Excellent Chicken, by all means!"

Monteblan dipped back momentarily, bringing us in line with the Rover's back windows. A beautiful woman looked at me, brown eyes solemn and deep. Long black hair flipped flying in the wind then a cloud passed over the sun, obscuring her in the blank reflection of glass. Monteblan pressed the gas, leaving house music in our wake as we left the Range Rover behind.

Eating up road he found French in their Citroen, passed Germans in a Mercedes then pulled past two Koreans piloting a retro future 70's dream. Angled and low, tinted windows and butterfly doors, the machine looked science fiction. In surprise the drivers registered us, then frowned in determination and fought to retake their position. All around us was speed. Gunning, weaving, dancing together like dolphins, drivers were grinning and challenging, pressing their limits; fast, alive and free.

Then a soft *thunk!* hit our roof, followed by the sight of a small red object with flashing fuse tumbling down the windshield.

"Holy Shit!" Monteblan shouted, recognizing the firework and swerving hard right, making it fall to the side. Behind us it bounced on the expressway before exploding with a loud

*Boom!*

"What the *fuck?!*" I yelled over screaming wind and 70s eight track pop. Another explosion just to our right blasted my ear, making it ring. We were overtaken then by the roaring red Camaro.

Reggie was at the wheel, a dark grin on his face while Mississippi Charlie, laughing, lit another M-80. Holding it out of the car window so his golden arm hairs danced wildly in the wind, he dropping the lit mini bomb to bounce on the expressway. The Brit behind us slowed then swerved in fine form, dodging the ordinance as it exploded just to the side of his Range Rover. Through the windshield I saw him raise his champagne glass in a smiling "cheers".

Mississippi Charlie lit another M 80, sky hooking it over their roof to land on the hood of the German's Mercedes. The firework bounced off, flying to the side and exploding. Blank faced Germans inside turned to each other, then looked back to the road. Inside the Camaro, Charlie and Reggie howled in laughter. The back windows, I noticed, were covered with chicken wire. Their stereo was a huge blast of subwoofer might, playing *The Boys are Back in Town* loud enough to drown out explosions. Not wishing to attract one, everyone gave them room to pass. Laughing loud while trading high fives, Charlie and Reggie gunned forward, leaving us behind as they roared north.

Watching them go, grinning ear to ear, I realized I loved this thing. The first five minutes were more action than I had seen in five years. Maybe Chicken 65 was what I had been looking for. I hadn't left America so much as fallen out of it. Bouncing from job to job, watching people get married, I didn't know where to belong. Choosing Thailand was chance, and stumbling into the race was entirely accidental. Or was it? Reggie had said I chose this. What did that mean? Right now, I didn't understand. But Mississippi Charlie had been right back at The Miami. Whatever this was, I was hooked. Flying over Thai highways, his southern drawl echoed in my mind.

*"Chicken got you bad."*

**The rest of the day blurred pleasantly by in humming high speed.** Monteblan searched for Monkey Beaches all the way, optimistically overlooking the absence of oceans. The rest of his attentions had been paid to the clutch, which he claimed was sticky. Whatever problems Pablo Cruise had didn't bother me. Rolling through eight tracks, flying on highways, I didn't want that first day of Chicken 65 to end. Finally, sky growing dark as we approached Chang Mai, it did. Closing in on the city, scooters joined the flow of traffic like birds signifying shore to homebound ships.

"We must be near Changers," I said. "Those scooters don't do long distances."

Many had three or more people on back, windbreakers rippling, heads leaning into the wind. Some wore cheap helmets made in China, notorious for disintegrating on impact. I had met a Dutch Harley Driver in Bangkok who had told me as much, explaining why he imported his helmets from America. Thais wore them more like a cosmetic affectation than anything else. Moving slowly now as traffic thickened, Monteblan watched as one more cheap helmet passed by on the shoulder, the driver's little child riding bareheaded behind him.

"Dude, you drive." I finally said.

I had been holding it back all day, waiting for the right time to crack this aspect of Monteblan's hidden life. Now I turned to face him fully.

"Can we talk about the fact that you drive, like, archetypically? That move on the bridge? What the hell was that?"

Monteblan smiled slyly from the side of his mouth. "What move?"

"When we hit the ground, you hit the gas. How did you know to do that?"

"Hit the brakes you freeze up." He shrugged. "Then you're skidding and we would have gone right into the dong."

"Klong," I corrected my friend, remembering our narrowly avoided river splash. "But how did you know? That's not the natural instinct. I wasn't even driving and my foot slammed down like there was a brake in front of me. That's what everybody would do."

"Everybody who doesn't know how to drive."

Monteblan didn't add more. Just shifted another gear and twitched the pedals, subtly swerving into lane while checking the rearview. Briefly flashing high beams and gassing forward, he braked to dodge a scooter then flicked right, finding open lane. Pablo Cruise responded beautifully, the entire sequence perfectly handled. It was like both were collaborating, thrilled to have met, eager to speed. All day such married moves had blended in smooth, fluid expression, racing us north while revealing my friend's intrinsic, instinctual feel for the road. Riding passenger, I struggled with the realization: my formerly ordinary friend possessed something exceptional.

"Dude, you *really* drive," I repeated. "What's up with that?"

Staring ahead, my friend's face was a blank. But flicks of expression chased each other through headlight shadows. Obscure and fleeting, suggesting regret and conflict, these depths were unsettling. My normally happy go lucky compadre rarely reflected in depth. The change was unnerving, although admittedly offset by the absurdity of his flak jacket and army helmet.

"Do you think they have a monkey beach in Chang Mai?" he replied, changing the subject.

"There's no beach in Chang Mai," I sighed, realizing Monteblan wasn't ready to talk.

Pointing out our turn, I directed Monteblan into town. Scooter thick local traffic clogged smoky streets. Food carts were suddenly everywhere, steaming under dangling light bulbs while surrounding tables spilled off the sidewalks. Following my map, we found the ancient city walls, circled the moat, and found our way into The General's residential neighborhood. Low houses were hidden behind cement walls with large iron gates. One was open, light spilling out onto the drive. A loosely parked lot of retro vehicles crowded the entrance, thronging the road and hanging off of curbs. Clearly the last to arrive, we stepped outside and stretched.

"I like parking in Thailand," Monteblan noting the casual crowd of cars. "Stop where you feel it."

Sounds of laughter, music, and party people drifted towards us from behind the house.

"Dude, our suits," I remembered.

We dressed behind the car, straightening lapels and shooting cuffs, stepping into patent leather shoes.

"Bring the whiskey," I told Monteblan. "I'll grab the food."

Wanting to make a good impression, I had stopped by a store on the way. Hefting the heavy box of grill-ready poultry on my shoulder, I smiled.

"This will make us Chicken."

**The General's yard was alive with chicken talk and a sizzling
grill.** A large photo of Somchai Kitapoon was positioned in respectful spotlight, flowers gathered below, incense sticks trailing. Trees all
round were decorated with lights. Racers stood with beers or drinks in
hand, drifting amidst Thai girls with back tattoos. All of them looked
at us and laughed.

Nobody was wearing suits. Mississippi Charlie had pranked us.

Fully formal in a sea of sloppy T-Shirts, flip flops, and cut offs,
my ears burned. Women's laughter surrounded us as men narrowed
their eyes in cool judgement. I had seen that look before: New Guy
worthiness weighed in the balance. Smiling, hoping to swing opinions
our way, I held up the box of meat.

"We brought chicken!"

The yard went silent. Mouths fell open in shock. The General appeared swiftly, dressed in pressed shorts and polo, snatching the box
of chicken from my arms.

"Nice going butt nuts." He muttered, shaking his head. "I'm trying
to like you two. Really, I am."

Chicken secured, the trim older man swiftly disappeared into the
house. Monteblan watched him go.

"I think he irons his socks."

"What'd I do?" I asked anyone and everyone around.

The reply was a collected turning of backs as Chicken 65 shut us out. We moved through chilly gazes, racers pretending not to see us. Their disgust, dismay, or dismissal was lit in flickers from hanging lamps all around: smirking German, astonished Japanese, sneering Koreans, bewildered French. A slightly different strain of sardonic *ennui* emanated from the tailored blonde Brit drinking champagne. Standing apart with a trio of tall, glamorous Thai women, he was the only other racer dressed formally. Eyebrows arched in languid amusement, he sighed in dismay then turned to his girls. From behind, a firm, strong hand slapped down on my back. I spun to see a forty something Asian man in blue jeans and T-shirt. His friendly voice was hard Chicago.

"Guys, bringing chicken to a Chicken 65 party is like showing up with hamburgers at a Hindu wedding. We don't touch the stuff till after the race."

"How was I supposed to know that?" I said.

"Well, you bought Sangsom, you're not all bad," the portly Japanese American added, taking the crate of Thai liquor from Monteblan. Trundling with it towards the house, he shook his head in wonder and dismay. "Chicken at a Chicken 65 party. *Damn.*"

"How was I supposed to know that?!"

Nobody answered and I turned to Monteblan. "We're those guys. The ones everybody hates."

"Don't worry about the suits, Charlie does that every year."

A short American man was standing beside me. Smiling politely, he had feathered, blown back hair. I hadn't seen a style like that since the 80s. But wearing full formal at a backyard bar-b-q, I wasn't one to judge. Relieved someone would talk to us, I reached out to shake hands. Instead the man clasped his hands together below his chin, Thai style.

"Baron." The voice was slight and high pitched. His athletic shoes were expensive. "*The* Baron, if you want to be formal with my full Chicken Name."

"This is Monteblan," I said, gesturing to my friend. "And I'm—.

"Asser," he told me. "I know. Chicken Names get around."

"Right, maybe you can help with that. I think there was a mistake. You see I was signing my name when—"

"If you're Asser, you're Asser." The man cut me off again. "Can't do anything about it but don't take it personally." Baron reached up, slapping the shoulder of my brand new suit. "People like to rattle the new guys. Gets worse on the road. You'll find that out after Vientiane. That's when the race gets real. These are the party laps. But don't be fooled. Everybody here hates everybody. Only thing special about your situation is that you're hated before the race starts. That's unique, really."

He frowned, as if considering the rarity of this.

"Thanks. We're kind of learning on the fly here. People are helping. Charlie let me read The Bible."

"Oh please," Barron winced. "That Bible should be burned before it gets half the race arrested. Old Charlie with his Chicken magic shit. What good's it done him? How the hell you run Chicken 65 *22 times* and never once bring back The Bird? Loser."

Shaking his head, Baron narrowed his eyes and stared at Mississippi Charlie across the yard. Happily flipping steaks on the grill, holding a beer, the paunchy old racer was puffing a stogie while telling jokes. Racers around him laughed, belly deep and loud. Baron turned away, shaking his head.

"Well, it takes all kinds out here. Even that kind."

Frowning, the feathered haired man now shot his eyes towards the dashing Brit with his trio of Thai women.

"What's wrong with him?"

"I wouldn't know where to start," Baron scoffed. "Maybe with the fact that his girls have wangs?"

Stunned, I spun back to the three tall Thai women, elegant and glamorous in form fitting dresses.

"Wait, those are—"

"Ladyboys," Barron interrupted once more. "And that's Ladyboy Man. Slick customer. Speaking of slick, I have an oil drip I want to check on. See ya on the road."

Placing his hands together, he bowed slightly and slipped away. Monteblan watched the man thread through the crowd.

"Probably the biggest dick here," he decided.

"Why do you say that?"

"Who else would talk to us?"

As if to confirm my friend's assessment, a voice spoke from the darkness just beyond the tree lights.

"Watch out for that one."

The heavy accent was almost comical, flashing me back to childhood cartoons where a chocolate cartoon vampire sold cereal. I turned to see a tanned man with cropped, salt and pepper hair, wearing a bright white T-shirt. The sleeves were turned up, showing well cut arms. He was fifty or so.

"I saw you this morning at the start," He said to Monteblan. "You know how to move. And you got a good car from Mr. Boom. The Datsun. How's it handling the highway?"

Monteblan nodded. "Decent."

"I looked at this but did not buy it." The tanned man shook his head, waving a finger. "I want the American cars. That is all. Otherwise you will have too much trouble finding any parts. European cars are like women. Fussy. Difficult. American cars you fix a fuel pan with a fucking pie tin and it doesn't mind. Plus rims. Stronger than other cars. They had richer metals then. Much stronger from Detroit or Pittsburgh than that shit from China. You'll need it. Forget about Laos. The roads, my God."

He shrugged, shaking his head before extending his hand to shake ours in turn.

"They call me Gears. Israeli Gears if you want to be formal but mostly just Gears. You are…?"

"Monteblan." My friend said.

"Ah, right, you don't have your Chicken Name yet. But you…" He pointed a finger at me. "Are the one they call Asshole."

"Asser," I corrected with a grimace. "But it's Archer, really."

"It's Asser now."

The Israeli dipped absently into his pocket and produced a small bottle of hand sanitizer. Glopping some into his hands, he briskly rubbed his palms.

"Tough name. Well, at least your friend can drive and the car is good. Chicken 65 is all about your ride. Your gear. Nothing else. You have to have the gear. Oh, look who it is!"

A trim, tan athletic man joined us. Mid-fifties with a full head of luxuriously thick black hair, his white T-shirt matched Gears. The easy grin was warm and brilliantly white. Gears threw an arm over the man's shoulder, patting his chest.

"Meet my map man. Moist Definitely."

"Now *that's* a Chicken name," Monteblan said.

"Moishe is my name," the well-built man smiled. "But…"

He laughed as Gears explained.

"This one here, the girls are all over him. Always. He walks in the room, it's wet panties all over: Moist Definitely."

As if to prove the point, a lovely set of fingers danced up Moist Definitely's arm, squeezing lightly. An exceptionally pretty, black banged Thai beauty appeared with them, pulling happily at the Israeli Map Man. Smiling with a shrug, he let the slim beauty pull him away.

"See what I mean?" Gears shook his head, watching his map man go. "She'll do him for free tonight. Everybody here wants to party. Nobody takes The Splits seriously anymore. But you..."

The Israeli leveled a finger at Monteblan.

"I saw you this morning. I thought: OK, this one knows how to drive. I'm not talking about circle burning on the track. I mean the road. You race?"

Monteblan didn't answer, just bit his lip and nodded slightly, tilting his head back and forth, telegraphing some kinda-maybe-I-don't-know thing.

The Israeli grinned. "Yes, OK, that means you do. Always the quiet ones you have to watch. That's good. I like competition. Like Reggie."

Gears raised his chin, gesturing to Reggie across the yard. Shirtless now, The Marine's broad back revealed the same squiggling Thai tattoos that prostitutes and working men had. I had learned from one of my Thai dates that these tattoos were made by the monk in their home village. Said with prayer and incantations meant to protect them in the evil clutches of Bangkok, it was all most had when they showed up in town. Sucked towards the city in waves every year, Northern people saw the place like some ancient, entrenched tarantula sitting on Thailand, feeding on people whose only protection was prayers said by an old monk while tapping tattoos into their back.

"That Camaro he drives can really move," Gears continued. "Ripped out the back seat and made it a chicken cage. Replaced the driving seats with airplane seats—they weigh less, see? Two seats on an engine with a chicken cage. That's what he drives. Not like it will help him. Not with Charlie in the car."

He shook his head in sad disgust, looking at the old Southern man at the grill. The faded Hawaiian shirt and happy, bottle battered face was the opposite of trim, grim Israeli Gears.

"He will never win. It is not possible."

"Why?"

"There is a curse," Our new friend said, stepping closer and lowering his voice. "Nobody speaks about this much but Charlie went north to learn some voodoo. Black magic to win the Chicken but it turned against him. Look at that face."

I looked back at Charlie's happy face in the grill smoke, trying to imagine it in veils of incense smoke amidst chanted incantations.

"And that Bible. Please. Half the race wants it burned." Gears looked at both of us, eyes wide. "Why write shit down? This can only lead to trouble."

"I thought it was kind of cool," I said. "I read some in the Miami."

"You don't know what you're talking about." Gears waved me away. "And Charlie knows he's fine because he's with Reggie. That one is a force of nature. They made him something in the military that is different from you and me. Four hours he sleeps. Nothing more. Drink all day, all night, never drunk. Forget about the road. He doesn't give a damn. He's been in more wrecks than anyone can count and walked away from all of them. That's Reggie. But Charlie? I don't know why he races with this loser."

He shook his head, then looked at Monteblan, eyes serious beneath close cropped, salt and pepper hair.

"You though, are not a loser. So you should do The Splits. I want some competition." He slapped Monteblan's shoulder warmly. "If you're in, find me tomorrow night at The Chantal. Everybody stays there. I'll be at the bar."

Before we could ask what he meant, the Israeli was pulled away. Lighting up with welcome surprise, he shook hands with an old friend. Walking away, we watched him shoot another glob of hand sanitizer into his palms, rubbing vigorously.

"Looks like Gears likes to keep his hands clean," I noted.

"Tough to do on these roads," Monteblan replied.

From the warm glow of hanging lanterns, a champagne glass raised in invitation. Pulling Monteblan with me, I joined Ladyboy Man and his trio of glamourous, not quite women.

Shunned by the rest, an island of debonair remove, Ladyboy Man stood alone. Dressed immaculately, relaxed and regal, his champagne hand showed smartly manicured nails. His ladyboys matched in decorative ensembles far more fetching then shorts and T-Shirts favored by tattooed Thai girls. Two were tall, with broad, elegantly proportioned shoulders and luxurious manes of shining black hair. The third was a tiny thing, wearing pearls and a simple black cocktail dress. Petite and withdrawn, her naturally feminine features required no make-up. Aside from her large feet, strategically angled to minimize their impression, it was hard to imagine she packed a dick. The realization put me off balance. The group we joined looked like men and women mingling at a party. In fact it was a sausage hang, half a dozen strong.

"Ladyboy Man," their leader said, extending his hand. "Godawful sobriquet, but thanks to Chicken 65, it's how I'm known in old Bangkok."

He pronounced the city as all the British did, stressing the *kok*.

"Yeah, I've got a lame name, too." I said.

"Own it old boy, that's the only way." Dipping into his pocket Ladyboy Man produced a silver case, tapping it open. "My card."

Monteblan pulled a card off the top. Cream colored, weight premium, the florid, elegant script spelled out *Ladyboy Man* and listed no contact information.

"The girls handle my business and calendar. We'll set an appointment should you care to."

"What do you do?"

"Oh this and that," he said dismissively. "There's always something that needs taking care of. South East Asia is filled with surprises.

Should you find yourself snookered, just ask around for Ladyboy Man. They'll find me."

A fast, bright Cheshire grin followed. It struck me that he had practiced it. Ladyboy Man, I imagined, was an entirely manufactured personality. While he rattled on, rocking grandly in Italian loafers, I lost focus. Something about him was disorienting. The charm, mannerisms, patter and wardrobe all worked together to disarm with bubbling lightness, like the champagne in his glass. Adding to the dizzy ambience were his trio of ladyboys. Their bodies shifted, angled and posed in mannerisms granting them an amplified femininity which charged the evening air. The little one, especially.

Twisting on one leg like a little girl who was bored, her brooding eyes kept catching mine. Thai girls didn't stare a man down like that. Thai girls were shy and giggly. But these weren't Thai girls. Glancing at their shapely forms, my body flooded with attraction and confusion. The little one picked it up. Smiling slyly, she flipped her hair, bathing me in a wave of light, expensive perfume. Responding automatically to these feminine signals, my blood rushed. When I realized the same thing might be happening under her dress, the excitement stopped suddenly. Troubled and confused, I turned brusquely back to Ladyboy Man.

"About the names," I cut in, too loud. "Yours is better than mine. They call me Asser."

My flat, blunt words smashed through his champagne patter. I immediately felt stupid and simple. Which was precisely how he saw me. The flash of contempt was just a blink, chased fast by that Cheshire smile.

"Asser, hmmm? There's a sticky wicket to play." Ladyboy Man raised one finger. "Felt the same with Ladyboy Man. But do understand it's quite a rough lot in Chicken 65. Animals, really. Show weakness and they move in for the kill. So next time they call you *Asshole*…"

"Asser," I corrected.

"Did I say Asshole?" He smiled, touching my hand. "Do forgive me, who could *ever* call you Asshole."

I smiled, nodding graciously before I realized The Brit had insulted me. Oblivious, Ladyboy Man carried on.

"Don't correct them, don't let it shake you. Next time they all you Asshat…"

"Asser," I grumbled.

"Do pardon me, Asser. Just take it all in stride. At least they don't call you mad, like Moon The Loon."

He lifted his champagne glass to gesture towards a tall Korean by the bar.

"Why do they call him that?" Monteblan asked.

"Terrible rumors about his propensities for high explosives." Ladyboy Man lowered his voice, stepping closer in a cloud of powerful cologne. "They say he blew up an elephant after winning The VV Splits."

"What *are* The VV Splits?" Monteblan said. "Gears told me I should race them."

British eyes flared in alarm. "He did what? Good God! Is the man trying to get you *killed*? Rubbish. Absolute rubbish. Don't touch The Splits until you've run them off the clock at least twice, please."

"What are they?"

"Just don't do them," He advised firmly. Stroking his chin, he thought again. "However… If you insist on such madness, do find Marcel. He'll be at the Hotel Chantal in Vientiane. We all stay there, you know. Look for a troglodyte Frenchmen, Chicken Name 'French Shrek'. Smells to high heaven but has *Le Chat Noir*."

We looked at him, confused.

"Black Cats," Ladyboy Man explained. "Military grade amphetamine left over from the Vietnam War. Priceless, really, but he'll find a number if you tell him I sent you. Mention my twenty percent referral, will you?"

Ladyboy Man thrust his chin forward and raised the champagne.

"Truly a pleasure, gentlemen. Now if you'll pardon us, the girls need some shopping time and I'm due for a rub down."

He stepped off. I felt a poke in my lower back and turned to see the little ladyboy walk past, pretending she hadn't touched me while suppressing a smile.

"She likes you," Monteblan said, watching her go.

"She's got a dork," I said.

"Amazing Thailand," Monteblan agreed.

"Well there goes a real cock sucker," a familiar, Chicago accented voice laughed.

I turned to see the portly Japanese American with the Chicago accent. He grinned.

"Ask him if he wants any chicken for dinner?"

I was about to try and explain things when the friendly man just threw his head back and laughed.

"Don't worry. The new guys always get fucked. The clown suit's a given. Mississippi Charlie always does that. But Chicken? At a Chicken 65 Party? No wonder the only person who will talk to you is Ladyboy Man. That prick doesn't have a friend in the race. But hey, when your broad's a guy, maybe you don't need any. By the way, I'm DTA."

He extended his hand, which we each shook.

"You're Asser," DTA said, grinning at me. "Everybody knows that. And you are...?"

"Monteblan," my friend replied. "But why are you talking to us? Everybody hates us."

"You're Americans, buddy, right off the boat. Been there. Don't want to see you guys getting played. Ladyboy Man is points against you."

"What, cause he likes ladyboys?"

"Nah, lots in Thailand do. Not me personally, but you won't be hard pressed to find a guy who came for the tacos and stayed for the hotdogs. Ladyboy Man's just shady. Cluster B motherfucker, all the way. Plus I saw you with Gears. Not a bad guy at all, but he probably tried to get you into The Splits, am I right?"

"Yeah, what are they?"

"Nothing you should get involved in, not your first Chicken. He knows as much. But hell, you *moved* at Democracy Monument this morning. Everybody saw you drive. Thais went crazy for you. Lots of money shifted towards you guys. Maybe Gears just wants a race through those damn Splits. Past five years, nobody's touched it. Shit. People die. Which is why he *also* might want you running the damn things. Get you out of the race. So don't listen to him. There's only one person you can trust in Chicken 65."

"Who's that?" Monteblan asked, swigging his beer.

"Him," DTA said, pointing at me. "Your shotgun and nobody else. You'll probably make some deals on the road, but make damn sure they're Chicken Promises. Personally, I've never done one. Never will. That's why my Chicken Name is DTA."

"What's that mean?" Monteblan asked.

"Don't Trust Anybody." He wiped his hands back and forth, as if cleaning dirt. "Not in Chicken 65. No way."

With a grin, the racer from Chicago disappeared into the throng, grabbing onto a girl's butt as she passed, pinching hard. The Thai girl turned around with an exaggerated frown. Slapping his hand while laughing, she pinched his butt back. DTA jumped like a cartoon character, really laying it on. Laughing together, the pair disappeared through the milling crowd towards the drinks.

"It's nice to see men and women pinch some ass without suing each other," Monteblan noted.

"And did you see his reaction?" I said. "I swear, the key to success with these bar girls is making a Muppet version of yourself. Just imagine yourself with big googly eyes and furry all over. That works in Thailand. Brooding intellects don't really fly out here."

"Which is why you're flying home?"

Ignoring my friend's remark, I headed towards the bar. A metal tub was filled with local brews, bobbing in ice. Cracking one, I drank it down.

"Nice suit, Asser!" Mississippi Charlie called in his friendly drawl. "How 'bout a steak with that beer?"

I walked over to his sizzling grill. Shaking my head as Charlie laughed, I shot the cuffs on my cheap suit and sat down beside him.

"Steak sounds good." I told him. "Chicken doesn't fly at a Chicken 65 party."

"Aw, don't worry about that." Mississippi Charlie winked. "You have entered unknowing into a realm of holy tradition. Lots of it has to do with Chicken. We don't eat a one except the Bird brought back to The Miami."

"You kill the chicken at end of the race?"

"That don't sound too respectful now, does it?" Charlie splashed beer on the steak then flipped it. "We have a monk at The Miami from Reggie's village. Says prayers over the bird, makes an offering, then slashes that neck fast as lighting."

"That's why I love Thailand," I told him. "Back in The States, they'd shut down a race that killed a chicken every year."

"No, son." he corrected me. "We don't kill a chicken every year. We kill *The* Chicken every year. Bird keeps coming back."

"What, like reincarnation?" I asked, taking the plate of steak Mississippi Charlie handed me.

"Yup," Charlie nodded. "Nothing else explains the way that Bird decides."

"Decides what?"

"Who's gonna win. Every year, that Bird just jumps right up in some fella's arms. No running, fussing, or fighting. You ever seen a Chicken like that? No sir. That's our Chicken. It comes back. Out there on the road, The Bird decides."

I nodded my head, sipping beer and eating steak. Charlie looked around, seeing that we were alone, then lowered his voice and lowered his spatula at me. Drops of grease slid off, hissing into the coals. His eyes sparkled with the red glow.

"Listen to me, Asser. What I'm telling you here is controversial in this crowd. Most people out there on the road think they're in control. Such illusions—along with others—are heightened during the intense exertions demanded by the Chicken. Racers will fight to maintain such illusions, which is why my Bible is downright despised. People round here, well, they don't much like the truth about Chicken 65."

"What's the truth?"

"It's The *Bird*." Whispering with a kind smile, Mississippi Charlie's goofy face glowed. "The Bird decides. Don't matter what you got planned for this race. The Bird has plans for you. *Especially* you, Asser. Hell, I ain't ever known somebody just stumble into Chicken 65. Chicken chose you. There's a part for you to play."

Lost in the sparkle of his eyes, the party disappeared.

"What part?" I heard myself say.

"Well son, that's what you're here to find out. But all that's up to The Bird. Chicken 65 going to show you something."

"What will it show me?"

"Bird decides." Charlie shrugged. "Ain't up to you. Just get yourself out there. Race don't much matter. Minute you step on the gas, it's already done. We're just going through the motions. Don't worry about winning or losing. Bird decides."

His gaze held mine through clouds of grill smoke. The sad, smiling eyes suggested hard lessons learned with great difficulty. Powerful lessons, perhaps, that others couldn't or wouldn't recognize about this race. Despite the heat, a shiver ran down my back. This man was close—perhaps dangerously so— to whatever Chicken 65 was all about. I was both frightened by this knowledge, and powerfully drawn to it. And I understood now why Reggie ran every race with the man. Mississippi Charlie was magic.

"Now get an old man a beer."

He winked and just like that the party came back. Startled to remember I was surrounded by people, I stumbled to my feet. Drifting through girls and laughter, I dipped my hand into the cold baptism of floating beers, picking one out for Charlie. Returning to him, I popped the top and passed it on. Pulling a deep, satisfying draft, Mississippi Charlie laughed.

"Chicken got you *bad*, Asser."

Shooing me away with the spatula, he lit another cigar and called out loudly to some girls. Through murmuring conversations and loosely gathered groups of racers, I walked nowhere in particular until an elbow pushed into my ribs.

"Hey." Monteblan's familiar voice cleared my brain fog. "Found out what The Splits are."

"What's the deal?"

"I really want to do it," he said wistfully. "Nobody else will be out there except Gears. I can beat that guy."

"Great. Let's rock."

My friend sighed. "It's not that simple."

"Alright, look." I said to my friend. "Something's been going on since you got behind the wheel. Are we going to talk about it?"

Slowly, Monteblan nodded his head.

"Let's find a titty bar." He said, walking towards the gate. "I want boobs around for this."

**The General, swordsman that he was, lived just a stumble from the Red Light District.** The street was dusty, lined with bars where uneven wooden front porches lead into dark air conditioned vaults, all black velvet and flashing lights. Monteblan and I had found one fast. Topless Thai girls in high heels and matching red bikini bottoms swayed listlessly as the entropic loops of 21$^{st}$ Century hip hop hammered reality with levels just shy of Abu Ghraib torture sets.

"None of these girls would last a night at *Jumps*," Monteblan shouted to me, sipping his beer while staring at the Thai go-go dancers. One smiled at him, giving half-hearted hip swirls and checking herself out in the mirror.

"You're right!" I agreed.

*Jumps* was a Bronx strip club down the block from a slaughter-house that Monteblan had found through what powers he possesses to find such places. The street was dirty and smelled like murder. There were chicken feathers in the gutter. Inside Jumps, the décor featured a motorcycle inexplicably crashing halfway through the ceiling, piloted, *cooch ex machina* style, by a lady mannequin's fishnet clad legs. Perhaps awaiting the arrival of her upper half, Jumps was packed at all hours. Black men preferred the place. Their flat brim Yankee caps lined the bar, dollar bills in stacks by cognacs. These patrons had a particular way of tipping strippers. Bills would be balled up into small, solid projectiles then dismissively tossed without a glance towards their target. Missing wasn't easy. Jumps girls were thick. The most popular dancers were pelted mercilessly through their act, bills bouncing from prodigious physical gifts that were worked in rippling, slapping, gyrating, pole grinding, floor humping power. Monteblan and I had passed many a dubious night in *Jumps,* marveling at their fleshy acrobatics. Every inch of them promised pounding release. Compared to these women, the aimlessly drifting Thais didn't hold a candle. Although in all fairness, just down the street was a place where women used their vaginas to blow them out.

"They look like sea weed," Monteblan observed, while thin girls swayed absently in the darkness.

"Seaweed you have sex with."

"Probably a club for that in Japan." My friend said. "Come on."

We left the air conditioned darkness for the bar's front porch. Across the dirt walkway, girls from another go-go caught Monteblan's eye. Waving and smiling, they invited him over. My friend raised his beer in salute. They shouted louder, calling out his tailored suit, saying they loved him. Monteblan smiled, turning back to me.

"It's not even the sex out here," Monteblan said. "Just them being nice I like. Women do this thing in New York where they shake their head "no" at you. Girls on the street. You're not even trying to pick them up. You just happen to glance their way. They don't look at you. They shake their head "no" without looking up from their phone. It's so rude. It's like a... *micro aggression,*" he said, satisfied at finding the word. "Out here is magical opposite land. Women smile and call me handsome."

"That's what they say to all people with a penis and a pulse. You know that right?"

"Sure. It's an act. But a good one."

"Talking about good ones," I said. "Your driving this morning was ridiculous. Can we get to that now? The most I've ever seen you do is run for the F train. Now you're…. *drifting*? Is that what you did under the expressway? You know, where we almost died this morning?"

"Come on…" he chided me.

"I stand corrected." Pulling up my chair, I raised two fingers. "That was in fact, the second time we almost died this morning. The first being the fully airborne leap we did over the klong bridge. *Bridge* being the word I would like to point out there. *Bridge* being something that makes it so you don't *have* to jump over a small body of water."

"Dude, chill."

"No, thank you, I'd like to have this Post Traumatic Stress Moment if you don't mind. The drifting? That's what we did under the overpass where we went sideways? That's in the movies. I've seen that. And apparently, you do that. Where did this come from?"

"Lubbock," Monteblan said.

I leaned back, nodding as the piece fell into place. "So that's what you did in Texas."

My friend had spent half his high school years in the same Texas town where Buddy Holly was born. He rarely mentioned it, but had a Texas license plate on the wall of his place in Brooklyn.

"That's where the license plate came from?"

"Yeah, it came from Lubbock." He nodded, sipping his beer. "Off a car I should have died in."

This sudden turn into a serious moment took me off guard. Monteblan didn't do deep. I recalled the conflicting emotions that had played on his face earlier that night, driving into Chang Mai. I suddenly wondered if forcing an explanation might bring us into territory best left alone.

"Look man, it's enough that you drive," I said. "It's cool. We don't have to go into it."

"No, you should know. They might be after us now."

"Who might be after us?"

I watched Monteblan frown, stroking his beard, hard at work trying to put something mushy and confusing together. When he finally spoke, he was still searching with his eyes, as if trying to find the first piece of a wet jig saw puzzle.

"Did you ever think there were... *forces* out there?"

"Explain?"

"Forget it." He shook his head. "What I mean is...were you ever the best at something, but it's not the best for you?"

I thought about that momentarily.

"I've never been the best at anything." I sipped my beer. "Never won anything, either."

"Well, I won a lot before. I was the best. I beat everybody. I drive."

He nodded to himself, confirming some distant version of Monteblan I had never met.

"When did this all start?" I asked.

"My brother got me into it."

"He's a mechanic, right?"

"Mechanics fix shit. Gordy's a master. Tuning Lambos at a dealership in La Jolla now. They drive down from Silicon Valley just for him. Back then, it was drift missiles. Beater bullshit cars made to crash. He was like a mad scientist. All over Texas scrapping for parts. Swapped out engines, hydro e-brakes, switches wired all over the place... Nothing was from the same car so we'd end up with like, the turn signal on the door handle. Frankenstein cars. Ugly. Dangerous. But damn, they went sideways fast."

Monteblan pulled down his beer.

"I'm the little brother, right? Just getting thrown into whatever my big brother needs me for. After I got my license, he'd throw me in the harness when it was time for fine tuning. It was a pain to jump in and out of the car, so he'd tune up and have me roll. So I start to drive these fucked up drift missiles. And he's telling me to push it this way, open up, test the suspension and whatever. But what happens is I get really good. We were all kind of surprised. One day I was like, the stupid little brother, next day I'm like…

"Monteblan Andretti?" I offered.

"That's Formula One. There wasn't any formula for what we were doing. But I was killing it. Gordy started putting me on the track and it was a wrap."

He shook his head, laughing to himself.

"We just won. Everything, everywhere. His cars? My driving? I don't want to sound like ego tripping or whatever, but I was like Napoleon out there."

"Napoleon Bonaparte," I clarified. "The French Emperor. In a car going sideways?"

"I remember this from school." A beer sign blinked slowly, reflecting in his eyes. "They said Napoleon was like Mozart on the battlefield. Like the way Mozart did all his music in one draft; just heard the entire thing and wrote it down? Napoleon was the same way, but with war. He would look at a battlefield, before the battle, and see the whole thing happen. That's what they said about him. When the battle started, he had already seen how everything would go. What general would move where, the ambushes, flank moves… he just *knew*. When I drive, it's like that. I see where people are going to go before they do. I know the road before it happens. I just know."

He shrugged.

"So these really heavy dudes who run for real money hear about my drift. I'm like, 17? They let me into their spot. These access roads to an old power station that went dark back in the 80's. So now I learn rally. Dirt roads that pass through two different parking lots. Asphalt dude, not concrete. That shit eats tires. This was like butter. Off road then cutting into these drifts? *Sick.* Gordy's making hybrid cars to handle the shit. I'm pushing them into pieces. Just breaking shit. Breaking cars. Breaking records. All over Texas."

"Sounds dangerous."

"It was. But what do they say? Young, dumb and…"

"Young, dumb, and full of enthusiasm?" I offered.

"That was me. Plus the whole point of a missile is you wreck it and build a new one. The harness was good. Gordy always doubled down on that shit. I had my helmet. And we were making *money.* That was what this whole track at the power station was about. Which meant gangs. They loved me. Seriously heavy dudes that were like: 'We'll put you in shit where you walk away 50 grand in your hand.' So this other world starts opening up, see? I was supposed to go to design school but all that is going away. I was gonna race. I was the best. Why wouldn't I?"

Lights from the go-go danced in his eyes. Sitting in his white tailored suit, my friend's face was glowing pride. But as the question hung there, the light slowly faded. This strange and shining Monteblan which I had hardly ever seen returned to his low key, indrawn self. As the transformation happened, I felt a sadness inside my friend. It spread to me. I almost didn't want to hear more. But Monteblan went on.

"There was this night." He blew a short sigh from the side of his mouth. He waited a moment. I wondered if he would go on. He did.

"I would run the track at night with one headlight to get the lines for my turns down. You see where that beam hits, follow it in, boom. That night I was like, scattered. Because I was trying to think how I would tell my mom that I wasn't going to design school, and I was going to race. That's where my head is, while I'm burning this padiddle missile…"

"Padiddle missile?"

"Car with one head light. We used to yell that when we were driving with my Mom. Whoever saw a car with one headlight yelled 'Padiddle!' You never did that?"

"No. But my Mom used to lock us in the car in the parking lot when she went to grab the dry cleaning. That used to be perfectly acceptable. Now it's a felony."

"She might have left you in there a little too long, buddy."

"Fuck you," I laughed, motioning with my beer. "Back to padiddles"

"Right. So I'm racking like a buck ten with one head light, having imaginary talks with my mom in one of these crazy Frankenstein half drift/half rally cars Gordy threw together. I take this turn I've took a million times, and a million times faster. But this time, a coyote comes out from the dark side—where I had my headlight taped up. I do the right tricks, but just a little too late and too hard and the suspension? It was just like: nope. Ripped right the hell out from underneath me. The car split in half. Like a cartoon. I look down, there's nothing underneath me. I'm flying sideways at like, a hundred miles an hour and then I flip over and I'm upside down and that's it man."

He paused for a moment, looking down at his beer.

"I knew I was dead. I *knew* it. And I saw my mom. I don't how, but I swear to you I did. She was crying in her room. Saying *Monty, Monty!* And crying. It was like the future, after I already died, and I saw her there. Crying over me being dead. And that was that."

"What was what?"

"I don't know." He laughed weakly. "I don't remember landing. Just woke up in the seat, still strapped in. Sitting there, like some hand just placed me there. The car is like, all over. Like an airplane crash. But I'm fine. Nobody there. I'm all alone, and I felt something. This is where it gets weird."

He breathed, looking at me, and I could tell he was debating whether to share what remained of his story.

"Tell me."

"I was *told* that this was over for me. That I shouldn't drive anymore."

"What do you mean told? Who told you?"

"Forces." Monteblan shook his head side to side, then slowly morphed it into a nod. "Good ones. I don't know what. I felt them there. I wasn't freaked out, but it was real heavy. There was this feeling that they had saved me. And they were smarter than me. And they knew things I didn't. And they didn't really talk they just like, put knowledge in you. Instantly. So I said OK. I said it out loud: 'I promise never to drive again.' And like that, they were gone. Whatever was there was gone. I was just sitting in the middle of the desert surrounded by a blown up padiddle missile. *Impossible* to survive. Gordy saw the wreck the next day and was like: 'Dude, you should be dead.' I didn't tell him what happened, like the X Files part of it, but I told him I wasn't driving anymore and I never did. I went to school. Took the bus or my girlfriend drove. Moved to New York. Didn't need a car. Never touched one."

He turned then, looking at me with a grim half smile.

"Until now," I said.

"Until now," he confirmed.

"So you think…"

"I don't know what I think." Monteblan said.

"There's like… *aliens* you're betraying… or..?"

"I didn't say aliens."

"You said X Files. That's like saying aliens."

"Forces. OK? Let's leave it at that. Don't make fun of me, man. The only other person I've ever told that story to is Rayne. Haven't even told my own brother. Don't give me shit."

"Dude." I pulled my chair closer on the uneven wooden porch, speaking soft. "I'm not giving you shit. Or if it sounds like I am, I'm sorry. That's not what I meant. Just trying to understand."

Monteblan shook his head. "I have too, for my whole life and there's no answer. I don't know what happened. I just don't drive. The Forces don't want me to."

"We can drop out bro." I reached out, grabbing his burly shoulder. "Don't worry."

"I'm not worried, I'm freaked out. Because this morning? When we hit that jump? I *knew* how to land, and how it was going to happen..."

"I thought you were looking at me because we were going to die."

"I looked at you to make sure I wasn't dreaming. I looked at you because I haven't been that happy in 15 years. I drive. Do you understand? It's who I am. I *drive*."

Before I could reply, Monteblan swiftly stood and stepped down the wooden stairs to the dusty street.

"Hey." I bolted up from my rickety chair. "Where are you going?"

Waving his hand dismissively, Monteblan slipped into the midst of wandering whoremongers. I watched his white suit disappear into the neon hued darkness, calling after him.

"Monteblan!"

He was gone. Frowning, settling back into my chair, I tried to process what my friend had just told me.

**"Fight with your girlfriend?"**

Reggie's grin appeared over the wooden rail of the bar. Blinking neon played on his face. The flip flop sea of meandering men moved from bar to bar behind him.

"Your boy tripping on The Splits?" Reggie said, squinting down the road to where Monteblan vanished. "Probably find a ladyboy bar to cry it out."

Mimicking a fist grip, Reggie opened his mouth, going down on an invisible prick while fake crying.

"Oh my God! I'm so lonely. This world so hard!"

"Fuck you, Reggie."

"Whoa!" The imaginary wang disappeared. "What?"

"Boys, come now." Charlie's hand appeared behind the marine, slapping him on the shoulder. He pointed a finger at me.

"Ain't a good look to let your wingman walk away like that. What're you boys having problems with? Maybe we can help you sort this out. Mind?"

I looked at Charlie, his eyebrows raised in question. He had been drinking and that red face was glowing, nose practically pulsing. A worn leather satchel hung from his shoulder.

"Sure, what the hell." I kicked out a chair for him. "Monteblan is tripping on the The Splits is all."

"Told you," Reggie said.

He lifted his large arm and a waitress appeared. He ordered in Thai and she disappeared through the curtains into the bar.

"First off, what are they?" I said.

"Split time in Laos," Reggie said. "Between Vientiane and the Vang Valley. Race within a race."

"Just one road between the two places." Charlie slung his satchel over the seat, settling in. "And it's a doozy. Animals all over. Tractors, cows. Busses. They laid about half it with pavement, the rest is dirt and rock."

"Ain't no plan how they did that," Reggie said. "Shit will just drop out right under you."

"You *can* dance your way through," Charlie added, swigging his beer. "Gears made a map that shows all the drop out points, which shoulder to take, and how to run the splits fast. Don't know why you'd want to, though. Vang Valley is cut into some real high terrain. Once you get close to town, road gets real tricky. Switchbacks on a drop off? *Mmm*. Not my cup of julep."

"So why do people run it?" I wondered out loud.

"They don't." Reggie answered. "Five years nobody touched The Splits. Motherfuckers were dying out there. Who was that last one, Charlie, five years back?"

"Childs," Mississippi said solemnly, eyes staring into distant memory. "Deceased in wretched fashion, a tangle of misadventure at the bottom of a cliff. Laos really ain't the proper place to wreck an automobile."

Reggie nodded in agreement. "Hospitals ain't shit. They gotta airlift you to Bangkok. But hell if any helicopter coming to Vang Valley. Throw your ass in a pickup, drive you all the way to Vientiane." With a whisk of his hand, Reggie dismissed me and the idea entirely. "Nah, nobody runs the Splits no more. That shit was old school."

"Why did people run if it was so dangerous?"

"Whole lot of money," Reggie told me. "VV Splits is the only money Chicken racers can win. Separate pool on the action, mixed in with outside bets. Everybody races the clock and whoever beats it best gets paid. Used to be the hottest action in the damn race. Shit just got too dangerous. But if somebody ran the Splits *this* Chicken? After five years of no action? Pull down some real money. But that road is wicked. Didn't even mention the murder vans."

"What the hell is a murder van?"

"Mini Vans," Mississippi grinned. "We call them murder vans out here 'cause they just flip off the road and burn."

"Drivers all up on *yaba*," Reggie said.

"Speed," Mississippi said.

"I know what *yaba* is," I said.

"Trust me," Reggie said. "You don't know *yaba* till you know Lao *yaba*. That shit is military grade. In Thailand they cook it up. In Laos they dig it up. CIA filled caves with the shit during Vietnam. Training the hill tribe soldiers, gakking those motherfuckers up and throwing weapons in their hands. Shit. They pulled out and left a mess of all that behind. It's *still* floating around out here."

"Those murder van drivers will be all wound up on it." Charlie explained. "Hightailing a van full of Koreans or Chinese tourists full speed into Vang. And the minute those fellas see a damn foreigner tearing up *their* road? *Whoooweee.* You got yourself problems. DO NOT get in the way of a Murder Van in Laos."

"We ain't even get into the snipers, have we Charlie?"

"No Reggie, I don't believe we have."

Suddenly it struck me what was happening. The porch rail of the bar transformed into some white picket fence down South. I saw Charlie and Reggie in checkered suits, holding carpet bags, talking circles around the yokel: *Me.*

"Wait a sec," I said. "This is some Tom Sawyer shit. You're running game, Charlie. You two don't *want* us in the Splits because you know Monteblan can drive."

"Who the hell is Montezuma?" Reggie's face screwed up.

"My friend's name is Monteblan."

"Please. That ain't no Chicken name." He turned to his friend. "Charlie?"

"Don't sound like one to me. What'd you call him at The Miami?"

"Grimace," Reggie replied. "Body built like the damn thing. Plus I ain't seen him smile once."

"Sold!" Laughing, Charlie slammed his beer down. "Grimace and Asser. Sounds like a law firm."

"Grimace?" I complained. "Come on. He can really drive. Can't he be like, I don't know, Sparkplug or Clutch or something?"

"This motherfucker here," Reggie laughed, shaking his head. "Trying to name his own wingman."

"That ain't the way it works, Asser." Mississippi Charlie explained, bar lights dancing in his eyes. "You are bequeathed your Chicken Name from your Chicken brethren."

"Well what about Reggie? You're Mississippi, how come Reggie doesn't have a name?"

"Oh." The combat vet leveled his look, staring right into my eyes. "You want to try and name me?"

Leaning back in the chair, I nodded. "Reggie works."

"Damn straight it does." Reggie glanced out over the sea of passing men, nodding to someone he knew. "And if you want both your legs working and your Asser shitting, let those Splits go. Gears trying to get you killed. I don't care how Grimace drives. Oh, and look who it is."

I looked up to see that Monteblan had found his way back. He ambled up slowly, default permafrown in place, bulk of a gut softly pressing from his suit. The Chicken Name, I realized, did resonate. Reggie pulled out a chair for him.

"How was that ladyboy, Grimace?"

"What ladyboy?" He turned to me. "Who's Grimace?"

"You are," I explained. "That's your chicken name."

"OK."

"We were just talking to your wingman here about The Splits," Charlie said.

As it always did, a beer appeared before Monteblan. He picked it up and fell right into the conversation.

"Yeah, back at the Bar B Q, Gears was trying to tell me all this shit you can win? Something about a license plate so you don't get arrested or something?"

"Serpico flaps, triple nine plates and The Mark." Reggie nodded. "You win The Splits, that's what you get. And that shit is gold, ain't it Charlie?"

Monteblan and I looked at each other, lost. Charlie leaned forward, placing his hands folded on his thighs before us, like a consultant.

"Start with the Serpico flaps. You must have seen some on the way up to Chang Mai."

My mind shot back to the road, and I remembered seeing a truck rumble past. The impossible non sequitur of Al Pacino's bearded face from the seventies film *Serpico* had been painted on two huge mud flaps behind the tires. "Yeah, I did see those. What's the deal?"

"Truckers love that movie. *Serpico's* their idol. Breaking corruption, standing up for the little guy, all that. Mafia was muscling in on trucking out here around the time the movie came out. *Serpico* ended up like a symbol for the drivers. You got *Serpico* flaps, truckers won't touch you."

"What, they will otherwise?"

"Box you in, run you off the road, yes sir." Mississippi followed up. "They know a Chicken racer when they see one. Last thing you want is a long haul trucker with a grudge against foreigners tearing up his road. You win The Splits, they put *Serpico* flaps on your ride. Truckers won't touch you."

"What about the plates?" Monteblan said.

"Triple Nine plates," Reggie replied. "Numerology. Only the biggest of the big noodles out here get plates for their car with triple nines. They have bidding wars for the shit, every year. Last year $500,000 paid for a license plate in Bangkok with 999.999."

"What does it mean?"

"Don't touch me," Charlie said. "Hell, *can't* touch me. If you're rich enough to get Triple Nine plates, you're of a class entirely beyond the law. No police or military out here going to mess with triple nine plates. It means you're old Thai money. Or mobbed up with it. That's not money to mess with."

"I still don't get the numbers," I asked. "What's up with the nines?"

"The word for nine in Thai is *gao*." Reggie said. "It sounds like the word for step, like when you're walking. So triple nine sounds like *step step step*. Which means walking into the future. 999's real good luck, and real hard to get. People don't mess with triple nine plates, because whoever's driving got pull. Cops lay off, military don't bother. Haul ass down highways, right through borders, nobody touch you."

"Which brings us to…" Mississippi slid in to finish up, lowering his voice into a hushed whisper. "The Mark."

Gazing between us in turn, he looked into our eyes. "The Mark gets you in with the Thai mafia. All these trucks out here running timber rackets or whatever, they got this little ol' mark on them. Changes monthly. That mark is a secret code sent on the roads. Lets people know you are connected and covered by the criminal underworld. Hell, you got The Mark, people run away from your car, let alone pull it over. Fill the damn thing up with drugs, guns and money, run it wherever you please."

Charlie stood up now, putting his finished beer down and waving his finger at us.

"But all of this is idle dreams. Nobody runs The Splits. Running the damn things *blind*, without knowing that terrain would be a reckless act which even The Bird would turn its back on. That infernal road will bring you well beyond the bounds of poultry providence. Don't do it gentlemen."

"But he can win!" I protested. "My friend drives. We'll get all that stuff and then we can win Chicken 65."

Charlie's smile slowly faded. He regarded me a moment, then lowered his voice, leaning forward on the table.

"Perhaps, Asser, there are treasures within the Chicken revealed only when one eliminates the persistently persnickety desire to win the damn fool thing, mmm?"

That question hung between us a moment. Whores laughed somewhere. Stepping from his stool, Reggie slid to the wooden floor in his flip flops, dusting off the back of his shorts.

"*Pooying* time."

Charlie dipped into his satchel and pulled out the Chicken Bible. The battered cover caught bar light and gleamed. He waggled it before me like a street preacher while prostitutes called out on the dusty streets.

"Greatly grim happenings and woeful events transpire on yon Chicken roads, Asser. This here book is full of 'em. Mostly, it's because a fella forces things. Tries to have *his* Chicken. Not what The Bird wants. What *he* wants."

Flipping The Bible open, Mississippi Charlie licked his finger and paged through, murmuring as he scanned the faded print.

"Splits be damned. You fellas have enough trouble waiting for you in Vang. Learn a little. Read this when you get there."

Ripping out a pair of pages, he folded them and produced a pen. I read his scrawled writing when he passed me the cheaply printed paper: *Read in Vang.* Sliding the Bible text into my suit pocket, still thinking about The Splits, I finished my beer.

"Grimace, Asser," Charlie tipped his imaginary hat. "Good evening."

Reggie and Charlie disappeared into the blinking lights and crowded streets. I sat with my friend listening to the girls call out to potential customers, laughing and teasing. When we left, they called to us, reaching for us as we passed, holding our arms, pulling us back. Shaking them off, we walked slowly up the crowded, bar lined road towards The General's.

"Do you want to drive this thing?" I finally asked.

"I don't know." Monteblan's eyes were thoughtful. "I think I shouldn't. But part of me wonders if I made the whole thing up: The Forces. That promise."

"Why would you make something like that up?"

He shrugged. "Maybe I was afraid to be the best at something. Maybe it was just me taking a dive. Look at me."

"What do you mean?"

"I mean my life. I'm along for the ride." My friend turned sideways to let loud Australians pass. "I used to drive."

"Yeah but you have Rayne, your work is always rolling. I mean, your life is really good. When I think of…" I stopped short before I could add *my life.*

"That's the weird thing." Monteblan said, missing what I hadn't said. "After I quit driving, life got really good. Because I did what I don't give a damn about. Design is just, whatever. They put it in front of me, I do it. So they put more in front of me. It all works out for me. That's how life is weird. They tell you all this shit about your dreams and trying your hardest and being the best but I don't believe any of it. If you want a good life, you should do what you don't give a damn about. Because what you love? *Man.*" He shook his head. "It will mess you up."

**The border crossing at Laos happened under a sign of Thai design, all yellow curly cues and royal celebration.** The drive there had been uneventful, Monteblan mostly withdrawn, brooding on The Splits. I took the time to mark our maps for Vietnam, still wearing my suit, enjoying the tailored fit. Monteblan had traded his for flak jacket and helmet again. Upon reaching the border checkpoint, I suggested he ditch the combat gear. My friend begrudgingly agreed. I was glad he did after what happened at immigration.

We had lined in front of the passport booths just after lunch. Inching forward in dead heat, we were processed through the slow, vaguely threatening shuffle of third world paperwork. The man in front of me was chain smoking. He was Chicken, but I didn't recognize him at first. Crew cut blonde hair, 30s, wearing an inexplicable wind breaker in the simmering heat, his eyes were hard. During one drag from his smoke I had seen a small black circle tattoo in the webbing between his thumb and forefinger. He saw me notice, then frowned, speaking with a thick Eastern Europe accent.

"Your first Chicken, yes?"

Looking fully at him now, the face fell into place. Tough and scowling, he had been lurking amidst a gang of hard looking Brits at The General's Bar B Q.

"Yeah," I answered.

He looked me up and down, barely holding back a smirk. "Well your friend at least, I hear he can drive."

He lifted his chin slightly, nodding towards Monteblan. Standing behind me, sweating and swaying, my pear shaped driver looked like he was falling asleep on his feet.

"Yeah, that's right," I said, realizing this man was competition. "You'll see out on the road."

"You won't see me on the road," the racer said flatly, looking into my eyes with a humorless smile. "You're not Chicken. But listen. If anything happens here, tell Mickey Stiches not to leave Laos. Tell him Vlad got pinched at the border."

Before I could reply, a light dinged on the immigration booth and he dropped his cigarette to the cement floor, grinding it out with his shoe. I watched him walk towards the window in the green border booth. An officer in tan army wear was waiting beside a camera and computer, processing travelers. The Eastern European Chicken Racer slid his passport under the glass and waited.

The process was slow going. I watched him rock slightly on his feet, looking distantly towards the bridge that crossed The Mekong into Laos. He didn't notice the two Thai men appear behind the immigration booth, moving smoothly towards him. One was holding a video phone high, filming. They closed in while two uniformed officers materialized silently from behind a black curtain. The startled racer didn't register what was happening until firm, coordinated hands clamped down simultaneously at different points of his body. In just a blink, all ability to escape was eliminated. Swiftly lead from line, the Chicken racer shot one last bitter glance towards freedom. Glaring at the sky, as if some celestial decision was responsible for his apprehension, he was pulled through black curtains into the bleak, dark grind of Third World justice.

The whole thing had transpired in surreal seconds, making no ripples, leaving no trace. I forced myself to look down at the cigarette the racer had dropped to the floor. Still smoking, it was the only proof he had existed. Jaw hanging wide in wonder, I turned to Monteblan.

"Did you see that?!"

Bleary eyed and tired, my driver looked up from his boater sneakers. "What?"

"They just seized someone at the border. I mean, that's *exactly* what they did. I just saw someone seized. Have you ever seen someone seized? I've never seen anything like that. He was Chicken, by the way. Fine company we're keeping."

"Well, what do you expect? Harvard grads?"

"I didn't expect to start the day chatting with someone who got seized!"

There was the soft tone of the light on the booth ahead.

"You're up." Monteblan said. "Seize ya later."

"Don't even joke. You did not see what I just saw."

There is a particular paranoia that can only be experienced on the other side of the planet. It happens when blank faced, uniformed people flick their fingers, ordering you forward. It descended upon me in force the instant the Lao border guard gestured me to the booth. For a moment, I was sure that all Chicken Racers were being arrested. Fighting panic, I produced my passport and waited. Pages flipped. Eyes flicked. Seconds ticked. This was followed by another feeling only understood while standing at obscure and distant borders, sweating in the dust: the flood of joy released by the hard *thunk!* of a stamped passport. Collecting it gratefully, I passed through iron guardrails to wait for my friend. Frowning, I thought about what the apprehended Racer had said.

"He said I wasn't Chicken," I told Monteblan while we walked towards Pablo Cruise.

"Passport dude?"

"No, the guy who got arrested. What did that mean? I mean, we're in Chicken 65. We signed the book. We're Chicken. Right?"

Monteblan shrugged, starting the car. Together we crossed the Friendship Bridge into new lands, gliding over the mud brown Mekong. It looked less poetic than other rivers. Mostly because The Mekong resembled a bad run of boundary defining diarrhea. Sun dazzled down on the shit brown tributary. I stared, mystified that I was actually crossing The Mekong. Flashes of patrol boats from Vietnam films flew through my mind. Shirtless soldiers standing at mounted machine guns while rock played loud and hapless peasant boats were capsized. We moved in a strange slant. I looked up to see Monteblan pilot us through a diagonal slice of road halfway across the bridge. With that we were back to the familiar side of the road, which was a relief after Thailand's British modeled traffic system.

Leaving the border behind, we plunged into partially paved roads, crowded with a circus of animals and scooters, layered in floating clouds of dust. Roadside shacks sold fans, cell phones, ever more scooters and food. Through it all, finding our way in dust and mayhem, Monteblan maintained a casual mastery of Pablo Cruise. Flexing through gears and touching brakes, tapping gas, taking us forward and threading us through the Chicken, Monteblan appeared entirely in tune with what he was born to do. I sat back, dismayed. My friend's driving was upending a tacit aspect of our relationship. Something never discussed and perhaps a part I hadn't known consciously until now.

Beer chilled, semi-mystical trajectory aside, Monteblan was like me: pointless. We weren't players. We were pieces to play with. Both of us were unexceptional portions of humanity, cannon fodder for the machine. Lacking that slash and grab fervor required to master the sleazy offal grab, we lived at lower tiers of corporate reality. There we existed as assets to be deployed. We knew this and didn't mind.

Work was shit we did and didn't like. We didn't want to advance because that would only lead to more of it. And we damn well never dreamed of Starting Some Business of Getting The Funding—those holy grails of capitalist salvation for every other squid trapped in the tank. My friend and I saw through that shit. We realized that capitalism's magnificent promise was also its most chilling scam: the only chance of finding freedom was by mastering moves so bastard that the real bastards would break off some action. A little piece of the Fuck You Machine that you'd keep greased and pounding, ploughing more profit into the insatiable anus void which had replaced the heart of America long ago.

Monteblan and I were off that table. Beyond our inability to slice metaphoric throats, we possessed no sharpened talents that would attract the blind idiot gods running shit. We showed up at the squid tank and were identified instantly: Interchangeable Graphic Designers 4,585 and 4,586. Dupes to be leveraged, doughboys to throw over the top. This didn't bother us. Monteblan and I were blessed with no illusions of greatness. And we shared a friendship based in the tacit understanding that neither would strive through the refining battery of challenges which might produce it.

As legion as the unremarkable are, this shared awareness is hard to find in The States. Most there are moaning for more or groaning for greatness, grinding themselves down to powder reaching for power. The unremarkable might be legion, but finding one in major American metropolitan regions who truly, utterly, year round and from top to bottom, at all angles and through all circumstances, entirely doesn't give a fuck about that—or want to fuck you over to change that—is rare. Mostly such people aggressively don't give a fuck, shooting up streets or shooting themselves up with shit. Finding someone on the je-ne-sais-qua side of the IDGAF spectrum is practically impossible. Which is why I cherished my friendship with Monteblan.

Evading whatever hellacious grey tomorrow this machine had planned for us, my friend and I made it a point to rip off pieces of fun. Hard, with both hands. Missions of precious, pointless joy. Things impossible to capitalize on. We didn't blog, share, or pitch the shit. Just did it. Darting trips to bright acid beachfronts and happenstance lap dance lairs. Jumps in rolling oceans of ass and laughter. Third world bars with dirt floors and whores. Cities of cigars and corruption. Days on dope in hammocks. Things that had nothing to show for them once they were over. Instances impossible to explain to those who hadn't been baptized in the beauty of not mattering. That was our mission. Those were our grails. And perhaps Chicken 65 was the greatest of all. Something we had been training for without even realizing.

And possibly, I realized while driving towards Vientiane, our last. Besides the external Fuck'emall landscape of 21st Century America, internal shifts of age were changing things between Monteblan and I. Already our trips and escapades were dwindling. My flight to Bangkok had split us for a year. He disappeared into his mists now for months at a time. His woman was murmuring of children. The job landscape was tightening. My ability to check in to the chain gang for freelance cameos was shrinking. Probably I'd have to go full time. In the dull mush of days that would follow, I would be forgotten. Just like everybody else. Like billions of others who had filled this planet, Monteblan and I were built to be forgotten. Only in America had that become criminal. The one thing you couldn't be there was unremarkable. Maybe that's why my friend and I were striving so hard to be nothing. Just to fuck with the place. This was our friendship. That was our bond. We didn't matter.

But Monteblan could drive.

Even I, who had never done lap one on a race track, recognized with every passing mile the talents that Monteblan possessed. Watching him drive from the corner of my eye, I sensed my friend somewhere beyond me. The crowded Third World road was filled with busses, cars, scooters, and trucks battling through a chaos of kicked up dust. Amidst them, Monteblan was playing. Playing with things like acceleration and physics, mechanization and vision, projection and estimation, spin and gear. Towards the obscure Asian capital city in gliding moves, feather light easing stops, casually gunned jumps and shifted lanes that effortlessly melded into advantageous positions within swiftly shifting traffic patterns, Monteblan was mastery.

Glimpses of whatever powers, Napoleonic or otherwise, my friend possessed were impossible not to sense. Sliding us fast towards a wall of traffic I would almost yell in alarm when suddenly, almost imperceptibly, an opening presented itself perfectly. Pablo Cruise slipping through like a minnow, I would swivel in my seat mystified, watching our passage instantly vanish. How Monteblan found these vehicular possibilities was impossible to ascertain. That he threaded us through them without scratches, dents or even the occasional jam of brakes wasn't so much impressive as unnatural. With Monteblan at the wheel we were mercury or some other inexplicable, uncontainable element. It didn't feel like we were driving through Laos. It felt like we were being poured through the place.

This was powerfully intriguing but also admittedly unsettling. In the passenger seat beside him, I remained unremarkable Rich Archer. Beside me, Monteblan was amazing. He had Value. Talent. Abilities people got drafted for. And this was just Third World crosstown traffic. What would my friend do on The Splits? As we shot through shoddy roads, I realized Monteblan was wondering the same. In the squint of his eyes, twist of lip, slight nod and tilt of head, he was registering all the car might do. My friend was not just driving now, but collecting information. Making mental tables and adjustments, estimating what was possible in Pablo Cruise, Monteblan collected an understanding of what statements of speed he might successfully express.

This silent conversation between vehicle and master continued all the way to the capital city of Vientiane. Twice I tried to interrupt and both times I was entirely ignored. Israeli Gears would be waiting at the Hotel Chantal bar tonight. He'd want our answer. Monteblan was deciding that answer while driving. It was his to deliver when we arrived. My job was just getting us there. Pointing out signs which were simple enough to see anyway, I directed us towards The Hotel Chantal.

We found it fast enough. The capital city was low built, quaintly constructed compared to the towering commerce of gritty, glittering Bangkok. I looked out the window at a brilliant sun hitting dusty pavement, bouncing off low buildings as tuk-tuks farted by, all ancient metal and painted wood. New, mid-range Japanese made cars dominated the road. Or maybe the Lao people were so psyched to have cars that they kept them all mint condition. Middle class was a new thing in this part of the planet. Pride went with it, as people looked forward to a brand new set of possibilities in life. The feeling was refreshing when I considered America's middle class, hammered and vanquished, looking back towards vanished Shangri-La.

Leaning out the window, sun bathed my face while parched scents from the city blew on hot breeze. Noodles from outdoor restaurants, coffee brewed street side, truck and tuk-tuk exhaust mixing with construction cement and street side dust. Trees flicked by as we moved in mellow traffic. Provincial seemed to sum up Vientiane in a word. Turning through a wide expanse of government boulevards, white buildings with golden rooftops flashed in the sun, guarded by ornamental military men. Gliding right, we turned into a block of coffee shops, travel agents, restaurants and travelers hotels. Low rent hostels hosted bombed out, drifting foreigners. White skinned with sunken eyes, smoking alone, beer bottles lined their slanted street side tables. Happier tourists passed by in purposeful strides: young women off to see temples, men with their wives, small groups of clean cut, backpacking Koreans.

"It'll be the first diagonal past the Buddhist temple," I told Monteblan. "Right there."

We swept past an enclosed city block where barefoot monks in bright orange saris were on a ladder at the walls. Pruning branches from a tree shading the sidewalk, other holy men swept limbs away. Passing them I wondered if the task held potential for transcendent Zen, or if the initiates were bitching under their breath like everybody else forced to do yardwork in the sun.

"Here?"

"Yup."

Monteblan veered left at the diagonal and our hotel was right there. The classical white façade matched the tone of Presidential palace we had passed earlier. A uniformed Lao man stood out front, shaded by an overhang of carved wood, stained with a lifetime of city smog. He wore a simple brown suit, squinting in the sun as we pulled up.

It wasn't Thailand; he didn't smile.

**Hotel Chantal was an elegant, throwback oasis.** Walking in, we passed between two large urns, filled with water and thick with lily pads. The lobby was a span of black and white marble. Slow fans circled from a wood carved ceiling. A vaulting, carpeted staircase lead upstairs to hidden rooms. Throughout the place were pieces of once modern furniture, now old and worn. Passing I noted tattered edges and sunken cushions, a battered elegance both sleazy and noble at once.

The reception desk we approached was made from old mahogany wood. Behind it stood two eminently graceful Lao women in traditional dress, hair swept up in pins behind their head. I blinked and pictured Hotel Chantal in the war era, filled with soldiers and spooks, reporters, photographers and whores. The same bell they had used to check in was probably the one before me now. The stretched reflection in its polished silver showed the lobby like an Escher print of infinite, spinning fans. Imagining every finger that ever hit it, I touched the metal button. A simple tone floated brightly in space than slowly melted into nothing.

Monteblan checked us in, paying with cash we had changed in Chang Mai. Details sorted, keys dispersed, we trudged up the carpeted stairs. Halls stretched long. Rooms were small. My friend found his and fell face first into bed, tired from the drive. The meeting with Gears happened this evening. I didn't ask Monteblan what he had decided, just let him sleep. The room next door was mine. Dropping my bag I shut the door, shooting my cuffs and wandering the hotel, remembering what I knew about Laos.

Little of it had been in school. My education about the region had been inspired entirely by an Australian I shot pool with in Bangkok. When he found out I was American he took me to task for guns, jails, our wars, our president, then dug into our history. I had the option of getting into his; letting him know that if there was one place more big and stupid than America, it was probably Australia. A barren chunk of desert rock spawned from the criminal rejects of Britain, red with the blood of Aborigine genocide, it hadn't done much for world culture outside of AC/DC. But as such insights don't lend themselves to pleasant banter, I merely listened.

This was something I got used to in Bangkok. People all over the world hate on the States. They'd corner me after a few drinks and mention shit like war and guns without remembering air conditioning, the blues, rock and roll and electric light, milk shakes, space travel, blue jeans, video games, reinforced steel concrete, tempered glass, Charlie Parker, personal computers and Snoopy. I don't take pains to point these things out, just listened to whatever got thrown my way. Over this particular game of nine ball, the lecture concerned US war atrocities in Laos. The heavily tattooed Australian was something of an expert in modern South East Asian history. I wasn't. Shocked and furious to learn how little I knew about Laos, he potted the nine then found a pen. Scribbling furiously on the back of a bar tab in CAPITALIZED AND UNDERLINED words he wrote the titles of three books I MUST READ. The following weekend, I found a bookstore, bought all three and read them cover to cover. When I was finished, the Australian's rage felt justified. I was furious myself for never having been taught what had happened in Laos.

What I had known was that during The Vietnam war, the Viet Cong took advantage of America's political position by hiding out in Laos. This little land locked country caught between Vietnam and

Thailand was the perfect place for them to evaporate after attacks against US soldiers in Vietnam. America had no legal right to fight in Laos. A ground presence there would have forced UN action. But that didn't stop us from bombing. First it was done casually; American fighter planes didn't like landing with bombs in the hold. So after they ran missions over Vietnam, they'd loop over Laos and dump leftovers there. This policy, which might have been called Operation Probably Maybe Hit Some Viet Cong Sometimes, began one of the century's most undiscussed crimes, which I was never taught.

During the Vietnam War, the US dropped more bombs on Laos—a country the size of Minnesota—then we did in the entire European theatre during all of World War 2. Thanks to us, Laos is the most bombed country in the history of the planet. There's been lots of wars. All of them filled with lots of bombs. None of them top what Laos absorbed from a country 40 times larger, that hadn't even declared war. To imagine what happened, picture living in Minnesota, while one bombing run, every ten minutes, 24 hours a day, went on for eight years. With the whole world not doing anything about it.

Towards the end of the war, the United States "secretly" got in on ground level. Ripping up Laos' mountains and valleys, we built huge CIA landing strips throughout their terrain. We fooled the UN by saying they were for hospital supplies, material to build schools, and repairing Laos' devastated infrastructure. (Which we had bombed.) In reality, these landing strips were a network of drop off and pick up spots for secret CIA soldiers, the weapons they needed, and Lao opium that funded their filthy racket.

These were the landing strips where we touched down to whisk illiterate hill tribe people into our war. Since we couldn't officially fight in Laos, we recruited Laos to do it for us. Most were agrarian tribal people. They went from doing rain dances for their crops to stripping down M-16s. Reporters from the time noted that most Lao people had never seen welded metal before. Let alone the airplanes we taught them to jump out of with machine guns in their hands. And while they were out there dying, who knows what we did to their women and children. All the while piling up opium and bombing away. Until we left. Just like that. Leaving all the soldiers we had trained to their own fate. Most of them hid out in the jungle, where they lived as outcasts dodging the communists. Lost and cut off from their land, doomed to die. The rest of the country enjoyed the pleasure of our after party presents. Out of the *two million tons* of bombs our country dropped on Laos, about a third of them failed to detonate upon impact. But they blow up now. Since the war ended, about 20,000 Lao people have been ripped to pieces by American bombs still hidden in their land. That's still happening today. Most of those hit are children, playing where they should be able to play, until they are murdered from the fragments of a war that never officially happened with a nation 40 times their size and synonymous with freedom.

That this happened is a shame beyond processing. That I had to learn this from an Australian with an Ankh tattoo over a pool table in Nana Plaza only extends that shame. In Europe, I had met young Germans who still hang their head in dismay about a war they had nothing to do with. Where was my shame about Laos? My country had decided it didn't matter enough to teach. Some groups get TV specials and movies made about their troubles. Others get days on the calendar and relentless, guilt building lessons in the nation's schools. What about Laos? How can you do a Never Forget moment for something people don't even learn in the first place? And how many more Laos don't I know about? What other places has America casually obliterated, smashing collective PTSD into generations forever?

These questions ran through my head morosely as I drank whiskey alone, sunken in a lobby settee. Normally my brooding insights would be brushed aside by Monteblan. (*Dude, it was war. Crazy shit happens.*) But my friend wasn't here to hear. Upstairs he was weighing

The Splits. And he hadn't asked me to help him. That depressed me further. Leaving The Chantal, I set out aimlessly, drifting through late afternoon Vientiane alone.

Frowning down dusty, sun baked streets, I wandered. Since Monteblan had told me his story in Chang Mai, the revelation hadn't brought us closer. I was weirdly angry that my friend had hidden that part of his life from me. This race had hardly started and already it was changing things between us. Charlie was right; The Bird had something to show me. Maybe I didn't want to see. Maybe Chicken 65, which I had imagined as some madcap, bro bonding adventure, was in fact the strain that would break a friendship already stretched thin by distance, threatened by time.

Brief as it had been, the road was already dividing us. Several times on the ride through Laos, I had brought up Chicken mysteries from Mississippi Charlie. Monteblan heard none of it. Listening to the engine, staring at the road, he had driven in rapture like I was absent. Now he was making decisions about our race without me. Big decisions about potentially terrible things. Chicken 65 was a gang of lunatics. *Reasonable Life Choices* wasn't the banner to hang on this bunch. These were people seized at borders. Still, The Splits had scared them off for years. With such powerful riches at stake for the winner, that was saying something. None of it good.

But Monteblan was more than good. He was great. There was something otherworldly about my friend's driving. What would those divine talents do when let loose in real, racing road? And what would they prove? I didn't like being told I wasn't Chicken. The Splits would show we were. That first dash of pure speed I had tasted in Bangkok had been exhilarating; addictive even. Truth was I wanted more. My friend knew how to score. But was the person capable of all that still my friend? I knew Monteblan. I knew him better than anyone on the planet. But Monteblan Driving wasn't just different. He was an entirely different version of my friend. I knew who I had started this race with. But who would I end it with? What was the Chicken showing him? What else would it show me? When this race was over, who would we be? *Would* we be? Charlie said people died...

Brooding through crowded noodle stands and open air bars, I found The Chantal by nightfall. Monteblan was descending the stairs as I entered. Freshly showered, oxford and madras, he hit the marble floor. I didn't ask where he was going, just fell in step beside. Together we crossed the lobby. Ceiling fans rotated silently. Passing under them I imagined others who had crossed this floor, wondering if they would die. Newsman, soldiers, and spooks from the war, warned not to fly somewhere, told not to drive someplace, doing it regardless because only other people died. All of us knew that. Trying to find words, I struggled for discussion. Striding decided, my friend was beyond me. This was destiny. It pulled us forward now, through dark curtains shrouding the lounge.

Dim, retro elegance of marble floors and deeply stained wood swallowed us. The circular bar held shelved galaxies of glittering glasses. Elegant whores lounged in shadows. Beyond them, a Lao house band was formally dressed while casually murdering an Eighties hit. Israeli Gears was watching.

Without a word, we joined the man. The racer turned to us, saying nothing. Yesterday's friendliness had been replaced with the cold, hard face of competition. A waitress slid a bowl of peanuts before us. Gears dipped into his pocket, producing a small bottle of hand sanitizer. Spurting some into his hands, he briskly rubbed his palms. Whiskey sodas appeared. We drank.

Gears watched Monteblan.

I watched Monteblan.

Monteblan stared at the floor.

Then slowly, my friend looked up. His face was different. Soft features were tempered with firm resolve. The normally placid eyes were slightly sharper. It might have been the bar lights, but I swear they flashed when he said the words.

"We're in."

**Everybody stayed at The Chantal. Racers partied till dawn.** Chicken 65 was watching when we checked out at five. Drifting in with mist from the pool, racers slowly materialized in the lobby. Some had women, others had bottles. All wore clothes rumpled from a rough all-nighter. Rubbing their eyes, swaying and tilted, they bore witness like some tragically hung over Greek Chorus. Marching past them in Madras shorts, Monteblan gripped his black army helmet secure. I wore my suit. Crossing the marble floor, it struck me as a funereal touch, rendering me ready for burial.

"Don't have to do this, Grimace."

Reggie's voice was low. Mississippi Charlie was at his side. The older man looked particularly wrecked from the excess of last night. Whiskey bottle dangling from his hand, the shade of his red face had transcended into some supernatural purple scarlet. Blonde hair disheveled, his head swiveled slowly, silently watching me leave. The pale blue eyes were mystified, then abruptly focused in anger.

*Fool!*

I could practically hear Charlie's drawl echo in my mind while we passed.

"Bird decides," I told him.

"Bird got nothing to do with this, son."

Waving me off angrily, the old racer turned his back and tottered down a long, dark hallway.

Remaining racers were grim. Ceiling fans slowly revolved, failing to disperse the heavy silence. Hungover to the point of shell shock, the Chicken witnesses looked lost in some emotionless fugue state. Faces slack, eyes bloodshot, hair in disarray, they watched us silently. I forced a smile. Nobody smiled back. Ladyboy Man raised a flat glass of champagne, voice hardly a whisper.

"God speed, old boy."

Behind me a wobbly whore tumbled from high heels. I glanced back to see her struggling up in thigh slit evening dress. She looked at the men bleary eyed, confused.

"Why you let them go die?"

The prostitute's plaintive question were the last words I heard. Sucked through the revolving doors, I was pulled from The Hotel Chantal into the misty dawn of Laos.

Outside, Pablo Cruise was angled like a knife. Jacked up and silent, windows lightly fogged, the dark vehicle looked malevolent. Monteblan took keys from our valet. The man backed away, melting into morning mist. Beyond us, Vientiane was an emptiness of silent streets. My friend and I were alone. Monteblan placed his helmet on the car roof then went to the trunk, pulling out his black flak jacket. Buying it in Bangkok had been funny; some over the top touch for our wacky bro-venture. Now in the misty dawn, unknown perils ahead, my friend's military vest looked unsettling.

"Is that really necessary?" I said.

"Snipers"

My mind, perhaps for the first time, fully processed the fact that we might be shot at today. As my driver snapped on Kevlar, something in me snapped.

"Hold it."

Monteblan looked up at me. "We'll be going fast. They're not gonna hit us."

I thought about this a moment. "What you mean is that we'll be driving the deadly road that everyone says is going to kill us *so fast* that the snipers shooting from the hills won't be able to murder us? That's your answer?"

He shrugged, reaching for his helmet. "Live a little."

"I don't want to live a little. I want to live a lot. As in a long peaceful life filled with fond memories and hey, Monteblan?"

My friend was ignoring me, adjusting the chin strap and carefully testing the fit of his army helmet. This type of meticulous attention— from a friend who remembered to pay his electric bills only when the power in his apartment was cut—was unnerving. I wondered where we were going. *Why* we were going. What were we after? A chance to be 'Real Chicken'? Why? What forces had brought us here? Just last week I was on a laptop looking at flights home. Now I was standing in Vientiane wearing a tailored suit and my friend had a flak jacket on. Lost in the grey mist, I reached for familiar morning routine to ground me.

"How about some coffee?"

"We're out of black coffee." Monteblan walked towards me, armored and helmeted, unfolding a Hotel Chantal Napkin. "Have a Black Cat."

He extended his hand, three gleaming black pills lying in the white napkin. I stared at them, already feeling slightly unhinged. Surely drugs wouldn't help.

"Found French Shrek last night," Monteblan told me. "Cost more than my plane ticket."

"I don't—"

"Let's go." Monteblan prompted. "One for you, two for the driver."

Slowly reaching for the fat black pill, I placed it in my mouth. Monteblan cracked open a warm beer from the back seat. He passed it over. Frowning in hesitation, I chased down the military grade speed with Beer Lao. Grabbing the can back, Monteblan threw the two remaining pills in his mouth. Sloshing them down, he rubbed the back of his hand over his beard, then slammed the trunk shut. Moments later, my friend was behind the wheel. Pablo turned over, engine throttle blasting. I opened the door and slid inside. Monteblan slipped into gear without a word.

At that precise instant, Israeli Gears emerged from the parking lot behind us, pulling up alongside. His matte black Mustang had shining silver trim. The car was immaculately clean, inside and out. Through lowered windows, Gears and Moist Definitely regarded us with grim faces. Both wore pressed black polo shirts. Gears had black fingerless driving gloves. There were aviators on their faces, goggles around their necks, and arrogance all over them. The Mustang had a fat, rich, roaring engine which Gears revved a few times for our benefit. When it idled back down to a throttle, he leaned forward, shouting with his heavy, old world accent.

"The Splits start 15 kilometers out of the city! Follow me there. You'll see him by the road: Thai guy with a Chicken flag. That's where the clock starts. Doesn't stop till you hit the end of the airstrip in Vang. Got it? And watch out for snipers. I heard they took a shot at Hans last night. Probably just some kid with a bottle of whiskey, but a bullet is a bullet, right?"

"A bullet is a bullet?" I said from the passenger seat. "What are you—"

A roaring blast of engine drowned my words and their muscle car slipped into empty city street. Monteblan followed. Vientiane was waking up as we wound through it. Greyish light lit the morning scenes. Barefoot monks in robes walked with silver bowls for alms. Steaming coffee carts ladled cups to early workers. Noodle shop owners hosed down the sidewalk. Tuk-tuks and a handful of bicycle rickshaws floated past.

Monteblan reached behind him, fishing in the back seat. His hand returned with a pair of binoculars. He tossed them at me without looking.

"You're going to need those in the Switchbacks." My normally *whatever* compadre spoke in cool, competent tones. "You're going to be calling out the turns. Before that, I want you wheel watching."

"Wheel watching?"

Monteblan downshifted, taking the turn smoothly after the matte black muscle car ahead. Traffic parted for us all around; some jungle understanding of raw power.

"That Mustang has rear wheel drive," he told me. "You'll see the wheels turn right before the car reacts. That split second matters. You shout them out. Got it? Right or Left. See there?"

He pointed to the mustang just ahead. Split seconds before the revving black car turned left on the next corner, I saw the wheels cut in.

"Yeah," I nodded, pulling my seatbelt tighter. "OK."

We passed a block of close apartment buildings, turned right at an intersection, and moved through a series of low office buildings heading out of the city. Looking down, I saw my feet were shaking in their shoes. My eyeballs hummed. I noticed my fingers, meticulously pulling invisible lint from my suit. My mouth was dry.

"This is fast speed." I rocked in my bucket seat. "I mean it's kicking in. Logically really when you think about it that makes sense because if you were pushed out of an airplane with a machine gun in your hands you'd want it fast acting ready for war and all." I breathed in deeply, shuddering slightly, air electric in my lungs. *"Whoa.* French Shrek Connection. Hey Marseille. Fucking *shit* this is speed.*"

"Mmmm!" Monteblan shook his head and shivered like he had just been plunged into freezing water. "God good speed. God speed. Good."

Wind rushed through the car as speed shot through my mind. Pablo Cruise hummed happily. Through tingling skin, I identified the feeling of each hair follicle on my head. Looking at the tires turning beneath the Mustang ahead, I suddenly gasped. *What focus!* The world turned HD plasma. My eyes roved with laser precision. Staring hard, I saw tire treads in a spinning pattern of blurring V's. They slightly shifted right.

"RIGHT!" I yelled.

"YES!" Monteblan yelled back, swerving with Gears as the Israeli changed lanes. Our hands flew instinctively up, high fiving with a sharp smack.

Vientiane was ending. We left hotels and offices behind. Up ahead, grass grew in dusty clumps beside the road. Shacks leaned against crudely poured cement stores selling fans, scooters, and food. Beyond them was a pole at the side of the road. A Thai man lounged at its base, yawning with a whiskey in his hand. Soft morning breeze blew the black flag in rippling display: Chicken gripping twin beer bottles, lighting bolts crisscross behind.

"Dude? Monteblan? It's on! We're here!"

The road raised up slightly, showing my first glimpse of The VV Splits. I thought there was some mistake. This wasn't a place to race. Below us in a bowl of confusion, clouds of dust hung over traffic kicking up dirt and gravel. Pickups and speeding scooters bounced and battled through bumps and pits. Shacks lined the ruptured road and cattle mooed throughout. Vehicles slid off sides of broken pavement, landing in muck and mire. Far ahead, the road leapt up in sudden inclines, split wide in separate lanes, or disappeared under mounds of construction gravel. Above the vehicular chaos, shining sun glared malevolent. Distant fields filled with buffalo stretched beyond. Passing through looked impossible. Surviving seemed debatable. Before I could protest, Pablo Cruise bucked and jerked, engine snarling hard, dropping us down into The VV Splits.

**The world blurred**. My head snapped back against the seat. Pablo chunked and jumped, metal grinding and gears jamming. Through billowing dust, the Mustang up ahead swerved suddenly right.

*"Wheels! Rich! Wheels!"*

Monteblan bellowed a thundering reminder of my task, just managing to swerve in line behind Gears. Bare inches beside us the road dropped out into ragged pits of debris. A dog shot from it in blurring fur. Monteblan swerved. Dust billowed. Sun glared. Horn blaring, a pickup raced towards us. Monteblan slid. Pablo Cruise spit gravel, fishtailing wild. We whiplashed forward through a mayhem of cars, trucks, swarming scooters and busses. Gears barreled ahead, spitting dust. My vision blazed in amphetamine focus. A flicker of tread betrayed his next turn.

"LEFT!"

Monteblan cut left close on Gears, just dodging a muddy hole.

"Left *Hard!*"

His hard swerve in unison with the muscle car just missed an oncoming bus. Forearms rigid with gripping fists, my friend held tight pursuit. Reading tread, I called out cues. Together we chased them like karma. Kicking up dust and tearing through Laos, Pablo Cruise roared. Window filthy now, I thrust my head from the car into blasting wind. Pebbles pinged off my glasses. Dust and smoke choked my lungs. Practically decapitated by a passing truck, I tracked the treads and shouted loud.

*"Left! Right HARD!"*

The world beyond my peripheral blurred. There was a tunnel with wheels at the end. Nothing else.

*"RIGHT HARD!"*

Speed sang through my being and God did Monteblan drive. My friends masterful hands blurred in shifting, spinning combos that punched us perfectly through the snares of The Splits. Feet below danced in patterns of brake clutch gas rhythm. Flooring through traffic I felt flashes of barely missed impact and total destruction all around. Nothing mattered. Speed had simplified existence. Confusions reduced, dreams discarded, my drifting personal mythology had been traded for this singularly singing, amphetamine pinned moment in time.

Until Gears figured us out.

Realizing his wheels telegraphed every turn, The Israeli downshifted hard. Swerving sharply they were suddenly beside us. Moist looked at us with *fuck you* all over his face. Then the Israelis vanished, breaking hard left towards a map memorized maneuver we missed entirely. Just ahead, the dusty road split suddenly in half. Five feet wide, the drop out ran twenty meters. Jumbled construction stones filled it. Rusted, brutal spears of reinforced steel shot up like swords. Rushing towards it I realized we would die. But my pear shaped friend had no such intentions. In the dark, twisted heart of The VV Splits, he bitch slapped physics to break our way.

Shifting stick and slamming gas, Monteblan yanked the wheel so hard it blurred. Our backside shot out sideways. Monteblan wrenched the parking brake. Pablo Cruise screamed. Sliding sideways full speed, we bridged the chasm. Tires spinning, dust pluming, we drifted past the Israelis. Through our filthy windshield, I watched Moist Definitely.

His hand raised in dumb wonder, pointing as we passed them perpendicular. Gears glanced. Gasped. Then it was done.

Roaring as he forced the shaking steering wheel, Monteblan punched the brake free. Pablo Cruise kicked straight and shot forward. Wind screamed as Laos blurred. Eyes wild, teeth clenched, my friend ripped through road furiously. Gears was behind us but we didn't need his wheels to read. Monteblan had cracked some code. He knew the road. Somehow it had soaked into him. All the turns. Every peril. Monteblan just knew.

Behind us, our rivals doubled down. Bellowing engine thundered, black bastard machine challenging. Fighting for leads, both cars roared. Maps were forgotten as The Israelis careened on pure instinct. Catching us then falling back, Gears appeared in flashes. The Israeli drove like he was fighting. Elbows up, chin down. Gears was good. He might have been great. But Monteblan was magic. Something from beyond. Gears felt it. Hated it and wanted to beat it. Gunned his machine. Gritted his teeth. Drove like hell, chasing heaven. Monteblan shut him down. Shook him off. Rivals finally swallowed in clouds of dust, we left them behind, lost.

Flawless macadam marked the end of The Splits and we hit it doing 150. Everything went suddenly smooth. Pablo Cruise's rattling, shaking conniptions stopped abruptly. I gasped. Monteblan yelled in triumph. My friend and I high fived. Pounding pavement we flew towards The Switchbacks ahead. Gears was somewhere behind. Victory ahead. Laughing, lifted on hands of angels we rose majestically up the hill, preparing to dive down into perilous hairpin turns beyond.

And then it happened.

**Hard to describe this sound.**

Mechanical, animal shrieking ripped from the engine like some wild predator snared. The whole car seized. Then we were spinning. 360 whirls that blurred the world. It stopped wickedly sudden: tires grabbing, car rocking, silent. Both of us sat frozen in shock. Crickets hummed at roadside. The sudden cessation of speed was like being ejected from heaven. Before us were the last five feet of rising road leading to The Switchbacks. Slowly, slinking back in fear, Pablo Cruise rolled backwards towards The Splits we had just barely escaped.

*"no no no no no no no NO!"*

Eyes wide, Monteblan stared at the wheel like it had shocked him. His hands hovered over it, unbelieving. Then he snapped into motion. Wrenching the stick into neutral, my friend hurtled out of the car yelling.

"Get out! Now!"

Screaming high on speed, I thought the thing would blow. Throwing myself into the roadside grass, racing fast I ran. Heart hammering under blinding sun, I pounded towards distant trees.

*"Get back here! Help me!"*

Monteblan's faint voice was far behind. Without stopping I turned in a wide loop, reversing my direction. Long legs bounding through hip high grass, I ran towards Pablo Cruise. Arriving breathless I found Monteblan pressed up against the back bumper like a linebacker. Pablo Cruise rolled slowly against him. Joining my friend I threw myself into the fight. Pushing, grunting, red faced under the sun, we struggled to halt the crippled machine. Slowly it rolled. Indifferent gods looked down at our Sisyphean travail.

"SHIT!"

Monteblan exploded in frustration, a gust of guttural exhalation, then leapt from the fender and ran to the driver side. Pulled parking brake halted the fall from grace. Pablo Cruise stopped, slightly rocking, ten steep feet from the unreachable peak.

*"What happened?!"*

I thrust my hands through my hair, gripping my tingling scalp. The shocking loss of our hurtling forward motion was tragedy beyond imagining. *Speed.* I wanted it back. Then an insight hit me like lighting. I looked up, eyes wide, remembering my friend's earlier tale.

"Is this The Forces? Did they do this?"

Monteblan shot up from the driver's seat, levelling a damning finger at me over the car roof. "Don't you bring The Forces into this!"

Spinning he threw open the back door, reached inside and started yanking things free. Beers and clothes flew wildly into the street.

"We're too heavy! Throw things out! NOW!"

Flipping the door open I struggled with a spare tire wedged behind the front seat. Prying it free I hurled it rolling down the hill to Splits far below. Monteblan was already at the trunk. The first suitcase was his, hitting the tarmac with a flat smack. Then came mine: all I had in Thailand, a bulking battered garment bag bursting with possessions.

*"Wait!* That's my stuff!"

His head jerked up wildly. "Do you want to win?!"

Frozen in place, sun burning down, my mouth opened without answering. Possessions from the bag flipped through my mind: Laptop, hard drive, cameras, vintage sunglasses, Italian handmade shoes, ring from the night market, shirts, jeans— *American jeans!* —more. Then Monteblan was there, grabbing my lapels, eyes wild in the hot Lao sun, sweat pouring from under his army helmet.

"Listen to me! That's not your stuff! That's Rich Archer's stuff! You're Asser now!" Inches from my face, shaking me by the lapels, Monteblan yelled. *"Are you Chicken 65?!"*

"Yes!" My triumphant shout floated over the open road.

"Damn right you are! Throw everything out except what you have on GO!"

Releasing me Monteblan shoved me forward. Then he pulled me back.

"Not the maps!"

He released me then yanked me back again.

"Or the binoculars!"

Wild eyes rolling, he spun away to leap sliding over the hood to the driver's side. Missing the landing, he face planted on the far side, disappearing from view. In a flash he popped up, helmet askew, lunging for the trunk.

I flung open the front passenger door, hurling out handfuls of eight track tapes. Monteblan was at the open trunk, items flying over his shoulder. Luggage, shoes, tools, flashlight, clothes, beer, bottles of whiskey all rolled or slid down the hill. Rounding the car I watched him salvage only the pellet gun, jamming the pistol into the back of his madras shorts. Then my friend slammed the trunk, bounding to the driver's side and yanking the parking brake free.

Pablo inched backwards. Monteblan scrambled back behind the slowly rolling Datsun, throwing his body up against the bumper, shouting mad.

"Push this thing Asser! Push if you want to be Chicken! Push if you're CHICKEN 65!!"

I joined him at the car, straining with my shoulder then turning backwards for more power. That's when I saw them.

"No..."

Bounding from the last pits of the ragged road below, Gears hit pavement and flew. Effortlessly eating road, the matte black machine shot uphill towards us. Sun glinted on the windshield. Fat engine roared. In a flicker while they passed I saw the racers' expressionless faces. Without looking, they flew past us over the hill and were gone. Left in the breeze from their sudden passing, I stood there dumbly.

*"Push!!"*

Monteblan bellowed and I snapped back to task. Lighter now, Pablo Cruise rolled up hill. Grunting moments later we were over the peak, rolling down. Monteblan shot to the front. The car sank and bounced as he shoved his bulk into the red bucket seat. I ran to the passenger side then jogged alongside, stunned momentarily at my first glimpse of what waited below.

Through dark green foliage in a murderous, coiling ribbon, The Switchbacks sat waiting like a python. My widening eyes saw cliffs and sharp drops, shadows and lost turns, curves both long and sudden. Then Monteblan yelled at me to jump in. My fingers fumbled for the door handle. Breathless and sweating I just managed to swing it open and leap in. The car was stifling hot but felt light and free. All was left behind.

"We blew the clutch," Monteblan said before I could ask. "That's what happened."

He was staring at the road ahead of us. Then at the dials on the dashboard. Then down at the stick shift positioned in neutral. Then back to the road we were rolling down with silent, increasing speed.

"So we roll now?" For a brief hallucinatory moment, this felt possible. With Monteblan at the wheel, even without an engine, I thought we'd still win The VV Splits. I thrust my hand up for a high five. "We roll!"

The high five didn't materialize. Monteblan ignored me, voice low and dangerously calm.

"You have to stop talking. I have to listen now."

We rolled a moment more, car gaining speed, trees passing outside, paved road pulling us down to the treacherous turns waiting below. When I spoke it was barely a whisper.

"Listen to what?"

Sweat ran down my friend's face from under his helmet. Beneath the beard, his jaw was grinding.

"The engine." Eyes darting from road to dials, Monteblan whispered more to himself than to me: "If I listen to the engine I can switch gears without the clutch if I can switch gears without the clutch I can beat Gears I can do it I can do it I can do it…"

Closing his eyes briefly, reverently, he turned the ignition, bringing the engine to life in neutral.

*"I can do it."*

The engine purred. We rolled faster towards the roads below. I belted up. Swallowed. Clicked my teeth. Cracked my neck. Turned to Monteblan.

"Can you? I mean can you… actually in reality… do that?"

His fingers rubbed in anticipation over the slightly shaking gear-shift. Monteblan licked his lips.

*"*I can do anything in a car. *Anything."*

Staring at the gear shift, then at the speedometer, he breathed in and out. Pablo Cruise gained momentum. Blowing sharp breaths like a cliff diver set to leap, Monteblan winced and slid the shift forward while pressing gas.

For a terrible, hovering moment, Pablo Cruise debated.

Then a roar filled our ears and all the dials on the dash danced tightly to life. Monteblan let out a long, pent up breath, sinking back into his seat. Needles danced and we jumped forward with a boost of acceleration. Listening closely, my driver found second gear. Holding his breath, he pushed the stick forward. Slight grinding made us both jump; then he did it. Dials on the dash slipped down out of the red. Third was hit with a flawless flick of the wrist. Dials to white, engine purring, he had it then. Driving without a clutch into the clutches of The Switchbacks, Monteblan turned to me.

"I have to watch the dials on the dash. You have to watch the roads. Get the glasses."

While wind raced through the window, I reached for the binoculars and fumbled them from their case. Monteblan sped us towards the first sloping switchback turn, shouting as he pushed Pablo Cruise forward.

"Tell me what's coming next! Tell me the turns! But for GOD'S SAKE don't say ANYTHING if I have to switch gears don't even BREATHE while I'm hearing it or we'll freeze up and fly off the cliff to our bullshit Grimace and Asser deaths GOT IT?!"

Before I could reply we were in. Dive bombing down the first curve, Monteblan spun the wheel and navigated the corner. Ragged, dusty green trees shot past. The world blurred. In the thrill of Speed once more, I forgot my job.

"Shout 'em out!" Monteblan yelled over racing wind and engine whine. "We're in this together, dammit!"

Grabbing the glasses from their case, I lowered them to the road. Vision magnified, I saw the layout of the upcoming turns just before an oncoming truck blotted them out.

"Right Hard Down!" I yelled while the whoosh of wind from the vehicle rocked Pablo Cruise. "Then Left Uphill!"

He sailed into them, catching a slight grind as he shifted into third, swinging us into perfectly swerving, smoke spinning skid. I laughed at the beauty of it. With Monteblan, I was listening to the engine, hearing that moment, understanding this language of Speed. Between shifts I shouted out directions. Sun shot through trees in slashes. Binoculars showed rushing road in shaking cinematic display. Farther we went, deeper into the switchbacks.

*"Right Down!*

*Left Down!*

*Right Up!"*

Moving faster, the smoother it all became. Perilous road transformed into something like a drumming roll. Monteblan responded with high speed jazz collaboration. Stick shift solo, blowing free. Tires spun. Sharp cliffs passed. Drop offs yawned below. All was well, speed our reason, planet spinning symmetry. But who was driving? My friend wasn't Monteblan anymore. The man beside me in body armor was Fast; living symbol, archetype incarnate. With a thrilling shudder of methamphetamine realization I understood what Chicken 65 was doing. Charlie said The Bird would show us things. I saw this now at high speeds. Flying with Monteblan, I was chasing what I wanted to be. While I was racing forwards, Monteblan was reaching back, retrieving who he had been. This wasn't a race. It was a revelation. We would find ourselves out here. *This is what Chicken 65 was all about.*

That's when the bullet shot out our back window.

**Shattered glass sprayed behind**. My hands thrust up instinctively. Monteblan yelled and swerved. We lurched past the Mustang. Stopped at roadside, oddly angled, the black car was abandoned. Dark marks in the pavement showed where Gears had jammed on the brakes like Monteblan was doing now. Skidding wild, my friend fought for control, sliding to a shuddering stop just ahead of our rivals.

"What are you doing?!" I yelled at him. "We'll never get going again!"

"Our boys need help."

"They didn't help us!"

"You're right." My friend spun to face me, eyes wild. "But this right here is damn fine Chicken."

With that he was gone. Left stunned in the empty car, my eyes shot up to the rearview mirror. Monteblan was hunkered low, jogging down the road towards a large boulder. The Israelis were there, taking cover from the sniper. Reaching out, they pulled Monteblan behind the looming stone. Moist slapping my friend's back, laughing, Gears shaking his head: *this guy's crazy.*

This was true. But Option B was a car full of broken glass and a sniper in the hills. I readied myself. Two fast in and out breaths. Heat buzzed and insects whirred. Then I threw myself outside to follow my lunatic friend.

Sun blazed. Full speed in a tailored suit I ran down the dusty road. Sparse tree branches flashed past. Through the jumping, jarring landscape of panic I saw Gears up ahead furiously signaling. I ran on, uncomprehending. Dark eyes blazing, the Israeli thrust his hands flat in front of him. Then he did it again. Frowning as I ran, trying to understand, the bright *aha!* finally hit me:

*He's telling me to stay—*

It was like a bee buzzing past my head.

*Fzzzttth!*

Bark blew from the tree just beyond me in splinters. Sound followed after: distant rifle crack floating ghostly downhill. Then everybody was shouting at once:

"Down! Get Down Asser! Down!"

I was. My body had thrown itself flat to dirty earth the minute the bullet hit the tree. Flooded with amphetamines and racing with adrenaline I pulled, crawled, and scrambled my way to the boulder. Sliding in on a cloud of dust, I tumbled into their midst. Head buzzing, disoriented, the world was brightly white. I heard my own voice from far away:

"I just got shot."

"You got shot *at*. You did not get shot!"

I heard Gears. Felt him grab my shoulders, shaking me.

"Look at me Asser! In the eyes!"

Gears was a shadow with brilliant light all round. Through the blurring white, I found his eyes. They blazed at me in black focus, boring through the haze. Desert warrior. Fierce. Slowly, world formed around those ferocious eyes. Pounding pulse in my ears lowered. Breathing deeply, I was back.

"Yeah," I said, shaking my head sharply to clear it. "I'm fine. All cool."

Orienting myself, I looked around. The four of us were crouched behind a large rock beside the road. Sparse bushes sprouted from the dust. Branches from a skeletal tree hung above. Sun blazed down, day's heat rising. The Israeli's Mustang was twenty meters away. I must have crawled past it in blind panic. Now I could see why it was slumped oddly: the right rear tire had been shot out. Up ahead, Pablo Cruise had a window shot out from the same side. My eyes jumped across the road, trying to find the sniper. A slowly rising, dusty grass incline lead up to the horizon line. He must have shot from there.

"Well," Moist Definitely said to Israeli Gears. "Now we can do something."

Tanned and athletic, squatting in their shorts and polos, The Israelis looked in control. Gears was scanning the sparse surroundings with roving eyes. Light sweat beaded his brow. Moist was relaxed, hair a thick black wave. Aviator shades hid his eyes. There was a handgun tucked neatly in the back of his shorts.

"Do what?" I said, still breathless.

"I'll do it!" Monteblan fairly shouted.

"Do what?" Gears said.

"I'll do it." Monteblan repeated. "Whatever. You know. The Mission. I'll do it."

Moist and Gears looked at each other, then back to look at us. I was wearing a rumpled black herringbone suit, necktie wrapped around my forehead. Monteblan was in madras shorts, helmet, boater shoes and body armor. Flying on the Black Cats, both of us were twitching and sweating, eyes wide, licking our lips and bouncing on our haunches.

"What the hell are you guys on?"

Gears fumbled in his pocket, pulling out hand sanitizer. He spurted out half the bottle and rubbed ferociously, like we might be contagious. A truck went speeding past, roaring towards Vientiane.

"That's the third one!" Gears said. "Two vans and that truck went right by. Cars on the side of the road and nobody stopping? They know! That fuck up there?" His finger shot out, pointing uphill. "He's after Chicken 65."

"Moist." My eyes shot to their Mustang with the flat tire. "You said now we can do something. Right. OK, we push your car. Change the flat from under cover."

Gears pierced me with fierce black eyes. "What, and leave him up there to shoot somebody else's brains out? Your friend Mississippi Charlie maybe?"

I was silent. The buzz of insects increased like some slowly rising alarm. Sweat ran down my back.

"We're first in." Moist Definitely's voice was slow and thick. "It's our get. That's how it goes."

I looked at both Israelis. They looked decided. My eyes moved to Monteblan. He was quietly nodding along. Throat dry, I gulped nervously.

"Don't worry." Moist waved his hand dismissively. "We did this bullshit in Lebanon before you were jerking off. But Gears and I can't clear the hill with two. We need three."

"Great," I said. "So we're fine if somebody dies."

Gears spun on me, practically shouting. "Nobody's dying today!"

Stunned at the Israeli's fury, I froze spellbound in his stare. While those eyes bored into mine, I suddenly wasn't afraid of dying anymore. I was afraid of what Gears would do if I dared get shot.

"Right," I said, "OK Gears. Sorry."

He considered me a moment, as if judging my conviction.

"Nobody's dying today," I repeated, with more strength. Part of me believed it, actually.

"Good." The Israeli slowly nodded his head. "Moist, break it down."

"Break it down for me Moisty!" Monteblan made *whick whick* DJ scratches.

Gears sighed and shook his head.

Moist Definitely took the gun from the back of his shorts. Finger extended along the smooth barrel, he used his weapon to trace the dirt.

"He's here, up that ridge." The barrel made a circle in the earth. "Five hundred meters probably, from the sound."

"I'll do it!" Monteblan burst forth.

"Do what?!" Gears was exasperated. "You don't even know. Shut up and let the man speak, will you?"

A bullet pinged off the top of the rock where we were hiding. Dust puffed up, chipped stone raining down. Startled, I turned to Monteblan. He stared at me, one eyebrow raised. The Israelis hardly cared. Gears glanced up, annoyed. Moist brushed rock chips from his hair and continued.

"We're here." Moist drew another circle for our location. Then he tapped his gun to the right of it. "That's his sightline; where both cars got hit coming in. The one at you running? He was fucking lucky. He doesn't have a clear shot left or he'd be shooting the shit out of our cars. So I go left. Low and fast, then up the hill, through those trees."

He casually gestured with the gun towards the distant hillside where dusty, scraggly trees dotted the incline.

"Cover!" I raised a fist, feeling militant. "Good thinking Moist."

"That shit's not cover," Gears said. "Not from sniper rounds. Your pal Reggie, that bullet he wears?"

My mind flashed back to the long, deadly looking round of ammo dangling from the neck of my nemesis.

"That's a sniper round. The shit he shot in Trashcanistan, running through the kill list for your fucking Vice President. Rounds like that go right through walls. Forget about trees. Just camouflage. But with that and distracting fire, Moist can get up the hill. Flank far left. Kick his ass."

"Distracting fire?" I said.

"From there." Moist pointed towards two large boulders to our right, twenty meters down the road. "That's where you fan out, firing. Make him think we're flanking right. This thing make noise?"

Monteblan's pellet gun was protruding from his pocket. Moist Definitely took it, turning the faux 9MM handgun over in his hands, then flicked off the safety. Pointing it through the trees behind us, he fired a round. The spitting, kicking cough wasn't much. Moist Definitely shrugged, flipping the safety and handing it handle first back to my friend.

"It's something. Looks real if he's on the scope. Noise will come from Gears."

I heard a metallic click and slide. Gears had pulled an automatic handgun from under his polo shirt. The weapon had a dull, mean gleam and looked well maintained. Nodding in satisfaction as he checked the action, Gears took over the map. From the circle representing our cover, he drew another line, hard right.

"One of you will—"

"I'll do it," Monteblan said fast.

"Fine! Grimace runs to that rock while I fire cover from here." He banged the rock lightly with his fist. "With Grimace in position firing that piece of shit, me here with the Glock, Moist will get up the hill fine."

"What," I said. "Like that sniper thinks you'll hit him uphill with a handgun?"

"Shit no." Gears said. "But he'll be distracted. A bullet's a bullet."

"A bullet's a bullet!" I lit up. "That's what you said this morning. Is that some Israeli Army thing?"

"You want to know an Israeli Army thing?" Moist Definitely said from behind his black shades. "Our secret weapon for surviving?"

Monteblan and I both nodded.

"No alternative," he said, voice slow and thick. "Out in that desert, we got nowhere to fucking go. That's the same way I want you thinking now. This is fucking *it*."

He pointed down to the dusty ground.

"Right here. Nowhere else. Think there's somewhere to go, some way out, you don't fight so good."

Sun blazed. Heat increased. Insects hummed in rising tension. Momentum had us that wouldn't be stopped. Some strange thing was taking shape and gaining speed. We were about to have a military operation. All guns and shots and bullets and... death? *No.* Nobody was dying today. Gears told me that. Made me say it. Now he was talking with Moist, chatting like this was a pickup ball game, making it all more surreal.

"What do you think," Moist said. "One over, one up?"

Gears laughed. "What is this, '92? You're going to do that incline in a minute?"

"Hey, I'm in shape." Moist Definitely slapped his flat, hard gut.

"You're in shape but you're not fucking 25. One minute over, two minutes up."

"Fine. It's almost lunch so let's get this banana off the hill. Synch."

Both Israelis looked at their watches. Holding them together, they pressed buttons simultaneously. Moist Definitely looked at Monteblan and me from behind his aviator shades and smiled.

"Chicken 65."

The trim, tanned man slipped the safety off his weapon and ran low down the road.

"What he's—?"

Gears snapped his fingers sharply. "Asser."

I spun to look at him. He was sweating now, looking down at his watch.

"On my mark, I'm up and shooting. When I do, Grimace goes right. That fucking vest is a piece of shit you bought on the streets of Bangkok so don't get shot."

"I'm not getting shot," Monteblan said surely, knowing it.

"Damn right you aren't," Gears agreed.

"Nobody's dying today," I piped in cheerfully.

Gears shot me a glance. Then he shook his head briefly and went back to his watch.

"Thirty seconds."

"By the way," I said. "What's my job, I mean, in the plan?"

"Back up distraction." Gears said, eyes focused on his watch. "If Grimace and me don't make enough noise, there's another rock out there with your name on it."

"What's my weapon?"

"Harsh language. Grimace. Ready?"

Monteblan was bouncing in place, squatting hunched like a runner at the starting block. Raising his pellet pistol affirmatively, he confirmed in rattling nonsense.

"That's go go Gears absolutely applesauce whiskey Mississippi Charlie."

Gears frowned. "It's that shit from those French motherfuckers. That's what you're on?"

Our heads nodded in unison, bobbing wildly like dashboard toys.

"Fuck me. That speed is dynamite. Don't lose your shit. Stay cool. Mark. 3, 2...1!"

Gears suddenly straightened up, reaching high to fire over the rock. Four shots popped from his Glock in loud, blasting reports. Ears ringing, I crouched down instinctively. Monteblan burst in a plaid blur towards the other boulders, bellowing with a roaring rage.

I had never seen Monteblan sprint. I was stunned. His body was shocked. Confused at this foreign motion, out of balance with the heavy helmet, my friend fell almost instantly. Rolling somersault through dusty grass, he tumbled all butt crack and bullet proof vest, a ridiculous madras mess. Sprawled in a tangled pile of limbs, boater shoes slipping, Monteblan struggled to rise. Just when he did, the sniper fired.

It looked like a giant invisible croquet mallet had swung down from the heavens. Monteblan was punched with a flat smack, hurled with an audible *oooof!* Flying ten feet through the air, turning slowly like an obese starfish, my friend hit the ground in a cloud of dust.

I heard Gears screaming at me even as I did it.

*"Draw fire! Move!"*

Bursting from the rock screaming, I raced through open space. The bullet hit the boulder just as I dove behind it, stone chips kicking free as the following report floated down the hill. Monteblan was motionless in the grass. Gears was pouring shots from the side of the rock now. The world was tilted and whirling.

*"Clear!"*

The familiar, low voice floated down from above us. Slowly, Gears lowered his pistol. Moist shouted again.

*"Just a damn kid!"*

Gears and I both bolted from our cover, rushing to Monteblan. My friend was groaning now, rolling slowly back and forth. Gears was there first, muttering as he searched my friend with quickly scanning eyes and roving hands.

"Fuck no fuck no fuck no fuck no…*What?!*"

His black eyes went wide in shock. Reaching down to the flak jacket, the Israeli pulled at a metal slug which moments before had been a bullet. It was stuck fast.

"Fuck me," Gears said relieved. Letting go he fell back into the grass. "You bought that vest on the *street?!*"

Monteblan coughed, nodding.

"That piece of shit saved your life, Grimace." He reached out to slap my shoulder. "Along with this crazy motherfucker."

Monteblan, wincing as he sat up, held his ribs under the vest.

"Thanks bro."

An old wooden rifle landed in the grass beside us.

We looked up. Moist Definitely had the Lao teen by the scruff of his neck. The kid's face was swollen and puffed from where The Israeli had punched him. His eyes were narrow slits of fear and anger; skin dark brown and streaked with dirt. His T-shirt was worn thin, showing an American hip hop star holding money and smoking a blunt. Some faded, traditional sarong hung around his skinny hips. The flip flops were rubber and dirt cheap.

"Want to kick his ass?" Moist said to Monteblan.

Monteblan winced, staggering to his feet. He took in a long breath, holding his side where the bullet had punched him. Then he shook his head.

"No."

'You should," Gears said. "If that rifle wasn't an old piece of shit, that round would have gone right through you. Sure you don't want to kick his ass?"

"No," Monteblan said again.

"Well I do." My fear had become fury, rising fast. "You just tried to kill my friend you little fuck plus shot me and our cars and what THE HELL ARE YOU DOING!!"

Raging waves rushed me. I stormed the sullen boy, watching his head lower to take the blow. My hand darted down instinctively. Grabbing the rifle I flipped it round, raising it high, ready to pound. But a soft touch reached out from behind.

"That's not you, Rich."

Monteblan was there. I spun to face him, breathing hard, shaking.

"That's not you, Rich," my friend repeated softly. "Come on. Don't."

I bit my lips, trembling. Sun blinded me, heat blazing, insects buzzing high.

"Do it Asser," Gears said grimly. "Blood for blood. That's all these people understand."

My eyes shot to the Israeli, standing there staring at the kid.

"Rich, listen." Monteblan's voice was clear and quiet. "You're freaked the fuck out and you're high and if you do this now you'll hate yourself for the rest of your life. I know you. This isn't you. Don't."

"Do it, Asser."

I wavered for a moment, all pinned up and loaded, then blew out a huge breath I didn't know I had been holding. Spinning from them I stormed away through the sparse trees, towards the cliff beyond. Hurling the weapon like a helicopter I launched it over the edge screaming.

*"Fuck! You!"*

I watched the old rifle sail down, my echoing curse following it into the blue. I shuddered. Sudden tears blurred my vision. I blinked them away, shaking my head sharply, biting my lip hard. Breathing fast in the sparse woods, I wiped my hands furiously on my suit jacket. It didn't wash away what I had almost done. I had almost brained a kid with a rifle butt. That was me. But I hadn't decided. Hadn't even thought. Just surged with situations which emerged with blinding speed. Charlie told me The Bird had something to show me. I just assumed it would be beautiful. Not ugly, not awful. The Bird had just shown me something terrible. It had shown... *me*. Without my friend I would have just—

*"Asser!"*

Spinning fast I blundered through trees, shaking off my troubled thoughts. Israeli Gears was standing alone, tucking his gun away. Moist had set the boy loose. The thin, forlorn figure was trudging uphill.

"You OK?" The Israeli asked me.

"Yeah."

He sniffed the air. "Smell that?"

I nodded, inhaling the light, smoky scent which shrouded Laos like rude perfume.

"That's their jungle being burned down." Gears slipped his sunglasses on, staring after the boy. "Chinese developers are buying everything around Vang. Lot of is it Hill Tribe lands, legally. But what the fuck is legal in Laos? And what are the Hill Tribes going to do with a patch of burned out brush? They're smoking these motherfuckers off their lands, then chopping down their trees. Timber rackets. Army sells it through the black market. Five years, that poor fuck will have nowhere to go. His sisters at least can go sell their ass in Bangkok. What's that one do?"

I watched the boy, now half way up the dusty hill. Head hanging, he climbed slowly under white, glaring sun.

"I don't know," I said, confused. "I can't believe what I just did."

"You didn't do shit, Asser." Gears headed back towards the cars, shaking his head. "Shot your driver and you didn't do shit. You're not built for this."

I turned to stare after him. "Built for what?"

He said it without looking at me. "Chicken 65."

**When we reached the road, Monteblan was watching Moist Definitely pull a tire from the Mustang's trunk.** Brand new, it hit the ground with a heavy bounce. Gears turned to help him, waving us away without looking.

"OK. Bye. Go win The Splits."

Monteblan and I looked at each other. Crouched beside the Mustang, Moist spun the jack handle with a clicking whirl. Gears was frowning at the tire, holding his chin. When he sensed us still standing there, he looked up.

"What?" His thick accent was edged with anger. "We fix the tire, you go win. The way you drive, it's done. Please…"

Smirking, the Israeli extended his hand down the empty road in mock cordiality. Moist spun the jack with clicking whirls, inching the car up in slight jerks.

"We can't. I mean, just go," Monteblan finally mumbled. "I blew the clutch."

There was a clink of metal as Moist Definitely dropped a tool on the pavement and stood up. The identically dressed racers stared at my friend from behind their black aviator shades. For a moment there was nothing but chirping birds and the hum of insects. Then Moist tilted his head towards Pablo Cruise, fifty meters up the road.

"You blew the clutch just now?" His low voice was slow. "That's why you stopped to help?"

"I stopped to help because…. I don't know. You needed it. We blew the clutch back on the hill. When you guys passed us?"

They looked at each other. Then back at Monteblan. When Gears spoke, his voice was a hostile whisper.

*"Fucking VV Splits without a clutch? That's what you just did?"*

"Yeah," Monteblan shrugged. "We got down the hill into first and from there I did it by ear. I mean, it's doable."

"It's… doable?" Gears tipped down his glasses, looking at Monteblan carefully. "You just did The VV Splits without a clutch and that's what you have to say about it? Doable?"

"Well…" Monteblan looked down at his boaters. He kicked at the road a little. "It is."

Israeli Gears and Moist Definitely turned to look at each other again. Moist spoke in fast quiet Hebrew. Gears nodded. Moist dropped quickly down beside the car. The high pitched whir of a drill hit our ears; lug nuts loosened in rapid bursts. New ones tightened on a swiftly mounted wheel.

"We just need, uh, a push." I pointed towards Pablo Cruise. "Into first."

Moist Definitely passed me, heaving the blown tire into the trunk. He slammed it shut.

"Yeah," he nodded. "You do."

Opening the car door, he knocked his fist twice on the roof and slipped inside.

Gears looked at us. "Good luck with that."

Then he was past us both, walking to the driver's side, opening the door, getting in.

"Um, Gears?" The realization of what might be happening slowly dawned. I walked to the window of the Mustang and looked in.

"We just—a push? I mean, we helped—"

Gears turned the ignition. The Mustang's ferocious engine roared to life. Exhaust blasted from behind in dark clouds. I heard Monteblan softly cough. Beside me, the black car trembled with the power of its throttling engine. Gears revved the gas. Squirting hand sanitizer in his palms, he rubbed them briskly.

"Gears, you're not..." I swallowed. "Are you?"

The Israeli ignored me. Moist Definitely handed him the fingerless driving gloves. Gears slipped them on precisely, staring at them, stretching his palms, testing the fit. He nodded, satisfied. Hands went to the wheel, fingers spreading slowly along the contoured plastic like he was touching something holy.

"All we need is—"

"Asser, Asser, Asser...." Gears sighed, shaking his head. "What you think you need and what you really need are two different things. You think you need my help. What you really need is to understand what this is all about."

The driver finally turned to look up at me. I saw myself reflected twice in the twin panes of his black glasses: eyes wide, mouth open, the portrait of played.

"The best teacher in Chicken 65 is experience." Gears revved the engine, hard. "Through *experience* you learn what this thing is all about. Don't you think Moist?"

He turned to Moist Definitely.

His map man nodded. "Yup."

Gears turned back to me. "So what'd you learn today, Asser?"

Stunned, I heard the choked words struggle from my mouth. "M-Make it a Ch-Chicken Promise?"

Israeli Gears grinned. His fingers formed a gun. With a click from the side of his mouth, he pulled the trigger.

"That's it."

Tires squealed. The black car roared forward. Blowing smoke, sliding in slight fishtail, The Mustang leapt past Pablo Cruise and shot down the long, sunlit road ahead. I stood there, watching the car get smaller, engine growing faint, until it disappeared around a faraway curve. Then I turned to Monteblan.

My friend was living up to his Chicken name. Grimace on his face, standing in the dust left hanging by the Israelis, Monteblan sighed.

"They... The...!" I finally stammered, still not believing. "*What!?*"

Monteblan trudged past me, shaking his head. I followed him towards Pablo Cruise, angry that my friend wasn't furious. Jumping ahead, I walked in front of him, backpedaling along the hot, dusty road.

"They were pinned behind a ROCK! We bailed them OUT! We stopped—you stopped!—to help. Shot at! Both of us! You! With a bullet! HIT! *And they left us?!*"

I halted, hands out, begging Monteblan, begging heaven to witness the injustice which had just transpired. Hostile sun stared down. Monteblan walked past, footsteps dogged and slow.

"Do you *care?!*" I called after his sloping shoulders. "You just took a bullet for them! We had The Splits! It was *ours!* What they just did was...."

Words failed me. I glared at the sun baked road. Fists clenched, enraged, I stomped my feet furiously in the dust. "*It's....! It's...!*"

"A race."

Monteblan's soft voice stopped me. I looked up from the dirt to see him at the car, driver side door open. Half in the car, my friend quietly repeated himself.

"It's a race, Rich."

For a moment I stared at him. Heat waves bent the road. Insects buzzed in their maddening, whirling hum. Monteblan dumped himself into the driver seat. I watched the vehicle buckle from his prodigious weight. The door shut. DTA's words floated back to me from a lost conversation at the General's in Chang Mai.

*"Is there anybody we don't have to watch out for here?"*

*"Your shotgun and nobody else. You'll have to make some pacts on the road, but make damn sure they're Chicken Promises."*

Then it hit me. There was nothing mystical about this road. Chicken 65 was a race. People tried to win races. That meant others had to lose. For a moment I stood stunned by how clearly this had just been illustrated. I blinked. Sweat ran down my temples. I brushed it away with the back of my suit sleeve. The heated road wavered before me. Walking slowly on shaky legs, I approached Pablo Cruise. Monteblan was staring blankly at the road ahead.

"You know—"

"No." He shook his head. "There's nothing to know right now."

I turned behind, taking in the distant ribbon of winding road we had travelled. Up ahead, more of that heat baked pavement stretched before us. With a sudden wave of fury, I strode behind the car and threw myself at the bumper. Angled like a sprinter stuck in his starting block, I hurled all my rage into the inert metal. Pablo Cruise rocked forward on the crumbling shoulder of the third world road. I leaned in harder.

Sliding in formal shoes on dirty gravel, dust kicked up and I cursed. Sweating and demented I struggled with what I had learned on this brutal road, far too late. *Chicken 65 was a race.* A filthy race littered with horrible others desperate to win. Charlie and his mystic shit could go to hell. Chicken 65 had no hidden mystery. Just nasty facts. People want you off the road. They want you out of the race. Don't trust them. Don't help them. Beat them. Ruin them. Destroy them. *Win.* Sun blazed shining on the bumper, blinding me. Swooning and slipping, pushing and kicking, I didn't register the growing noise from behind until it was almost upon me.

Spinning in surprise I saw the machine. Under dazzling sun on deserted road it approached like a hallucination. The naked engine showed shooting pistons all coughing smoke. Two huge tractor tires were on either side. A ten foot pole extended from the engine's rear, ending in a handle. Held by a Lao man on a flat platform, he stood between two more tractor tires. Puttering and bouncing towards me, face tanned by the sun and creased, he wore a battered old flopping hat. A little boy in shorts and a T-shirt was clinging to his legs.

Arriving beside Pablo Cruise, the contraption rattled and coughed to a loud, idling stop. The Lao man pointed at the car and made a flicking motion with his hand. I thought he wanted us off the road. My flooding surge of bitter curses were ready to fly when he did it again. This time, he pointed to the front of his engine. Then down the road, straight ahead. With one hand, he mimicked a push. Unable to comprehend kindness on this forlorn road, I just stared. Peering over his engine, the old Lao released his clutch with the hand lever and lurched forward, thunking into our bumper with his dirty machine. Pablo Cruise jumped forward with a startled lurch. The strange machine pressed in behind, maintaining contact, gaining speed down the road.

*"Rich! Get in!"*

If Monteblan hadn't yelled, I might have just watched him drive away. Snapped into action I jogged beside the tractor, frantically patting my pockets and jacket searching for money. Squinting in the sun, the tan old man waved his hand at me, shaking his head. The little boy beside him held one finger in his mouth, pulling down his lip. I stared at them both a moment, standing on that rattling metal platform. My mouth formed two words that didn't do justice to the depth of my feeling: *Thank you.* The old man nodded briefly and I darted ahead towards the Datsun.

Flinging open the door, I jumped in. Monteblan's palm hovered over the gearshift stuck in neutral. Blinking sweat from his eyes, licking his lips, my friend turned over the engine as the trembling needle showed slowly growing speed. Monteblan turned to look at me. *This is it.* I nodded, message received. With three short, sharp breaths he pushed the stick.

First fell into place effortlessly. Wheels grabbed road and the engine thundered in road burning fury. The same turn which had swallowed the black Mustang minutes before pulled us into The Switchbacks, closing in on the Israelis under the glaring white eye of a furious sun. Monteblan drove like murder. When we found them they weren't even racing. The sniper shot had shattered any chance of a decent split time. Gears was going easy; something like a Sunday drive. Window open, arm casually dangling out the side. We passed them like a shot. Leaning back, I smiled. Wind rushed over my face and I imagined the crisp, cold taste of whiskey soda following our victory: deliciously chilled bubbles of bitter delight, downed by the winners of The VV Splits.

A fat, charging roar jolted me from my dream. Gears had bounded right besides us, engine bellowing like a throttled beast. Monteblan barely smirked, expecting the monster. Moist Definitely looked deadly calm. That lack of emotion frightened me until I saw Gears. The glasses were gone and his dark eyes glinted with throat slashing fury. King David descending on chariots type shit, Yahweh's smiting force, chosen and set aside, right there by our side, driven to annihilate.

Side by side we shot through a deathly blur of turns and straightaways. Sliding in drift, billowing smoke, twin engines thundered power. Monteblan and Gears traded leads. Gears with gloves on, elbows out. Monteblan belly fat and helmeted, Datsun Golem. Not out of control but far beyond it. Threatening Gears. Frightening me. Searing through Laos in lethal velocity. As wind screamed through the window, it felt entirely impossible that anything in God's brutal universe might possibly move faster.

Until the murder van overtook us both.

The white van floated in between the battling cars like a dream. Gears almost lost control in shock. Even Monteblan swerved. The Lao driver barely looked at us. Deeply tanned with wisps of thinned black hair, the wiry old man wore glasses tinted green. Energy drink bottles danced on the dashboard. His chin was set in grim resolve. The old van rattled and shook, straining to handle the speed. Behind him, passengers were screaming.

His tourist load of Korean moms wore floppy straw hats with flowers. Their moon shape faces were pale with terror, pressed against the window. Weeping, screaming, they banged the glass frantically. Oblivious to their hysterics, the old Lao bent unrelenting over the trembling wheel. Flooring through straightaways, dive bombing turns, the murder van added random horror to the already deadly proceedings. With the reckless attack of a man who had been driving The Splits since childhood, he throttled his shaking machine. Behind him, Korean moms screamed. Deaf to their lament, staring over the dashboard of dancing energy drink bottles, the Lao's sharp frown was a hard line of unrelenting pride: *my road.*

Side by side, three vehicles shot towards Vang. Windshields glinting. Pavement flying. Enemies absolute. Moist a frozen statue. Gears glaring. Monteblan mumbling. Korean moms wailing. Lao driver relentless. Pushing karma, pressing fate, we raced. Then before us, distant but rushing closer, the tunnel into town appeared. Its dark mouth drilled through the hillside like a tomb. Beyond was the Vang Valley and victory. Blinking, I squinted from my jumping, rattling seat to be sure that what I saw was really happening.

It was.

The tunnel into town was a single lane, one car wide.

"Monteblan?!" I shouted in real fear.

His answer was a low grumble, blending with the engine growl. "It's a race."

The murder van was the first to go.

It was a matter of equipment not skill. Had the old man been handling either Pablo Cruise or The Mustang, he would have made paste of us. Maybe that was all he wanted to prove. Roaming unregulated, his murder van was like all the others: driven till things broke. That happened now at 150 KPH. The wrenching sound of whatever went wrong sent him swerving. I saw the swaying terror of Korean moms. Gears swung to the far shoulder while the murder van jerked back spinning like a top. With a sharp intake of breath my eyes looked to the rattling rearview mirror. Behind us the thing was spinning in oblivion, lost in clouds of dust. Monteblan hardly glanced. Gears swooped back in, reappearing right beside us.

*500 meters.*

Both drivers shot neck and neck towards the single lane tunnel rushing closer ahead. A high speed poker hand where someone would fold.

*200 meters.*

Or bend, twisting in a burning wreck of metal as the other shot through the tunnel. I looked through the windows at Gears. His eyes were straight ahead. I turned to Monteblan. So were his.

*100 meters.*

I shut mine.

In that suspended moment, memory bloomed. I saw the old coffin maker in Bangkok. We had shot past his shop the first day of Chicken 65. Through unknown quantum capacities my mind retrieved everything. Barreling towards death, I recalled details registered but not seen: old radio in the corner, royal portrait on the wall, slowly blowing fan, simple tools in sure old hands. Those hands, I saw now, had been carving our coffin. I watched him tap tableau moments of our journey into unfinished grain: Brain The Dane at the bar, a battered Chicken Bible, Ladyboy Man with champagne, Pablo Cruise, Charlie grilling steaks, Hotel Chantal whiskey, sniper shots, Gears... Wood carved relief showed our Chicken; the tapestry of happenings hammered into being before we began.

Beyond my vision, the race went on. I sensed the Thai master's hands descending from heaven: chipping pieces of reality just ahead, tapping what would happen into shape. His random tumble of masterful strikes was shaping our oncoming death as it formed. Eyes closed but seeing, I hovered as my life's final moment was made. Then beyond those working hands I sensed a spanning stretch remaining. More to be carved. More Chicken. I knew this. I opened my eyes.

"We don't die here."

The instant I said it Gears was gone. Pulling hard left The Israelis vanished. Tunnel swallowed us whole. Through darkness we thrust suddenly into bright sunlight. Blaring bus. Monteblan swerved just. Side view mirror exploded in a pulverized puff. We shot past dingy cement stores with dirty drooping signs showing soda and beer. Skidding through gravel past the dilapidated bus depot, we almost missed the airstrip.

*"Right Hard!"*

I screamed it and Monteblan wrenched the rattling Datsun. The abandoned CIA airstrip ripped like a scar through the jungle valley. We hit in in a cloud of white dust. Monteblan roared, mouth open, howling. Pressing for everything he floored in fifth, flying over white gravel under blinding sun. The whole car seemed to rise just off the earth. We floated. Monteblan didn't stop shouting. The tension, The Forces, The Splits and their terrors now flooded from him in primal, animal release. Faster we screamed, every needle pinned right and trembling at highest possible speed.

The Chicken flag rippled ahead. We passed in a whipping rush of wind then bounded down into a raw, rugged ribbon of dirt road snaking towards the river. Humps and bumps, trees flashing past. Monteblan slowing, groaning now, shifting through grinding gears of sharp metal gnashing. Clattering, shuddering, Pablo Cruise chewed through a tortured revving of brutal downshifts:

4,

3,

2….

*Done.*

The car didn't stop. It died. Engine cut, Pablo Cruise rolled forward in exhausted, crawling meters. Then all was still. The silence was shocking. Trees all around. Leaves rippling in soft wind. Chirping birds. The meandering river before us sparkled in sunlight. Distant cliffs yawned up beyond. I blinked, heart still hammering. Blood pounded in my ears. My body was shaking. For a moment, I didn't believe it all. Then I turned to Monteblan. Staring straight ahead, he spoke softly.

"Beer."

**The glovebox held a single can.** Fingers trembling, I handed it to him. Monteblan took it without looking and popped the top. The beer hissed with flooding foam, spraying his body armor and dribbling onto his madras shorts. Monteblan chugged half down, fast. Then he wiped his beard. Birds chirped. The river flowed. My friend opened his door. He took one step outside then collapsed.

I leapt from Pablo Cruise and found Monteblan spread eagled on his back. Staring up at the whispering jungle leaves, drained entirely, the sun reflected in his vacant brown eyes. Shaking him for response, I received nothing. His beer lie tilted on the dirt road, silently pouring suds into the earth. Panicking, I grabbed the can and poured small sips into Monteblan's half open mouth.

*"Hold on man!"* I said desperately. "Don't you fucking die on me!"

Beer splashed in his mouth. The rest ran down his beard. Then it was gone. I hunched over my friend.

"Is this you dying?"

Slowly, staring up at the sun, Monteblan shook his head no.

With a huge sigh, I fell back into the road. Still shaking with Black Cat adrenaline, I rocked quietly in the dirt. Birds chirped all around. Staring at the swiftly flowing river through the foliage, time passed slowly. Naturally. Then the Israelis were there.

Moist and Gears came striding down the jungle road leading an ancient black tow truck, dented and greasy. The Lao driving it stopped before Pablo Cruise. With Israelis supervising, he managed a laborious three point turn. I moved Monteblan from the road with a few hard pulls and pushes. He watched vacantly while Pablo Cruise was hoisted on ancient rigging. Gears directed the driver with hard-ass commands, shouting, stopping, double and triple checking the hitch. Finally satisfied, he punched the truck door go and shot a fat glop of hand sanitizer into his palms. Rubbing them briskly, the vanquished Israeli approached us with his map man trailing.

I didn't know what to expect, but it sure as hell wasn't a hug. I almost jumped back in defense when Gears stepped in and embraced me like a brother on that quiet dirt road. Holding tight, he let me go with a soft pat on the back. Moist did the same. Then both men hefted Monteblan to his feet. I watched while Moist Definitely peered into his eyes, testing reflex response with finger snaps. Satisfied, he nodded and Gears stepped forward. For a long moment, the rival racer held my friend by the shoulders at arm's length. Looking him in the eye, nodding silently in respect, The Israeli finally found words.

"How did you know? How did you fucking *know* I would drop out from the tunnel?"

We all looked at Monteblan. There was a long silence of chirping birds. Then my friend smiled.

"Hand sanitizer."

Gears looked at him incredulously. "What, you want some?"

Digging in his pocket, he thrust the small bottle at Monteblan.

Monteblan looked at it, then shook his head.

"That's how I knew you'd pull out." Gazing at Gears, my friend squinted in the sun. "Anybody that worried about getting their hands dirty doesn't die in a third world car wreck. Too messy."

Gears looked at him blankly a moment, then slowly replied. "Son of a bitch."

Moist laughed. "Good shit, brother."

"Hand sanitizer?" Gears shook his head, recovering. "The VV Splits without a clutch? That's one for the Bible. You two are Chicken legends now."

I grinned, pleased at being legendary. "Where'd our car go?"

"Chicken Garage," Moist told us. "Mr. Boom's brother in law runs it."

"Here's the card." Gears handed a business card to Monteblan, tapping it with his finger. "He'll tune you up and trick it out: Serpico Flaps, trip nine plates and the mark. Plus big money in the trunk. This year's pool was large. Fifty K."

"*Whoa!*" My face lit up, thrilled. "Nobody will steal it?"

"Not with The Mark they won't," Gears said. "Nobody will touch you this Chicken. And you earned it."

"Hey." Moist was tapping his watch. "Time for my jerk off massage. Let's go."

"Listen guys," Gears slipped his sunglasses on. "Let me buy some harnesses for you both. Five point belts, real shit. I don't want you bouncing around out there with those bullshit Datsun seatbelts. We'll stop by the garage on the way to the hotel. That OK with you?"

"Sure Gears." Squinting in the jungle sun, Monteblan nodded. "Thanks."

"You bet."

With that, the two Israelis turned down the jungle road. I watched them walk away in white shorts and matching black polo shirts. They had looked crisp this morning. Now tails hung out, dust streaked the black fabric, and shorts were rumpled. Gears reached absently into his pocket, pulling out hand sanitizer. Just when he was about to shoot a palm full he stopped, looked at the bottle, then throw it in the dust. Moist laughed, slapping his friend on the shoulder. Then without breaking stride, the trim map man turned towards us, walking backwards while calling out from a distance.

"Watch out for Vang, fellas! This place swallows people alive. Get fixed up and get the hell out!"

He pointed beyond the trees, past the airstrip, where faraway road wound up through the mountains out of town. I shot him a thumbs up. With a last wave, the beaten racers rounded a rough turn, swallowed by the jungle.

**Vang was wild east.** The sun was blinding and dust was everywhere. We walked past small restaurants, storefronts selling tourist shirts, and run down wooden bars. Mopeds flew by with drivers wearing windbreakers, surgical masks and sunglasses. Half the road was paved, divided right down the middle. Every four wheeled vehicle passed in a perilous side wheelie, dropping down hard at road's end. Massage girls waved from windows. Day drinkers hunched ornery at road side bars. Above me was a strange sound like some great beast exhaling and I was suddenly cast in shadow. Looking up startled, I watched a hot air balloon slowly gaining loft towards the distant cliffs. Pounding electronic music made me jump. A covered pickup truck lined with empty seats flew past, blasting dance music. The crudely painted sign read *Jungle Rave!,* showing a wall-eyed Alice in Wonderland white rabbit with Down's syndrome. Then buzzing thunder overtook us as middle age Chinese tourists ploughed past in dune buggies, twenty vehicles strong. A young Lao boy followed slowly on a bicycle, coughing in their dust, case of beer balanced precariously on his cross bar.

Across the street, an army of sandwich makers were set up with sizzling grills under dirty, dilapidated umbrellas. Monteblan slowly floated towards them in his body armor and helmet. While my friend negotiated his lunch, I slipped into a tourist shop festooned with fanny packs, wide brim hats, flip flops, carved statues and shirts of glorious error. I passed on *Pink Floyd's The Well*, almost bought an *Ample Computers*, then settled on two *Beer Lao* T-Shirts for my driver and myself. Picking up toothbrushes and pens, notebooks and deodorant, I paid in US dollars and found Monteblan outside, double fisting a pair of sandwiches.

Leaving a trail of fallen onions and stringy lettuce, he walked us randomly down a shaded drive. I followed him between high bushes, down a path which lead us to a quiet hotel. The front stoop had tingling wind chimes and another urn of swirling fish. Sliding our shoes in the rack of jumbled footwear, we walked into the lobby of brown wood and stone. Paying the night in advance, we wandered towards our room, Monteblan spilling sandwich debris all the way.

The hotel was an unfathomable Laotian Escher layout. The owner had expanded impulsively. Buying buildings behind and beside, holes had been hammered through walls. Random, three step staircases bridged formerly unrelated halls. Hairpin turns lead to abrupt walls. Inexplicable motorcycles sat parked on a second floor landing. Mismatched architecture formed random rhombus courtyards, where seraphic cats dashed through sun shafts. Room numbers throughout the hallucination jumped with quantum logic: 12 to 48, 3 to 212. Filthy and exhausted, I finally found 8. The old fashioned key looked archetypal. Pushing beveled metal through the tumblers, I felt the latch click and our door groaned open.

The dusty chamber had two beds, cement floors, tile walls, and a high ceiling.

"That's a blood stain," Monteblan said, walking towards the far wall.

He tapped his finger on the faint streak of a scrubbed blood stain, neck high, which arced down in ominous descent to the floor.

"Just a small one," I nodded, peering at the red streak. "At least they got rid of the body."

Both of us were too tired to care. I slumped in a misshapen wicker chair while Monteblan collapsed on one of the twin beds.

"Ow!"

He cringed at the rigid and unyielding surface. I left the rickety chair to test my sleeping arrangements, sitting down on cheap, worn sheets. Beneath them, my mattress had the approximate depth of cheese spread on a cracker. Imagining a night of fitful turning, followed by a harrowing tomorrow of lower lumbar agony, I volunteered to leave.

"There's other hotels," I suggested.

The idea was answered by silence. I turned to see Monteblan on his side, breathing heavily. Taxed totally from his astounding feat in The Splits, my driver was out. Half an unfinished sandwich was stashed in his upturned helmet. Turning off the light, I stepped to my bed and laid myself down. It was like reclining on a subway bench. Flipping to one side, I stared through gloom at the blood stain. Ruined by exhaustion but unable to sleep, I took a physical inventory.

The race's ravages had been overpowered by adrenaline and a Black Cat rush. But now the toll was slowly emerging. Each hard bouncing bump in that long and savage race had made my ass a welt of ache. Wrenching drifts had punched me hard against the metal car door, leaving shoulders bruised. There were twin points of real pain on each hip from the seatbelt strain. My leg muscles were sore from springing past sniper bullets. The sharp slice in my cheek was a burning line. Each eye socket ached from the strain of staring at tires and turns. Through this wreckage, my mind remained lit by amphetamine hum. Like a building half demolished with lightbulbs flickering in smashed and gutted rooms, thoughts blinked erratically. Sleep was impossible.

"Monteblan?" I said softly.

My friend shifted in his palette, turning on his side in the dim dusty room. I was on my own.

Stepping quietly through the gloom I walked into the bathroom, prepared for whatever third world bugs waited. Flicking the light, I was pleased to find myself the only living creature there. I washed quickly with a cracked plastic hand held shower head. Water drained through a rusty corner grate. I skipped shaving, glanced at the cut on my face in the mirror, shrugging it off before drying with a thread bare towel. By the bed I slipped into shorts, found flip flops, then donned my *Beer Lao* shirt. Floating in oversized casual wear, I missed the sharp, tailored poise of last night. Dusty and probably ruined, my first tailored suit lay in a forlorn heap by the bed. Gathering it up, something slipped from the pocket and fell to the floor with a whisper. Glancing down, I saw the faded Bible pages Charlie had passed me in Chang Mai. Stooping down on aching legs, I snatched them up and stared at his scrawled handwriting:

## Read in Vang

Slipping the missive into my pocket, I made my way into the staircase labyrinth. After 12 wrong turns I named the place *Hotel Laoifornia* and wondered if I would ever leave. Finally landing in the lobby, my relieved appearance generated a tired glance from the moribund old Lao lady tallying papers at the desk. Her black hair was drawn in a bun, her skin tanned a deep brown, wrinkled and sagging. Looking at her as she wrote up a laundry receipt, I wondered where she had been during the US bombing. What had she lived through? Who had she lost? What horror had been burned into her brain by my nation's flying machines? My people had murdered her people. Now here I was, showing up with a suit to wash. What cosmic logic scripted such things? Instead of addressing this, she asked if I wanted ironing. I paid in advance, tipped hard and walked outside.

Sun hit me like a trashcan lid. Distant cliffs loomed softly in the distance. Toned in shades of tan stone, lush green foliage spilled from their tops. The strange gasping sound of a helium blast floated towards me, as another rainbow hued balloon wafted past. I stepped under the tinkling wind chimes and down the walkway into the traffic thick road. At a small, dark café with Bob Marley posters, reggae music broadcast the international signal for dope spot. I stepped in out of the sun. The wooden floor creaked beneath my feet. A sleeping black dog shifted. One other traveler, tattooed and twenty, kicked back with his spliff. I took a table deep in the shadows and ordered weed. A Lao Rasta in skinny jeans delivered it moments later. Lighting up, I took a long pull, hoping the dope would dull my Black Cat buzz.

After a few long puffs, I remembered the pages which Charlie had ripped from the bible. Opening one as a pleasant high clouded my mind, I found **Vang Valley** printed in large block letters at the top, followed by poorly copied, hardly legible text. Squinting to focus, I read.

Vang Valley is an armpit of narcotics. Every cop, hotel owner and whore is on the take. Tip hard to survive and lie about everything. If you speak Thai it helps as the Laos understand and will respect you slightly more. Might make them think of turning somebody else in for drugs after they sell them to you. If you're doing drugs, lie about everything. Lie about what hotel you're staying at. That way they won't send police. Lie about when you're leaving. Make them think you'll be there, buying drugs for at least two or three days past your planned departure. Tip large. They will keep the heat off to take money from you before they bust you. Be vague at the hotel desk when you check in. Tell them you might stay a few days, a week or more. If you're busted you're fucked. Leg irons in a room filled with opium addicts who skipped out on hotel bills, yaba heads who dismembered their uncle, ladyboy prostitutes, drunks who started fights or crashed motorbikes, etc. They'll hold you for days then spring you for an indeterminate amount of American dollars, which escalates every year. The last 65er who got pinched in Laos was Randall Riggs from Surrey, in 2016. His plight was predictable and par for the course: paid 500 American, cash after three days sitting in a room with 15 people, back to the wall, legs in irons, pounding bugs on the fl oor and eating them to survive. But Randall's case showed a new peril for 65ers nabbed in Vang. After being bailed he was blackballed from the country, escorted to the Thai border, and therefore eliminated from the Chicken due to his inability to traverse Laos. So don't get busted.

That said, there's fun to be had in the Valley. The opium is clean, the women are dirty, the weed doesn't come smoother, and the mushroom omelets are brain blasters. Shakes are hit or miss. When they miss, you'll wish you bought smoke and saved your money. When they hit, you might start talking to God. Or think you are one. Don't do that in public. Streets are slanted in Vang Valley. Shady landlords are looking for people to toss to the boys in brown. Whores are slick. Lots of girls in on the take. Watch your passport, put your money in your shoe than leave your shoe in the hotel safe.

Whatever you do, never EVER admit to running the Chicken. They'll shake you down for everything just to keep driving through Laos. Beware. Many a fl ne Chicken has fl nished in the alluring ides of the tempting Valley of Vang. The one who is most dangerous still lurks in this valley. One to watch out for at all costs. His name is

I was just turning the page when a loud, scraping noise at the table made me jump in paranoid fear. I snapped up from my pages expecting to see a Lao police officer with handcuffs. Instead it was Monteblan, large and lumbering, pulling in his chair.

"How's the weed?"

"I thought you were sleeping,"

"Nah, those Black Cats got me pinned."

Monteblan had changed into his *Beer Lao* T-shirt and a white pair of drawstring pants. His hair had been washed, and all pieces of sandwich removed from his beard. The army helmet dangled at his side. Setting it under the table, he sat down beside me.

"Cock blocking my drunk, too," he continued. "I had like ten beers between the hotel and here and don't feel a thing."

"With some drugs…" I held out the butt end of my joint. "The only thing that helps is other drugs."

Monteblan took the remains between his thumb and finger. Puffing briefly, he exploded in racking coughs that filled his eyes with tears.

"Whoa! That's some shit."

Drawn by the explosion of coughs, our Lao Rasta waiter appeared with water.

"We have shakes." the Asian Rasta said.

"So do we," Monteblan said. "That's why we're smoking."

"No like smoke try weed shakes." The waiter explained. "Good. Very good."

Monteblan's eyebrow arched at the thought of not just doing drugs, but having them in a shake. The waiter produced a menu and left it between us, then disappeared through the ratty curtain with a pot leaf emblazoned on it.

"What do you think about a shromelet?" my friend asked.

"What's that?"

"Mushroom omelet."

"You just had two sandwiches big enough to feed half the children in this town for a month."

"They didn't get me high."

"Oh," I said. "That type of omelet."

He nodded. "That type of omelet."

Before I could debate the matter, the waiter had returned.

Monteblan ordered profusely. Large beers, chicken dishes and pork, sticky rice, a side of soup, ribs, two weed shakes and a pair of shromelets. The beers arrived first, poured into frosted mugs. Toasting cheers over the reggae, I leaned back pleasantly stoned. Long, lingering moments of sunlight and silence passed in empty perfection. Food arrived and we dug in, shoveling through plates while reggae played. Sticky rice, shromelet, chicken and ribs were washed down with beer and weed shakes. By the time the food was winding down, I felt my high morphing into the first faint strands of psychedelic goo. Clearing my throat, I drained my beer and spoke.

"Look man, I don't want to take anything—*anything*—away from your driving. Because what you did out there is poetry I don't understand. But..."

Monteblan looked up, voice flat. "What?"

"We can't win this thing. There's lots more to Chicken 65 than driving. All the Chicken Promises, the deals, the allies... There is critical information we don't have. History we're not part of. They don't even want us here. We're trash!"

"It's garbage can, my friend." Monteblan burped loudly. "Not garbage can't."

He pushed his plates away, patting his gut, and surveyed the wreckage of our table.

"Still got some shake and half a shromelet. Shame to waste good drugs."

"Yeah," I said, staring at rainbows which had started shooting from the ceiling fan. "It is."

Monteblan smiled. "Which is why we won't."

Reaching under the table, he produced a hidden item and placed it proudly down with a heavy thump.

"The Hideki!" I said in awe, staring at the tall, black oblong cylinder.

"Had it stashed in the back of Pablo Cruise." Monteblan said proudly. "Couldn't throw it away,"

It was a thermos. But saying the Hideki 3000 is a thermos is like calling a Lamborghini a car. This Japanese state of the art thermos was the holy grail of beverage containers. I had learned this during Monteblan's trip to Portland. He had passed out after a night of heavy drinking in front of the computer. Waking up first the following morning, I went to shut off the machine. Expecting porn, I had found my friend face down in front of browser windows filled with thermoses.

There were chic urban thermoses pictured with dapper commuters on subways in Munich. Hardy thermoses of the American West, glistening in the shining sun. Sleek, Zen style thermoses sipped on Mount Fuji... Amidst them in forum posts, the chat was ballistic. *Brothermos* dismissed product post '99 from the US, citing unilateral adaption of a despised hybrid plastic which compromised heat retention. *ThermoSlutz's* praise of an obscure soup-specific thermos from Norway had entangled her in vicious battle with *ThermosBmore*, who stridently celebrated an Austrian model for identical purposes. In the high corner of the screen was a looping window, where an expertly lit video clip showed loops of a high caliber handgun firing repeated shots into a thermos. At point blank range, the glistening metallic finish remained flawless.

Mystified at the depth and breadth of this thermos world, I had shaken Monteblan awake. Bleary eyed and confused, he had looked down at the credit card in his hand and groaned.

"Shit, I finally did it."

"Did what?" I said.

"Bought the Hideki 3000."

"So you got a thermos. No biggie."

"There's cars that cost less."

His head had fallen to the desk with a thump. But next time I was in New York, Monteblan was rocking his thermos with pride. Held around his neck with a cord made from the same material that NASA used for astronaut lifelines, the Hideki 3000 hit the town. Emitting some silent ohm of perfection, Monteblan's thermos drew compliments at every party, bar, and restaurant we went. Used for unfinished asparagus, slices of meat, splashes of bisque, spare ends of sushi or the last swallow of some rarely refined whiskey, the Hideki 3000's hermetically sealed hold (proven to deflect radiation from the Van Allen Belt) kept Monteblan's leftovers fresh... for 3000 calendar days, if necessary. From then on, he always had his thermos wherever we dined.

In Laos, this ritual continued. Our psychedelic leftovers were chopped into pieces, slopped together with the weed shake then poured into the regal keep of the Hideki 3000. As Monteblan screwed the cap in place, I noticed increasing swirls in my world. The walls looked like they were crawling with small lizards. I blinked and they were gone. Then I looked at my friend.

"It's kicking in."

"Kicking in? Try kicking my head," Monteblan said. He looked up at me, eyes black balls. "I want my body armor."

I inhaled deeply, nodding in agreement. "Kevlar protection seems perfectly sensible for this one. Wow. We're really going to trip. Hard."

I said this trying to be nonchalant. After what I had just read about Vang, I was just short of flipping over the placemats looking for microphones. Tipping generously, I spoke loudly in stage voice, hoping the bartender heard.

"Let's go. The *hotel near the river* that we're leaving *next week* is this way!"

Turning the wrong way out the restaurant, I dragged a frowning, confused Monteblan down the dusty road.

"It's that way, dude," Monteblan said, pointing over his shoulder with his thumb. "And we're not staying a week."

"Shhh!" I said, casting glances over my shoulder. "This whole town is a racket. They lock up Chicken racers. Spies everywhere."

"Oh, no. Don't go there. Not yet."

"It is written!" I produced the pages from Charlie, holding them up like holy writ. "Heed the Chicken Bible! Beware this valley of ill repute!"

"What are you talking about?"

"This whole place is slanted," I said. "That's what I'm talking about. Don't trust anyone and above all tell *no one* we're running Chicken 65. Turn here."

Hanging right down a pebbled side street, we doubled back behind the restaurant. Finding our hotel, my friend froze on the stoop.

"Hold it."

"What?"

"I'm tripping."

Monteblan pushed the helmet back on his head, staring wide eyed at the Laos chaos beyond. Trucks, busses, and buzzing blasts of dune buggies kicked up swirls of loose, gritty earth. From above, another strange, monstrous exhalation made us jump. We looked up at the helium balloon as its shadow loomed over our hotel courtyard. Dangerously low to the building tops, it trailed an errant rope from the basket, practically skimming the ground. A blast of techno music from the *Jungle Rave!* van shot past. The Down Syndrome White Rabbit whisked past staring.

"This is as far as I go." Monteblan sank back on the porch steps, leaning against the fish urn. "It's too Laos out there."

"What about some activity?" I said, world swirling hard for myself as well. "Bikes or something?"

"Not happening." He reached up, pulling the goggles down over his face. "I'll be lucky if I don't fall off this step."

I left him there and walked inside the lobby, world spinning in melting patterns all around the woman at the desk.

"Bicycle rental?" I said.

She stared at me blankly.

I tried to pantomime riding a bike. Everything was off. I could have been relating my desire for a hovercraft eggbeater. Somehow she understood. Finding a key under the desk, she pointed to a bike chained by the bushes outside. Overjoyed, I pulled a pile of colored money from my pocket and put it on the desk. Then I reached into a nearby glass refrigerator, pulling forth a frosty six pack. She took bills from the pile and I took the beer out to Monteblan.

My friend was rocking slightly, hands around his knees, peering through his goggles at the world beyond. I placed the beers beside him like a security blanket.

"You going to be OK?" I asked him.

"I have my helmet and I have my thermos too." He rocked gently, staring straight ahead.

Satisfied my friend would survive, I turned towards the carnival chaos of the dirty road beyond. The distant cliffs were majestic and silent, emanating some powerful pull. Saluting Monteblan silently, I strode heroically towards the bike. After two bewildering minutes trying to unlock the chain with my room key, I realized that I was in no condition to operate anything with wheels. Silently, stoically, I walked past my friend and without explanation, returned the bike key. The woman took it with no questions, as if this happened all the time. Then I walked outside, sitting down beside my friend.

Monteblan looked at me curiously. "What happened?"

I opened my mouth, trying to explain. Words were a swirl. They moved like vapors through my mind but none lined up. Mouth hanging open, I tried to speak. I couldn't. Then four words I hadn't planned leapt out desperately fast.

"Freddiehubbardskydive!"

Monteblan looked at me without understanding. I didn't understand either. *Sky Dive* was a 70s jazz track by the trumpeter Freddie Hubbard. Jumping inexplicably to mind, remembered from the record collection left behind in Portland, I said it again.

"Freddie Hubbard *Sky Dive.*"

"What's that?"

"It's a-a—" My voice struggled to explain. "*S-s- song.*"

But in this melting moment of heavy psychedelics on the far side of the planet, *Sky Dive* was more than a song. It was salvation. Frying in the Far East, Freddie Hubbard's trumpet promised True North. Freddie would direct me. Playing *Sky Dive* would save me. This was realized religiously. Lost in swirling Laotian goo, half remembered fragments floated, chords inchoate, riffs just beyond recall. Hearing them in strident clarity was life's vital mission. My clarion call. *Sky Dive* was all. I knew this absolutely.

"Freddie Hubbard Sky Dive," I repeated.

"You want to hear it?" Monteblan asked.

I nodded, shell shocked. "Freddie Hubbard Sky Dive."

"OK, buddy. You can stop saying it."

I shook my head slowly. "Freddie Hubbard Sky Dive."

Monteblan frowned in waves of warping Laos.

"So this is what's happening. You're tripping so hard that the only thing you can say is 'Freddie Hubbard Sky Dive'. Is that what's happening?"

I nodded.

"Are you sure that's all you can say?"

I frowned. Screwing up my face, trying to form new words, I spoke.

"Freddie Hubbard Sky Dive."

"Alright…" Monteblan pulled up the goggles, fixing them atop his helmet. "Don't panic. We're on lots of drugs. This shit happens. We'll find a bar, play Freddie Hubbard Sky Dive and you'll be fine. I'm with you, buddy."

Rising to his feet, Monteblan slapped his belly with authority and plucked up what was left of the six pack. Twin beers dangled from one hand as the other secured his helmet strap. My possible implosion had pulled Monteblan together. My friend radiated control. Bro powers hummed. Nodding firmly, he waved his arm forward while striding towards town.

"Let's move 'em out!"

I frowned, wondering how I would manage moving through public space. Following him cautiously, the world dipped beneath me like a trampoline. All around me was a bafflingly beautiful masterwork. Each detail elucidated masterful attention of some Great Creator. The perfectly crushed shape of a discarded tuna can. The zig zag streak of paint on a distant restaurant wall. Clouds above like floating Roman busts. Rapt in revelation, I perceived beauty pouring everywhere into form, wrought by whatever engine brought it into being. Flattened with rapture, stopped spellbound in my tracks, I stared at one more wonder on the ground before me.

"Dude, that's a dirty sock."

Looking up from the discarded tube sock, I tried to explain.

"Freddie Hubbard Sky Dive."

"Yup." Monteblan pulled me away. "We're getting there."

We passed one of the tourist shops, storefront filled with faded posters of daily excursions. Monteblan stood, swaying slightly, staring at the area's glorious offerings: underwater grottos, mountain trails, balloon rides, dune buggy adventures, zip lines, more.

"See any monkeys?" Tripping hard, my friend scanned the daytrips furiously. "Monkey beach monkey beach monkey beach... Damn! Where are you!?"

"Hey! Asser! Grimace!"

We swiveled in unison to see the Koreans from Chicken 65. Both were standing in front of a small, brightly painted bar. There was a bird cage and a bottle of whiskey in the middle of the road between them. The tiny bird fluttered behind the bars. Two beautiful, expensive looking young Korean women in bikini tops and corn rowed hair sipped cocktails just inside the bar. Smoke drifted from a tall hookah at their side. Downtempo lounge oozed slinky from ceiling mounted speakers. Moon The Loon walked towards us, smile wide, towering over us both, hand extended.

"You guys won The Splits! Without a clutch? What the fuck!" He shook Monteblan's hand vigorously. "Is that true? We ran into Gears at the hotel. He won't shut up about it! Man, you blew his mind!"

His race partner approached, the shorter one with the bright red K Pop glasses and impossibly processed hair. Staring at the swirling gel waves, sculpted tails, and triumphant spikes of heavily processed haircitecture, I beheld worlds being born. Jet black waves crashing, cosmic wheels turning, life forming, civilization rising, empires falling, wars, ruin, and renaissance all happening in his hair. Staring at it open mouthed, I saw him laugh.

"Dude, what are you *on?*"

"Freddie Hubbard Sky Dive," I mumbled.

"What's that?" Moon said. "I want to try."

Behind him, the bird jumped fluttering in its cage; fast, rapid motions painting space.

"He means shromelets," Monteblan offered. "Mushroom omelets."

"Um, wait…" Seoul Brother's eyes narrowed within the bright red K Pop frames. "Gears told me you guys were rolling on *le chat noir*, right?"

We nodded.

His eyes widened. "And *then* you did mushrooms?"

We both nodded.

"Whoa. I analyzed Black Cats one year because we were thinking of rebatching them in Korea. Like, um, I do chemistry and everything? They have a tetramethylaniline base. That amplifies dephosphorylation metabolism."

We stared at him blankly.

"In the mushrooms," he explained.

We stared at him blankly.

"It's really going to fuck you up," he told us.

Monteblan and I looked at each other, then back to the Korean chemist.

"Right," my friend said. "We're kind of getting that. I hope he's not like, looking too much at your hair or anything."

"Forget it." Seoul Brother laughed. "I've watched Moon trip way harder and lots worse. Just drink lots of water, and get sleep. That's really important. If you um, stay up and drink beer instead of water you're really going to be dehydrated and *really* trip out. Like not in a fun way. You'll shit."

"Thanks." Monteblan was breathing deeply and twisting oddly at the hip, trying to maintain balance. "What's up with the bird?"

Moon The Loon grinned. "I bought a box of dynamite in the hills. There was this temple up there. They sell birds that you set free so it takes all your bad karma away with them. We're going to let it go later. *Wait.* Is that a Hideki 3000?"

Stunned, the large Korean peered closer at the thermos around Monteblan's neck.

Monteblan just grinned.

"That's a great thermos," Moon said with respect. "I have three of them back in Korea. It's true what they say, you can shoot them. I shot mine. Maybe we should blow yours up with my dynamite. What do you think?"

Monteblan considered this. I was tilting sideways now, staring at the bird but unable to turn my feet. The affect made me twist like a piece of licorice. The Korean girls with the hookah were laughing at me. I smiled.

"Man, you got to get this guy off the road," Seoul Brother said, shooting a concerned look at me.

"Yeah guys." Moon raised his eyebrows, nodding. "Vang cops are no joke. I mean, in the bars OK, but not out on the streets."

"That place over there has good ketamine." Seoul Brother nodded his Origins Of The Universe hair towards a forlorn little shack on a rising patch of dirt rock road by the river. "Not like you need anything. But you know, for later if you want. With The Mark and the plates, you can fill your car to the roof with drugs."

"Shit," Moon said. "Wish we could do that."

"We did that, remember?" Seoul Brother said with a touch of irritation. "The General almost executed us."

"Whatever," Moon shrugged, staring at his feet.

"Freddie Hubbard Sky Dive," I said, understanding.

Moon The Loon looked up. "Do you smoke it?"

One of the girls at the bar called to him in Korean.

"That's our food," Seoul Brother said, reaching down and picking up the bird cage. "See you on the road."

With a wave he walked away, karma bird fluttering in the cage. Monteblan waved goodbye and turned down the road. With great determination I uprooted my legs, which had melted into the core of the earth, forming twin Doric columns. Moving unsure, testing each step, I caught up with my friend.

"Those guys are cool," he said. "I don't know why people were talking shit about them at the General's Bar B Q."

"Freddie Hubbard Sky Dive," I shrugged.

By now, the panic had passed. I had gotten used to my limited vocabulary. Adapting to the condition, I was learning to use intonation and spacing of the words to convey a limited set of feelings.

"Freddie Hubbard Sky Dive?" I asked, looking toward the dark and shadowed bar on the river.

"Why not. Trying Ketamine is on my Fuckit List."

Up the jagged slant of rocky road we entered the tilted, dirt floor bar. At a warped pool table with ripped felt, a dreadlocked Lao looked up from his bank shot. Passing him we found some bean bag lumps that swallowed us whole. A woman in traditional Lao robe looked up from behind a wooden bar of hammered boards. She moved towards us under dirty Christmas lights sagging from a warped roof beam. Smoke parted in the air as she moved through it, floating in a traditional Lao dress sashed about her slim body. She laid down menus and smiled, eyes shining.

"Some drink?"

"Beers," Monteblan said, instantly forgetting Seoul Brother's advice. "Big and dark."

She drifted off in patterned waves of silver, blue, and purple, reappearing with two large frosted bottles of Beer Lao. After pouring the beers, she took a small menu from the folds of her robe and placed it on the warped wooden table before us.

"Check it out," Monteblan told me, leaning the menu towards me.

Hidden inside was a laminated piece of paper with various narcotics in scrawled handwriting.

Ketamine

Meth

Opium (tea and shake)

Weed

Mushroom (Muffin Shake and Tea)

Turning to the waitress, Monteblan furrowed his brow, stroking his beard in debate.

"Uhh, yeah, I was, umm wondering. Is this ketamine fresh?"

She looked at him. She looked at me.

"Yes Ketamine." Then she held her finger up before her lips. "Shh. Police."

Shot through with panic, I swiveled in my lumpen bean bag, taking in the dingy, empty bar. Everything looked slanted. The floor was tilted. The pool table was slightly askew. The bar was leaning towards the river and had splinters. Not a pleasant place. And thankfully, not a place with any police. I sighed in relief. Monteblan lowered his voice.

"Is it fresh Ketamine?"

"Yes, Ketamine," she answered.

"I mean has it been lying around in the sun for like a year?"

"Yes, Ketamine."

"Wow," Monteblan said. "You two should get together. Yes Ketamine, meet Freddie Hubbard Sky Dive."

"Yes Ketamine?" she asked, confirming the order.

"Freddie Hubbard Sky Dive," I replied.

"Yes Ketamine," Monteblan said. "And a mushroom muffin. Let's call that a shmuffin. Throw in some opium tea— when's the next time you'll see that on a menu? — and we're good."

Our waitress floated away in purple and silver geometric patterns. Beside me, Monteblan sighed.

"When drugs are food, it's a problem."

Moments later, the shmuffin arrived, sunken and slumping. One rarely hears the words "sinister" and "muffin" together, but in this case, they applied. The yellow hued dough looked dubious, perhaps demented. Monteblan took a small bite that broke into crumbs. Frowning in distaste, he uncapped the Hideki and crumbled the rest inside. A small plate appeared before him next, filled with fat white lines.

"Yes, Ketamine," Monteblan said.

"Yes, Ketamine," our waitress answered before disappearing.

Monteblan dabbed his finger into the stuff, rubbing it liberally into his gums.

"I have no idea if that's what you do with Ketamine," Monteblan said. "But nothing from this place goes up my nose."

Tilting the plate, brushing it with his hand, Monteblan deposited what was left of yes ketamine into the brewing sludge of drugs now stewing in his designer thermos. Just when he finished dusting off the plate, opium tea arrived.

"Try some?"

Monteblan offered me the warm cup. I held it in my hands, staring into the light brown liquid. Lowering my head, I sipped just the lightest bit. Violently bitter, the liquid swirled up some race-memory montage of bones, skulls, chains, graveyards, and half sunken ships groaning in midnight harbors. Flashing like primal warning, they vanished in an instant. I passed the cup. Monteblan frowned darkly upon tasting, shivered, then shook his head. Into the Hideki it went, opium tea splashing together with the weed shake, shromelets, shmuffin, ketamine, and a few chaser splashes of Beer Lao. Fitting the top tightly, Monteblan nodded with satisfaction.

"That should get somebody through the war."

Then we were up out of the shapeless soft sacks, past the tilted pool table and down the dirty road into night.

Crowds of people ambled from dirt floor bar to dirt floor bar. Motorcycles in the darkness buzzed past. The *Jungle Rave!* truck passed in a pound of techno, back section now crowded with partygoers. I watched them disappear around the corner, weaving in inebriation as the truck turned out of town. We passed a few ratty hookah lounges, strewn with cushions, plastered with TVs. All were inexplicably playing the old sitcom *Friends*.

"Is it just me," Monteblan said. "Or do we have lots of *Friends* in this town?"

"Freddie Hubbard Skydive," I agreed, passing two more bars showing the 90's hit show.

"Bad trip material. *Real* bad. Let's move."

Detouring between bars, Monteblan lead us down a creaking wooden bridge of crisscross slats and missing planks that sagged over a shallow stream. Leaving the lights of town behind, we entering a lush hollow of jungle fronds and bushes. The starry night above looked like a piece of black velvet with holes poked in it. I half expected some huge magician's hand to whisk it away, showing the bright white nothing behind it all.

Distant laugh tracks from absent *Friends* floated behind us. I followed my friend through the night. There were no shows about us. Friends of mine would never be on TV. My friends were poetry. Impossible to understand and dangerously true. Lyrical fragments inscribed through psychedelic jungles bathed in South East Asian moons. My friends set land speed records and materialized beers magically. Dreamed of monkey beaches. My friends had thousand dollar thermoses filled with five different drugs and understood the one single jazz song that *must* be heard. They drew sniper fire. My friends were underestimated and overweight, obscurely brilliant, shining in shadows. My friends were unscripted. Beyond broadcast. My friends were known only to those who dared follow them through darkness while the moon glowed mad above.

"Whoa."

Monteblan's gentle wonder at what lay before us was softly echoed by my whisper of reverence.

"Freddie. Hubbard. Sky. *Dive.*"

Set like a mantle beneath the moon, the place looked created for us. An outdoor bar with soft yellow light played deep house grooves through crystal clear speakers. The river ran silver and rushing beyond. Hammocks swung in slight breeze on the banks; two dozen at least. Slung up in small open bungalows, they looked over the flowing river. Dark and rushing, reflecting the moonlight, water splashed and babbled. Mist gathered on the far bank, shrouding lush bushes and trees. Above and beyond, the cliffs of Vang towered in stone mystery. Monteblan turned to me, face lit glowing by the moon.

"Can you hold on the Freddie a minute?"

I nodded, following him towards the most distant hammocks. The river murmured louder there, chilled air from the surface floating towards shore. I fell into my hammock. Monteblan swung into another by my side. Lizards darted in quick patterns on the bungalow roof. Breathing clean night air, I stared into darkness. Then a shooting missile burst from the banks upstream, followed by distant cheers.

"Holy Shit!" Monteblan tracked the pattern of flight with his upturned face. The missile's distant light played softly on his features like a war film.

"Signal to the rain gods."

A smiling, middle aged American raised up from a hammock nearby, eyes hidden behind sunglasses. There was a battered straw cowboy hat on his head. Thin blonde hair fell in greasy strands behind his ears.

"Shoot 'em up there this time of year to get some rain," he continued. "Tribute to the Gods. Something, isn't it?"

"Yeah," Monteblan said.

"Still waiting for one to hit those moonlight balloon rides."

He pointed up, over the river. The hot air balloon drifted up, lit and glowing from the flame within. Helium released in a rough gust, like the breath of some mythic beast. The basket of travelers jumped up, floating higher. The man laughed.

"It'll happen someday. And nobody will give a damn. Laos..." He shook his head with a rueful laugh. "The land lawsuits forgot."

The man disappeared back into his hammock. Empty ones beyond him swung like ghosts in the wind. The river rushed by. Monteblan turned to me.

"We could try to get Freddie on the system here, but that DJ looks pretty… French."

I followed his gaze to the Gallic faced, sunken eyed French DJ near the bar. He had standard issue hipster *fuck off* face, clearly visible at a hundred yards. Sighing with the realization that Freddie Hubbard would never find its way onto his playlist, Monteblan cursed.

"We need the damn internet."

The guy in the far hammock called over to us. "Can't get the internet down here. Have to be up in town."

"Doesn't matter," Monteblan said. "We can't get on the internet anywhere. Part of the rules."

"Rules?"

A long pair of skinny legs unfolded from the hammock. The man sat facing us now, wearing nothing but a speedo swimsuit and his beat up old hat. Grinning from behind sunglasses, he folded his hands over his potbelly.

"What type of rules?"

"For the race it's—"

Remembering warnings from the Chicken Bible, I lurched up shouting.

"Freddie Hubbard Sky Dive!"

Taken aback, the stranger frowned. "Freddie Hubbard Sky Dive?"

"Yeah," Monteblan started to explain. "It's the—"

"Second Freddie Hubbard record on the CTI label, right?" The stranger leaned forward, rubbing his chin. "Or is that *Red Clay*?"

"Holy shit!" Monteblan shouted in surprise, struggling up from his hammock in wild swings. "You know Freddie Hubbard *Sky Dive*?"

"Sure I do. That's good jazz. I used to play in LA back in the 80s. Conga drums. You know I toured with Stevie Wonder one summer?"

"Shit really?" Monteblan said. "What's he like?"

The man laughed. "All over the damn place. Used to call him Stevie Wonder What The Hell Happens Next." He waved his hand dismissively. "But *Sky Dive*, shit. That's real music. Ever hear *Sunflower?* By Milt Jackson? Now *that's* a track."

"Freddie Hubbard Sky Dive," I agreed, nodding.

"Well, really now," the lanky stranger said sourly. "We don't have compare them. It's not a contest or anything."

"No, that's all he can say," Monteblan explained. "We did a lot of mushrooms and he can't really say anything except Freddie Hubbard Sky Dive. He has to hear it. But we can't get on the internet that's the thing."

I reached out, punching Monteblan's arm, just out of sight.

"Down here, I mean," Monteblan mumbled lamely. "We can't get on the internet down here."

The stranger regarded us. Behind his sunglasses, I sensed him thinking. Then with loose, swinging gestures he swung his limbs free from the hammock to stand. Reaching up, he pressed the crushed cowboy hat firmly into greasy blonde hair. He stepped into cheap, battered flip flops and nodded his head up the hill behind the bar.

"Up away on the hill, there's a little place overlooking the river. Guy's my buddy up there. Got one of those internet jukebox thinga-bobs. He'll play your Freddie Hubbard."

"Wow," Monteblan replied. "Thanks man. You'll take us there?"

"Will do. And uh, well, maybe you can buy me a cup of tea for my troubles?"

He grinned widely, head sticking forward, hands on his hips.

"Sure man," Monteblan said. "OK."

"Then we're on."

Happily, the tall lanky man in speedos and cowboy hat flip flopped towards the hill. We followed him, leaving the light of the hammock bar. In darkness, our swimsuit guide picked his way carefully forward over one more creaking, wooden bridge. Up steep, crumbling cement steps we scrambled to an empty ridge. The dirt road was quiet, far from tourists. The river was far below now. Turning us away from town, the man shot a grin over his shoulder.

"Tea's a little stronger up this way," he said.

Bars were empty and quiet, shrouded in shadows. Tough Lao faces looked up from pool games, peering as we passed. The unwelcome feeling increased with every ragged block of buildings. Just when I was about to say Freddie Hubbard Sky Dive and call it off, our flip flop guide slipped inside a dingy, empty bar.

**The place was made of planks**. Hammered roughly together, large gaps showed in the floor. Rusted nails stuck out from the walls. Everything creaked. The far end was an open balcony strewn with dirty cushions. The distant river was far below, silver moon hanging full. Blue flame heated a black pot in the filthy kitchen behind the bar. A wiry, squinting Lao man emerged from the gloom, wiping his hands on a rag. He shot a few fast words to our friend, who grinned and responded in words I didn't understand. For a moment, the bartender debated our presence. Then nodding tersely, he flipped the dishrag over his shoulder and popped open a round of beers. Our flip flop guide rubbed his hands briskly, grinning.

"Best tea in Vang Valley here, fellas. Mucho obliged. Now let's see to this internety jukeboxish thingamahoo we got here…"

Slipping from the stool in his frayed and faded Speedos, the long legged man flip flopped to the bar's far corner.

"Now what about this 'you can't get on the internet' thing?" he called out casually over his shoulder.

"Just the rules for some—"

I punched Monteblan on the knee, frowning.

"Uh, dumb bet," he recovered. "About, uh, how far we could go without being online."

"I see." In the bar's far corner, a dusty old PC screen came to life, lighting our friend's face in blue. "How far you planning on going out here?"

"Vietnam then back to Bangkok," Monteblan told him.

Then heaven descended. From hidden speakers deep in the gloom, the patter of 70s conga drums blended with warm guitar chords. A trumpet's noble notes heralded the arrival of Freddie Hubbard *Sky Dive*. Forgetting Monteblan's slip, I melted in gratification. Displaced 70s memories swirled. Brown corduroy world filled with rotary phones. For a long time I listened in silence, losing myself completely.

The sharp clink of porcelain and silverware rattled me from my reverie. Before us on the bar I saw a steaming teacup filled with dark brown tea. Our guide rubbed his hands and smiled. Picking up the cup, he sipped. Shivering with a wince as the opium hit, he turned to Monteblan.

"Have some yourself?"

Monteblan shook his head. "We did our drugs."

The teacup tilted towards me. "How about you?"

"Nah, I'm good."

Monteblan turned to me, mouth open in amazement. I signed in relief, finally hitting verbal *terra firma* after hours of skydive.

"Well that worked," our new friend remarked, sipping more tea.

Monteblan slapped me on the back. I made small talk to be sure my new found powers held.

"Nice view." I picked up a beer and gestured towards the open balcony, overlooking the valley below.

"Big drop off," the opium drinker said. "Used to have a zip line to the river but too many damn kids hit the rocks. I swear about twenty of them died out here last year."

The thin bartender leaned out from the gloomy kitchen. He looked at Monteblan and I with barely hidden contempt then said something to the lanky American. He pointed to the clock. Closing my eyes, lost in the anchoring groove of my jazz song, I watched the swirling play of hallucinated mushroom shapes.

"There you go, friend."

I was hit by a tap on the shoulder from the grinning tea drinker. I opened my eyes to see the bartender before me, holding up two joints in front of me and Monteblan.

"No thanks," I shook my head. "I did so many drugs today all I could say was—"

Monteblan clapped his hand over my mouth.

"*Don't* say it," my friend pleaded. "Please. You might get stuck again."

I nodded. Monteblan slowly removed his hand.

"We're going to pass on the weed," he said.

The bartender frowned, squinting mean. He glanced up at a clock on the wall: black plastic cat with swinging tail. The eyes looked left and right. Joker cards from different decks were pinned to the wooden wall around it, dusty and old. The man in the cowboy hat leaned in, speaking low.

"Uh, boys? When a bartender in Vang gives you a joint on the house, he loses face if you turn him down. Not good."

"We can't do any more drugs," Monteblan whispered.

"This is *not* the man in town you want to offend." Our new friend spoke through a smile; soft words tinged with tension. "Take the joints. Put them in your pocket and smile."

I looked away from his dark sunglasses. The wiry Lao with the microstashe held the joints out, unmoving. Slowly, smiling, I reached for mine while Monteblan did the same. Maintaining eye contact, I placed the joint in my pocket, patting it carefully and smiling wider.

"Thanks man. I like to smoke when I'm home."

The man looked at me with narrowed eyes, not happy I wasn't smoking, but accepting the excuse. Spitting into the sink, he washed it down with a twist of the tap then turned and disappeared in the darkness of his kitchen. The opium drinker nodded in satisfaction, then stepped off his stool and stretched.

"Fellas, a friend of mine is swinging by. Always misses this place. I'll be right out front there to flag him down. Don't move."

Grinning with a tip of his hat, he moved with a groovy, fluid stride towards the bar's open front. When he was out of earshot, I spun to Monteblan, whispering furiously.

*"We're not supposed to tell anybody about Chicken 65!"*

"Relax, the guy's walking around in grape smugglers. What's he gonna do? Besides, without him you'd still be saying Fab 5 Freddy."

With a thunk, a huge bowl of greasy soup, lumpen noodles, and chunks of grey meat and carrot slices was set before my friend. A wave of queasiness oozed through me.

"When did you order *that?*"

Another plate appeared, skewered meat in thin, greasy sauce. Monteblan smacked his lips.

"While you went all Rain Man with your song."

"Didn't we just eat?" I said.

"Yeah, about 389 Freddie Hubbard Sky Dives ago."

Without another word, my friend dug in with fork and spoon, noodles twisting with flat slapping sounds. Splats of warm broth hit the bar. Mushrooms churned up in my gut. The rising bile of impending vomit seeped onto my tongue. Sliding from my chair, I called to the bartender as cold sweat broke out on my body.

"Hello, toilet Please?!"

"Whole place is one, bro," Monteblan mumbled.

Then I saw the sign across the room. Running towards it through a jumbled chaos of piled furniture, my guts roiled in mushroom indigestion. I raced through a dusty limbo of broken washing machines, kids' bikes, slanted tables and chairs. Bursting down a cement hall lit by a single bulb, I threw myself into a filthy bathroom. Braced over the squat hole in the floor, I heaved fat, splattering chunks of shromelet and beer. Somewhere in the distance, I thought I heard Monteblan laughing.

When it finally passed, I felt like I had run a marathon. Exhausted, sweating, I scooped pans of water from the nearby drum, splashing the shit hole clean. Legs weak I went to the sink, splashing water on my face. There were no paper towels or toilet paper to dry. Then I remembered the pages from Charlie.

Pulling them from my pocket, I ripped out the first two sheets and wiped my face and hands clean. I left the bathroom with a last remaining page in hand. Glancing at it in the dim light of the hall's single bulb, I squinted at the Xerox copy. A dark, shadowed image of a smiling face was barely clear. Peering closer, the grin suddenly ignited a flame of recognition. Frozen in my tracks, I read faint text below the picture.

## *Flip Flop Earl*

## *Chicken 1997*

Flip Flop Earl had been a contender. Everybody thought so when he joined the race. Paired with an Australian rig monkey known to run his chickens fast and dark, their odds were favorable. More money was put down on the two after a wild, pre-race bar fight they won in Gold Fingers. Taking on five Thais, both held their own till the boys in Brown showed up. At that point, Flip Flop Earl showed an uncanny ability to reason with the forces of law. Paying them all off- including the bar's mamasan- Earl demonstrated a keen understanding of how things get done in Thailand. This combination of finesse and fighting power made Flip Flop a favorite for Chicken '97.

All that changed when Earl hit The Vang Valley and tried opium for the fi rst time. Addicted in a sip, the rest is history. Dropping out of the Chicken, Flip Flop Earl has remained in the Vang Valley ever since. The only 65er to never fi nish the race, this hop head has eluded every posse that tried to bring him in. His connections and ability to manipulate them have let Flip Flop earl remain in Vang with a visa that expired twenty years back. He sleeps behind the bars and sweeps fl oors for opium tea. About all he has left in the world is the fl ip fl ops that have earned him his name.

Flip Flop Earl has been known to set up racers with the local boys in brown. Part of it is money but most of is for revenge. The Chicken made Earl face himself, and he didn't like what he saw. Furious at his fate, Flip Flop has sworn vengeance on all Chicken Racers. Through the years this devious speedo wearing ex-conga player from West Hollywood has run his racket. Fixing up racers with drugs in local bars, he then drops a dime and has police round them up.

One of the most treacherous fi gures in The Vang Valley, Flip Flop Earl is to be avoided at all costs.

The page fell from my frozen fingers. I stood silently, swaying slightly while my heart hammered. The dank cement hall with the single lightbulb tunneled before me. With a few deep breaths, I calmed my panicked mind. Forcing myself to walk slowly, I left the dim hallway and passed the jumble of piled appliances and unused furniture. Walking over creaking wood to the bar, I heard Monteblan talking to Flip Flop Earl.

"It's just a little hotel right off the air strip. Got all these crazy stairways in it. Mango House? I think that's what it's called."

"Sure, Mango House," Flip Flop Earl answered, sipping his opium tea. "That's a great place if you can find your room."

He laughed loudly and Monteblan joined in, turning to me as I pulled out my bar stool.

"What's up with you?" He frowned, looking at my pale face. "You alright?"

"Yeah... I just, got a little sick."

I glanced outside. The bartender stood smoking under a lone streetlight, peering down the road as if expecting somebody.

"We should probably go," I told Monteblan. "Like, now."

"Hold your horses, partner!" Flip Flop Earl grinned. "Have some tea. Always helps me."

Without answering, I pulled Monteblan off his stool. My heart was thudding, matching the beat of distant techno music which was slowly approaching from outside. Through the door, just down the hill, I saw the shape of the *Jungle Rave!* van approaching.

*"Dude what's going on?"* Monteblan whispered, concerned.

*"We have to get the hell out of here,"* I whispered back. *"They're setting us up."*

"Hey!" Earl frowned hard. "You planning to pay, or what?"

I turned back to Earl, smiling.

"Sorry." Digging in my pocket, I pulled out an incomprehensible wad of foreign notes and slapped them on the bar.

"Now hold it..." Flip Flop Earl held his hands up plaintively. "Let's just count this out."

Outside, the music was growing louder.

"Whatever's over, tip the bar and have some tea. Thanks for *Sky Dive*."

I spun back to Monteblan, hustling my friend towards the open bar front. The owner was blocking the doorway, standing hands on hips, glaring. Techno music from outside blasted full volume now, and I saw the dancing lights of the *Jungle Rave!* bus behind him.

"Move!"

Pushing Monteblan, we lunged past the bartender. Knocked hard by Monteblan's shoulder, the man spun sideways and fell. Moonlight shone down as we chased the thumping techno bus down the dirt road. Tattooed ravers shouted, pounding the van to stop. The driver braked momentarily, lighting us in red. I pushed Monteblan up inside. Tattooed arms pulled him deep into the van of partygoers. Someone punched the roof and the driver punched gas. The vehicle jumped forward. Laughing trippers reached for me. I ran for the speeding vehicle, desperate hands outstretched.

Feet ran up behind. One jammed down hard on the back of my lower calf. The sabotage step collapsed me. Slipping from the ravers fingers, I fell face first into the dirt. Tumbling at full speed, wind knocked out of me, I watched the van disappear. Techno music faded as trippers waved. Gasping for air, I was swung up to my feet and pushed roughly back towards the bar. The wiry bar tender had an iron grip. Spitting unfathomable curses, he yanked me towards the dingy darkness of his wood plank bar. Over his shoulder, down the hill, the slowly approaching form of a police van came into view.

Flip Flop Earl was waiting in the door frame. He greeted my arrival with a swift cuff to the head, ushering me into doom. Instinctively backing away, I edged towards the rickety balcony. The night sky hovered over a steep drop to rocks and dirt below. Stars that had earlier flickered mystically now winked laughing at my fate. With nothing but a drop to death behind me, I turned to face the foes before me.

The bartender had a long, heavy stick in his hand now. His eyes had narrowed to livid slits, and his thin body trembled with adrenaline and rage. The lanky, speedo wearing villain beside him smiled wickedly.

"No internet? Bangkok to Vietnam and back? Hell, I know that route." He laughed. "You're going down, Chicken man."

Over their shoulders, the dark police van pulled up outside. I saw officers step from their van, hats pressed down, two frowns wearing brown. The bartender spit a final curse at me, turning to meet them. Before me in the gloom, Earl laughed loudly.

"What'd I tell you about this bartender? Oh, boy are you fucked! Making him run after you? Shit, we just wanted to set you up. Now you're going down. You're doing time, Mr. Chicken 65." He spit on the floor with derision. "Serves you right for running that damn race. Piece of shit ruined my life."

Searching frantically, knowing there was no escape but looking for it anyway, I answered Earl. "It's not the Chicken's fault."

"*What* did you say?"

Lao police walked into the bar, strides tight and militant. Polished shoes hammered on wooden boards. Fierce eyes glittered beneath their hat brims. Fear rising, I spit my words at Flip Flop Earl.

"What happened to you isn't the Chicken's fault! It's yours. This is who you are. The Chicken just shows you who you really are!"

"I heard that shit before!" Flip Flop Earl spit back. "You're talking Mississippi Charlie shit! That old fool still alive? Still talking his Chicken crap?! And you believe the old drunk?"

Closer now, one of the cops raised his hand in a *come here* gesture, curt and fierce. I backed desperately against the balcony banister, one arm looping over it to anchor me. Earl saw what I was doing and laughed.

"That ain't gonna help. You're going down. The Chicken's showing you who you really are..." Flip Flop Earl grinned darkly. "*Fucked.*"

The strange sound like some mythical beast breathing fire burst behind me in the night. I spun startled and saw the balloon basket rising fast just beyond the balcony. It trailed a dangling rope. Without thinking I spun vaulting up onto the banister and leapt.

Flying through the starry night, life paused. Reaching out, extended totally, the sound of a single exhalation—perhaps my last breath—was the world's only sound. Glowing moon filled my wild eyes. Hanging in lunacy before Fate and physics decided, I watched my hand reaching for the swaying rope. Leaping through Laos, hovering over hard, horrible earth, it all felt strangely reasonable. This was my race. My Chicken 65. Win or lose, live or die, The Bird would decide.

With a grunt I grasped rope magically. Fingers seized manically. Swinging wildly, I whisked up wickedly fast. Stunned at the speed of ascent, I saw furious faces upturned below, shouts lost in the balloons' hot air blasts. Then they were gone. Lifted quickly into the night the moon grew so large I gasped in wonder. Dangling one handed, silently speeding, wind rippled my clothes. I laughed. Stars surrounded me. World raced below. Turning in slow circles, I watched the river winding through jungle darkness. Then reaching with my other hand, I pulled myself up the rope, finally looking above.

Four round faces stared down at me over the basket edge. I recognized the flat daffodils pressed in the upturned hat brims immediately. Their shocked expressions had been identical that morning. Korean moms from the murder van. Together in a row, staring down at me gasping, the light of recognition lit their eyes. *The white man from the car that nearly killed them!* The women turned to each other, chattering fast in Korean. Then all eyes were back on me, furious. Handbags raised high like siege weapons, they brought them down in fury.

While the basket bobbed and swung dangerously, Asian moms battled me in blind panic. Screaming Korean filled my ears as handbags rained down. The flashing face of the Lao balloon captain appeared suddenly over the side—shocked at what he saw— then disappeared. Huge bursts of sound breathed overhead as he desperately let out air. I struggled for grip as the balloon dropped down in sharp, dangerous dips. Then a final handbag hit just right. Struck squarely, my hand opened in reflex. I gasped. Grasped. Trying desperately to regain hold, I felt the rope burn through my palm. Then it was gone and I was falling through space astonished, shouting up at the shining moon.

**I splashed down hard in cold water.** River current churned me blindly. End over end, tumbling underwater, scraping rocks in the roaring rapids I was rushed in a swirling flail of limbs. Punching through the surface, gasping for air, pulled back down, I bobbed and kicked, fighting for control. Slowing finally, able to swim, the thunder of rapids faded from my ears as I paddled towards the bank, gasping for air. Reaching wet earth I pulled myself up from the river, drenched and shaking. Breathing deeply, flopping on my back, I grabbed the ground as if someone might pry me away. Cold mud oozed through my fingers. Just above was a wooden bridge, filled with foot traffic heading into Vang's bar zone. Distant music played faintly. Laughter and voices floated in the night. I lay there for a long time, not knowing what to do. Exhaustion caught up with me. My eyes fluttered. And just when sleep was taking me under, I heard it.

Hardly believing, I snapped up staring towards town. The sound was louder now, unmistakable, growing closer. Crawling first, then pulling myself up, I ran crouched through reeds. Diving flat beside the dirt road, I peered towards the sound. Rolling slowly down Vang's main road of party bars, the *Jungle Rave!* van approached. Empty of its previous load, blasting techno to lure the next, I watched it crawl towards me. People waved the vehicle down, staggering aboard. Reaching the end of the main drag, its headlights passed over me as the van turned. I pressed myself into dirt, hidden by reeds. Dance music thumped past. Looking up, I saw the wall-eyed, Down Syndrome White Rabbit staring at me. When it passed I sprang to my feet. Crouched like a fugitive, I ran beside the van, reached for a metal hand rail and swung myself inside.

A half dozen tattooed travelers, hair in knotted dreads, stared at me with drug glazed eyes. Streaked with mud, dripping water, I offered no explanations. Sitting on the rough wooden bench, I rode head down while we rumbled through the nightly loop of hostels, hotels, and bars. A pack of loud Australians loaded with six packs jumped inside. With rowdy cheers, they guzzled down beers. One of them fell stumbling out the back. With a darting arm I grabbed him, yanking him back. He grinned his thanks on wobbly legs. I pressed myself deeper into the crowded vehicle. Glancing up I saw a Buddhist temple. Cursing myself for not renouncing life when I had the chance, I suffered in the crush of sweaty, unwashed bodies. The van hit open road and picked up speed. A thudding din grew louder then totally swallowed us, as we rolled to a stop in the heart of the jungle rave.

Pouring from the van into strobe lights, ravers were lost in the flashing mayhem. I stumbled in the stream of them, eyes shielded with a raised hand, surrounded by halos and shadows. The distant dance floor was spot lit white. Like lost souls collected for some chaotic afterlife, we moved towards the light. Dazed with one flip flopped foot, I roamed through stacks of paint streaked amplifiers. Day-Glo mushrooms and lightning bolts, butterflies and video game icons. Cords snaked towards banged up generators. Pounding music pulsed in my teeth. People froze like hieroglyphs all around me, captured in strobe light blasts. Overloaded with unknowing, I found myself turning in slow, bewildered circles when a hard hand grabbed my shoulder, spinning me around.

Monteblan looked insane. His shirt was ripped. The combat helmet was tilted absurdly. Both eyes were black basketballs, panicked and wide. Without a word he yanked me behind a wall of speakers, pressing me hidden behind the thudding cabinets. Instants later, two police patrolled swiftly past. Both officers from the bar. Eyes glittering with rage beneath their stiff caps, they peered through the stream of party people, pushing ravers angrily aside, searching intently through shadows and light. Fanning out through the amplifiers, both officers disappeared in the distance. Breathing in relief, I rose up. Monteblan pulled me violently down, eyes wild with fright. Jabbing his finger towards hazy clouds floating from a smoke machine, he stared petrified.

I turned to see. At first it was a shadow, ominous and rippling in the mist. Then a man stepped slowly through the fog. Hands on hips, Flip Flop Earl surveyed the jungle rave. Cowboy hat jammed down, speedos pulled up high, dance lights flashed wickedly on his sunglasses. Scanning the landscape of jumbled amplifiers, his head turned in predatory circles. Ravers streamed past. Music thundered all around. Monteblan shifted beside me, knocking a row of empty beers off the amp. Flip Flop Earl's head turned sharply towards our hiding place. His nostrils flared, sniffing the air. We pressed our bodies flat. Slowly, the opium addict approached through floating clouds of smoke. Frozen in fear, I watched him like a dream. Beside me, Monteblan was shaking. With one more long leg step, Earl found his sight line. Exploding strobes illuminated us in white lightning. Flip Flop Earl grinned. Then the drunken Australians blasted past in a bro storm.

Shouting with their six packs, hands darted out in classic frat boy prank. Earl's speedos were yanked to his ankles. For a moment he stood stunned, tiny penis exposed. Laughing bros disappeared in high fives, swallowed by the smoke machine. Earl recovered from his shock, fumbling desperately in the flashing lights. The battered cowboy hat fell, revealing his bald head. A trio of tanned girls lit past laughing, jeering at his shrinking junk. Earl spun away in shame. Fumbling for his suit, our naked nemesis fell off balance, limbs thrashing, howling in animal rage. Monteblan and I darted into darkness, swallowed by the jungle, leaving him behind.

Racing though slapping leaves, lights from behind flashed wildly. Music thundered at our backs. Rushing through bushes and trees, Monteblan pivoted in sudden, random turns to shake pursuit. Chasing him blindly, I lost my flip flop and ran barefoot. Baptized in madness, crouched low and streaked with mud, I plunged farther into darkness. Rough roots took me for stumbling falls. Bashing branches struck me. Slicing leaves slashed. Mushroom buzz swirling, senses alive, I charged through wilderness until the jungle stopped suddenly. Launched from thick brush onto open dirt road, my cartwheeling limbs spun me colliding into Monteblan. The impact sent us both reeling. Landing heavy in the dirt, panting wildly in the moonlight, we stared at each other in animal fear.

*"Move!"*

Monteblan lurched to his feet and rushed downhill, away from the rave. Jogging after him, lungs burning, I shot glances over my shoulder. The road was empty, showing nothing but the huge silver moon. Brush disappeared and we found ourselves winding through barren rice fields. Sun baked all day, the cracked dirt still emanated heat. Insects whirred from thin, dusty grass. Far ahead of us, the cliffs of Vang loomed in shadows that blotted out stars. On the far edge of a distant field, I saw a small structure built from bamboo.

"There," I panted, pointing towards it.

Slat floor with no walls, the woven roof provided workers with shade during the day. Trudging towards it now under star light, far from town in the shadows of towering cliffs, we made our way to the structure and collapsed. Lying on his back, words interrupted by deep, desperate breaths, my friend's voice was rasping gasps.

"Chicken… 65…. what… the… Fuck!"

"They warned us about Vang," I moaned. "Everybody did. *Shit!* We have to get out of here."

"We can't leave Pablo Cruise."

"We can't get him now."

"We can't go back to the hotel." Monteblan sat up, suddenly realizing our plight. "I told that flip flop fuck where we're staying."

"Tomorrow morning," I said, gasping for another breath. "We go to the garage. Once we're in the car, we're OK, right? The marks, the flap? All that shit? We just get in and go."

"OK…" Monteblan was too tired to think or argue. "OK… Just let me sleep. Keep watch for like an hour. Then wake me up."

"Sure," I said. "OK."

Monteblan fell back like strings had been cut. With a thump he splayed on the dirty bamboo. Looking around in the dark, I hocked a thick glob of spit into the bushes. My throat burned. All I wanted was water. All we had was a thermos filled with drugs. *Drugs.* What had Seoul Brother said? Something about the Black Cats and mushrooms…. drinking lots of water and sleeping? We were supposed to do that. Instead we drank beer and ran all night. I felt my mind fumbling for bearings now, still humming in mushroom buzz. Simple tasks seemed complicated. It took me one full and very difficult minute to understand how to hang my wet T-shirt on a bamboo banister.

Staring in the darkness, I considered our plight. Behind us, distant flashes from the jungle rave lit the night like silent lighting. Before us, black cliff walls towered ominously. Still high, mind swirling, I stared at the cliffs until dawn.

**It might have been a moment or it might have been hours**. Light didn't rise so much as seep into being. The faintest of illumination, mere breath of suggestion, emerged in stealthy play. Squinting for vision, I watched the cliffs before me clarify. In barely perceptual stages, details emerged. Lines carved by time, wind blasted planes, sharp outcrops and shadowed coves. Then suddenly they were there and I gasped.

Ancient faces like towering Easter Island visages stared down at me from the stone. Frowning down at me, alive and massive, I trembled in tribal realization.

*The Forces.*

I rose slowly, stupefied, leaving my small shelter to behold my stone overlords. The Forces stared down at me, waiting. Barefoot through the dirt I approached. From them came silent emanations, messages sent in waves of vibrating stone. Impressing me with information, I resonated with cellular understanding. Mouth agape in the Lao dawn, I realized everything.

Two Forces were fighting on earth. One was Light. The other Dark. Both were at war. Theirs was an eternal battle played out through planets and eons. Time beyond measure. The path of a single punch might span five hundred human empires. Fighting through dimensions, they tumbled into realties. Like bar fighting movie cowboys smashing through tavern windows, they had crashed into ours.

The Forces fought. They fought through us and in us. Forces of Light were the whispering impressions that inspired our greatest art. Holy notions that lead to achievement. Inspired dreams that anointed princes of peace. Forces of Dark did likewise. Hissing slithers that stirred up wars. Unheard utterances that drove maniacs to murder. Leering evil that pillaged innocence. This is how The Forces fought here. Winning our world for Light or Dark.

Then I saw the Chicken.

Streaking in a jagged path of feathers, Chicken 65 ripped right through reality between them. Reeling between Light and Dark, the Chicken was a race between both, owned by neither. The Chicken was its own spirit. A jagged path of happenings arranged by Fate. Chicken 65 wasn't a race. It wasn't a chase. It was a choice. The choice between Forces. Man could run with the Light and win. Man could run with Dark and win. But man could not run with both the Light and Dark. During the race, he would speed between both. Circumstances would arise, forcing him to decide. And that choice would define him. That was the point of this. Chicken 65 was where a man decided what he was in this world. Light or Dark. Some knew this. Most didn't. All fumbled, and many fell trying to learn.

Helping them was my Destiny.

Chicken Wisdom was My Mission.

In total, humbling knowledge, I lowered my head. A long moment passed. When I finally lifted my face, The Forces had vanished. What had been clearly chiseled visions were now just walls of rock. Slashed from great blasts of ancient winds, eroded and empty, the cliffs loomed over me. Reality saddened me. After The Forces, life felt cheap and cardboard. People all cartoon. Dazed and ruminating, my body brought me back to the simple shelter in the fields.

Wearily, I climbed short steps up the wooden floor, surrounded by empty fields. Monteblan turned over. I looked down at him a moment, feeling far away. We had different Chickens now. He had Driving. I had Wisdom. Sadness washed through me, at all my friend would never understand. I tapped him lightly with my toe. He didn't rouse. I poked him harder. He rolled over.

"Life's a dick," Monteblan groaned. "It's always hard in the morning."

Standing silently, I stood with my hands on my hips. Monteblan pulled himself to his feet, standing in his torn T-shirt, staring at me concerned.

"We're not back to Freddie Hubbard, are we?"

"We're way past Freddie Hubbard."

"What's going on?"

"I saw Them." Turning to my friend, I stared deeply into his eyes. "The Forces."

Monteblan's mouth fell open in awe. "What did they tell you?"

I just shook my head.

For a long time, we stood in silence.

Then Monteblan spoke.

"I know what it's like. There's nothing to say. Let's just go."

Peeling my crusty *Beer Lao* T-shirt from the bamboo bannister, I felt the damp material. Too wet to wear, I tied the two short sleeves around my neck. It draped behind me like a cape. Barefoot, following my friend from our shelter, I set off with him in the rising dawn towards the distant town.

Through vacant back road intersections, we found silent sleeping neighborhoods. The longer we walked, the more the villages woke up. Children ran from porches, finding bicycles and riding in uniform to school. Adults with tools dispersed into fields. The sun rose higher. Heat came down. My mind was strange and loose, jarred from the message of stone revelation. I had my role in this race. Chicken Wisdom.

"I think it's farther than we thought," Monteblan said.

"It is," I agreed. "But We'll Get There."

"Aww, dude…" Monteblan said with evident pain. "Don't talk like that. You're not even talking. You're like, intoning or something. Plus you're wearing a cape. What the fuck?"

"Fear Not, My Friend," I intoned.

Looking down as we crossed a dirt field, I found a perfectly sized stick. This was a sign. Set there by calculated variables of time and nature, it was precisely placed to propel my mission. I took it up, walking barefoot over the earth. A gathering sense of greatness surrounded me. The *Beer Lao* T-shirt rippled in my wake. I stared forward towards civilization, at the humble hamlet where my Chicken ministry would bloom.

"Rich, please. I mean, you're wearing a cape. And now you've got a stick?"

"This is no stick," I said nobly. "It is The Staff of Chicken Wisdom."

"It's a stick, Rich!" Monteblan was exhausted, frustrated. "And you're *really* intoning now. This is bad. Could you lose the cape maybe?"

I smiled gently, giving my friend a reassuring pat on the shoulder. The sun was higher now, growing hotter. The work day had begun for Laos. A cowherd in the distance was leading his slowly ambling beasts to graze on the dry grass of the barren rice fields. Small groups of workers with tills and ploughs were turning the earth. Barefoot with my staff, I hailed them all.

"Stop waving!" Monteblan hissed.

"I'm not waving, friend. I'm Hailing."

"Stop calling me Friend!"

"You are," I said simply.

"I'm going to be a foot in your ass if you don't shut up!" Monteblan spun me by the shoulder to face him. "We're wanted men! Do you understand? You have totally turned a corner here. You're out of your freaking mind. We have *got* to get you home!"

"This is my home," I said with great peace.

"Listen to me!" My friend shook me hard. "This is Laos! You've got two cops and a flip flop opium addict chasing you! And *will* you stop hailing!?"

Monteblan grabbed my hand, which had raised in benediction, hailing all around. Some farmers stopped, curiously watching from distant ploughs. Monteblan hustled me from their dusty fields onto a dirt road. Cliffs to our back, the town before us, we trudged under the blazing sun. Then we heard voices up ahead.

"This way," Monteblan grunted, pulled me forward. "Maybe we can buy a ride into town. Just shut up and let me do the talking. OK?"

I didn't reply. Something about the voices ahead was calling me. Through a bleak cornfield of scraggly stalks, I saw Lao farmers standing in a large circle. They were watching something, cheering it on, shouting excitedly. Striding ahead of Monteblan, I moved towards them quickly, understanding intrinsically that my mission of Chicken Wisdom was starting here.

"*Rich!*"

Monteblan shouted in a loud whisper but I didn't stop. Head held high, shirt like a cape on my shoulders, I moved in purposeful strides towards the gathered group of men in the hot, barren field. Their shouts grew louder. I saw bills in their hand, money in fists. Cans of beer glinted in the sun. Cigarette smoke plumed in the dust. Sharp, shouting words erupted as they stared intently at some spectacle hidden in their midst.

"*Rich!*"

Monteblan's fierce, whispered shout from behind was desperate. Raising my staff, I hailed him absently, assuring my friend that all was fine. Then calmly, as if I belonged, I joined the circle of Lao farmers.

Gently laying my hands on their backs and shoulders, I cleared myself a path through clouds of cigarette smoke. The air reeked of sweat, spilled beer, and the sharp, metallic smell of hot blood.

Between the men, sun blazed down on two birds locked in battle. Circled by the shouting farmers and shrouded in clouds of dust, the roosters fought for life. With a savage flurry of pecks and kicking claws, they ripped each other in feathered shreds. The men cheered roaring with each landed strike. One rooster was drenched in blood that poured streaming from deep wounds. It walked with a jerking limp. The other bird darted in for clawing kicks and vicious pecks, ripping flesh anew. The men screamed in bloodthirsty excitement, waving money and upping bets. The bleeding bird whirled to escape, met with the men's nasty kicks. The bird shuddered, shedding feathers. Life nothing more than a drunken bet between red faced, savage Gods.

Calmly, holding my staff, I stepped barefoot into the ring.

A shocked silence descended at once. Farmers stared at me, stunned. The birds fluffed feathers softly, shaking wings and strutting in place. Hot sun blasted down. I raised my hands high.

"Friends," I intoned. "This Is Wrong."

The men looked confused. Frowning, they turned to each other. Then they turned back to me. With a roar, they rushed as one. Punched, kicked and cursed, I fell to the bloody dirt. Dust erupted all around. Yelling farmers battered me. Through the forest of lashing feet, I watched the bleeding bird limp fluttering away. I smiled.

Then a flat, heavy blow turned the whole world black.

**It smelled like feet and sweaty balls.** I gagged. Sharp pain stabbed my ribs with the breath. I shifted on a stone floor. Head throbbing, I struggled to orient myself in dim light. The room was rectangular. Slits near the ceiling let in weak beams of light. People were outlined in shadow shapes across from me. Struggling to rise, I reached behind me for balance. My hand found a cement wall. Moving my feet to stand, I felt the heavy weight of metal cut into my bone. I stared down in alarm. Heavy metal cuffs bound my ankles, threaded through with chains.

"Don't freak out," a friendly, distant voice said.

I did, heart hammering as I looked around at bodies chained together all around. My eyes narrowed to focus in the shadows. Our fellow foreign inmate was twenty something in a trippy rave shirt. He had long dreadlocked hair.

"Your buddy doesn't look that good," he said.

I looked to my right. Monteblan was chained to me. Shaking and sweating, Monteblan managed an urgent whisper.

"Must… *shit.*"

I turned quickly to the other foreigner in chains.

"My friend has to go. Like, *now.*"

"Stay chill, man. Everybody wants out."

"You don't understand…"

I looked around me at the faces of imprisoned Laos. Chained together and staring at nothing, their blank acceptance of fate emanated in Zen dismay. None understood the horror brewing in Monteblan's butt. Stalwart toilets answering to the highest standards of first world plumbing barely handled the worst of my friend's movements. The thought of such defecation splattering free within this third world prison was terrifying.

"I mean *go!*" I clarified, urgency straining my voice. "Like go to the bathroom. *Now.*"

"Cool it, man."

Through the gloom, the locked up, dread locked traveler had a slight edge to his voice. Beside me, Monteblan whimpered, straining with the effort of holding his shit together.

"*Please.*"

My friend stared at me terrified, eyes pleading like a hostage strapped to a slowly ticking time bomb.

"Guards!" I called out. "GUARDS!"

"Hey!" The chained raver's voice rose harshly in alarm. "Do *not* call them in here. Someone always gets hit."

Frowns materialized in the dim light around me from the prisoners. Monteblan's bowels rumbled like distant mortars of impending Assmageddon. Then a dark shape flew through the air. It landed with a soft metallic clunk on the cement before me. Incredulous, I stared at it.

"Are you kidding me?"

The rusted, dented coffee can emanated phantom strains of untold prison shits.

"That's what we got." The voice from the corner wasn't friendly anymore. "Do it in the can and pass it down the line. She'll dump it in the drain."

He nodded towards a dark, dank corner. The Lao ladyboy there had missed several weeks of hormones and makeup application. Looking far more boy than lady, she huffed and folded her arms.

"Put me near shit drain since I ladyboy. So bad here."

Monteblan groaned beside me, staring at the coffee can with bulging eyes. Then without warning, he lurched for it. Pants yanked down with wildly fumbling hands. A furious brown geyser exploded, hot shit ripping wickedly through the windowless room.

The Ladyboy screamed.

Thundering turds roared forth, monster plops splattering flecks of shit. Prisoners shouted, straining to escape the shit storm. Crouched and grunting, Monteblan moaned with eyes closed. Brown substance slid loose and splattered forth, farts gasping like primal animal forces. Poop mountains slid into level plains which were superseded by still more formations of piling dump. The fury of all watching transformed into terrible awe. Nobody had ever see shit like this. Revolting reek choked the air. Prisoners moved through rage, passed awe, and started yelling in horror. Rattling chains, banging the prison door with their fist, they screamed for release. Weeping now, Monteblan apologized while shit poured relentlessly.

*"Sorry! Sorry!"*

Metal keys were shoved into tumblers and the door slammed open. The Lao guard physically recoiled from the wretched smell, throwing a hand up instinctively as if warding off physical attack. Chained at the ankles, haunches above the mountainous mound of brown, Monteblan looked up. The guard's eyes were wide circles of disbelief. Tense silence strained the air between them. Monteblan's butt blew a low, forlorn fart. The single sustained note sounded mournfully through the gloom. Prisoners stared. The guard gaped. For a long, poignant moment, Monteblan's fart held pitch. Then fading sadly, followed by a final, tender plop, it finished.

The shit was done.

The fury of Lao law descended in full. Matched with backup now, the guard stormed towards the shit and screamed hideously at my friend. His hand pointed to the dump, then the door, then at Monteblan. Hot spit shot in foaming fury as undecipherable Laotian curses erupted from the man's reddening face. Keys were produced by an underling. Frowning in distaste, the low ranking officer hunched by Monteblan's ankle cuffs, face turned away from the lake of waste while he fumbled to release my friend from the others.

Dragging Monteblan up by the arms, pants still down at his ankles, I saw my friend hauled away, backside smeared brown.

"Where are you taking him?!" I yelled. "That's my friend! We're together, dammit!"

A sharp slap from another guard whacked my head. I flinched back, covering my head from further blows, hearing the jingling of keys near my ankles. Snatched up by both armpits, I was dragged heedlessly through the hot pile of excrement towards the door.

"Hey! We could have gone around that just—"

Another sharp smack hit my head, harder than before. My eyes blurred and I learned to shut up. Hauled away, I saw the other chained white guy wave his hand, mouthing *bye bye* with malicious light in his eyes. Then the cell door slammed behind me and shouts crowded my ears, guards yelling at me while dragging me down a narrow cement hallway.

Struggling with my ankles chained, feet slick with hot shit, I was dragged, pushed and shoved in a cloud of shouts towards a low door at hallway's end. Shoved through before ducking my head, I banged hard against the metal frame with a sharp smack that made me cry out.

Hallway light illuminated a stark cement room with chains hanging from the walls. Monteblan was already being bound to them. Pressed to the wall with a billy club against his throat, my friend stood at squatting height, gasping for air as chains were wound through rings positioned in the wall. Thrown against the opposite wall, I was pinned in similar fashion. Billy club to the neck, short of full standing height, I gasped for air while a tight metal belt was clamped around my waist. Wincing as it pinched my hips, I felt chains threaded through it, attaching to my ankle cuffs then running through rings on the wall. Something broke inside me and I started crying. Disgusted, one of the guards spit on me. The other kicked my feet out from under me and I fell forward, hung in space by the chains, unable to reach the floor. Laughing, they left me struggling to stand, bound in chains. The door shut with a thundering boom. Guards gone, alone in total darkness, I moaned miserably at Monteblan.

"We had it all! You won The VV Splits! We had The Mark, The Flaps, The Triple Nine Plates! We would have won!"

"You did this!" Monteblan yelled furiously through the blackness. "You turned into some Chicken Apostle!"

Lashing at his heavy chains, my friend fought desperately and futilely. I yelled back at him.

"You put me on drugs! The Black Cats! All the Mushrooms! Opium?! That was you! *You!*"

Thrashing in my bindings, I turned my head up towards far away heavens.

"I know who you are! I know why you did this! We flew to high! We saw too much!"

"Don't blame The Forces!" Monteblan yelled back. "They told us! They warned us!"

"Your shit got us here!" I lashed out in nasty rage. "Why didn't you go when we were processed?"

"Processed!?" My friend roared back through the blackness. "They threw us in a van, then threw us in a cell! *That's* being processed in Vang! You were passed out after being Jesus! I was scared shitless!

*Literally.* How could I crap when I thought you were permanently brain damaged?! This is *not* my fault! This is you and all that Chicken magic Tallahassee Charlie whatever shit!"

"Mississippi!" I yelled back.

"I don't care if it's Alabama!" Monteblan thundered. "He's a liar! There is no Chicken Magic! This is Real Chicken! Right here! *This* is Chicken 65!"

All the mystic clarity from my Chicken dawn had evaporated entirely. Helpless in chains, broken and afraid, I stared into empty blackness. My brain racked in ragged panting. There was a long, pained silence. Then Monteblan softly repeated himself in anger.

"*This* is Chicken 65."

I frowned in the darkness. Then surprising myself, laughed out loud.

"Chicken 65," I said, as if that explained it all.

There was a heavy silence. Then Monteblan agreed.

"Chicken 65."

Through the darkness, I sensed his smile. Like someone giving up on all logic and sense, everything bad and good in the world, Monteblan called out loudly.

"Once you're in, you're in for it all!"

"The whole Chicken!" I called back, laughing.

"Chicken 65!" my friend howled.

"Chicken 65!" I whooped, pulling at my chains and rattling the rings.

Chained to the wall, smeared in shit, laughing in darkness like demented lunatics, we shouted the only words that explained the world we had found ourselves in.

"*Chicken 65!*"

"*Chicken 65!*"

"*Chicken 65!*"

*"Chicken 65!"*

*"Chicken 65!"*

*"Chicken 65!"*

The cell door slammed open. Squinting in the sudden blast of light, I cringed automatically. Keys rattled, damning metal bindings fell away. Hard hands gripped my arms. Dragged from the cell with my eyes still adjusting, I blinked confused in the bright hall lights as Monteblan was dragged out behind me.

"Where are you taking us?"

Frowning guards didn't reply. Barefoot and terrified, I was pushed down the hall towards a distant wooden door. Dark and foreboding, it filled me with dread. Struggling helplessly, I twisted and writhed.

"No!" I called out. "Please!"

"We're Americans!" I heard Monteblan bellow behind me. "There's a Geneva Convention!"

Guards dragged us closer to the door. Strange lines streaked the wood. Shock hit me as I recognized the scraping trails left by human fingernails. Others had been dragged through screaming. I screamed too, pushing my bare, shit stained feet into the floor. Pulled forward by hard polished boots, I was thrust hard against the dreadful door, slamming it open with the impact of my body. Monteblan was hustled in roughly beside me, ankle chains clanging. The guards disappeared, slamming the door shut hard. Behind us it boomed in a resounding note of doom.

We stood in a room. It was a simple place where brutal things happened. The large wooden table was scuffed and splintered. Ancient blood stains had seeped into the surface, marking it like maps of human pain. Atop them our passports and wallets were laid out neatly, with bank cards, licenses, photos and spare change lined up precisely in rows. The two joints from the bar were laid neatly parallel. Monteblan's thermos stood silently. My walking staff was positioned crosswise. Light shone down from a single, wired window just beyond.

Beneath it, a high backed chair was turned away, hiding our interrogator. Smoke from his cigarette drifted in slow, swirling patterns through the shaft of sunlight. For a long moment, there was no other motion in the room. Then slowly, the chair turned round.

"Let's talk Chicken, shall we?"

Ladyboy Man smiled.

**The tan suit was pressed.** The bright blue shirt was starched, tie notched perfectly. His white boutonniere was fresh. Casually hitching his slacks, the tailored Brit crossed his legs. A manicured hand slipped into his jacket pocket, producing a small bottle. Ladyboy Man pressed the top smartly, releasing clouds of thickly sweet cologne.

"No offense old boys. I'm afraid you smell as bad as you look."

Stunned and unable to respond, we both stood in dumb shock. Regarding us for a moment, Ladyboy Man let cigarette smoke drift up from his mouth, then inhaled it smoothly into his nose.

"Either of you injured?"

"I've been hit," I said, rubbing my head. "A lot."

"Of course you have." Ladyboy Man said with a dismissive wave. "This is Laos and you're in prison. What I mean is *injured*. Internal organs ruptured. Fingernails pulled. Genital malfeasance. Any such unfortunate business while detained?"

He arched his eyebrows, tapping ash on the floor.

Monteblan and I both shook our heads.

"Well, that's both good and bad. Good that you won't need hospital. Bad that I won't have anything to parley with. If either of you had your testicles attached to a car battery, I might be in the position to bargain. Depends really. Every situation is different. Which is why I *so* enjoy my work."

He smiled, golden in the sun. Pressed and crisp in our world of shit and dismay, Ladyboy Man was like a dream.

"How did you find us?" I said, disoriented.

Leaning forward in the chair, Ladyboy Man tapped his business card on the table. Set next to Monteblan's license, the cream colored card with swirling *Ladyboy Man* script brought me back to The General's Bar- B Q, where we had first met.

"Lucky you had my card." He stood from the chair, holding court and gesturing expansively with his cigarette. "The Vang Valley tends to be a bit of a dust bin. Every Chicken, something needs sweeping up. To such ends, I have cultivated personal relationships with more than a few Lao police. Bottles of whiskey here, university tutoring for a daughter there. One saw my card in your belongings and put out word for my services. And oh, don't you need them!"

The Blonde British man laughed in delight, placing both hands on the table, leaning his weight forward and looking at us both.

"In this race I've seen everything from detonated overpasses to stolen tanks, redirected satellites and routine decapitation, but never, *ever*, have I found a pair of poor buggers on the wrong side of both the police and the mafia in Vang." Squinting at us as if studying rare specimens, his blue eyes glittered. "What's this about breaking up a cock fight?"

"I thought I was Jesus," I said.

"Indeed. Well, they do warn us about Lao mushrooms. Did you know they grow in buffalo piles by the river? Puts the phrase "Holy Shit" in a whole new light, shouldn't you say?"

Laughing breezily, Ladyboy Man strolled around the table, hands clasped behind his back.

"But as you've no doubt learned, the dear Lord won't help in old Vang. Out here..." He pivoted sharply, fixing us with a brilliant smile. "You need Ladyboy Man."

For a moment he froze there posing. I imagined he had practiced the move.

"We've got the embassy," I said, repelled by his airs. "When I left the states they said I could always call the embassy."

"That was then and this is Laos," Ladyboy Man informed me, casually pacing the room again. "With the mafia involved, I'm your only chance. That wasn't just a cock fight, you see. That was a mafia cock fight."

"In a field with a bunch of farmers?" I mumbled, incredulously. "How was I supposed to know that?"

"Where there's money, there's mafia. Mind that from now on, will you?"

Staring down at the curling, expansive script of the *Ladyboy Man* card, I nodded dumbly. I had never felt more lost. Hours ago stone cliffs had been beaming telepathic wisdom. Now I was chained in a third world prison. Besides me, Monteblan shuffled, rattling his ankle cuffs and sniffling.

"Oh come now!" the Brit said, noting the funereal mood in the room. "It's not all bad, you've had quite a stroke of luck you don't even know about!"

We both looked up as Ladyboy Man strolled back to his chair, easing into the seat. I sensed his enjoyment of the situation. Holding court in tailored delight, lording over two chained, shit stained Americans gave him palpable satisfaction. Ladyboy Man was intent on drawing forth all the dramatic potential the moment possessed. I imagined him placing the chair precisely for theatrical effect. Practicing his turn before we arrived. Clearly, he was the star. We were captive audience. With no other option for deliverance, I played my part in the prat's performance.

"Luck?" I said, cueing the next monologue.

"Very much so." Ladyboy Man smiled with immense pleasure at my leading question. "Not three minutes ago I was in here arguing.

Ever so politely of course, but in terribly insufficient Lao. I'm simply godawful in these hillside dialects. In Vientiane, mind you, I muddle through quite alright, but out here in the valley is another thing entirely. You'd think one land should have one language, don't you? But that's all bother. The point is..."

Producing another cigarette, the Brit frowned in concentration, sparked his LBM monogrammed lighter, inhaled theatrically, and blew smoke from the side of his mouth.

"The point is, not three minutes ago I was standing where you were, and the Vang chief of Police was sitting *here*." He tapped his lighter on the chair's armrest. "Maintaining that he had absolutely no knowledge whatsoever of any Americans in his possession and *quite* certainly no foreigners at all involved in this Chicken 65 business. A race which couldn't possibly exist due to the fact that it's *highly* illegal and no such motorized mayhem would ever dare dally through his little Bailiwick. Oh, these Laos..."

Laughing in patrician affection, Ladyboy Man twirled in his chair, looking up at the sun.

"Well then, at the precise moment we're going back and forth like a Wimbledon volley where I know he's lying and he knows he's lying, and he *knows* that I know he's lying, and *I* know that he knows that I know that he's lying but won't stop lying and—

"AND WHAT?"

Monteblan's voice thundered through the room, startling Ladyboy Man into silence. Turning in his chair, the charming blonde looked distinctly upset at not hearing himself talk. Regarding the burly, defecation encrusted Monteblan for a blank moment, he recovered with a thin smile. Producing his cologne bottle, Ladyboy Man pressed the spray smartly.

"And at that precise moment, old boy, what should we hear but two lunatics in the bowels of this godawful place singing out *Chicken 65* at the top of their bloody lungs. Whatever possessed you, surely I don't know. But you'd remain in possession indefinitely if you hadn't. Good Chicken timing, I'd say. Or perhaps… Chicken magic?"

Ladyboy Man raised his eyebrows.

"How much?" Monteblan said.

"Americans!" Ladyboy man laughed. "Right to the point. You know I admire that terribly about you? None of this fussing about with bothersome civilities and godawful courtesy. We British are terribly old fashioned about all that. But I dare say the Thais top us all at being inefficiently pleasant. The last thing a Thai *ever* wants to get to is the blasted point. Doing business with them is like trying to push a wet noodle through a plate of papaya. Laos lack their polish but possess the same paralyzing dread of direct confrontation. Understanding these differences, you see, is part of the talents I possess. You have nothing to fear. Did you know I once negotiated—"

"How much." Monteblan repeated.

Unruffled by another brusque interruption, Ladyboy Man blew yet another extravagant plume of smoke.

"That's what I'm trying to ascertain, you see. This is more than a law being broken. There's issues of face involved. Sticky wicket to play. One doesn't just break up a mafia cockfight and walk away. What kind of mafia would allow that to happen? This is why legs are broken, fingers removed, people loaded into oil barrels and shipped off to Burma and so forth. You're lucky the police from the night before were looking for you on charges of trafficking narcotics."

"Trafficking narcotics!" I cried out.

"Exhibit A." Ladyboy Man nodded towards the two joints on the table. "It's all in the report, along with one additional charge of— what did they call it? Ah yes! Institutional Damage of People's Democratic Property."

He smiled proudly at recalling the offence.

"What does that mean?" I said.

"It means…" Ladyboy Man shot his cuffs, then adjusted his boutonniere. "One rather large shit in their jail."

"Busted," Monteblan mumbled.

"Come on!" I yelled. "He was chained to the wall!"

Ladyboy Man shrugged. "Surely I don't run the facility and I'm not aware of the sanitary arrangements, but the charge has been levelled. And in all fairness, you both reek of the offense."

Kicking lightly with his polished loafer, Ladyboy Man twirled slowly in his chair. Gazing up at the sun, he frowned while calculating out loud.

"With this additional political infraction, in concert with narcotic trafficking and mafia considerations—not to mention the highly detested and patently illegal tradition of Chicken 65—mitigated of course by my refined skill set, extensively cultivated local network, and the intricate knowledge of native nuance required to—"

"How *much.*"

Monteblan seethed the words. I saw violence in his eyes. Ladyboy Man must have seen it too. Covering quickly with the broadest of smiles, he spoke the words brightly.

"Ten thousand US cash."

"Done," Monteblan grumbled. "Get us out of here."

"Ten Thousand?" I said the words in strained unbelief. "Wait, hey! Monteblan? You never take the first offer. Let's bargain, we should—"

"There is a time and place to bargain." Ladyboy Man interrupted softly, gazing disinterestedly at his nails. "I dare say covered with shit in a Lao prison isn't one of them."

"He's right," Monteblan said, shoving his wallet into his pants pocket. "We have the cash in the car—if they haven't impounded it."

"Nobody's touched your vehicle," the loquacious Brit was chipper. "I've already checked. Mr. Boom's brother in law had already placed The Mark and fixed The Plates before this dreadful business began.

We'll be escorted to the garage, you'll produce the payment and you'll be off to the races. Oh, except for one more slight detail."

Monteblan and I, in the middle of collecting our things, froze. Both of us looked up at the man.

Producing the bottle of cologne, Ladyboy Man sprayed a single spritz.

"My fee."

"Wait…" I stopped, throwing things down on the table. "You want *more* money?"

"Not at all. I want a Chicken Promise."

Ladyboy Man's request hung in the air between us with the sweet cloud of his cologne.

"Let's just pay you," Monteblan said. "Honestly, I don't want to owe you anything bro."

"Despite how flattered I am to be considered brethren, the only way out of this… *shit,* shall we say? Is a Chicken Promise. And a Chicken Promise is a Chicken Promise. I'll collect it wherever I like, anywhere in the race, regardless of the circumstances, and you shall comply." Eyebrows arched, he folded his arms. "Have we a deal?"

I stared at him simmering. Monteblan slumped in resignation.

"Fine."

Ladyboy Man beamed. "Splendid!"

**One hour later, Monteblan, Ladyboy Man and I stood staring down at the open trunk of Pablo Cruise.** The beaten brown leather suitcase was lying there with a new spare tire. Monteblan reached down and snapped the old varnished catches. The top sprung open. Neat stacks of US Dollars were lined up in rows. I whistled. Ladyboy Man's hand snaked down and grasped a thick stack of hundred dollar bills.

"Hey!" I said sharply. "A moment to admire 50,000 dollars, if you will?"

"Why of course," Ladyboy Man shot back. "Let me just tell the police escort waiting outside the garage that you'd like a moment to appreciate your undeclared winnings from the illegal race that doesn't exist!"

I didn't like his manicured hands on our money. Or the way he pronounced "garage" to rhyme with "marriage." But Ladyboy Man had a point. The wheels of justice grind slow, but bribery was a fast, greasy slide. After striking our deal at the prison, we were hustled quickly to the garage in a waiting police car. Blankets were thrown over our heads to evade Mafia lookouts. Lead by Ladyboy Man to the Chicken garage, we were rushed inside to collect the payoff and hightail it out of Vang.

Thankfully, Pablo Cruise looked more than ready to roll. New five point harnesses were affixed in the front seats. Precise metal welding had impressed arcane Thai lettering in front and back fenders. With

The Mark were new white plates numbered **999 999**. Al Pacino's face hung over both back tires, *Serpico* mud-flaps completing our trifecta transformation. But despite these modifications, Pablo wasn't mobile. We had been told that the replacement clutch was still *en route* from Bangkok. Driven full speed by special Chicken courier, it was set to arrive any hour. The news hadn't pleased Ladyboy Man. Standing at the trunk counting out ten thousand US Cash, he muttered to himself while organizing the bribe.

"Well, we can't just jolly well wait." Flicking through bills, he shot me a glance. "I struck a deal to get you out of town, *tout suite.*"

"Why me?" I said, pointing at Monteblan. "He's one who shit on the People's Property of Glorious Tomorrows."

"That being what it may," Ladyboy Man muttered, "If I don't deliver, it just isn't cricket."

Then he lit up with an idea. Looking towards his idling Range Rover, the Brit snapped his fingers sharply.

"Ploy!"

The little Ladyboy who looked like Audrey Hepburn with big feet slipped out of the vehicle. She was wearing a white one piece dress with pearls. Crossing the garage to Pablo Cruise, her feet were deliberately placed one in front of the other. The moving pose was calculated to accentuate her slight hips. Her large brown eyes were downcast. Thick black hair spilled over her bare shoulders. She held a clutch Chanel handbag under one thin arm. Stopping before Ladyboy Man, the light scent of her perfume played in the air. Without looking from his money counting, Ladyboy Man spoke to her quickly in Thai. She shrugged her slim shoulders and then stood twisting one foot behind the other, looking bored.

"It's settled then," Ladyboy Man slid the thick payoff into his breast pocket. "I'll pay off the police while Grimace waits here for the clutch. Ploy will take Asser up ahead."

His hands dipped into the briefcase again, pulling out five more hundred dollar bills. Speaking fast in Thai, he pressed the money into Ploy's hand.

"What the hell?" Monteblan said. "We're not paying for your girlfriend's sex change."

"Indeed." Ladyboy Man smirked. "I *detest* post-ops. Designer vaginas are strictly for the Japanese. Ploy will disperse these funds to purchase a scooter, upon which she and Asser will ride into the proverbial sunset and out of Vang."

"Why can't you drive us?"

I looked towards the immaculate Range Rover. House music played inside, while the air conditioner blasted behind tinted windows.

"I'm afraid there's more business to drum up in Vang," he replied. "Plus you're notorious. Facilitating bail is one thing. Personally transporting a mafia target out of Vang would have grave repercussions on my standing in the community, such as is."

He flashed his grin.

"Besides, Ploy will be more than happy at the chance to ride with a handsome American. Show a ladyboy a good time, why don't you?"

Ladyboy man winked. Ploy smiled with a slight twist of her lips. Patting her on the behind, the Brit propelled her towards the large open door of the garage. Passing the Range Rover, the petite kathoey smiled in triumph, counting the money in obvious pride.

The instant she passed, tinted windows descended. Two ladyboys, all lipstick and sunglasses, thrust their heads out the Range Rover. Pointing towards Ploy as she disappeared out the garage door, bracelets jangled angrily while throaty voices rose sharply in confrontation.

Rushing towards them, our advocate raised his hands in placating gestures.

"Ladyboys! Ladyboys! *Please!*"

Overriding their argument in flowing Thai, he talked them down. Frowning and fuming, the windows went up and the girls disappeared inside the idling machine. Holding his head, the Brit returned to us muttering in dismay.

"No difference, I tell you! Put a dress on someone and they're difficult. Women are a headache and ladyboys are a pain in the arse."

A hard, barking command from the garage door set Ladyboy Man spinning in his loafers. The police officer who had driven us to the garage was shouting angrily, hands on hips. Lighting up in a diplomatic grin, our advocate oozed subservient charm, repeating Laotian phrases until the man in brown withdrew. Watching him step into the dusty heat, the blonde Brit sighed in relief. Rushing back, looking physically taxed, Ladyboy Man patted his forehead with the perfumed handkerchief. Slipping it into his pocket, he clapped sharply.

"Chop chop, then! Another five thousands if we don't sort this out fast. There are showers in the back. One of the girls got your belongings from the hotel. Dress yourself and let's move."

Sliding one more manicured hand into the trunk, Ladyboy Man drew out a few more hundred dollar bills.

"Dude!" I shouted. "You already have ten thousand!"

"A minor but prudent investment, I assure you." Waving the bills theatrically, the Brit walked briskly towards the door. "There are neighbors who saw you arrive. This will assure they don't see which way you depart."

Slipping smartly outside, he disappeared in the blinding heat. I looked at Monteblan and he shrugged. We walked together past oil slicks and strewn tools, finding a dirty doorway that lead to a dirtier shower.

The harsh soap, designed to cut engine grease, was just strong enough to scour away the humiliations from Lao prison. My suit was waiting miraculously, draped over a tire iron jammed between stacked tires. A cracked mirror, dusty and chipped, showed my reflection in dim, flickering fluorescents. I smiled, admiring the cut.

"The problems all started when I got out of my suit." I told Monteblan. "For the rest of this Chicken, I'm not taking it off."

Monteblan was just stepping out of the spitting shower. Drying with a threadbare towel, he stepped commando into his madras. He pulled on another *Beer Lao* shirt, following up with body armor.

"Yeah, this shit ain't coming off either." Tightening a side strap, he punched the plates. "Chicken ain't no joke."

Pleased at my friend's reverence, I wondered if his understanding of Chicken 65 was deepening. For a moment, I thought of preaching. Then I felt opportunist. Like a born again Christian—Born Again Chicken?—sizing up a spiritual mark to hustle. Letting the issue rest, I imagined Monteblan had his own journey towards Chicken meaning. If there were real powers at play, I shouldn't have to point them out. Even Ladyboy man—a sleazy wheel spinner steeped in the race's dirty practicalities—had noted some magical Chicken coincidence. Before us wound untold miles of road. Along the way were many chances for The Bird to illuminate my friend. Satisfied with the decision, suited up, I walked confidently into the garage.

Ladyboy Man looked up tensely the instant we appeared.

"You." He pointed at Monteblan. "In the car."

The British voice held such authority that Monteblan merely complied. Sliding into the safety of the Marked car, he dumped his body in the driver side bucket seat. The car rocked happily. Monteblan slammed his door. The sound boomed in the empty garage. Reaching forward, he held the wheel. Brown eyes softened. Staring ahead through the windshield, my friend focused on things unseen.

"It doesn't have a clutch," I said.

"That's the safest place to wait for it." Ladyboy Man pointed at the front fender, welded with arcane Thai letters. "If worse comes to worse, The Mark will protect him."

"Great, so let me stay, too."

"You're another story entirely."

"Look, back in the Chantal, they told us that—"

"Listen to me, *please!*" Pleading with both hands in a prayer gesture, Ladyboy man looked positively frightened. "We're not in the Hotel Chantal! We're in the Vang Valley! And it's all over town that a foreigner broke up a cock fight. You made the local Mafia Don lose Face. Half your bribe is going to him and it *still* might not be enough! If you try and hide in that car, The Mark might be overlooked in order to make a mark on you— in terribly unpleasant ways! That, in turn, will ignite a Thai Lao mafia war, which I assure you is not conducive to pleasant Chickening. So please, for God's sake, let me do my job and *get you out of town!*"

His words died in the empty garage, bright blue eyes begging me in the gloom.

"Fine," I said. "Where do I go?"

Sighing in relief, Ladyboy Man produced the perfumed handkerchief and blotted more sweat from his brow. Striding towards Pablo's trunk, he pulled another few hundred dollars. Stuffing them in my suit pocket, he led me by the elbow towards the garage door.

"You have money for the road. There's a string of hotels overlooking the Valley. Ploy will show you the way. You'll be fine up there—out of sight, out of mind. Have a drink, relax, discuss particle physics…"

"Ploy knows physics?"

"Why *yes.*" Hustling me across the floor, his voice dripped sarcasm. "We met at the *Fisica d'Italia* symposium in Brindisi. Ploy had a riveting lecture on the valence properties of electron bonding and I was instantly smitten. *What* an intellect. Do let me know if she uses any two syllable words, will you? I'd like to mark the occasion in my diary. Ah, there she is!"

The little Ladyboy was waiting at the open garage door, hips cocked, twirling a pair of keys on her finger. Ladyboy Man ushered her out into the glaring heat, drawing me along by the elbow.

The sun hit with white hot malice. Traffic thundered on the road beyond. Squinting through glare and dust, I saw a shining red motorbike waiting. The Vang police officer was parked nearby, staring from behind mirrored glasses. Ladyboy Man gave him a friendly wave, sat on the bike, twisted the keys, pressed the ignition, and kicked it into gear. Stepping off adeptly, he smiled at me grandly and gestured to the idling machine.

"There you are, old boy!"

For a moment, I looked at it.

Ploy, Ladyboy Man and the police officer stared at me.

I gulped. "I've never driven one."

Ladyboy Man stepped forward, spitting through his smile.

*"For God's sake, drunken three year olds drive them out here!* Right is the throttle and that's how you go. You won't need the brake because once you get on that thing you're not stopping, are you?"

I looked out at the chaotic upheaval of traffic blasting past on the glaring, sun hammered road. Busses and trucks thundered with rattling metal tonnage. Tiny figures raced alongside, unprotected on plastic scooters. Weaving through the huge vehicles in smooth, instinctive trajectories, they evaded death in ways I didn't understand. Looking back at the bike, I then turned to Ploy.

"Why don't you drive? You're Thai. You've done it lots, right?"

"I not drive." Ploy frowned. "You are the man."

Beside us in his idling car, The Lao officer cleared his throat and spat noisily into the dust. Ladyboy Man turned to him, smiling, spouting Laotian pleasantries while pushing me on the bike. Then he turned to Ploy.

"Get on."

Ploy didn't move.

*"What?"* Ladyboy Man hissed desperately.

"I need some things," she said sullenly. "For the sun."

"Thais and sun!" Ladyboy Man laughed in dismay. "Of course! Forget the mafia! The slightest suntan will drop you three levels in the social hierarchy! Asser, give her your jacket! *Now!*"

I slipped out of my jacket. Ladyboy Man grinned to the officer while Ploy pulled on the large black coat. Frowning as she rolled up the sleeves, Ladyboy pushed her towards the bike.

"Off we go!"

Behind me, Ploy sat sidesaddle. One of her small, dainty arms went around my waist, holding secure. Her perfume and shampoo rushed me in light scent. Throttling much too hard, I lurched us into traffic. Ploy screamed. A barreling truck with rusted undercarriage rushed us in fumes of petrol. Just flicking the wheel, I kept us alive while two Al Pacinos swept past, staring at me from Serpico mud flaps. Ploys arm tightened hard around my waist. Protective instinct kicked in. Leaning forward, I punched the gas for steadying velocity and shot us forward down the hot, glaring road out of Vang.

"Good boy," Ploy whispered appreciatively in my ear.

We were off.

**Flooring along the shoulder, holding my breath while huge vehicles kicked up dust, I ploughed out of town.** For ten tense minutes I pressed on, white knuckling until we hit open road. There another lane was added and the shoulder expanded. Swerving to the far side, I drove diligently away from the impending mafia hit. Kilometers passed. The road took us higher. Laos shot past. In shuttering view through passing trees, the valley we had left behind stretched out below. Ploy leaned her head gently against my back. Her perfume smelled stronger. There had been lots of sex in Bangkok, but not much affection. Something as simple as a ride through the country with a woman had eluded me. Her pleasant smile, gentle manners and light, affectionate body contact felt more erotic than most of the fast, slamming encounters I had pulled from nights in town. There was no doubting my attraction. But this attraction made me doubt myself in ways I didn't want to consider. Shaking off the confusion, I focused on the road.

"Hot," the little voice behind me said, leaning into my ear.

Despite the rushing wind, I was sweating. Hot sun beat down on my suit's black fabric, increasing the heat.

"Me too!" I shouted back over the wind.

"Maybe you want to stop and rest?"

Her Thai style made me smile. Instead of telling me what she wanted, Ploy made it seem like my idea. I had been in Bangkok long enough to understand why Thais played this game. First, we avoided conflict. If Ploy had told me she wanted to stop, but I didn't, we would have been at odds. In the West, conflict sets the stage for dialogue and resolution. In Thailand, it sets the stage for somebody losing face. That's to be avoided at all costs, which is why her question worked on another level. In Thailand, the man would never tell his woman he was tired and wanted to stop. He would lose face by looking weak. Ploy was doing her job of monitoring my condition and making suggestions. Wonderfully pleasant stuff if you think of the thoughtfulness involved. Slightly maddening stuff when you're hearing thoughts put in your head. But in this case, Ploy was right. It was hot and I wanted a break.

Just up ahead was a low, open building that passed for a highway rest stop. I pulled into the dusty gravel lot. The open air, tile floor structure was filled with blessed shade. Heavy wooden chairs sat at polished dark tables. A fridge full of sodas and beers waited inside, where a few different vendors sold meat on grills, corn on spits, and different pans of stir fried food. There was a TV in the far corner, where kids sat sprawled watching static fuzzed cartoons. Draping her handbag over one of the chairs, Ploy indicated our table.

"I take care you," she told me. "Sit."

She moved towards the grills and I slipped into the polished wooden chair. Body still buzzing from the roar of the open road, I relaxed in the cooling shade. Moments later my passenger reappeared with two cool bottles of water. Screwing off the caps, she slipped straws inside and handed me one.

"Thanks, Ploy."

"You nice man." She slipped into the chair beside me. "He never say thank you. Just tell us what to do."

"Who, Ladyboy Man?"

She nodded with a frown. "Don't like this name."

"Sorry. Do you like him?"

She shrugged, looking off into space. Behind her, a slowly rotating fan blew breeze that rippled her silken black hair.

"So why do you stay with him?"

"He take care me," she said.

This phrase described many Thai relationships with foreigners, but the details were often different.

"How does it work with him?"

Reaching into her designer handbag, Ploy shuffled through make-up, sunglasses, credit cards, and a long tube of what I thought was lube before finding a laminated square of paper. Slightly larger than an index card, it was neatly labeled PLOY. She placed it before me and I leaned closer to read. Printed by computer, the card showed a neatly organized month of days. Each day had a column running under it. Some squares were filled with letters. Others were empty. Frowning, I tried to decipher the organized boxes.

"What's Iffy?" I said, reading one day marked *IFY*.

"I fuck you." Ploy replied.

"He schedules this shit out?!" Peering closer at another square, I read the letters aloud. "YFM?"

"You fuck me," she shrugged.

"What a prick," I said. "All the girls have one of these?"

She nodded. "Cannot be busy or go home see family and miss some sex. Then he not pay us that month and very mad."

"What's this?"

I pointed to the box on Saturday: *16:00- 18:00/PMFM.*

"Ploy and Mint Fuck Me."

My eyebrows shot up in disbelief, picturing the irrepressibly dapper Ladyboy Man banged from both ends by a pair of well hung kathoeys.

"I don't like." Ploy frowned distastefully. "This one worse."

Her finger, sparkling with jewelry and a bright red painted fingernail, pointed out Sunday.

*19:00-21:00/PMJFM*

The clusterfuck of letters didn't have to be explained. Shaking away the image of Ladyboy Man rocked by a power trio of lady boners, I looked up at Ploy with concern.

"You don't have to do this," I told her. "There's nice guys out there. They won't put you on a schedule."

"He take care me." Flipping her hair in a dismissive wave, she slipped the laminated booty calendar into her designer bag. "My family too."

Ending the discussion with that, Ploy turned her attention to the food which had just been set down. The server was a bored looking Lao who broadcast open contempt at my gender bending companion. She pretended not to notice. Picking up utensils, Ploy dipped delicately into the dishes. Loading a spoon with rice and meat, she topped it with a dash of sauce.

"Careful," she said. "Hot."

Holding up the spoon, she moved it toward me. Highly pleased, I leaned in and let her feed me. While eating, Ploy watched, carefully gauging my reaction. Reaching up with a napkin to dab an errant fleck of rice from my stubble, she sat back, eyebrows raised for my verdict on her food choices.

"*Aroi mak,*" I said, telling her in Thai it was tasty.

"I think you speak Thai too good," she said, with a coy smile. "Maybe understand Thai people too much."

"Don't worry," I shook my head. "There's no threat of me understanding Thai people. You guys aren't even opposite of Americans. You're like another shape entirely, on a different plane of reality."

She frowned. "I don't understand what this means."

"*Aroi mak,*" I repeated, filling another spoon.

"Good." Ploy smiled.

Now that she knew I approved of the food, Ploy fed herself. She ate in tiny, dainty bites, sitting up straight, poised and lady like. Or, more accurately, like a lady. Now that I was looking closely, I could see minor tells that suggested her sex. The bones were just a little more angular at her shoulders. The arms slightly proportioned different. When her hands had brushed my skin, they weren't as soft. But still, it was hard to imagine her with... Shaking my head, I just laughed.

"What?" she said.

"Nothing," I replied.

"No, I think something." She playfully reached out with her free hand, poking me in the stomach. "You laugh same way before. What?"

The question which had been thrusting at me since our ride began was just too awkward. Setting my fork and spoon down before the array of plates, I leaned back in my wooden chair. The fan whirled in circles behind me. Outside, the late afternoon road was quietly empty. Soft sunlight played within the open air plaza. Ploy's oval face caught the glow perfectly, features cast soft, brown eyes questioning. Eyebrows arched, she smiled then playfully touched my thigh.

"What? You tell me."

My attraction surged. I shifted to hide it, sliding forward and leaning my elbows on the table.

"What I'm trying to say is... uh, well. It's hard to believe you have..." I cleared my throat, lowering my voice. "I mean, what I'm trying to ask is, do you have a...umm..."

My voice trailed off as I struggled to find the polite way to find out if Ploy had a prick. The most feminine looking ladyboys had them removed. She might be one of them. I wanted to know. But I didn't want to embarrass us. Then a phrase overheard in Bangkok's Patpong district leapt to mind. In that grimy red light maze where female, ladyboy, and post-op hustlers mingled freely, the beautiful girl grinding in one's lap sometimes started life as a bouncing baby boy. Prudent patrons deployed a *de rigueur* question to avoid unwanted surprises from popping up later. Remembering it now, I finessed the phrase for my dining companion's consideration.

"Did you have The Operation?"

Ploy smiled, pointing to my lap. "I same same you."

"*OH!*" I said too loudly. "OK then. Right. Hey. Chicken 65. Something else, huh?"

"What you mean?"

"This race, it's really something. Lots of new experiences." I sipped long and deep from my water, flicking through questions which might change the subject further.

"There's something else I wondered..." *Aside from how big your cock is.* "Why aren't there many Thai people in Chicken 65?"

"*Bah,*" Ploy said, frowning in distaste. "Too crazy for Thai people. Plus very dirty. Thai people don't like."

She scooted back in her chair, sipping her drink through the straw. Awkward subject cleared entirely, I sat back in relief. Once more, I admired Thai style. Ploy was entirely unfazed about my penis inquiry. In The States, there would have been a tirade on gender identity politics plus a shaming session, followed by a trip to the police station to file an "indecent questioning" incident, chased by a blizzard of social media posts that probably would have cost me my job. All that went out the window in this part of the world. In Thailand, girls with a dick really understood a guy.

"Come on," I said. "Let's go."

At the old fashioned register by the cola fridge, a pair of women registered my ladyboy friend with smirks of disapproval. I frowned at the instant prejudice. Ploy didn't notice it at all. She paid for our food. I tried insisting, but she refused.

"His money anyway." Threading her arm through mine again, she added softly. "I don't like him. I like you."

I looked down to see her wide brown eyes looking up at me, warm and beautiful. My semi thickened into a chubby and I wondered if she had one too. Outside, I started the bike on the first try. She slipped on the seat behind me, this time leaving her hand on my stomach. I stoked the engine. Stroking me slightly, she gently undid one of my shirt buttons. I roared the throttle and sped us out onto the open road. Her small hand slid in against my skin, rubbing in delicious, meandering circles as the road blurred fast below.

My blood raced with the landscape. Wind rushed through my hair. Ploy loosened another button, gaining access to more skin. Now she was pressed tightly to my body, perfume clouding my mind, wind whipping her hair in luxurious waves. Her hand danced gently up and down my bare side. The world felt soft around us. Crickets hummed from dusty green brush all around. My heart hammered while the bike vibrated between our legs. Losing concentration, I drifted lazily into oncoming lanes. It didn't matter. The road was practically empty. Even it if wasn't, nothing would touch us. Some glow had formed around us. Ploy and I raced breathlessly fast, bodies pressed together, world a flying rush.

"Maybe you are tired?" She whispered in my ear. "You want to stop and rest maybe?"

Her hand withdrew from my shirt, pointing ahead to a small hotel on the left. I didn't reply. Just turned the wheel when we reached it and stopped us in the lot. Ploy slipped off one side of the bike. I turned towards the other, trying to hide the hard on pressing through my pants. Flipping it up in a masterful move employed since grade school, I strode towards the lot's edge. Then I laughed. If anyone would understand a boner, it was a girl who had one herself. Shaking my head once more at the surreal twists of my Chicken, I gazed out at the beautiful view beyond.

Just across the road, earth ended in a sharp drop off. Blue sky showed bright, and far below, the Vang Valley glowed in the afternoon's fading light. Rainbow colored balloons floated bright and distant. The river sparkled winding through the canyon, jungle pressing up to the banks. Mists danced up from the river, making the treacherous town look like lost paradise. From high above, it was hard to match this beautiful vision with the roaring chaos of our arrival there. I strained to connect the serene display with chains and jails, psychedelic mayhem, twisted treachery and the malice of lost souls. Then I felt a finger trace lightly down my back.

Ploy was there. Legs crossed, feet precisely positioned to diminish their size, she reached for my hand and tugged it playfully.

"Ya kit mak."

"What does that mean?" I asked.

"Don't think so much," the girl with the penis replied.

I smiled.

She did too.

Together we turned and walked towards the hotel.

**The room cost seven dollars.** Simple and tidy, holding a queen sized bed, the window looked out at trees. The bathroom was clean. It had a toilet on tiled floor with a sink, and a shower nozzle positioned over the corner drain. Ploy took one of the folded towels from the bed.

"Wait. I go shower."

Slipping into the bathroom, she closed the door softly behind her. Moments later, the sound of running water drummed faintly on tiles.

It hit me then. She was in the shower washing her balls. A girl with a boner was about to walk into the room. Having no reference, I wondered what to do with a dick. Pussy I had been hitting left right and center since high school. Despite being somewhat dorky and an average earner, my rap was solid, I lifted weights and was tall. With a few drinks in a girl, I didn't look bad. With dedicated footwork, my bedroom had never been empty and I had enjoyed a healthy array of relationships and hook ups. All had been women. I had never been in bed with another wang. Hadn't even thought of it. I was the type of guy who closed his eyes in movies where two men kissed. Not because it was wrong. Not because I didn't think they should. Just because it made me really uncomfortable. Dudes were friends. Dudes were dudes. Kissing one had never crossed my mind. Dudes didn't do it for me.

Dudettes, evidentially, were another story.

I sat there rock hard waiting for Ploy. Slim, petite, sly and subtly seductive, she had totally turned me on. Her perfume was perfect. The

long, gently swaying black hair hypnotic. The manner she carried herself with endeared her to me. Ploy had grace. She had style. That little
white dress, simply cut. Her pearls.

Her prick.

The thought of it made my hard on slightly fade. My eyes drifted
towards the shoes she had left by the door— Ploy's only tell.

The flat soled, black pumps were slightly worn down and awkwardly large. Positioned beside my shining black shoes, they were not
nearly as small as a woman's should be. Dust from the road had faded
their luster. People said you judged a man by the shoes he wore. What
if the man wore a dress and looked like a hot little broad? How did
you judge those shoes, or the person who wore them? Sitting tensely
on the bed, I tried to imagine the proverbial miles Ploy had walked in
them. Just one afternoon of sideways glances and mocking smirks had
made me want to punch walls. What happened when those afternoons
stacked up into years, then stretching into a lifetime? What effect did
that have on a person, even if they pretended not to notice? Before the
perfume went on in the morning, after the dress slipped off at night,
what was it like to walk that road? It was bad enough living in a hard
world. What would it be like living with hard-ons you didn't want?
Fighting the wrong body while everybody laughed at you for trying
to escape?

Before I could think more, the shower stopped. Silence followed. I
wondered if she had the same problem I always had, forgetting to dry
behind my balls. With the thought, my mast dipped lower. The thought
of her prick was confusing things. I wanted to leave. I almost did. Then
the door opened.

Ploy emerged from the light in a small cloud of steam. She looked
utterly delicious. Her long black hair was knotted casually up over
her head. Wisps of it trailed down along her graceful neck. Her chest
was small, nearly flat. The tiny white towel covered her lithe body and

lead down below her waist. Lovely thin legs with smooth, bare thighs gleamed with the glow of freshly lathered soap. Her feet played awkwardly, hiding one behind the other in a manner more endearing then anything. The soft flowered scent of her perfume, playing now with light soap, drifted towards me. Brown eyes, deep and quiet, held mine in the silent room.

"You shower now," she said.

"Wait."

Her voice was instantly defensive. "What?"

"Come... sit here a minute."

"You go shower," she repeated.

"Just come here a minute."

I patted the bed beside me. She didn't move. Then frowning like she understood something that had happened before, her head dropped and she sighed. Staring down at the floor, Ploy walked towards me in the small white towel. Closer now, her smooth skin emanated the sweet smell of soap. Legs held tightly together, rigidly sitting at the very edge of the bed, Ploy stared down at the floor.

"What?"

"Look, I think you're... beautiful. Really."

"What?" she said flatly.

"I just.... I like you. Really. I think you're amazing. You know, in that restaurant? The way you handled it?"

Her eyes flicked up with a trace of hostility. "What you mean handle?"

"People looking at you, being mean, the way you handled it. I mean deal with them."

"Always like this." She shrugged. "I ladyboy."

"You have grace," I told her. "Many people don't. Your parents. Did they support you?"

She frowned in distaste, head pulled back. "They don't like that I ladyboy. Brother and father hit me so much. I leave I 12."

"That's terrible."

Reaching out, I placed my hand on her shoulder. Holding her, I felt her relax slightly. Ploy moved slightly on the bed. Not next to me, but closer. She stared at the floor. I couldn't help but be moved. I edged closer. With my hand on her shoulder, I brought her next to me. She resisted a moment, then melted. Leaning her body against mine, Ploy let her head rest on my shoulder. I reached up and stroked her hair, silken and fine.

"Sometimes difficult for Ladyboy. Not like *falang* think. Not so happy all the time."

"I'm sorry," I said.

"OK," she said. "You don't like me. I know. We go now."

"Wait, that's not what I'm trying to tell you. Just…"

"What?" She looked at me flatly.

I thought back to her calendar with Ladyboy Man and felt angry.

"Just talk to me. I want to know you a little."

"Why you want to know me?"

"I just do. So your parents kicked you out of the house, but you still say that Lady—" I cut myself off, remembering she didn't like the name. "That he still helps you support your family? That he takes care of them?"

She nodded.

"What the hell would you do that for? They beat you, they told you to leave when you were just a child."

She shrugged. "All Thai people take care their parents."

Leaning against me again, her body felt pathetically small. I wondered how many hits and kicks her little frame had taken. My arm went down her back. Sitting side by side, I hugged her closely. The final rays of afternoon sun were dying outside. We sat in silence for a long while in the dim room.

"What you want to say to me?"

Her voice was so small, so quiet, that I barely heard her.

I moved away so I could see her better. Tracing my hand from her shoulder down one arm, I held her hand in mine. Then I reached out for the other. She had relaxed now, looking slightly defeated, sad, but accepting of whatever was happening. Slumping a bit, legs no longer crossed, she wasn't posing. She wasn't guarded. This was her. This was Ploy. Looking at her like that, I felt a huge wave of affection for her.

"Ploy, listen to me."

She looked up with those wide brown eyes.

"I've never been with a woman like you."

"I not real woman."

"Hey..." I reached out, loosening her hair, and it tumbled down over her shoulders. "To me, you are a really beautiful woman."

She smiled just barely. Her eyes held me with strong, magnetic power. Our gaze lasted for long moments.

"Probably you want babies," she told me. "I cannot do this."

"Let's slow down here." I squeezed her hands, breathing deeply. "I just want to tell you that all this is confusing for me. I want to be honest. But I'm really attracted to you. You're beautiful, you're sexy. You have this strength inside you. I mean, you are so strong. I don't really know you? But what I do know, I think you're really an amazing person. And I'm really, *really* attracted to you."

She looked into my eyes so deeply, so strongly, that I almost missed it. But the strange movement caught the corner of my eye. I looked down. Ploy's boner was rising up from out of the towel. My huge wave of affection was inspiring her huge erection. Pulsing slightly, thick and absurdly large, it pressed up through the part of the towel, head rising. Staring at it in fascination, my words trailed off.

"I like you," she said, voice a husky whisper.

250

I was stunned. I had never been in the room with a boner other than my own. I reached down and touched it. Strange. Both soft and thickly strong. I withdrew my hand. She was looking into my eyes and hadn't moved. I reached for the top of her towel. With the lightest of touches, I unwrapped the binding folds, letting it fall away.

Ploy had small breasts, like a pubescent girl. The nipples were brown on tiny cones of flesh. Below this was zero body fat and a fat boner. This thing was large. It curved slightly to the right, a strong snake of flesh, head visible and pulsing. Small, tight balls anchored the base. The entire unit was shaved clean. I caught scent and thought she might have perfumed it. Tentatively touching, I grasped and let it go, watching the thing boing back and forth. It didn't freak me out.

She moaned, kissed my throat, sniffed my skin, then reached with frantic, fumbling fingers for my belt. Staring intently at my crotch, she pulled at the leather. Yanking my pants down frantically, pulling everything to the floor she had me naked from the waist down. Her silken cascade of black, perfumed hair swept my skin. She leaned down moaning, thrusting me in her mouth. I watched the lips grip me, pulling expertly and had to push her shoulders, shove her away before I orgasmed. Smiling coyly she looked up beautifully, licking my shaft, her own dick hidden somewhere below.

"So big," she said, kissing my prick.

The slim body turned, butt tight and young, bounding up on the bed on her knees. Pressing her face to the mattress, she reached behind with both hands, pulling cheeks wide, baring her hole. It was like something out of a nature program. One animal presenting itself to another. The stark suddenness of it drained the eroticism entirely. All her feminine charms had vanished. The hair, the curves, the scent, the nails were obscured. Dangling man meat met my eyes. Looking at it, my hard on wavered, faded and confused.

"Condom," she whispered thickly, not moving, not seeing, not knowing my conflict. "My bag."

I fumbled for her bag by the bed, signals mixed, overwhelmed by scents, sights, motions that didn't match and never went together before. Managing the condom on, I stood behind her, poking and pressing, failing to enter. She moaned, grinding back into me. It didn't work. After a few fumbling, folded tries, I finally stopped.

"Sorry," I said, peeling off the condom, casting it off like a curse. "I can't."

She whipped her head around in a flash of black hair, eyes blazing in the dim room.

"What wrong?"

"I don't know," I said. "I don't know."

Riven with humiliation, I collapsed on the bed beside her. My dick looked shrunken and pathetically small. Hers was still huge. Shaking my head, I repeated myself.

"I don't know. I'm sorry."

Ploy spun frowning, eyes narrowed, staring at my dick. Her hand darted out. She reached down like she was testing mechanical equipment. Squeezing. Judging. It was done. There was no charge between us now. It had all gone away. Like some wild hurricane that had burst through the room, all the wild sexuality had vanished. We sat as two strangers in the dark. I looked at Ploy's angular shoulders and narrow waist. She wasn't a woman anymore. What had happened to the fascinating attraction of moments before? Trying to capture it, I reached for her shlong. It felt like a toy I had tired of. I wished I was drunk. I wanted to be away. Gone.

"You don't like me."

"I do like you," I said. "This is just something I haven't done before. It's just... different. Really different. I don't know."

"Why you say I don't know?" she shot back. "All you say I don't know. What you don't know?"

I reached out to put my arm around her bony shoulders. She shrugged it off. I sighed with exasperation. We lay in silence and then she turned in a fast spin. Laying her head on my chest, she stroked me silently. Fingers dancing optimistically on my gear, she tried to revive it to life.

*"What I supposed to do?"* she whispered. "Make me so horny. What I supposed to do? Hmmm?"

Stretching like some strange sphinx, Ploy moved her face right to mine, brows practically touching, brown eyes boring into mine. The throbbing boner slid against my thigh.

*"What I supposed to do?"* she repeated in a whisper.

Feeling more sympathetic the erotic, I started jerking her off. Dutifully remembering all the women who had given me blue balls in high school, I did what I could for the little ladyboy. She shut her eyes, pressing her body to mine. I yanked. I tugged. I felt wildly ineffective from this new, unknown angle. Ploy pressed her body, flexing and trying to orgasm. Then she slapped my hand away and sat beside me, drawing my head down.

"Here," she said hotly. "Here."

"No," I said, staring at the quivering wang.

*"What I supposed to do?"* she whispered tensely.

She pressed me to her small breasts.

"My tits. Lick my tits. Yes."

What the hell. It was better than sucking her dick. While I did, her hands shot down to her prick, pumping wildly. I watched the blurring rush of painted fingernails. Small hands pumped that huge wang. The irony made me question creation. That someone who wanted to be a woman would be given such a huge rod seemed wickedly cruel. There was no God. Not here. Who would make someone like this then set them free in the world, expecting them to bloom? I hated everything. She came.

"Yesssss!" Ploy hissed, lithe body arched, while the thinnest trail of white semen traced down over her red finger nailed hands.

It wasn't much at all. But then remembering the calendar she had showed me, I imagined the tap ran pretty frequently. Ploy collapsed back in the bed. She panted in satisfaction a moment. Then she whisked up and away, tiny body bounding towards the bathroom, grabbing all her things, slamming the door. The shower started. I frowned, totally confused, feeling used in ways that had eluded me in life up until now.

"What the fuck was *that?*" I heard myself say out loud.

Ploy heard too. The shower stopped. Wrapped in a towel, the lady-boy thrust the door open and put her head out.

"What you say?"

"Nothing."

"Tell me," she said sharply, head in profile, looking down in the darkness.

I didn't like her tone. I didn't answer.

"It not matter," she said. "You are the gay anyway."

Slipping her head back through the door, she slammed it shut.

For a moment, I was too stunned to respond. Then furiously I leapt to my feet. Reaching the bathroom door I banged hard with my fist.

"Open up!"

She did. Standing naked with her huge, draping penis, Ploy stared up insolently while casually drying her nuts.

"What do you mean by that?" I said.

"You want I fuck you," she told me. "You are the gay. That's what you like. That's why you not finish. You want I fuck you. You are the gay. All *falang* the gay."

Reaching out, she pushed the door shut.

I stood too confused to move or speak. Finally, the only thing I could come up with was grammatical.

"It's not 'the' gay. It's just gay."

The door opened and her head poked out.

"See, you say it. You are the gay."

The door slammed shut in my face.

The sudden roar of rage within me was startling. Never before had such fury throttled me. I wanted to murder her. Shred her things. In wild, whipping motions, I scanned the room. She had been ready for this. Ploy had taken everything inside the bathroom. Even her oversize shoes. With nothing to work with, I cursed.

"*Shit!* Little bitch!"

I lurched away, thrust my clothes on angrily. Pushing my legs into pants, I zipped them tight. Throwing on my shirt, I wrenched on the jacket. In my fury, I didn't notice her emerge. But she was there when I finished, simple dress neat, pearls on her neck, looking at her nails.

"Let's go," I told her.

Ploy didn't move. "What you pay me."

That took a minute to register. When it did, I had never been so mad. For the first time ever, I saw red. Staring at Ploy, it glowed like a murderous frame on the edges of vision. *Hustling little prick in a dress and pearls. Hurt her. Hit her. Hard.*

Breathing deeply, I fought it all back. I waited. I stood. Vision cleared. I spoke.

"You just whacked off and made me suck your tits. I am not paying you for that. *No Way.*"

"Don't be angry," she huffed. "Everybody so angry."

"Probably because you jerk off on people and call them gay!"

Ploy smoothed her dress tensely. "How much you pay me."

"But..! But..!"

Losing words, I struggled through the hours that had flashed past on the road. The wonderful emotions this little person had stirred up in me. Things I had missed. Things I had needed.

"I thought you liked me!" I yelled. "The bike? Eating? All that… that…the… *us?*"

My voice faded pathetically like my prick had before.

"I think you in Thailand long enough to understand this," she said. "How much you pay me?"

Her voice was strangely thick. The handbag clutched tight. Rock rigid on the bed, Ploy didn't look at me. Danger registered. Thais had an invisible line. Perhaps the most graciously accommodating people on the planet, their love of harmony made them let 90% of things slide. But that ten percent that didn't had the danger of triggering something wild. When that line was crossed, all bets were off. I had heard stories. Smashed apartments. Ruined lives. Grievous bodily harm exploding in frenzied, primal Thai freak out mode. In that dim, tense hotel room, I sensed the line in Ploy, growing sharper every second.

When crossed, I imagined anything was possible. I didn't know Ploy. What little I did know wasn't good. Born a pretty dude who wanted to wear dresses. Hit by everyone. Leaving at 12 to survive. Three guesses on how that was done. Surviving it all to face a lifetime of smirks. Ending up on some jackass Brit's fuck calendar. All that fury bottled up. I sensed it simmering in that little person. I imagined it unleashed in this hotel in the middle of Laos. All she needed was a target. She deserved one. But wouldn't get one. Unless people like me showed up to stand in. Breathing deeply, I tried hard to take the edge from my voice, backing down.

"I don't have Thai money."

"American money OK."

She didn't look at me. She was trembling. I recognized someone trying to restrain themselves with all the control they possessed.

"All I have is hundreds," I said.

"Why you disrespect me?" She whipped her face to glare at me, brown eyes blazing. *"You think I cheap?"*

The fury I had felt was entirely eclipsed by what raged in those eyes. Moments before I had never been so angry. Now I had never seen such anger. The depths of it frightened me. There was something in those eyes I would never, ever understand. Something to step slowly, cautiously away from. But I didn't want to. Staring at the little person in the dress, all my anger washed away. In swooping misery, I felt totally sorry for Ploy. So tremendously, achingly sorry. For a crazy minute I wanted to hug her. I wanted to start again. I had a driving, thundering urge not to fuck her but to love her. Strong and as hard as I could. It struck me that I had never seen someone who needed it more. And someone least likely to find it. Or hold onto it, should the stuff ever arrive.

"Ploy," I sighed. "Can we—"

"One hundred US fine," She cut me off, staring straight ahead. "OK then we go."

I stood with her in the dim room. The little body was rigid and cold, withdrawn someplace I wouldn't reach. So I reached into my suit pocket. Ladyboy Man had filled it with bills. I took out a hundred and held it between us.

"Thank you," she said, nodding towards the bed beside her.

I stepped forward and laid it down. Then I backed away. Picking up the money she stood swiftly. Tucking the bill into her hand bag, Ploy ran hands imperiously through her black mane, shaking it behind her, smoothing it out. Adjusting her dress, eyes cold, she looked up at me.

"We go now?"

There was nothing in those eyes for me. Nothing I could do for them. Nothing I would change.

"Sure Ploy," I said. "We go now."

**I followed Ploy's calculated stride down the hall.** In exchange for the room key I received the clerk's smirk of disdain. Outside was a different world. Light had left the sky. No colorful balloons floating magically. Gone were gorgeous greens and shimmering, faraway rivers. Draped in descending dusk, the landscape shifted with shadows. Ploy rode without touching me. Slipping on the back, she held herself secure by gripping the seat. I drove fast, flashing past the string of hotels on the ridge. Any of them would be fine. I didn't stop driving. I needed something to do. I wanted distance from that room of confusion and fumbled consummation. Escape from strange sadness and rage.

"Not stop here. *Falang* no good."

She said it before I saw them. My eyes flicked to the rearview, where Ploy's hair danced wildly in the wind. Her narrowed gaze was staring towards the road ahead. I looked forward and saw the cluster of battered Chicken cars parked by a gnarled tree twenty meters from the road. High grass rippled in wind and a shadowed old hotel loomed beyond. An open door cast slashes of light into the gathering darkness.

"*Yes*" I said in relief. "Chicken 65."

Throttling down, I slowed to a stop behind the cars. From the hotel I heard rough laughter and shouting.

"No," Ploy said. "*Falang* no good. We go."

"Just wait here a sec," I said, getting off the bike.

"I no like," she said.

"Too bad," I told her. "Wait."

"*Falang* no good," she repeated.

"Whatever," I shot back, walking away.

I had hardly left the shoulder before the engine roared behind me. Spinning in the gravel, I saw Ploy with a determined frown, turning the bike around.

"Hey!" I shouted, running back towards her. "Wait!"

The Ladyboy punched it. Leaning forward in her little white dress, black hair flew as she shot towards Vang. Vanishing around a curve, engine faded in descending night, leaving me stranded. Crickets chirped. I stood disoriented in the night.

Then a strange noise floated towards me from the hotel. Loud, rhythmic and clapping, it spilled out from the half open door. Rough laughter followed. Crossing the road, I headed towards the slash of light spilling out onto the hotel porch. Following the winding path that lead to the building, the strange clapping sound pulled me forward. Hard to place, it struck me as oddly familiar. Chirring crickets filled the night. Shouting grew louder, followed by mocking laughter. A bottle shattered. Closer now, I saw shadows of men in profile through the half open door. The flat, heavy clapping was loud and insistent. Rowdy British jeers chanted with it in time:

> *"No one likes us!*
> *No one likes us!*
> *No one likes us!*
> *We don't care!"*

Slowly I mounted creaky steps. Spilled liquor and hash smoke floated in the night. Hiding from view, I looked into the room.

A white naked ass was pounding into a drunken woman on the dirty floor. Racers cheered every loud, slapping thrust of the man. Brown thighs stretched wide around him. An old, wrinkled face shot up shining over his hairy shoulder, grinning hideously with missing teeth. Red faced Lao women clapped and laughed drunken by the TV. Bottles tipped from the nearby table, spilling liquor. Rolling metal pieces tinkled to the ground. The bullets didn't register until I saw the guns. With them were bags of white dust and piles of playing cards. Children's toys were scattered just beyond a sunken sofa. A child's head darted up from behind it, eyes wide, then disappeared fast. Yells, jeers and chaos thundered all around, while thrown money rained down on the fucking couple.

*"He won't finish!"*

*"Too drunk, I tell you!"*

*"Ten to one!"*

*"TWENTY!"*

Turning from the noxious scene, a hard hand clamped my arm. Yanked roughly from the door, I was pulled into shadows then slammed into the outside wall. Before me, the short Irish racer grinned. Bats dipped erratically in the night beyond him.

"What have we here?"

Sharp suspicion carved his craggy, weather beaten features. White hair, slicked and combed, topped a pair of piercing pale blue eyes. Half one eyebrow was missing from a faint scar. Decades of cigarettes emanated like pungent, thick cologne. Pushing forward, he pinned my chest with his forearm.

"Just leaving," I said, struggling with the rough wall at my back.

The grim racer leaned in, elbow grinding precisely. Pain stabbed down my side. I cried out, shouts lost in thundering, drunken cheers from the mayhem inside. Shadows bobbed and danced on the harsh slash of light at our feet. Cold sweat bloomed all over my body.

"Nobody leaves who seen how we run," he told me in thick brogue. "You got yourself a new race now, lad. You're with us."

The short, powerful man stepped back. Pressure on my chest let up. The sharp snap of a struck match flared. Rough hands cupped a cigarette. Dancing flame illuminated the Irishman's craggy face. Pale blue eyes held mine, quietly violent. Thick, nicotine stained fingers shifted his cigarette. The black, tattooed dot between his thumb and forefinger was barely visible. But I saw it and had seen one before. Memory triggered of the border. A crewcut Eastern European, seized in silent concert by iron Thai hands. *Tell Mickey Stiches Vlad got pinched at the border.* Heart hammering, I forced my voice calm.

"Mickey I know what happened to Vlad."

Lurching forward, he slammed me into the wall. His voice was frighteningly low.

"Hell you know my name?" The cigarette danced on his lips. "Where's Vlad?"

"Chicken Promise." My eyes darted right and left, staring into his. "I'll tell you for a Chicken Promise."

The Irishman's hand shot out of sight. There was a flicking noise. Blurring fast it stopped right before my eye. Too close to see, I sensed the blade just breaths away.

"Take your bleeding eye out I will," Mickey said calmly. "Good with me knife. *Talk.*"

My whole body froze. Behind us, the hotel room erupted in rhythmic shouts, feet stomping floor in time with slapping flesh. The chant returned, loud voices shaking the walls:

> *"No one likes us!*
> *No one likes us!*
> *No one likes us!*
> *We don't care!"*

"This is Chicken 65," I finally managed through clenched teeth. "I want a Chicken Promise."

For a long hard moment, he looked at me. Chanting filled our ears. Floorboards shook beneath our feet. Then Mickey stepped back, flicking his knife shut with a flourish.

"So be it. Road rules. Talk."

Rubbing my neck, stunned to be let go, I cleared my throat and told him.

"I was with him at the border. He got pulled out of the immigration line by five cops. He told me to tell Mickey Stiches Vlad got pinched at the border. Tell him to watch out."

"Shite." he murmured. "Be waiting for me at the border they will."

Arms folded, stroking his chin, the compact man didn't move. Mickey stood looking at me while bats looped erratically in darkness just beyond. Moments passed tensely while he stared.

"Got yer car sorted didya with all the gear the mark and flaps and that didya?"

I struggled to decipher his words; brogue so thick I hardly understood.

"Yeah, we won The Splits," I nodded. "That's what we got."

Stepping forward, his arm reached up and slapped my shoulder. "Well that's old Mickey's ride out of town. You'll be rolling meself and some gear into Bangkok for me then. Come now. Say hello to the lads."

He started forward toward the bawdy chaos but I didn't move.

"I want my promise."

Spinning sharply, the short man frowned. "The fook you want then?"

"To walk away. Right now. That's your promise and we're good."

A roaring cheer went forth as the couple on the filthy hotel floor finally finished. The Irishman stared me down, eyes pale fire. Then he spit on the floor.

"Then walk you ladyboy ponce fuck." Raising a finger, he pointed. "We'll find you down the road."

With a shove, Mickey launched me down the stairs. Fumbling, half falling, I heard the hotel door slam shut behind me. Leaving him behind I ran. Stumbling through the winding path, lost in thick darkness, crickets pierced the night. Swooping bats looped in. I ducked, lurching forward to find the road. My feet hit pavement. I ran panting in the moonlight until burning lungs made me stop. Exhausted then, I walked alone. But not for long.

When headlights lit up slowly from behind I wasn't surprised. My shadow hit the road and stretched. The Chicken Promise hadn't meant shit. Running was pointless. They had me. This was my Chicken. It would be ugly. I wondered how I would survive their movable beast. What happened? Things had started in sunshine with laughs. Bikini girls drinking Bellinis poolside. We had wanted to leave them all behind. Find something real. I had thought real Fun. I had pictured real Good. But Bad was just as real. I hadn't thought of that. Forgot death was real, too. Maybe never knew. Things were happening too fast to learn. Fate thrown down, Karma handed out, all of it blurring in a whirl. We all had our Chicken and mine was out there to find. Blindly, I trudged towards it. Behind me, blazing headlights shot my shadow down the lonely road. I didn't stop walking. The car pulled up alongside. It idled while rolling, engine finely tuned.

"Want to grab some chicken?"

I looked up.

Monteblan was driving and Pablo Cruise gleamed.

**Robotic with shock, I walked numbly round the car.** Wind kicked up from the cliffs. Long grass rippled and whipped. My hand felt the familiar handle of Pablo Cruise. Pulling open the door I stared at the red and black leather bucket seat. Twin seatbelt straps draped down vertically. I stared them without understanding.

"That's the five point harness from Gears," Monteblan told me. "Put it on like a shirt. Slip your arms through... there you go."

Both arms through the straps, I buckled them together with the band that crossed my hips. Securely fixed, Monteblan shifted into first. The body armor was back, along with his helmet. He wore his madras shorts. There was a beer between his legs.

"New clutch is butter."

The car had been cleaned, inside and out. More beers sat chill in the back. Rolling down the window, I let rushing wind tousle my hair. Watched headlights push through late night darkness. Monteblan eased through gears, gaining speed.

"You OK there, Asser?"

I didn't say anything. We drove a while. Sparse traffic passed in the night. Trucks. Empty bus. Flocks of Scooters. Laos unfolded with cliffs to the right, high stone walls to the left, curves of nothing for a long time. I stared at darkness unthinking, then heard myself speak.

"I touched a penis and someone put a knife in my eye."

The engine hummed.

"Want to talk about it?"

"Yes, I do. With a therapist for five years. Right now, a beer will do."

Monteblan fished around with his free hand, finding a beer. I opened it gratefully, drinking long and deep.

"Got drugs, too." Monteblan sipped from his can. "Opium if we wreck, weed if we're bored. Passed on the mushrooms."

"Good call," I nodded. "Got pretty gooey out there. Sorry about being God and all."

He shrugged. "Shit happens."

I finished the beer and found another. "How was your day?"

"Decent." Relaxed in his driving seat, chilled in control, Monteblan recalled his afternoon. "Slept in the ride. Had a Ladyboy score narcotics. Paid some kid to clean the car. Bought a CB."

Reaching from the gearshift, my friend tapped a flat black box fixed to the dashboard. Dials of numbers showed on the front. A coil of wire like old telephone cord lead to a hand held talk piece, clipped to the side.

"Pretty much all the Chicken has one. Different bandwidths. Found Gears and Moist. They're still back in Vang. Trouble with the intake valve."

His words danced past me, meaningless. I gazed ahead at the winding road that wasn't moving fast enough. I turned to my friend.

"I really want to get out of Laos."

"Sure buddy." Monteblan punched the gas. Needles danced on the dash. "You kinda have to get out of Laos, actually."

Pablo picked up speed whining high before dropping into low, satisfied growls. Blurring through turns we raced into darkness.

"I thought I just had to get out of Vang?"

"There was some action in the garage after you left. Microstache Lao dudes showed up. Weird scene. Ladyboy Man handled it. Told me to get you over the border tonight."

We drove in silence for a while.

"Who put a knife in your eye?" my friend asked me.

"Mickey Stiches. Runs with those Brit thugs we met in Bangkok."

"Shit." Monteblan took a sip from his beer. "It wasn't his penis, was it?"

I turned with a frown. "What?"

"You said you touched a penis and someone put a knife in your eye."

"Two separate instances," I said. "Unrelated entirely."

"So how was the dick?"

"I'm not talking about that."

He grinned a little. "Ploy was smiling when she came back to the garage."

"What did she say?"

"What was it?" Monteblan stroked his beard, squinting to remember. "Oh, right: *scooter you.*"

"Dude!" I called out loudly. "She did *not* scooter me."

"Relax." Monteblan laughed. "She was dropping off the bike. Parked it next to Pablo and said 'scooter you'. That's all."

I slumped back in my seat, staring grimly ahead at the road. "How long till we're out of Laos?"

"It's this road for a while, then we hang a right. Want to check the maps?"

Thrusting my hand into the pocket on the passenger door, I pulled out a fistful of maps. Scattered pages flapped wildly in the rushing wind. I rolled up my window, seeing the dimly curved reflection of my dirt streaked suit. Brushing off dust, I shot my cuffs and tried to order our erratic charts. Yanking through the pages, shifting through

Thailand, Vietnam and Laos, I hunted for bearings in the bleak glow of dashboard lights. My eyes just stared. Color coded grids, numbered margins, thin print, triangular mountain symbols… The abstraction of our landscape failed to process. My day had been too real. Thrusting them messily into erratic sections, I shoved the pages back.

Holding my chin, gazing darkly ahead at the winding road, I felt the nudge of something cold hit my arm. I looked down to see Monteblan handing me a fresh beer.

"Have another brew. Don't sweat the maps. We'll find it."

Taking the beer gratefully, I watched him shift smoothly, gunning the gas to overtake a rumbling truck. Floating past the large, half rusted beast, I vaguely wondered if our *Serpico* mud flaps were getting us cred with the driver. He tooted his horn and I imagined that meant they did. Monteblan beeped back, raising a hand in the rearview then sliding back into our empty lane. Winding cliff side road unfurled ahead. He smiled.

"What?" I said.

"Are you 100% sure that you are not going to talk about the Thai ladyboy you just banged?"

"How about we talk about your humiliating prison shit instead?"

He shrugged. "Had to go."

"You were crying."

"Tears of relief."

"Too bad," I drank more beer. "I was hoping to mine your personal trauma instead of my own."

"It was traumatic?"

I tried to recall the furious whirl of strangeness that had been Ploy. "More like confusing."

"She do you?"

"No! She didn't do me."

"Blow her?"

"The fuck! What do you think I am?"

"Well…" he moved his head side to side.

"What?" I pressed.

"Mmmmmm…." he debated. "Nothing."

"That's not the Nothing Noise," I said, testily. "That's the Should I Say This Noise. Say it."

He sighed. "I just wouldn't be surprised. Nobody would, really. I mean, everybody kinda just thinks you're gay, you know?"

"No, I don't know this." Straightening up in my seat, I turned to look at Monteblan directly. "Who's everyone?"

"People we know? Like everyone? I mean, not like they care, or they make fun of you, they just figure you are."

"I'm not gay! She was all over me! I've been lonely out here. Alone all year. And that shit in Vang? I was shook the hell up. She took advantage of me. I was… vulnerable."

Monteblan laughed. "He's not gay, he's just vulnerable."

"I mean it!"

"Best line ever!" My friend laughed louder, pounding the wheel. "I almost want to blow a dude and have Rayne walk in, just so I can take the dick out of my mouth and say: 'I'm not gay, babe. Just vulnerable.'"

"Go to hell," I had to laugh some. "And as far this *everyone* you're talking about. Please. American dudes are paranoid that every guy is gay. You try and meet someone for a beer, he thinks you're gay."

"Why would you ask a dude for a drink?" He frowned. "I'd think you're gay."

"Work! Networking! New friends, you know? It's this whole attitude in America! If you're different, they say you're gay! You're not married, you're gay! Tuck in your shirt and know who Renoir is, people think you take it up the ass!"

"I know who Renoir is, nobody thinks I juggle nuts."

"Do you tuck in your shirt?"

"Got a point there." He pulled from his beer and burped. "Was she hung?"

"You're not going to let this go, are you?"

"Nope." Monteblan shook his head. "We got lotsa road and you just fucked a dude in a dress. Give it up."

I looked out the window. Half embarrassed, half relieved to speak. Then I shrugged, drank more beer, and told him.

"First of all, Ploy wasn't a dude. I don't know what she was. They are not women, and they are not men. Something entirely different. Like, spiritual imprint? Genetic identity? No idea. That was some different shit."

"Come on," Monteblan said. "She had balls. There had to be one point when you were like: this is a dude."

"Yes." Nodding, I recalled the moment. "When she left right after coming."

"Rub one out for her?"

"I tried. Wasn't that good."

"What are you talking about? It's a dick. Been practicing with one your whole life."

"That was someone else's dick. Big difference."

"Was it big?"

"Pretty damn large."

"That had to be weird. Like, your girl's dick is bigger than yours?"

"Probably a support group for that."

"And you couldn't wack her off?"

"The angle is everything. Imagine having to drive while sitting on the dashboard facing backwards. Challenging maneuver." I shook my head. "I sympathize for every lame hand job I had from old girlfriends."

"So she's not going to be your girlfriend?"

"Ploy?" Cliffs raced past in the darkness. "Are you kidding?"

"I don't know." My friend shrugged. "Gotta have its upsides. Like a chick you can jerk off with when you don't feel like having sex? That wouldn't be bad."

"I know. I half went into it hoping the shit might work. Some alternative to what women put you through."

"Yeah, you were in a bad place with that when you left the States. Sent me those links of girls falling down and breaking their legs."

"Hot Girl Fails." I corrected him. "No one broke their legs. You make it sound sadistic. It's a comedy genre. I'm not alone. Those videos have millions of hits. It's funny watching hot girls fuck up. Slipping off yachts, twerking on kitchen counters and falling into the sink, farting during yoga, whatever. I was watching lots of them before I left the States."

"Why?"

"I just got sick of them always winning." I shrugged. "You don't get what it's like out there now. You and Rayne met young, been together forever, you're set. But it's not just dating. It's the whole thing for dudes these days."

"What whole thing?"

He took a curve with high speed panache. We emerged into empty straightaway. Dark shadows of mountains loomed to our left. The cliff fell off right. I stared into nothing.

"Everything," I finally said. "I don't know where to start."

"Hit me, come on."

"What? Everything. Like the girl who sat next to me in our last job in New York. Remember her? Wore the shirt that said *Boys Make Nice Pets*?

"She was a twat."

"We would have gotten fired if we wore a *Girls Make Nice Pets* shirt. She got compliments."

"Probably didn't pull any decent dick. Who'd fuck a chick wearing that shit?"

"They all wear that shit! Their entire wardrobe is telling them how great they are. Shirts with *Goddess*, and *Hot* and *Pretty* all over it. Imagine getting to walk around wearing advertisements for how awesome you are? What about us? How far would I get wearing a shirt that said *Handsome* or *Strong* before I got punched in the face?"

Monteblan thought a moment. "Half a block in New York. Maybe two in L.A."

"LA! Please, West Coast is even worse! You know that burning man thing? That festival in the desert?"

"Little hippie for me." He slowed slightly as an oncoming truck barreled past. "Never went. Why?"

"Did you ever think about the name? Burning Man. Because it's perfectly acceptable to light a man on fire and watch him burn. How long would Burning Woman last?"

"Come on, where are you going with this?"

"Seriously man, every feminist in the planet would be in the desert with bullhorns. They'd shut that shit down. You can't burn a woman. But you can burn a man. Burn a man and cheer it on! Charge tickets! It's all fun and games! That's what we're here for! What about war movies?"

We shot past a trio of scooters, entire families dangling from each. Swallowed in darkness they vanished behind us.

"What about war movies?" Monteblan said.

"Burning men! Blown up men! Stabbed men! Trampled men! Men getting ripped up, eviscerated, shot from the sky, flamed alive and dismembered!"

"That's just the movies man. And war is war."

"Fine, but how many women have you seen graphically murdered in the movies? When's the last time you saw a bunch of women just mown the fuck down? Your whole life, you probably saw ten of them get rubbed out on film."

"Slasher movies."

"Point well taken." I raised a finger. "But those are singular murders. When men get murdered, it's like a harvest. And the baseline for family entertainment. Slasher films are a genre. Speaking of genres, let's talk about Man Impaled."

"What's this?"

"Every action movie today has a scene where a man gets impaled with a piece of something. Then he has to pull it out. Sadistic fucking scenes where a dude is sweating and trying not to scream while pulling a piece of a car out of his thigh. *Every* fucking movie. Probably fucked up homoerotic shit. Who knows. But I'm sick of watching movies with men getting painfully impaled then brutally unimpaling themselves."

"Watch TV then."

"You can't! TV today is like The Broken Man Channel. There's not one show with a dialed dude just nailing shit. They're all conflicted and tragically flawed."

Monteblan turned and just looked at me. His eyebrow raised.

"OK, fine. So I'm conflicted and tragically flawed. But what about dudes who aren't? They're out there. Where's their shows? Why can't we just see dialed dudes nailing shit?"

"Simple solution." Monteblan swigged some beer. "Don't think so much."

"That's what the girl with the penis told me."

"Maybe she had something there."

"She *did* have something there. It was huge. Now listen…"

Turning in my seat to face him, I made my final point.

"So what if you grow up as a girl, watching a bunch of movies of men getting mowed down or impaled. I mean, countless thousands of men being murdered or beaten up before your young impressionable eyes. Then TV shows of them all broken and fucked up and ruined.

What do you grow up thinking if you're a girl? I'll tell you what you think: *Those are the ones that die and do things for me."*

Monteblan didn't answer. He drove.

"Well, think about them for a second," he finally said. "They don't have it easy."

"Aha! And that's the other thing. When dudes talk about women, there's always a guy who comes in and sticks up for them. I have it on fact, from *five* ex-girlfriends that no woman ever does that for a dude. None! It's like betrayal of the sisterhood."

"Do you want to let me at least say what I was going to say?"

"If you want to," I moped.

"A little pissy there, Asser."

"What do you want? There was a boner in my hands two hours ago. It wasn't mine and I'm a little rattled."

Folding my arms, I sat back in my seat, looking out the window. Then I looked back at my friend.

"Sorry for being a dick. Today fucked me up. What were you going to say?"

Some road went by.

"What I was going to say…" Monteblan softly resumed. "Was that this whole thing we're rolling on now? Chicken 65? A woman couldn't do this. They can't. They'd be like all freaked out about getting raped. We have more freedom."

"To get thrown in jail," I told him. "Sniped at or chained to the wall while people shove a knife in your eye."

"Race against Gears kinda kicked ass."

"Mmm." I nodded slightly. "OK."

"Mushrooms were fun till we met Earl the banana hammock guy. Holy shit, that trip? And how good did Freddie Hubbard *Sky Dive* sound when you finally put it on?"

I smiled at the memory of the first notes. "Amazing."

"And how about Freddie Hubbard? Where's the bad ass woman jazz lady? All the good music is made by dudes jamming. Imagine if every record you ever put on that rocked was made by women. Wouldn't you feel lame? Like: *Oh shit—they can do that and I can't?* They can't. Give them five hundred years of feminism and free guitar lessons and they *still* won't bang out anything to beat Led Zeppelin."

"I think you got something."

"What I got is this..." He drank his beer and crushed the can. "Dudes rock. Women rule. Let them. I'd rather rock than rule."

Tossing the can into the back, he stepped on the gas. Pablo Cruise raced faster. Flying through the night. I scrambled for some injustice to counter his logic.

"But... But..."

"But nothing!" Monteblan raised his voice over the rushing wind. "Butt fuck a ladyboy! Rent a 'ho! You got options out here, bro. And who cares about some twat in the West Village with her *I'm Hot* shirt. Look at this."

I turned to look. My friend kicked back, driving expansively.

"I'm wearing a flak jacket with a bullet in it, driving around with a beer in my hand. You've got a tailored suit and there's opium in the back plus weed that you will not *believe*. We got thirty five grand in the trunk and I can hit a buck seventy five and nobody's doing shit about it since we got Joe Pesci mud flaps!" He concluded with a triumphant grin. "This *rocks*."

"Al Pacino," I corrected, grinning with him.

"He rocks too!"

"Mud flaps, I mean. They're from *Serpico*."

"I don't care if they're from Syria! This is the shit, man." He pr' the gas harder and we flew. "Chicken 65 rocks. Don't think '

"That's what she said," I reminded him.

"Who?"

I reached in back for beers. "The ladyboy I tried to jerk off."

"Is that where this started?"

"I told you I didn't want to talk about it."

"Next time I won't press."

The CB crackled:

*"Grimace? This is Seoul Brother, do you copy? Over."*

We both jumped at the sound. Sudden, unfamiliar static filled the car. Monteblan reached down, unhinged the mouth piece and spoke.

"Grimace. Go."

Lights flicked behind us, hitting our rearview.

*"We're right behind you. Saw the Serpicos. Moon won't shut up about it. He should tell you, over."*

There was a break of static.

*"Grimace? It's Moon. Over."*

"What's up player? Over."

There was a long, static silence.

*"I want to blow up your thermos. Over."*

Monteblan didn't press in the speech button. He turned to me instead.

"That sounds really gay."

"See!" I shouted, exasperated. "All he wants to do is blow up your thermos and you think it's homo."

"What? Might be Korean gay slang. Some guy said he wants to blow up my thermos. It's weird."

*"Grimace? Do you read me? We have dynamite. You have the Hideki. We can make history here. Over."*

"Yeah, roger that Moon. Just discussing with my map man, over." Holding the receiver against his body armor, Monteblan turned to me. "What do you think?"

"I really want to get out of Laos."

"Could be cool. People shoot them online. Never saw someone blow up a Hideki 3000. Never lit dynamite before, either. Probably fun."

"Don't I *have* to get out of Laos?"

"Go out with a bang," Monteblan said. "Let's pull a Chicken Promise from these clowns. What do you think?"

"Didn't he blow up an elephant? That's the story about him."

"There's stories about everyone." Monteblan shrugged. "But you had a rough day. I mean, girl with a penis and all. If you don't want to blow up my thermos I understand."

I frowned. "What does that have to do with anything?"

"You told me you were traumatized because her wang was bigger than yours."

"That's not why I was traumatized!" I told him. "There was a lot more to my day. Death, knives, people—"

"People fucking on the floor, right I heard you. Blow up a thermos. Take your mind off things. Come on. It'll be fun."

His eyes held mine in the pale light of the car.

"OK," I agreed. "I'll watch. Just don't die."

"I don't die blowing up thermoses." Monteblan raised the CB receiver. "Affirmative, Moon. For a Chicken Promise. Let's light this candle."

We didn't get an answer. Just Moon's ecstatic woops through the CB, so loud they made the speakers break up. Then Monteblan was pulling over, slowing to a stop on the crumbling shoulder of the old, poorly paved mountain road.

**The Koreans pulled up from some future dimension that could only have been imagined in the 1970s.** The entire front of their classic car was slanted glass. An angled machine of various planes, it looked like origami made from credit cards. Rolling to a stop, opera music cut ignominiously short. The doors went up, winged and silent, sighing like some pristine goddess revealing rich leather interior. Moon leapt out wearing a racing suit of blue and silver, custom made and scripted *Moon*. His huge, excited grin beamed happiness. The tall Korean darted towards us with hands held up for high fives.

"Dudes we're doing this!"

Slapping fives, he laughed wildly, enthusiasm total and instantly contagious. Seoul brother slipped out from the other side of their machine, hair a gel masterpiece, lime green sweater vest, red framed glasses large.

"Chicken 65."

"Chicken 65." Monteblan returned the salute. "Nice Bertone."

"Thanks," Seoul Brother said. "Useless in Laos. Thing's fiberglass. Splits nearly ripped it in half. We did the whole thing at like, 20."

"Heard you won The VV Splits before," Monteblan said.

"Yeah," Moon nodded. "Had the Lancia Stratos that year."

"'75?" Monteblan asked.

"I wish," Moon said. "'74."

"Still the shit." Monteblan nodded. "Independent suspension."

"Yup. Part jet, half tank. Loved that car. Wrecked it on Phetchaburi Road." He frowned remembering, then lit up smiling. "Let's blow up your thermos."

"Yeah, umm, away from the cars?" Seoul Brother suggested

"Give the bird some air?" Moon suggested.

"Right." Seoul Brother reached into the back of the car, pulling out the bird cage from Vang. The bird inside fluttered nervously while the styled Korean set it on the roof. Smirking as he walked to the trunk, he explained.

"Moon wants to rack up more karma before we let it go."

"Karma's real!" Moon protested. "My cousin!"

"What happened to your cousin?" I asked.

"Drink?" Seoul Brother offered.

Standing behind their car, he raised a bottle of black label whiskey. Monteblan and I walked down the empty road to join him. The trunk held a velvet case with four highball glasses. A small bucket of ice chilled beside it. Next to that was a dusty wooden crate, half filled with loose sticks of dynamite. Seoul Brother took ice with tongs, dropping them pinging in a glass and poured my drink.

"Thanks. Nice bar car." I turned to Moon. "What about your cousin and karma?"

Moon dashed over, absently snatching the Black Label as Seoul Brother was pouring Monteblan's drink. Seoul Brother stared at his now empty hand.

"Not like I was pouring a drink or anything."

"Oh!" Moon froze. "Were you? Sorry!"

"No sweat," Monteblan said. "Had lots of beer anyway. Tell us the karma thing."

Drinking straight from the bottle, Moon wiped his mouth then shook his head. "Sad story. My cousin is crazy. *Was*."

"And stupid rich," Seoul Brother. "One of the top five families in Korea."

"Top Three," Moon said. "When he was 15 he wanted a Lambo. And my uncle says no."

Finished with the whiskey, he set it on the roof.

"So my cousin is real mad and takes one of my uncle's birds. He collects them. Tropical, endangered, flown in from Costa Rica, Africa, everywhere. My cousin takes my uncle's favorite bird and throws it in the drier. Kills it since he can't have his Lambo. My uncle is like, OK, I'm frightened. You can have your car. Buys my cousin the Lambo. Has it one week. Full of friends flips it off the highway. Flips 18 times. In flames. They have it on CCTV. All over the internet. Everybody in Korea knows it. All his friends die except him. He's alive but totally paralyzed. All he can do now is blink. He's lying in my uncle's house staring at the ceiling and blinking. That's his life. Can't even kill himself. Family said it's karma. Like that bird he killed? It flipped over and over burning up in the drier. That's *exactly* what happened to him in the Lambo. Nice five points man!"

Moon had drifted over to Pablo Cruise and pointed out the new harnesses on our seats.

"I have to get out of Laos," I reminded Monteblan.

"So what about getting this thermos blown?" Monteblan called out.

"Yeah!" Moon beamed excitedly. "Let's find the right place!"

Waving my friend to join, the tall Korean jogged up the road. Monteblan followed and Seoul Brother reached for the whiskey on the roof.

"Asser, I need a favor," he said, refilling my glass.

"What's up?"

"Umm… this dynamite?"

I eyed the box of old, dusty sticks.

"If I don't get it away from Moon, he's going to blow up everything between here and Bangkok. Would you, like, add it to the Chicken Promise? Tell him you want the dynamite? He won't say no. All he's been talking about since Vang is blowing up that thermos. He's obsessed."

"I don't think I want a box of dynamite." I said.

"Just leave it on the side of the road, then. You can do that. I can't. He'll never let it go. But if I don't get it away from him he'll blow shit up all Chicken."

"Well…" I said.

"Do you want a separate Chicken Promise?"

"How about a trade?" I said, raising my glass. "I like this blend. Throw in what's left of that Black Label and we're on."

Seoul Brother smiled. "Done."

We clinked cheers as Moon came bounding back.

"You know about the Hideki, right?" He said to me, beaming with excitement. "Indestructible! They shoot them! Throw them off cliffs. It's all over the thermosnet."

"Thermosnet?" I said.

"Thermos sites on the internet. There's so many!" Bent over the trunk now, Moon rooted through the dynamite, inspecting different sticks like fruit in the market. "We're on all the same boards! Grimace and me. We didn't know it but now we do! This is history. We're going to blow up a Hideki 3000."

Emerging with his dynamite, Moon flipped the stick twirling in a circle. Catching it smartly, he started up the road. Monteblan was rooting in Pablo Cruise for the thermos. I felt a nudge from Seoul Brother and called out after his driver

"Hey, Moon!"

Moon turned, grinning while flipping the dynamite and walking backwards. "What's up Asser?"

"That thermos is everything to him. I want more for it."

The tall Korean stopped in his tracks. "You're getting a Chicken Promise. That's huge."

"Throw in the dynamite," I said. "You blow up the Hideki, we get a Chicken Promise and the box of dynamite, too."

"Sure!" His big grin returned. "I have long range mortars waiting for me in Cambodia."

Spinning again, the towering driver loped up towards Monteblan, slapping him on the back as my friend showed him the thermos.

"We have to get the kick right." I heard Moon tell him. "We want to blow it up. Like, *up*. In the sky."

"There's stuff in it," Monteblan told him. "Should we dump it?"

"No, leave it in!" Moon said excitedly. "Stuff in it is good! Real world conditions."

Dynamite and thermos in hand, the racers walked up the deserted road. We followed their forms melting into the darkness, searching for a suitable roadside patch. Before us on the Bertone, Moon's karma bird fluttered its wings. I turned to Seoul Brother.

"Did he blow up an elephant?"

"Ummm...yeah." Seoul Brother swirled his scotch. "But there's blowing up an elephant, and there's blowing up an elephant. Nobody tells the whole story."

"So what's the whole story?"

"Well, we were—

***BOOM!***

Like some massive, slamming hammer, dynamite pounded the night. Light flashed and I cringed instinctively. Seoul Brother spilled his scotch. Up ahead, dirt rained down on the pavement. Dust cleared. Moon's laughter howled. Monteblan faint voice floated in the air.

*"Where's the Hideki?"*

Strange, crumbling sounds of shifting earth drowned out any answer. Ground trembled. The karma bird fluttered and jumped nervously in its cage. Peering fearfully through the night, I watched Monteblan and Moon rushing towards us from the blast site. Faces white with fear, bounding full speed, they outran huge clouds of dust blooming in their wake. Flat impacts of falling stone crumbled with groaning earth. Outrunning the shaking chaos, our panicked friends flew past us breathless. The rumble slowly faded. Silent country night returned. Seoul Brother and I exchanged looks. Together, we walked cautiously up the road.

Then we couldn't anymore.

Dynamite had undone the pavement like some giant biting off a mouthful of road. The jagged edge of a ragged sink hole stopped just ten feet short of Pablo Cruise. Concrete torn, dirt exposed, the hole stretched long as a tennis court. With stunned eyes, we watched the last pieces of pavement slide on rivers of shifting dirt, crumbling into the dark void below. Monteblan and Moon, breathing heavily, joined us at the edge of the chasm. We all looked at each other.

"That's the road out of Laos," Seoul Brother said.

"I have to get out of Laos," I told them.

"How are you going to get out of Laos?" Moon said.

"Where's my thermos?" Monteblan asked.

*Ponk!*

The sharp, metallic impact hit the road just behind us. Jumping in shock, we turned as one. Slightly smoking, the indestructible Japanese thermos rolled in a lazy circle on the pavement. Spellbound, we turned to each other in awe.

"There is one perfect thing in this world," Monteblan said softly. "The Hideki 3000 thermos."

"That was in space." Seoul Brother looked up. "Did that just go up in space?"

Moon was too overwhelmed to speak. Eyes wide, he held both hands to his head as if it might fly off his body.

Then static hissed from Pablo Cruise, as a familiar, heavy accent crackled through the CB.

*"Grimace? Asser? Do you copy? Over."*

"Gears," I said, moving towards the car.

Behind me, Moon finally broke from his stunned astonishment.

"YESSSS!!!!"

Reaching Pablo Cruise, I turned to see the Korean racer fist pumping in triumph, jumping wildly in his custom jump suit. Throwing his arms around Seoul Brother, he swung his map man in a delirious circle. Monteblan held his flawless thermos high, roaring in triumph.

"HIIIDDDDEECCCKKKIIII!!!"

Breathless from the excitement, I picked up the CB, yelling over the celebration.

"Asser! Over!"

*"What the fuck is going on out there? Over."*

"Moon blew up Grimace's thermos. Over."

There was a long moment of static.

*"What is that, some gay shit? Over."*

"Chicken Promise," I told him. "You had to be there, over."

*"Well you have to be out of there. Listen to me: Mickey Stiches is after you. Whole crew. You fucked with that piece of shit? Over."*

"I kinda had a run in with them, yeah. Over."

*"We're driving out of Vang. They passed us in formation. All over the CB about the Yanks and their car. How they're taking it and you're fucked. Over."*

"The cliff road?" I asked, spinning in place and squinting through the darkness in panic. "They passed you on the cliff road? Over."

*"Five minutes ago, over."*

I focused my eyes down the long, winding road that followed the cliff edge. Far below us—but not far enough— a string of headlights was racing together in formation.

*"Asser, you there? Get the fuck out of Laos. Over."*

"Shit. Yeah Gears, got it, thanks." I was about to say 'over' when I remembered the fallen road gaping before us. I looked at it, debating. This was a race. Gears taught me that. Why should I tell him?

*"Asser? You read me? Copy!"*

For a moment I tried. But I wasn't the race. I was me.

"Find another way to Vietnam," I told him. "The road up here fell through. There's no way out. Over."

*"That's real Chicken, Asser. You're alright. Over and out."*

Stashing the CB receiver, I looked up to see Seoul Brother with the box of dynamite, whiskey bottle lying on top.

"Pop the trunk?"

I reached down through the driver side, hitting the button. Seoul Brother stashed the whiskey and dynamite and slammed the trunk.

"What did Gears have to say?"

"Nothing good." I pointed down towards the distant headlights. "Trouble incoming."

"Let's take a look."

I followed him back towards their futuristic ride. Seoul Brother rummaged beside the scotch bar, pulling out a hand crafted leather case. Unzipping the side, he produced an expensive pair of binoculars.

"You're going to want the infrareds."

He handed them to me and I pointed the glasses down the road. Darting them up and down, trying to orient my line of sight, I finally found the fast moving posse. Ominously silent, tinted red in the night vision glasses, their old, dented cars powered up the cliff road. Mickey Stiches lead them. Driving alone in a boat size old Chrysler, the tiny

Irish thug looked like he was floating. White leather interior matched his snow white hair. Dashboard lights set his face in dramatic shadows. Chin lowered, eyes blazing, he promised terrible things.

Lowering the glasses sharply, I spun towards Monteblan. Still laughing with Moon, reenacting the explosion, The Hideki swung proudly from his neck.

"We have to get out of Laos!" I told my driver. "*Now.*"

"What's up?" Seoul Brother said.

I turned to the Korean racer, handing him the field glasses.

"See for yourself."

Taking the binoculars, he focused on the line of lights heading up the dark road below.

"Mickey Stiches?" His usually nonchalant voice had an edge of concern. "Damn. He's got his whole gang. They run one fucked up Chicken."

"They're kind of after us."

"*Kind of* after you?" Lowering the infrared binoculars, Seoul Brother looked at me. "Those guys don't do 'kind of'."

I sighed. "They're after me."

"Wow." Seoul Brother said. "Then you really want to be gone when they get here."

"How? We just blew up a thermos and took out the road." I spun in anger, hands balled into fists. "I *knew* we should have gotten out of Laos."

"Don't worry." The stylish Korean racer packed his field glasses neatly into their leather case. "Pull off road till they go past. Then head back to Vang. Take the East Road to Vietnam instead of North. That's all."

"Back to Vang?" I said. "Like through town?"

He nodded. "By the airstrip where you come in. The road branches out from the tunnel into town."

"Ha!" I laughed in sharp dismay. "That's perfect. We're black balled from Vang. The Lao mafia's waiting for us there."

"Shit." His eyes were wide with concern. "What did you guys do?"

"Shit," Monteblan had floated over, now picking up the conversation. "That's pretty much it. I shit in their jail and Ladyboy Man bailed us out for a Chicken Promise."

Seoul Brother's face went slack in dismay. "You owe *him* a Chicken Promise?"

We both nodded. Moon, still beaming from his thermos explosion, joined us near the futuristic car.

"What's up guys?"

Seoul Brother turned to his driver. "They owe Ladyboy Man a Chicken Promise."

"That's bad," the looming Korean frowned. "He'll collect it at the worst time you know. Nobody makes a Chicken Promise with Ladyboy Man."

"Yeah, well…" I sighed. "We're getting lots of information out here behind the curve."

"Help me understand this." Seoul Brother crossed his arms, leaning on the car. "You owe Ladyboy Man a Chicken Promise. Mickey Stiches is chasing you and the mafia wants you dead. Plus you're blackballed from Vang?"

We looked at him and nodded.

The Koreans looked at each other and shook their heads.

"That's some Chicken you guys are running," Moon said. "We're hardly out of Bangkok. Wow."

"Plus he fucked a ladyboy," Monteblan added.

"Shut up!" I yelled.

"You already fucked a ladyboy?" Moon's eyebrows rose. "Most people don't get drunk enough to do that till Cambodia."

"I didn't fuck her!" I snapped. "Can we get back to how we're going to not die tonight?"

"She fucked you?" Moon said. "What's that like?"

"Nobody fucked anybody! She had a boner! I touched it! I touched her boner, that's all that happened!"

My face burned in the night. Crickets chirped. Everybody looked at me.

"He's not gay," Monteblan mumbled. "Just vulnerable."

I shot him a look. He laughed. Moon cracked up. Seoul Brother smirked.

"Ummm, OK then." The Korean racer took off his red framed designer glasses, polishing them with his shirt. "On to getting you out of here."

"What about that way?"

Moon pointed down the road. A barely visible track branched off into dark jungle.

"Where does that go?" I said.

"Somewhere," Seoul Brother said. "Just get on it."

"Yeah!" Moon said, suddenly excited. "Then blow it up behind you! That way they can't follow you!"

"No." I shook my head. "I'm not blowing up any more Laos. People need that road to get to work or the hospital."

"I'll do it." Moon spun towards me, grinning. "I'll blow up more Laos! That way you don't have to."

"Nobody's blowing up more Laos," I walked towards Pablo Cruise. "Monteblan drives. We'll lose them that way."

"Don't end up in Burma," Seoul Brother called after me.

"Where's Burma?" Monteblan asked, giving Moon a bro hug.

"Burma's left," Seoul Brother. "Vietnam's right."

"Thanks." Monteblan shook his hand. "Want to roll with us a while?"

"Not in this thing," Seoul Brother knocked his fist on the car. "Fiberglass. We'll rip up on that road. You better watch it, too. Don't bend your rims."

Monteblan gave him a thumbs up and walked away.

"And guys, seriously?" Moon swung the bird cage off the roof of their sports car. "Blow up the road."

He tucked his fluttering karma bird carefully into the sleek machine. Monteblan got into Pablo Cruise, starting up the engine. I slipped inside, strapping the harness and calling out the window to Moon.

"I don't want to be another American blowing up Laos!"

"America blew up Laos?" Moon frowned, sliding into the leather cockpit. "I thought you guys blew up Vietnam."

Monteblan tugged at his harness, revving the engine. Across the road, Moon's silently descending doors slowly closed him in.

"Yes! And Laos!" I shouted, lowering my head to maintain eye contact while doors fell shut. "It's one of the great unknown crimes of the 20th Century! Laos is the most bombed country on the planet! There were more bombs dropped on Laos then during—"

Wing doors secured. Opera music blasted from high end speakers. Moon thrummed the engine, rocket roars of pure power. Spinning the wheel deftly, he whipped the Bertone round parallel with Pablo Cruise. Seoul Brother's window went down.

"Think Chicken," he said. "Blow up the road."

Rear wheels spun and they shot into the night, trailing soprano arias.

**With a trunk full of dynamite we blasted forward.** The road was hacked through enclosing foliage, pitted with fall outs and ditches. Monteblan navigated them diligently, applying speed to outpace our pursuers, simultaneously dodging sporadic drop outs. The task was entirely absorbing and I maintained silence while Pablo Cruise prowled and bounded. Glowing with pride from the Hideki's performance under fire, my friend wore the indestructible thermos slung round his neck. Swinging slightly with the rocking vehicle, the inviolate vessel emanated the faintly sinister smell of blast residue. The thing unnerved me.

By all means it should be shattered. I pondered what forces the Japanese engineers had brokered with in order to fashion the Hideki. Nefarious jinns perhaps, conjured from alternate realms in Faustian thermos bargains. Why something for soup was wrought to withstand the full blast of a TNT charge eluded me. Maybe they knew something we didn't. Or perhaps Nagasaki had something to do with it; atom bomb race memory inspiring apocalypse proof beverage standards. Regardless, the astounding construction struck me as tragic rather than miraculous. If every brilliant mind involved in producing the Hideki 3000 were set loose in Laos, the entire infrastructure would be integrated; indestructibly, probably. But our Empire of Stuff would never allow this. Bullied or lulled, all were hurled into product propaganda.

The finest minds of my generation might remake the world. Instead we made thermoses that people blew up for internet likes.

"Fuck this road," Monteblan said, wrenching the wheel to dodge a drop out.

"This road is our fault," I said.

He jammed gas and downshifted. "How is this bullshit third world road our fault?"

"US bombing," I said, sipping warm beer. "The whole country has PTSD. Mass destruction fucks shit up. People don't want to rebuild after something like that. They figure why bother, if some planes can just fly overhead and ruin everything again."

"Dude, that was what, fifty years ago?"

"We're talking genetic memory here. You have to understand the way DNA encodes memory and—"

*Whump!*

Monteblan cursed as we thumped hard into an unseen drop out. My head whiplashed, smacking the seat. Beers in the backseat fell rattling to the floor. My friend snarled, pushing gears and gunning gas. Pablo Cruise grabbed traction and snapped us up onto level road. Fishtailing slightly, we shot forward, lurching with a strange, groaning metal grind. Another revolution of wheels produced the same scraping moan. I spun to my friend in dismay. Monteblan pounded the dash with his fist, slamming the brakes.

"You can't stop!"

"We can't *go!* That's a bent rim."

"Mickey Stiches!" I spun in my seat, turning to find the headlights that I was sure would sweep the hidden road. "He wants Pablo Cruise. He won't stop. It's his only way out of Laos!"

"We have to pound the rim out."

"With what? Dynamite and your thermos?"

"Nah." Monteblan missed my sarcasm. "We need a garage."

"Here?" I swept my arm at hanging jungle leaves and deserted dirt road. *"How?"*

"I don't know." Monteblan sat back, exhaling in frustration. "Work some Chicken Magic why don't you."

Unsnapping my harness, I pushed open my door. It swung into heavy foliage. I had hardly placed one foot on the ground when the sound of distant engines floated towards us in the darkness. I froze. The whirling flicker of Mickey Stiches' knife spun through my memory. I turned to my friend.

"That's them. We have to get off this road. *Now.*"

Letting out a sigh, Monteblan started up the car. "C'mon bro, they're whore mongers in flip flops. We got a trunk full of dynamite. What are they gonna pull?"

"You haven't seen these guys in action," I said, buckling my harness. "They're forces of dark karma or something. Believe me. Just go."

Easing into first, wincing with the grinding metal groan, Monteblan pressed us forward slowly. I thrust my head out the window, looking behind us. Jungle leaves slapped the back of my head. First flickers of headlights traced the road. I darted my head back in the green glow of Pablo Cruise. Heart hammering as our car groaned forward, I peered through the windshield.

"There!" I said, pointing to a dark opening up ahead on the left. "Take it."

"We don't know where that goes."

"We know who's behind us," I said. *"Please."*

"Fine."

Reaching the opening, Monteblan turned the wheel. We rolled through a tight opening of screening leaves, disappearing into the darkness of a barren dirt field. Rolling forward cautiously, our lights stabbed through the murky night. Flies swarmed the bright tunnels of illumination. A grungy, empty expanse of dirt stretched out to no-where before us.

"Kill the lights," I muttered. "Engine too."

Monteblan did both and I unsnapped the harness. Darting out of the vehicle, I crouched low and ran towards the road. Sliding behind a dirt mound, I raised my head just enough to see. The headlights of the leading vehicle stabbed through the tunnel of jungle leaves. Pressing myself to the dirt, I didn't dare watch. Lights grew brighter over my head, illuminating the trees. Engines rumbled louder now, passing in a slowly moving caravan of menace. Faint music came from one; old rockabilly. I heard shocks squeak and tires crunch dirt, as powerful vehicles slowly, cautiously took the road. When all had passed, I lifted up slowly from the dirt. Glowing red tail lights receded down the choking tunnel of jungle foliage. Crawling first, then standing up to run, I made it back to Pablo Cruise.

"We're clear." Sweating, heart racing from the run, I spoke to Monteblan through his open window. "Now what?"

"I saw some lights that way." Monteblan pointed through the wind-shield down the dark field. "Looks like a village or something."

Through distant brush I saw the faintest glimmer of illumination.

"Drive across the field?" I said.

"Better than that damn road."

"What about their crops?"

Monteblan sighed. "What are you, Chicken Jesus again?"

"I'm thinking about our karmic footprint. We already blew up a road."

"I'll steer around the crickets. Get in."

I did. With the same grinding, metallic groan, we rolled through unmarked terrain. Monteblan drove without headlights. The moon lit dirt before us. Soft earth crunched under our tires. Lights ahead grew brighter as we approached, slowly forming through the scrub of bushes at field's edge. I saw homes and stores arrayed along a road. Some were lit, others dark. Televisions babbled softly. Voices from open doors floated over the field. Monteblan rolled to a stop on the edge of the darkness, peering at the village.

"Think there's a garage?" I asked him.

"They're farmers. They have tools."

"Think they'll help us?"

"What I think," he pushed the car into first. "Is that we have 35 thousand dollars in the trunk. That's Get Shit Done money."

Off the field, down through a slight dip, we popped up into the single road that made the small town. Our sudden arrival was an event. Heads poked out of windows. Children ran around the corners of homes. All were dusty wooden structures, some raised on stilts. Piles of discarded wood and pieces of old, rusted farm machines littered their dirty yards. Rolling painfully with our grinding vehicle, we slowed to a stop in the middle of their road. Stepping out of the car, I waved hello to an older Lao man who was approaching us. Shuffling in flip flops, wearing a T-shirt and baggy shorts, he walked cautiously, eyeing me first, then Monteblan.

"Good evening," I smiled. "You might have heard the extravagant pains of our arrival. Fate has been cruel. Our rim is bent."

He looked at me.

"Bent rim." Monteblan clarified from the driver's window. "And money to fix it. US Dollars."

The old man looked at Monteblan.

Then a sharp Laotian voice called out from a dark house, telling him something. The old villager bent lower, peering at our bumper. The Mark had instant impact. When the curiously welded letters registered with the old man, he nearly jumped. Eyes wide, running stiffly back towards the closest house, he waved his hands, calling out to the village. Doors slammed shut all around. Windows went dark. People vanished. Children were pulled inside. Within moments of arrival, Monteblan and I were left standing in the dark, deserted village. We looked at each other in stunned confusion, while the creak of a distant fence gate swung squeaking. Then lights swept the distant curve. Engines growled towards us as the pursuing racers wound around the field from another road, prowling towards the village.

"Go! Go!"

Monteblan didn't wait for me, just punched the car into reverse and backed it fast. Flying off the road, bouncing down into the dirty field, he shot through the inky blackness while I ran after him. Both of us were swallowed in shadows as the throttling cars rumbled into the village. Mickey Stiches lead the posse, floating in the white interior of his boat like Chrysler. Peering into darkness, ominous rockabilly drifted from his radio. Tattooed Brits trailed in their ruined Mini Cooper. Rough Australians followed driving a battered jeep. Moving slowly through the now deserted town, the procession paused. Mickey Stiches leaned from the window, shouting over idling engines.

*"Break apart, lads! Move right, I'll be off left. No way out but through us!"*

With that, the Irishman stepped on the gas and throttled ahead. At road's end he turned one way. Following cars fanned out in the alternate direction, dispersing in the night. We watched their headlights sweep distant dirt roads. Rounding unseen turns, they disappeared, leaving us alone in the empty dirt field.

"No way out?" I frowned to Monteblan. "What did he mean by that?"

"I don't know," Monteblan said. "What the fuck happened back there with the village people?"

"The Mark. Freaks out civilians. Reggie said something about that in Chang Mai."

"I thought this shit was supposed to help us?"

"With cops, mafia and army, yeah." I boosted myself up and sat on the hood of Pablo Cruise. "Not in the village. People see mafia marks and want nothing to do with us."

"That's the bad news." Monteblan got out of the car, stretching in the stifling heat. "Good news is we got the best weed I ever smoked in my life."

A lighter sparked. Thick sweet stench wafted heavy in the night. Coughing a plume, my friend passed the J. I hit it, erupting in a cascade of coughs. Leaning against Pablo Cruise, burning through half the joint, we went through ideas. Wait out the night. Push our luck with the rim. Split up while one walked to the next village. Try to ride back to Vang undetected...

"What about our Chicken Favor?" Head spinning, body tingling, I blew a curling plume of smoke. "We could get Seoul Brother and Moon on the CB."

"How are they going to find us?" Monteblan said, taking the joint. "And what if Fucky Charms is listening?"

"Fucky Charms?" I frowned.

"Aya Boyo!" Monteblan imitated Mickey's Irish brogue. "I'll be breaking your arms with me Fucky Charms I will!"

Laughter hit so hard I slid off the car into the dirt. Holding my stomach, rolling on the ground, I watched Monteblan kick up dirt in a Fucky Charms jig. Holding up fists like an old fashioned boxer, he jabbed and feinted, pattering madly in stoned brogue.

"Throw me cow at you I will. Through the green ceiling! Finnegan's wank! Angela's acid! Oh me Fucky Charms!"

"Stop!" I pleaded, weeping with tears of laughter. "You're every one of my drunk Irish uncles!"

"Like there's another type of Irish uncle?"

"Fuck you!" I yelled through laughter. "Stop!

Weaving and dancing in the moonlight, Monteblan doubled down on his brogue, singing louder:

*"Fucky Charms, Fucky Charms!*
*Smack yer face and break yer arms!*
*Take a rainbow from the sky*
*Stab it in yer fucking eye*
*Chase you on me unicorn*
*All the way to Vietnam*
*Punch yer dad and do yer mom*
*Fucky Fucky Charms!"*

Laughing too hard to breathe, I pulled myself to my feet while Monteblan jigged and bobbed.

"Must be good smoke."

The stranger's rough, rasping voice froze us instantly. Looking up from our absurdity, we turned towards the bushes where he had emerged. His voice was American. His luck, by the looks of it, had been bad. Standing barefoot in ripped cargo shorts, a raggedy T-shirt hung from his skinny frame. Flies and mosquitoes darted about him in the dark.

"Smell that shit a mile away. Get a hit?"

"Sure," Monteblan said, holding the joint out. "American?"

Stepping in to take the smoke, he nodded. "Yeah."

The glow of embers lit his features. White guy, thirties, buzz cut that needed trimming, face streaked with dirt. Strong brow, chiseled chin. Puffing deeply, holding back a cough, he handed the joint back to Monteblan, pointing at it.

"That's the shit I came out here for, right there."

Flipping into Alpha mode, the stranger extended his hand rigidly, staring Monteblan right in the eyes.

"Mike."

"Monteblan." My friend shook the stranger's hand, which then moved towards me.

"Asser," I told him, receiving his bone crusher handshake and iron gaze.

Standing back, folding his arms across his chest, the stranger looked at Monteblan.

"Hell of a thermos you got there, bro."

"Thanks," Monteblan smiled, holding it up. "It's a Hideki."

"I know a 3000 when I see one. Fucking nice. What the hell you guys doing out here?"

Monteblan and I exchanged glances. We turned back to the shadowed man standing rigidly in the moonlight.

"Just kinda chillin'," Monteblan replied. "You know."

"Right." Mike laughed harshly. "In the middle of a field in fucking Laos. Shit, you don't want to tell me how you're fucked, I'll tell you how *I'm* fucked."

"You're fucked?" I said, feeling earth swirl in the stoned night.

"Look at me, I got no shoes."

"How'd that happen?"

Peering beyond us at the distant, shuttered village, his eyes narrowed. *"These people."*

"Well, uh, you need some help there, buddy?" Monteblan said. "We're Americans. Heading towards Vietnam."

"Sure," Mike said. "You got a spare passport let me know."

"Where's your passport?" I said, passing him the joint.

"Thanks bro." He took another hit in the empty field. "Passports in my house."

His face glowed, frowning and intense, pulling hard on the weed. He exhaled without further explanation. Crickets chirped in the darkness. A lone bat looped surreal and shot into trees.

"OK," I shrugged. "Well, um. Our fucked is we got a bent rim."

"That's all?" He smirked, eyebrows questioning.

"Well it's kind of a deal since no one will fix it," Monteblan said.

"Bro." The American smiled, visibly mellowing with the smoke. "The first thing you learn living here is how to hammer out a rim. Roads are shit all over. I can do that in my sleep. There's a site I can grab some tools. My place is right by the river. Through there. Come on."

Waving towards the bushes he had emerged from, he headed forward. Standing by Pablo Cruise, we didn't move.

"Dudes!" He called back, walking backwards, hands held wide. "Come on, I'll get you out of here! You can do me a solid when you get to Vietnam."

Turning again, he slipped into the bushes, disappearing with a rustle of branches. Monteblan and I looked at each other in the moonlight.

"You think he's cool?"

"He's probably insane." My friend snubbed the joint in the dust and shrugged. "Who else shows up in the middle of the night in Laos?"

"We did."

"We have a reason," Monteblan replied.

"Right. We blew the road detonating a thermos, while on our way to get a chicken in Vietnam."

Monteblan opened up the car door and slipped into the bucket. "Don't forget the ladyboy."

"I'm trying to. Why do you keep bringing it up?"

"Cause you did it and I'm never letting you live it down."

"Who says I have to live it down? It's a cosmopolitan life experience. I'm a Citizen of the World." Pleasantly high, I floated around the back of the car. "Cosmonaut of Life. Scholar of Chicken."

"Holder of Boner." Monteblan added, popping the trunk release. "Grab the jack and throw it in the back, will you?"

"Why?"

"So the probably insane stranger we just met doesn't find out we have 35 thousand dollars and a box full of dynamite in the trunk."

"Good thinking," Throwing the requested item in the back seat, I slammed the trunk. "You really think it's alright?"

"How the hell should I know?" Monteblan started the car. "But how else do we get out of here?"

**A half hour later we were kicked back with whiskey.** Pablo Cruise was jacked up, front wheel gone. Water rushed in soothing streams through a narrow river. Fire burned brightly by the banks, where Mike stared down at a heating iron hammer. Pulling it glowing red from flames, he turned towards the car rim. Wedged tight between two large stones, it took the first blow with a rain of sparks. Mike eyed the impact and nodded in satisfaction.

"You guys are set. This shit's alloy. No problem."

In a hammering rain of dancing sparks, the stranger pounded metal. Then rotating the wheel slightly, he threw the hammer back in the fire to reheat. Turning towards Monteblan, he stretched out his hand.

"Whiskey."

Monteblan lobbed him the bottle. Unscrewing the cap, the gruff stranger drank down a deep pull.

"Nice place you got here, Mike," Monteblan said.

We were sitting open air, in old abandoned car seats. A lean-to nearby drooped with plastic tarps. A single pair of underwear hung from a scraggly line tied between two oil cans. Wiping his mouth with the back of his hand, Mike pointed up stream into the darkness.

*"That's* my place."

Taking the extended bottle, I followed his gesture. Far up the river, set on a distant rise, a decent sized house was freshly painted and warmly lit.

"What happened?"

For a long time there was silence. Fire crackled. River streamed. Crickets chirred. Monteblan and I exchanged glances.

"These people," Mike finally muttered.

Returning to the fire, he grasped the hot metal hammer. Stalking back towards us, he held the hissing instrument up before us, face lit red with the glow.

"You believe these people? Leave their tools lying all over the site. Just walked up and took it. There are *children* around here. Fucking bulldozer is sitting there with the keys in the damn ignition! *These people!*"

Turning furiously back to the rim, Mike raised the hammer high. Sparks flew as he pounded out the metal. Rotating the wheel further, he tossed the tool into flames. Joining us again, sinking into a sunken car seat, Mike stared up at the stars.

"Good upcountry girl, that's what I wanted. Burned out on that American shit. Buddy of mine lived out here. Told me out here women were real. Found her in Bangkok. 19. Selling her ass but she just started. One month she told me. That's what they always say. I didn't know it then. Didn't know them. Didn't know these people."

He lurched up from the seat, stalking back to the fire, staring at the flames.

"Pulled her out of the bar." he said ruefully. "Out of my mind for that shit. Teen pussy is like crack. Don't fuck with it. Moved her into my place. Married her in Bangkok. Met the family. *There.*"

Lifting the red hot hammer, Mike pointed in vengeful fury towards the village that had just shut us out. For a moment the glowing weapon trembled in his hand. Then he lowered it sadly, dropping it in the flames.

"Out here, man? It's the life. Start drinking at noon. Women pour the whiskey. Her brother was my man. Cop out here. All connected. We partied. *Coolest* dude. Roll down to Vang and blow off steam. Ass on the side? That's not a problem. That's being a man. You pay the bills, you dip where you want. I start running numbers. I can buy a house here. *Build* a house. Own something. Raise a family. Fuck America. Transgender kindergarten coloring books? Don't get me started. Do not *fucking* get me started on America. Divorce courts. It's like Stalin. Guys are lighting themselves on fire. Wealth transference. Systemized, socialized—"

"Right, Mike." Monteblan said. "You were talking about these people?"

"Yeah." Mike pulled the hammer from the flames. "*These people.*"

He went to the wheel. Painting the night with sparks, our furious savior pounded hard and long. Then panting, sweating in the flames, he tossed the tool back in the fire. Coming towards us, Mike reached for the whiskey. I handed him the bottle and he drank. Throwing it back to me, the stranded American stood staring at us both.

"Built us a house. Her brother helps manage the construction. Local cop making sure I don't get fucked? What luck. But it's leased land. Lao laws. I own the house. Not the land. Foreigners can't own land. So you know what happened, right? Because you know how these people do it, right?"

Mike jabbed his finger furiously towards the distant house.

"She made like it was *my* idea. That's what these people do. They put *their* ideas in *your* head." Eyes wild, he stabbed his head with his finger. "Make you believe they're yours. Make you say it!"

"Say what, Mike?" I asked.

The stranger held his face in the flickering firelight, grinning grotesquely, voice a mocking tone.

"Darling wife, why don't *you* buy the land? I'll give you the money. Then the house is in my name, and the land is yours. We'll raise our family there. *Together.*"

He laughed out loud ruefully, reaching for the whiskey bottle, swigging a hard swallow.

"Sign the papers. Back and forth, here and Bangkok. My online business turns over. Hand it off to managers. Sign that shit off. Finished. Off to Laos. My house. My wife. My life. One night I get. Best sleep of my life. Come down in the morning. Her brother the cop is sitting in the kitchen. Wearing his browns. Gun on the table. Right beside his coffee. I'm like: What's up bro? Trouble in town? I got your back. What's up?"

Eyes wide, Mike stared at us. Sparks popped softly from the fire. The river murmured quietly. Darkness all around. The man squatted low. Crept towards us. Whispered.

"*This* is what's up. He's not her brother. He's her *husband*. Sent her to fuck foreigners in Bangkok. Find one to build them a house. *Me.* Our marriage in Bangkok doesn't mean shit in Laos. Little bitch is *his* wife. And my house is on *his wife's* land. That makes it his land. Tells me to get off his land. *Now.*"

Mike bolted upright, eyes tearing up, staring into the dark river.

"I say this can't be happening, no. We partied together! She loves me! You're lying! Then she walks in. Doesn't say anything. Doesn't have to. The look in her eyes. *Hate.* 19 year old, *young girl* hate. I...I..."

He broke a moment, voice cracking, snuffling back tears, then shook it away.

"You know those alien movies? When this predator alien thing is standing there dripping acid and the dude can't move? Like it's so far from fucking believable that he just stares at it, like: *What the fuck IS this thing?!* That's what it was like. I didn't know who I was looking at. *What* I was looking at. A year? A year of... *us?* And now you hate me and there's a husband and he's got a gun telling me to get out of my house? MY HOUSE? *MY! HOUSE!"*

Spinning in fury on the gravel by the river, he clutched his hands in trembling fists. Staring at the fire, the man hissed.

*"These people."*

For a long moment, the only sound was running water and the cracking sparks from the fire. Monteblan and I looked at each other. There was nothing to say. So I said the dumb thing you say.

"I'm really sorry."

The man was lost. He didn't respond. Squatting by the river, flames flickered as he held his head in his hands.

"When did all this happen?" Monteblan asked softly. "Hey...Mike?"

Hearing his name, confused a moment, the man looked up. "Few days ago."

He rubbed his hand over his close cropped hair. Walking to the fire, Mike picked up the red hot hammer and held it close to the rim. Peering in the soft glow, he nodded in satisfaction. With a kick, he knocked the rim free. It rolled into the water, tipping over and lying in the running stream.

"Rim's good to go. Give it five to cool and you're rolling."

He walked closer, sitting down heavy in one of the seats and continued.

"Here's what I need from you. I got a buddy in Nam, he's in law. NGOs. All that shit. You're gonna—"

"Come with us," Monteblan said. "We can get you out of here."

"Didn't you hear me?" His rage flared up. "My passport, my money. *Everything* is in that house. They're in that fucking house right now! He's a cop! You know about cops out here?"

"We can get you out of here without a passport," I told him.

He laughed bitterly. "What are you guys, CIA?"

"Better." I smiled. I wanted to tell him. I almost did. I opened my mouth to start but Monteblan stopped me.

"Just this thing we're in. It's pretty connected. You won't have a problem at the border. Promise."

For a long time there was just the sound of rippling river water. Then Mike shook his head and spoke softly.

"I'm not fucking running bricks for you or taking shit across the border. Fuck that."

"Dude, it's not like that. At all. We'll be in the car with you. I mean, if you don't want to, no problem. We'll find your guy in Vietnam."

He looked at us long and hard in the night.

"No. I just saw you dancing leprechaun songs. You're not going to fuck me. And I can fuck with them better once I have my passport. You guys can get me over the border? You're sure?"

We nodded.

"OK." He looked up the river. "We have to go by the house."

My friend and I glanced at each other in the flickering firelight.

"Look man, we can't help with setting all that straight," Monteblan said softly. "All we can do is get you out of Laos."

"*All* you can do?" Mike laughed. "What, like that's not a miracle?! No, you don't understand, we have to go by the house. That's the only way out. This area? It's built like a basket. All the roads go crisscross. How did you even find this shit hole?"

I told him about driving through the field to dodge Mickey Stiches.

"Fuck me. And those guys are driving around here looking for you?"

Monteblan and I nodded.

"Well they're not going to find their way out of here. People who *live* here get fucking lost. They all drive drunk, though. You don't understand these people. Have you ever driven in a car with these people? Do you know how these people—"

"Uh yeah, that road out?" Monteblan said.

"Right, yeah," Mike said. "We have to go past my house. Only way out. There's a road you can't even see unless you get up the ridge. It's why I built there. So I could fuck off out of this crap basket when I wanted. Sure shot to Nam. One hour. Tops. And we go right over the border? You sure?"

"For sure. We owe you for the rim. Let us help you out."

"You bros are the first good people I have seen in a year." He pointed his finger fiercely at us. "Fucking *love* Americans!"

Bounding from the seat, Mike stepped to the river and fished the rim from the water. Holding it up in the moonlight, he examined his work. Nodding in satisfaction, he turned and stared upriver. The distant, softly lit house floated in the darkness. He looked at it a long time. When he whispered, I barely heard it.

*"These people."*

**We piled into Pablo Cruise.** Mike took a last look over his shoulder at his shanty by the river. Underwear still hanging, fire ashes smoking, the sagging lean-to was a snapshot of defeat. Grim faced, he shook it off. Forward over the dusty field, we rolled towards the still shuttered town. Crickets purred in the hot, silent night. Eyes roving, I scanned the terrain for Chicken predators. Roads were empty. Pablo Cruise pulled us up through the last ditch, popping us into the village.

Rolling slowly past the silent, clapboard homes, Mike shook his head muttering *these people*. Pointing out a hardly visible turn, he directed us down a narrow dirt path. Lights off, led by moonlight, we left the village behind. Winding through turns slowly, drifting closer to the river, we drove uphill towards the freshly painted house in the distance. Construction equipment lay dormant in shadows. I saw the dark shape of a bulldozer, backhoes, and mounds of piled dirt. Lights were on upstairs, throwing warm glow into the desolate darkness. We drove closer. Soft tunes of foreign pop music floated towards us, drifting in the silent night.

"One last look," Mike uttered, staring transfixed at his stolen dream. "My house."

Monteblan slowed to a stop in shadows, gently pulling the handbrake. We idled quietly, sweating in the tropic heat. Mike was gripping the back seat, eyes sharp and piercing. Behind the house was a range of distant mountains. The view of the river was probably fantastic. Mike had chosen a good spot to build.

"Over the ridge?" I turned in my seat, pointing out the rise behind the house. "That's the road out to Nam?"

He didn't hear me, lost staring at his house, fury in his eyes.

"Mike?" I said.

Snapping out of his trance, the American looked at me as if I had appeared out of thin air. Sweat ran in silent streams down his temples. The weak light of the dashboard made him glow pale green.

"What?"

"Where's the road to Vietnam?"

"Past my house on the right," he muttered. "Follow the tire tracks. Over the ridge it turns into the access road."

Monteblan slid Pablo Cruise into first. Lurking in shadows, the black car rounded Mike's house. Crunching quietly over ground, we passed the scattered array of abandoned tools, littered amidst hulking shadows of construction machines. Nestled securely in hushed, up-country darkness, the new house emanated security. Modestly built, it looked like the local mansion when compared to village shacks. We had almost passed when the childish, beguiling giggles of a young woman drifted out with the floating music. Mike bolted straight as if struck by an arrow.

*"Her!"* he whispered fiercely. *"Stop."*

Monteblan stopped. His eyes flicked up in the rearview, catching Mike.

"Hey buddy," my friend said kindly. "We're just about at that road. I can see the tracks up there."

Mike shut his eyes while the young woman's laughter danced softly in the night. Breathing in short, fast breaths, the vein in his temple throbbed ominously.

"We'll get you right over the border," I said softly. "Promise."

Mike didn't answer. Like moving in a dream, his hand lifted slowly, resting on the door handle. I watched the knuckles whiten as his grip tightened.

"You have to let it go man," I gently urged. "Or you won't get out."

Tense breaths passed. Then his grip loosened. I watched the hand float down from the door handle. Eyes still closed, Mike nodded slowly. He let out a long, slow breath. Then the woman's light, distant laughter was joined by a man's. The young couple broadcast delight through the dark, empty night. Their shared domestic bliss sheared Mike raw. His eyes shot open.

*"These people."*

Silently springing from the car, the stranger darted into the darkness.

*"The fuck?!"* Monteblan whispered to me. *"What's he doing?"*

I strained my eyes through shadows, trying to find his form in the looming construction equipment. Music and laughter played lightly in the night air. Mike was nowhere.

"Dude." Monteblan tapped me on the arm, pointing out my window. "Look."

I swiveled from the house, looking out my passenger window towards the town. Bright headlights of a large old American car were prowling through the strip below. The faint, jangling rattle of rockabilly music hovered over the low rumble of Mickey Stiches powerful engine. I spun back to Monteblan, face blank with fear.

"Fucky Charms."

Night exploded with blasting throttle. A bulldozer lunged from the shadows, barreling towards the house. Hunched over the controls, Mike raised the plough, smashing with gusto directly through his freshly painted dream. The raw, wrenching scream of bent boards ripped the night like a wounded animal. The roaring engine blasted puffs of angry smoke. Straight through the front door, the thundering machine snapped it sharply, pushing a ragged hole directly into an exposed staircase. Steps exploded in split, spinning boards. A woman screamed. Grinding into reverse, the demented American backed up for another run.

"Mike!" I yelled out through the destructive din.

Covered with white construction dust, Mike laughed manically from the jerking bulldozer seat. Slamming gears in a destructive, spinning whirl, he raised the blade. Debris rained down. Shattered dry wall, wooden planks, frayed wires, crumbled cement and dust erupted in chaos. Appliances crushed under heavy treads, scraped walls exposed electrical wires that popped with sparks. Bright white drapes ignited in flame while severed pipes sprayed water in wild bursts. The second floor buckled and dipped, dangerously close to collapse. I looked up.

Two panicked figures that had been laughing were now dangling half naked from the upstairs window. Man and wife let go, falling roughly to the ground. Mike rumbled obliviously, ploughing through rattling circles of ruin. He missed the Lao man darting in his underwear. Didn't see him run for his pickup truck. Rifling through the passenger side door, popping open the glove, the Lao spun furiously with his pistol and pulled off shots towards the raw, open wound that had moments before been his home.

*Bam! Bam! Bam!*

Like wild punches thrown through the night, angry shots blasted erratically at the house. Singing sparks danced on the dented metal back of the bulldozer. Mike dashed off in a flash, leaving the machine circling like a blind, dumb beast in the ruins. Ducked low and running, he darted through hedges just as the decimated structure collapsed with tearing, terrible groans. Screeching with visceral loss, the half-naked young woman hugged herself tightly. Through streaming tears, she screamed for vengeance as her husband sprinted past in underwear. Arm outstretched, firing shots blindly towards the bushes where the American had vanished, the outraged Lao chased his prey into the wild.

"There goes Mike," Monteblan said.

Bright lights suddenly blazed the scene. Spinning in my seat, I saw the great white beast driven by Mickey Stiches. Drawn by the noise and chaos, grinning from behind the wheel, he gunned the great engine and lunged up over the rise.

"Move!"

Monteblan hit the gas. Thrust into gear, wheels spinning dirt, Pablo Cruise was hungry for speed. Traction grabbed. We flew. Darting over the rise we went airborne, landing in a cloud of dust. Lights flicked on. Monteblan shifted form. Bro traveler to poet warrior. Owning motion, he shot us surely through unknown roads. Headlights stabbing, engine revving, needles danced wildly on dash mounted dials.

Mickey Stiches drove faster. Rammed us. Banging impact shocked my driver. Shouting curses, skidding wild, Monteblan fought for control. His eyes flicked to the rearview, slits of rage. Up ahead, road widened. Monteblan punched it. From the darkness of the narrow access trail we leapt onto deserted lanes, flooring towards Vietnam.

"What did he say?!" Monteblan shouted. "An hour?!"

"Not this fast!" I yelled over roaring engine. "We'll be there sooner!"

*BANG!*

The huge, heavy American machine slammed the back of Pablo Cruise once more.

"Shit!" Monteblan swerved, maintaining control. "He's crazy! You can't race Crazy!"

The white beast shot forward, pulling up beside us. Squinting in wind, gripping the wheel, The Irishman shouted.

"That's me only way out of Laos and I'm taking it lads!"

Wrenching the wheel he lunged at us. Monteblan predicted the maneuver. With breathtaking precision my driver shifted while ripping the parking brake. Shock hit Mickey's face as he rammed into nothing. Dropping behind, we watched his large car rock on its axels. Swerving drunkenly, the terrible white machine spit dust in thundering rage.

"Dynamite!" Monteblan shouted.

"The hell are you talking about?!" I yelled back.

"If we don't wreck him, he'll wreck us! That's how Crazy races! He's Crazy!"

Swerving sharply, Monteblan dodged while Mickey Stiches slammed the brakes. Nicking our side with a pinging dent, the white whale groaned. We scraped sides, metal screeching, then shot ahead. World a reckless blur, Monteblan shouted.

"Dynamite!"

"No! Drive faster! Lose him!"

"You don't know driving, Rich! You don't know how Crazy races! I do! Throw that dynamite or we *die!* Kick through the back seat! *MOVE!*"

Startled to action, I undid the harness. Floating in velocity, I drifted like an astronaut. Landing in back I pulled at seat cushions, struggling for the explosives trapped in our trunk.

*"Dynamite!"* Monteblan screamed, hitting gas harder.

The world shot past in streaks. I fought to breach the seat. Punching wildly, a dull glint winked from the floor. Squinting I saw a Rambo knife from Bangkok's weapons bazar. Grabbing it I lunged, stabbing through backseat cushions. Pleather stripped away, baring springs and foam like muscle and bone. Ripping an opening, I reached for the old crate. Snatching twin sticks of dynamite, I heard Monteblan shout.

*"Hold on!"*

My friend hit sideways drift. Mike hadn't locked the door when he left to bulldoze his house. I flew right out. Halfway through, some ruined spring from Pablo Cruise grabbed my suit. Dangled over blurring road, I watched drifting, spinning wheel. Slow motion surreal, tire blooming smoke, life's final realization dawned. *This is where the rubber meets the road.* Monteblan straightened sharply then, hurling me inside. Pablo's door slammed shut. I shook off my brush with metaphoric death. Our winnings from The Splits had fluttered free from the savaged trunk. Gripping dynamite in the swirl of hundred dollar bills, I shouted.

"How do we do this?!"

"It's a five second fuse! I'll tell you when! You light it! You count to three! Drop it out the window! Don't throw it! *Drop it!* On the road! Got it?!"

I looked at the explosive in my hand. Then up at Monteblan. "I can't blow someone up."

*Bang!*

Mickey rammed from behind. Pablo's engine flared. Our car was furious. I felt it; Datsun rage.

"We'll *die!*" Monteblan spun the wheel for control. "That's what happens on the road with Crazy! Crazy wins or kills you!"

I leaned up to the front seat, shouting.

"Know what happens with karma and murder? What Buddhists say? You kill someone, you're bound to them for eternity! Fucky Charms forever? *Are you kidding me?!*"

*Thud!*

Mickey's ramming impact bounced me to the back seat. The Irishman's heavier car held ground while we danced wildly in skidding hops. Monteblan fought for control. Terrified eyes flared in the rearview mirror. My friend had never looked so frightened. It registered then. Like a stone dropped into my soul, simple truth rippled cold. This road was death. Someone was surviving Chicken 65, and someone wasn't. Nodding in realization, I shouted over racing wind.

"Dynamite! Next straightaway!"

Gripping two sticks, I wedged myself by the window. Monteblan floored us forward and screamed.

*"Now!"*

Stunned at how fast it was happening, I sparked my lighter. Fuse exploded in hissing sparks. Panicking instantly, I threw the dynamite.

"What the hell was that?!"

Eyes in the rearview, furious now.

"It's dynamite! I was—"

***Boom!***

The thundering flash behind us was breathtakingly loud. Ringing left my ears and rushing wind returned. I spun to find the Irishman behind us. Dynamite didn't shake him off. What would? Closer now, floating like a shark, his old car drifted in. Grim decision filled Mickey's eyes. With it I saw Crazy. My friend was right.

"Let me get farther up ahead!"

Monteblan hit gas harder. Tapping unknown capacities, Pablo Cruise hurtled forward. High velocity lifted me lightly, floating with swirling hundred dollar bills. In this floating came knowing. Staring at the dynamite in my hand, I knew what would happen. Just like that. Saw the whole thing. Stunned, I lit the stick.

"Wait!" Monteblan yelled. "Not yet! He's right there!"

Hissing sparks spit from the lit explosive. Sitting in my suit I calmly counted, measuring seconds with an old grade school counting trick.

5 Mississippi

*This was my Chicken.*

4 Mississippi

*Charlie smiling: "Race already run before it starts."*

3 Mississippi

*Monteblan from far away: "That's three! Throw it Rich! Now!"*

2 Mississippi

*Mickey pulling up next to us. Like I knew he would. Holding dynamite up I smile. Irish eyes go wide. Whole world slows.*

1 Missssss—

*Reach out the window with spark-spitting stick.*

—isssssssss—

*Mickey Stiches jams the brakes, disappearing.*

—ippppppppppp—

*Drop my dynamite and*

**BOOM!**

The pounding explosion just behind us hammered our car forward, lifting the back of Pablo Cruise. Front ending, spitting sparks, we surfed the wave of explosive heat. Slamming down hard, holding road, we flew. Spinning in my seat, I saw what I had known would happen behind us:

Mickey Stiches trapped behind a blown crater of road. Cursing, punching his car, horrible but unharmed.

Rounding a curve, the Irishman vanished. Pablo Cruise charged forward under dawning skies. Monteblan whooped from the front seat. Monteblan pounded the ceiling with his fist. Monteblan tipped back his head, opened his mouth and bellowed to the heavens:

"My motherfucking *MAN!!!!!*"

Grinning wildly, my best friend in the whole world spun around and shouted:

"What the *hell* was that?!"

Smiling, I shot my cuffs.

"Chicken 65."

**We hit the border at dawn.** Our obscure Northern crossing was noted by the crisp inhabitant of a dilapidated booth. The Vietnamese official stepped smartly forward, halting us at a barrier. Pablo Cruise rolled to a respectful stop and quietly idled. The guard's eyes flickered as triple nine plates and The Mark registered. His flat, expressionless gaze took me in. Slumped in my suit, I smiled amidst lunatic debris. Ripped out seats and hundred dollar bills, opium bags and scattered joints mixed with loose sticks of dynamite. Raising the whiskey bottle high, I smiled. Muscle twitched at the man's lip. But arcane mafia codes prevailed, and the barrier was lifted. Leaning out the window, Monteblan held a hundred dollar bill folded neatly between his fingers. The guard collected it wordlessly and we rolled into Vietnam.

"Why'd you bribe him?" I leaned forward as wind rustled my hair. "The Mark got us through."

"Call it Chicken diplomacy," Monteblan called back over the wind.

Satisfied with that answer, I leaned back in my seat, looking out the window. Vietnam looked different. It smelled different; rich and loamy. The dust of Laos had been replaced by lush green. Emerald foliage ran rampant. Pablo Cruise shot through morning misted road. I lit the joint resting between my fingers. Monteblan reached down and punched in the single eight track that had survived our purge in The VV Splits. Orchestration swelled and a smooth crooner floated in from another era, singing of the moon while we flew through jungle green.

"What happened to songs like this?" I wondered aloud.

"Songs like what?"

"Pleasant people in V neck sweaters." I passed the spliff forward. "Singing little ditties."

Monteblan took a hit. "You looked at his picture on the cover and called him a lizard person."

"That was before I heard him sing. This is wholesome entertainment. I grew up singing *Don't Fear The Reaper*. That was my favorite song when I was little. A power ballad telling people to go kill themselves. Who flipped that switch? You have one generation that grows up listening to songs about the moon and rivers, and people like us who sang songs about shooting ourselves."

"What did the girl with the penis say again?"

I sighed in exasperation. "Are you just going to keep going back to that?"

"The gift that keeps on giving." Monteblan slowed down for a tractor up ahead. "Remember what she said to you? *Don't think so much*."

"That's probably what she says to every dude," I grumbled. "*It's just my dick. Don't think so much.*"

"No, bro. That little ladyboy was The Universe talking to you. You have a thinking problem."

"That's ridiculous!" I shouted up over the wind. "How can I have a thinking problem?"

"Some people have drinking problems. You have a thinking problem."

More open country rolled past, green loping hills, backed by distant rocky mountains.

"Thinking is life," I told him. "Great things start as great thoughts. I love thinking. I can't live without it."

"That's what drunks say. They can't imagine life without drinking!" He shouted over his shoulder while a truck roared past from the other lane. "Put down the think, Rich. Shit's too fucked. Don't think about life. Just deal with it. That's what I do. And I do pretty well. Everything I have is because I don't think. Try it sometime. I'll help you. Be your sponsor and shit."

For a moment, I was literally stricken dumb. When I finally regained my voice, it was quiet and slow. "That was the most ridiculous thing you've ever said in your life."

He shot his eyes to the rearview. "Why don't you have a steady job?"

"Because I like to do my own thing!"

"Because you walk into places and think too much. Pisses people off. Girlfriend?"

"What are you talking about?"

"I'm talking about the fact that you never have one. Why?"

Gentle hills rose up to the right, where the road turned around unseen bends. Stammering nervously, I gave my standard line. "I... I haven't met the right woman."

"Wrong. You meet as many right women as anybody else. It's your thinking problem. You think about them too much. Thinking about women leads nowhere."

"I think about the relationship!" I said, defending myself. "About the give and take, the back and forth. Where she's coming from, where I'm coming from. That stuff."

Old pavement crumbled on the sides into dirt shoulders, where low built, slat wooden houses leaned at angles. Far beyond, a river wound lazy under the rising sun. Monteblan raced us through it all.

"You shouldn't think about women," he told me. "Just appreciate them."

"Ridiculous. Interpersonal relationship dynamics require reflection, and thought and—"

He cut me off. "Who has a girlfriend for twelve years and who doesn't?"

I stopped talking.

"That's right. And here's what I think about women," Monteblan told me. "Women rattle your cage. If you let them, they rattle harder. That's it."

"That's it? Your entire theory on women?"

Monteblan nodded proudly, piloting us down the early morning country road.

"Well then why? Have you thought about reasons for this essential truth of yours? Why do they rattle the cage?"

"Testing the merchandise, my friend." Monteblan grinned broadly, fielding an easy question. "The world throws shit at dudes. That's all it does. Women need to know her man can handle it. So she throws shit at him to check his reflexes."

"Sure," I agreed. "First few dates, I get that. But they never stop."

"Of course they don't." Monteblan waved his hand dismissively. "It's like checking the door every night before bed. You rattle the knob to make sure it's locked. Same thing with women. They rattle you up just to check. All the time. Because this world never stops throwing shit at a dude."

"This is where I have the problem. Look." I pointed out the window to the winding road. "The world throws shit at me at every turn. Why do I need it happening when I go home, too?"

"What can I say," Monteblan sipped some beer. "The world doesn't blow you on your birthday."

"I just don't think that—"

"Aha!" He lifted the beer with his finger extended. "There you go again. Thinking."

"I'm not going to stop thinking."

"Then stop talking, how about that? Can I get that?" His eyes pleaded with me from the rearview. "It's dawn dude, I don't do morning. Driver's call: no talking till Chicken Town."

"Fine," I grumbled, staring out the window.

We rolled on. The map had been marked before leaving, and Monteblan had it spread on the seat beside him while I rode in back. Every so often he glanced at it, getting bearings, taking us through increasingly crowded roads. The velocity of Laos has been quashed entirely. Vietnam was waking up, with roads filled in morning traffic. Our speed dropped drastically, as the narrow lanes filled with slowly moving busses, trucks, farm tractors and honking scooters. The mundane motion of it faded the riotous fury of our border escape. Excitement waned, snarled in commuter tangles that thwarted speed's freedom. My vibe dropped with the slower pace. Regular people living at daily speeds; I wanted nothing to do with it. The whirl of high speed Chicken had been narcotic. But Traffic was traffic, a universal law onto itself.

Vietnam, LA, Bangkok or New York, there was no difference. People fuming and fighting, polluting and plotting, trying their best to find the opening, hating the ones who beat them to it, surrounded by strangers all grinding along. Slow down and they'll hate you. Break down and they'll leave you behind. Slowing now, stuck in the midst of traffic, Chicken 65's wild velocity faded like a drug. For the first time since we left Bangkok, I thought of what I had tried to outrun when I left The States. What was waiting for me once this mad, magic moment finished. As Monteblan plodded us through upcountry snarls, I shut my eyes. This reminded me of home. The place and pace I would return to after Chicken 65.

For the first time, I truly wondered if there was a way I could actually go back to real life. Living the way they told you to. Just getting by. Grinding it out with others. A crawling, grasping procession of hustle and butt kiss, chasing the checks, sweating the rent, fighting for crumbs I didn't like the taste of. Page after strategic page made for people I didn't like in places I didn't want to be. None of it anything but miasma. Totally disposable, hyper accelerated pointlessness. I didn't design. My job was making mist. Stuff to obscure the monsters who lumbered through glass buildings running things. We sensed but never saw these fucks. They had flipped the market, taken the cake, then slithered up the walls long ago, kicking the ladder away. Looking down they laughed while we fought through traffic, struggling towards places we hated. What a racket. Chicken 65 had made me forget it all a minute.

"Can we go any faster?" I said.

Monteblan glanced at the clock on the dashboard.

"15 minutes. I had 15 minutes of silence. It was like heaven came down."

"Come on man, we're... we're..."

Struggling to find some escape from the prison of thinking, I scrambled for reasons to speak. Part of me was afraid of losing my friend. It was like I already sensed him leaving. The race halfway done. Him gone. Me alone on the other side of the world, until who knows when we met again. I didn't want silence between us. I felt that talking might chase something away. The fear. The fear which our crawling traffic had triggered. Fear for the end of this moment of fast insanity and escape. Dread for the grim lines of order waiting back home. Monteblan vanished then, back to his mists again. When would he reappear? Would he? How many trips did we have left? I didn't know. Depression spread. We raced through beautiful green. Vietnam War movie memories bloomed. Burning hills, tumbling napalm, machine gun jungles. Then I had it. Something to say.

"We're driving through Vietnam," I told Monteblan. "This is a historic scar on our collective national psyche. As Americans, we should discuss this."

"What? Are you kidding me?" Monteblan winced, shooting me a glance. "That was fifty years ago."

"Time doesn't exist in memory!"

"Wow." Monteblan shook his head. "You're high."

"I'm not high!"

"Dude, that was the most high thing you ever said. It was so high I can't even remember how to start to *tell* you what you just said. That's how high it was."

"All I said is that history resonates through the present. This is Vietnam. We're driving through history."

"I don't care if we're driving through geometry. It's morning. I don't do morning."

"Come on. This is a once in a lifetime opportunity to examine the hobbling of a great empire, on the battleground where that... that... um, hobbling was...uh, hobbled."

A moment of silence passed. I took a deep breath, agreeing.

"OK, so I am high. But so was every soldier fighting this war. Come on man, work with me here."

Monteblan stared ahead at the road. He drove a little, then spoke.

"Ten minutes. You get ten minutes to trip out on Vietnam, then I get silence all the way until Chicken Town."

"Ten minutes?" I moaned, raising my hands. "Ten minutes to dissect the essential crippling moral blow of—

"Driver calls it." He squinted at the clock. "Nine minutes and forty eight seconds."

"Wait, no, I wasn't ready. Rewind. From the top."

"Nine forty," Monteblan said, staring ahead.

"Damn! OK, look..."

I rubbed my face, trying to get in all the speaking I could while my friend would still listen. Glancing out the window, I saw a million scenes in a blur. Waves of flame destruction. Naked girl screaming running down the road. A man shot point blank in the head on foreign city streets. Body counts and body bags. Rock and Roll montages in movies that turned it into war porn: hip music video of jungles and junkies, machine guns and monsoons. We had pulled this place apart. We had murdered and stabbed and altered it. We had drenched the place in flames. Still, we had lost. How? A fact came jumping out at me from high school history class.

"We'll start with the drivers. Alright? On the Ho Chi Minh trail. The truck drivers moving supplies were chained to the steering column of the truck. You're chained to the truck, you don't let that thing get blown up. That's how they won. They could chain their people to the truck, we couldn't. Plus the underwater bridges."

Monteblan reached over, taking the extinguished joint from my fingers. Relighting it and taking a pull, he coughed out a large cloud of the stuff.

"What underwater bridges?"

"Across the rivers," I told him. "What they did was pile up stones under the water, just below the surface. Went across the whole river. Trucks drove right over them. Planes were looking for bridges to bomb. There weren't any."

"Dope." My friend nodded. "Five minutes."

"Genius. Simplicity defined. We were flying in million dollar mine detecting radar bridges. They were piling up rocks. But my favorite story about that war is the negotiations..."

I thought a while, trying to remember through my pot clouded, exhausted mind the details. Scenery went by cinematically and I lost myself for a long time, imaging a time when people were flown out here and dumped into the jungle to kill or be killed. We passed a KFC, and I wondered who really won.

"Three minutes 18 seconds." Monteblan stared ahead, stoned and smiling, flying through the green tunnel of bushes and trees, sun rising higher, heat coming up through the day.

"Come on! You don't find this interesting?"

"I don't find anything interesting at seven AM." He yawned. "Three minutes five."

"OK, fine. So the war was grinding on and we wanted out. We were done, but we couldn't just walk away. So we finally agreed to meet their representatives in Paris to make a treaty to end the war. The US delegates rent suites at the most expensive hotel in the middle of Paris. Running up room service bills, champagne, ambassador parties, the works. The Vietnamese don't rent a nice suite. They don't even rent a place at all. They buy some shitty little house in the suburbs of Paris. *Buy it.* The negotiations go on, and the Americans start sweating it out since they're running up this huge bill in the middle of Paris. The Vietnamese aren't giving in on anything. They don't care. They bought a damn house. They don't have bills. They don't have to concede on anything. Just wait the Americans out. How do you beat people like that?"

Monteblan didn't answer so I did.

"You don't. Which means there's always hope. That was a country with Stone Age technology that beat the most technologically power-ful force on the planet. So there's hope! Don't you see? No matter how big it gets, this whole thing they're building, we can beat it!"

My friend frowned. "Beat what?"

"You know, the… *it.* The whole thing. This entire global hyper capitalist dystopian 21st Century, Guy DefuckingBord nightmare—

"Aaaannnnd we're done." Monteblan said, pulling around another truck. "That's your ten."

I opened my mouth to protest and he thrust his hand out, palm facing me.

"That's what I'm talking about," Monteblan told me. "That's your thinking problem. We always end up at Dystopian. You can start talking about a strawberry milk shake, and we end up at dystopian. I don't even know what dystopian means. It's like, machines shooting lasers at people who live under rocks that used to be Los Angeles. Is that right? I should know by now because you say it all the time. Do you realize how much you say dystopian, Rich? Have you gone a day without saying dystopian?"

"It's true."

"How is this dystopian?" Monteblan said, gesturing around at the open landscape. "We're flying through Vietnam smoking a j. Used to be war out here. The whole place was up in flames."

"I'm talking about the global economic model. It's entirely inhuman."

"Europe!" Monteblan shouted back. "I saw bar graphs on the internet! Europe has never, *ever* had less people dying and less wars than today. EVER. How is that dystopian?"

"Control," I shrugged. "A neo feudal corporate construct that grinds people into paralysis through a perfectly engineered social paradigm."

"Did you just throw paradigm at me?" He sighed with disgust. "I should stop the car and make you walk."

"Listen man. My opinion is based on well researched, documented facts. You're just throwing shit out there. What's your point? You never have one."

"Right now I have two of them."

"What?"

He held out a finger. "One, stop talking because your ten minutes are up. Two…"

"But this is a separate talking situation. I talked about Vietnam. Yes. But now we're —

"*Two…*" He held out another finger, looking at me in the rearview. "You have a thinking problem. We're on a morning drive through the country. That's all. But you just turned it into history class meets *1984* goes War of The Machines. How do you even get there? Can't you just look out the window and be cool with shit? *Don't think so much.* Remember your ladyboy wisdom."

"That's more than point two! That was like 2, 3, 4, and—"

"It's The No Talking Show!" Monteblan shouted. "Starring Rich Archer! Welcome to the show where we say *absolutely NOTHING!*"

We took a long curve. I just looked at him, smirking.

"Great, glad to hear it. And we have *so much* to not talk about. Won't it be wonderful?"

Monteblan drove us onwards, punching the eight track. Old crooner music flowed through the speakers. I sank back in my seat and the day slouched forward. My driver remained true to our bargain; wordlessly weaving us past shacks and high grass, down crowded roads towards distant rivers. I flickered in and out of sleep, head banging the window, sweat seeping into my clothes, body getting stiffer. Hours limped past. Then by late afternoon, my friend finally slowed, pulling into graveled asphalt crumbling to the roadside. Peering at a sign sticking up from bushes, he spoke slowly.

"We're here."

"What? Already?"

Monteblan pointed out a crossroad sign nearly obscured by drooping green jungle bushes, *Sabon Sai* showed through in crudely painted English letters under Vietnamese characters.

"This is it." He turned to me. "This is Chicken Town."

He pulled back onto the empty road. Two lanes of rough pavement lead through high grass on either side. Scraggly forest revealed a distant, sparkling river to our left. Gentle hills rose up to our right. I scrambled from back seat to front, grasping at maps. Wind whipped up as speed increased, pages flapping in the breeze. Pinning them with beers, I finger traced our path. Sabon Sai had been marked before leaving Bangkok. A much lower border crossing had been anticipated at the time. Pushed north by thermos demolition, our evasive maneuvers to shake Fucky Charms had further obscured our journey. Measuring distance, estimating time, I spun to my friend grinning.

"We're going to be first," I said. "Everyone else had to use the lower border crossing near Vang."

Monteblan frowned, tugging his beard. "I don't like it. We shouldn't get this close. Not this easy. Something's not right."

"Easy? Laos was easy? What are you talking about?" I slapped the maps sharply. "*This* is Chicken Magic. What Charlie talks about! This is how the good guys win."

"Good guys?" He downshifted. "You smell like dynamite and the car's full of drugs. We bribed our way out of jail and just crossed the Vietnam border with mafia plates. Not sure if we're the Good Guys, buddy."

I frowned, considering the transgressions we had effortlessly racked up while chasing the Chicken.

"Plus don't forget sodomy," Monteblan added.

"Touching a boner isn't sodomy."

"Technicality." Then Monteblan frowned. "Shit. What's this?"

Up ahead, glowing sun dying down behind him, someone was standing in the middle of the road.

**He focused in degrees as speed brought us towards him.** Broad, strong arms waved overhead, signaling us to stop. Large shoulders in a neatly tucked T-shirt. Cargo shorts. Clean white track shoes and low cut socks. Finally the hard, frowning face I had first seen at The Miami hotel.

"Reggie." I turned to Monteblan. "Don't stop. Remember The Israelis."

Monteblan squinted in the sun. "Maybe he needs help."

We raced closer to the Marine in the middle of the road.

"Last time we helped someone in Chicken 65 they laughed at us. Forget him. Go."

Wincing uncomfortably, Monteblan whisked past Reggie. Flicking my eyes to the side view, I saw the Marine squinting in the sun's glare, watching us leave. Feeling satisfied at outsmarting him, my eyed darted ahead. The road turned sharply around a large, rocky hill. Tall, thick grass swayed on the roadside. It was a blind turn into Chicken Town. Monteblan shifted into it when a thought shot through me and I shouted.

"Stop!"

Pablo Cruise slid to a skidding stop on the empty road. I turned in my seat, looking back. Reggie stood, hands on hips, watching us from afar. Grinning, I turned to my driver.

"Let's help. We'll get a Chicken Promise out of him."

Monteblan frowned, looking at me strangely. "That's a guy we know in the middle of nowhere, waving his hands for help. First you say don't stop. Now you say stop because we can get something out of him?"

"Think Chicken!" I shot back. "Seoul Brother told us that and he was right!"

He shook his head. "This race is changing you."

"This isn't about helping people." I turned to look at the Marine, still standing, still staring on the deserted road. "It's winning the damn race. That's all that matters out here. Getting that chicken and not getting screwed while you do. Turn around. Let's see what we can get here."

Monteblan stared at the wheel a moment. Sweat dripped down from his chin. Then he shook his head and let out a sigh. Hitting the gas, he whipped us in a fishtail kicking up gravel. Slowly down the crumbling road, high grass thick on either side, we rolled right up to Reggie. The Marine watched us approach without expression. We stopped. He walked to the driver's side window. Leaning down, he looked in. The long bullet hung swinging from his neck. Reggie wiped sweat from his forehead, squinting in the sun.

"Damn lucky you stopped, Grimace."

Punching the hood, Reggie pointed us towards a hardly visible opening in scraggly bush. Monteblan turned off the road and eased through. Hard branches scratched windows and paint in faint, painful scrawls. High grass swallowed us completely in impenetrable walls of green. Punching the trunk, Reggie urged us forward. Pressing through the bending stalks, Monteblan drove blind through the sea of grass until it vanished suddenly, leaving us in a sparse forest of rough, scraggly trees. Through them, I saw the rushing flow of a distant river. Reggie walked ahead, waving us to follow, and disappeared down an incline. Monteblan piloted Pablo Cruise through the trees, angled down the hill, and rolled us over bumping jungle into cleared terrain.

Reggie's camp was a sharp square of order in the wild. Flames had scorched jungle away precisely. Twin tents were pegged diligently, ropes taught, olive canvas crisp. The Camaro was draped with camouflage netting. A large canvas stretched from the roof. Two poles held it up like a porch. Charlie sat under it, smoking a cigar and marveling at our arrival. Face blazing red in the heat, dripping with sweat, the blaring bright tropical shirt he wore screamed through jungle green. Grasping a whisky bottle he pulled himself up groaning from the dust, shaking his head with a smile.

"Well look here what The Bird delivered."

"Won those Splits." I grinned, stepping out of Pablo Cruise. "How about that?"

"Impressive, I do admit. Chicken 65 always surprises."

Blowing a blue plume of smoke from his stogie, the racer handed me his whiskey. The bottle was plain glass, no label, corked instead of capped. I looked at it dubiously.

"Go on there," he said in his drawl. "No better way to celebrate your vehicular triumph then a blast of premium Lao hooch. Brew it like moonshine up in the hills."

I pulled from the rough, misshapen bottle. The stuff exploded in my throat, burning like fire. Coughing, eyes watering, I passed it to Monteblan. My friend took a sip and sprayed it back out, coughing in surprise, wincing in pain.

"Charlie, they can't even drink your damn whiskey." Reggie swiped the bottle from my coughing friend. "How the hell they gonna help us get the bird?"

"Ah," I raised my finger. "There it is. You need our help. Which we will gladly supply in return for a Chicken Promise."

For a long moment, Reggie stared at me through buzzing jungle heat. Pressing like a wet blanket, slowing movements, the soupy humidity drenched us with sweat. Distant canopy hid the sun, trapping stale air that breathed in heavy and thick. Mosquitos swirled in the moist, dim surroundings.

"Chicken Promise?" The Marine finally said, incredulously. "Asser, this here is a Chicken Opportunity."

"That might well be. But we learned a few things while ahem, *winning* The VV Splits. Like never help someone without a Chicken Promise."

"Did I ask for a Chicken Promise before I stopped you from driving into a military roadblock back there?"

I looked at Charlie. He nodded, shifting the stogie in his mouth.

"That's the truth, Asser. Chicken Town been locked down this year by the local militia." Leaning on the camouflaged Camaro, Charlie blew out a plume of smoke. "Had you not heeded the roadside warnings of my compatriot here, your chicken would have been duly cooked. Both you boys be in jail right now."

"We have the Plates," Monteblan said. "The uh, Slurpy Cone flaps or whatever. We won The Splits. We can just drive through."

"Wouldn't risk it, Grimace," Charlie said. "There is a measure of historic instability in this year's Chicken. Due to fomenting rebellion in the city of Bangkok, payments promised from parties in the army have not been rendered unto Sabon Sai."

"What are you talking about?"

"Bribes." Reggie cut in gruffly. "Chicken 65 pays them motherfuckers off every year. That lets us tear ass through their town. This year, that money didn't make it to Sabon Sai. Shit in Bangkok is too damn hot."

I slapped at a mosquito. "What's going on in Bangkok?"

"That's to be ascertained upon our return, Asser." Charlie said, puffing smoke. "For now we are in the proverbial and literal jungle. Perhaps you recall The General's warning of an impending *coup*. Such shit may indeed have transpired. Not a soul knows. All efforts to raise The General on our radio have been fruitless. Nobody can get a word out of Bangkok. But the fact that tea money was overlooked…"

"Who gets money for tea?" Monteblan said.

"Bribe money, son," Charlie said, tapping ash. "They call it tea money out here. This whole race runs on it. And the fact that it didn't make its way to Sabon Sai makes this a difficult Chicken."

"Damn near impossible. One road into Chicken Town," Reggie said. "They got it locked down tight. Jeeps, trucks, soldiers, all that. I stopped you two from rolling right up into it. Shit…"

He shook his head, turning to Mississippi Charlie.

"C'mon Charlie. Let's hold tight for Gears and Moist. Those boys military. They'll be up here soon enough and you know they ain't having problems handling what we have to do."

With that, Reggie walked from the camp, heading through the trees towards the river.

"Can't wait another night!" Charlie called after him. "Patrol last night was right up on us, Reg. You heard them on the CB! North Road out of Laos got blown, Moist and Gears had to double back!"

Reggie just waved his hand, disgusted, then disappeared through the trees.

"Patrol?"

"They maintain an ever widening perimeter," Charlie answered me. Then flicked ash and spoke to my friend.

"Grimace, help Reggie down there, will you? The man needs a hand but damn if he'll ask for it."

Monteblan nodded, walking silently and heavily through the brush, crashing and stumbling down the hill.

Mississippi Charlie and I were left standing in the heat. The older racer walked over to the Camaro, ducking down under the shade of the canvas. Leaning back on the fat mag tire, he pulled at his shirt, fanning at the thick jungle heat. I joined him, sitting in the dirt by the front door.

"How about Full Metal Jackass?" I suggested. "That's a good Chicken Name for Reggie."

"Never to judge a man till you've walked a mile in his shoes." Charlie winked. "Then you're a mile away and you have his shoes. Here, puff on this."

He handed me a cigar. Flicking open an old zippo, he lit the flame and we puffed deeply on the rich, thick smoke.

"Keeps them mosquitos away," Charlie told me. "Damn if I'm laying down another night by the river. Sure you won't do this without a promise?"

"Maybe for you," I muttered, blowing out smoke, swirling in a shaft of sunlight. "Not for Reggie."

"I admit my compadre is rough around the edges," Charlie drawled. "But you don't know what the man been through. Scraping out Trashcanistan two tours? Iraq before that? Mmmm."

Pursing his lips, Charlie shook his head with a grave look in his eyes.

"Here's the trick on Reggie. Listen to what he says. Then do what he says. If there's one thing that man knows, it's hostile terrain. And what we are facing this year in yon Chicken Town is indeed that."

The jungle buzzed around us, birds high up calling in piercing, distant cries. Sweat rolled from my armpits and I shrugged.

"We're not doing it," I shrugged. "If I've learned one thing out here it's getting a Chicken Promise."

"Oh, Asser." Charlie shook his head, disappointed. "You do sound amateur."

He stretched out the last word, pronouncing the last syllable strangely. Both what he was saying and how he said it bothered me.

"No, you know what's ama*toor*?" I glared at his red face, that purple veined nose blooming beads of sweat. "Ama*toor* is standing on the side of the road with nothing but your dick in your hand, watching someone drive away after risking your life to help them."

"That happens from time to time. But don't you worry. The Bird keeps score." Charlie eased back on the tire, folding his arms propped up over his gut. "Broad and arcane are the balances, my friend. Running through all the races. Bird keeps score. Chicken Promise is a Chicken Promise, sure. But what's that really mean?"

"I was told that's everything out here."

Charlie blew out a long, leisurely plume of smoke. The scraggly brush around us muttered with the buzz of unseen birds and bugs.

"Listen Asser. If I do something for you, and I get a Chicken Promise, who am I really doing it for?"

I thought of that for a minute. "Me. You. A deal. That's what this road runs on."

The racer from Mississippi squinted at me. "So what makes that special? It's people just looking out for themselves. But when you help a fella out just for helping a fella out, well, that's another thing. That's doing it for the Chicken. The spirit of the thing. Bird *loves* that. Run your race thusly, and you get beyond Chicken Promises into the higher realities of Chicken 65. And I promise you my friend…"

Charlie reached for the whiskey bottle, popped the cork and took a pull, wincing at the hit.

"This road *will* lean your way. You'll feel it. You'll be out there with the Chicken. Different race, entirely. Bird will show you things, son. Things you gotta get out of the Chicken Promise mentality to see."

"Like what?"

He raised his eyebrows, blue eyes dancing magically.

"That's hard to tell you. It is a rare and elusive road. Difficult to find out here. Especially if you're busy adding up all those promises, trying to win."

Insects whirred around us. Charlie puffed his cigar. The ember glowed red.

"You've never won, have you?"

"Son, I never tried to win the Chicken. I tried being *with* the Chicken. World a' difference."

"Different how?"

With a heave, he pushed himself up, grunting with the effort. "Don't trouble yourself with such musings, Asser. I imagine I was wrong about you."

Bottle dangling from his hand, trailing blue cigar smoke, Charlie ambled off through the jungle. I watched him grow dim in the shadows of the trees.

"Wrong about me?" I called out after him. "Wrong about what?"

Like Reggie before, Charlie didn't bother answering. Just waved his hand and disappeared in the dim jungle, vanishing through the trees. I looked after him, frowning and confused. Sweat stung my eyes and I rubbed it away. Then Monteblan came crashing through the branches, reaching me out of breath.

"Dude, we gotta do this." My friend grinned. "It's really good Chicken."

"OK..." Ten minutes later I holding my head, overwhelmed with it all. "Tell me what a boom can is again?"

"Hand grenade in gasoline." Reggie told me matter-of-factly. "Duct tape the handle. Pull the pin. Drop it in. Gas eats through the tape. 10, 12 minutes, can goes boom. Double tape it for 20."

He wiped beads of sweat from his mocha colored skin. Squatting over a spread of detailed maps, he shifted through the pages. Just beyond him, the Mekong River rushed in murky brown swirls. A large, roughly built wooden raft bobbed on the currents, lashed firmly together from fallen trees. Ropes extended to a pair of bankside trees, holding it fast. I pointed to it.

"And that will hold both cars?"

"No Asser, you swim with yours. What the fuck?!" Reggie glared at me, snapping up from the maps. "I damn told you the plan!"

"Well tell me again," I told him. "I want to know details because we got screwed out here before."

"No, really?" Reggie made a mock concerned face. "Charlie, did you hear that? Someone ran Chicken 65 and got screwed. Believe that?"

"We did," I said, missing the sarcasm. "We were in a firefight with—"

"Welcome to Chicken 65," Charlie drawled. "Till you get fucked, you're just visiting."

Passing me the whiskey, Charlie lit another cigar. Speaking from the side of his mouth, he puffed the flame.

"Reg, run through it again, huh?"

We gathered closer round the maps. Reggie had reams of them. Some were black and white, others were colored. There were maps with graphs and elevation numbers. Maps with roads and directional marking. Some maps were close ups of buildings. Others showed paths through the jungle. All of them looked like something from a spy film.

"Nobody out here got a better look at Sabon Sai," Reggie said. "I got my boy in the NSA, we toured together. Pulled me this satellite shit back in Bangkok. Terrain, heat mapping, river currents, all that. I know this piece of shit town better than anybody grown up in it. Right here..."

He tapped one of the maps with his finger.

"Is where they got the bird. And this is where their people will be. See, they expecting us from here or here."

Clearing the dirt, Reggie placed another map, this one a larger overhead view of the town marked *Sabon Sai* in clean block letters. Reggie pointed to two roads in and out of the small town. Both were marked with circles and Xs. Far behind the buildings, beyond forest was the thick stripe of the Mekong River. A circle was there. He tapped it.

"That's where the cars float in. We got flow estimates this time of year, plus weight of the vehicles, add that up and Charlie, we looking at 20 minutes maximum. Maybe more depending on whether you catch a current in the middle. Best to stay by the banks. Ain't real deep, but shit, we don't want to play around."

"What happens if we play around?"

"On that river?" Reggie glanced at the current. "Nothing good. Miss the landing, you be gone on the Mekong. Good for getting the hell outta dodge. Not shit we want on the insert."

"OK," I said, picturing a spinning raft adrift through the heart of Vietnam darkness. "No playing around."

"So right *here*," Reggie tapped that space by the river again on the map. "Is where we land the vehicles. Charlie and one of you motherfuckers doing that. I insert round here, overland."

He pointed to a rough edge of satellite mapped jungle, dark and foreboding, then tapped spots on the map, slashed with red marker.

"Boom cans go here. Two timed out at 10, the last at 20. First two booms for distraction. That lets us get the bird."

In my mind I imagined how loud a hand grenade would sound, blasting in a can of gasoline. Reggie continued.

"That shit flames up like crazy with the gasoline. Looks lots worse than it is. Have them all running for it, firing like crazy, running around the jungle here...."

He gestured over a large part of distant terrain, then moved his hand to a cleared area.

"While we up here, on the scope for any loose ends."

"And uh, what would be a loose end in this type of situation?" I asked, trying to sound casual.

"Ain't going to be loose ends, Asser," Reggie replied, voice tight with control. "Those boys gonna run towards the boom like good motherfucking soldiers while we go down, get the damn bird and fuck off outta Sabon Sai down the river."

"Right, it's just loose ends? Like when things are blowing up and people have guns? It's just that you mentioned it, and since I'm—"

"YOU," he said loudly, standing up full height and pointing squarely at my chest. "YOU are the loose end here. You out here in the jungle wearing a damn suit like we going for appletinis. Can't even drink our damn whiskey. I run a million ops like this with *lives* on the line, not a damn chicken. And you here second guessing me?"

His glare was impossible to confront. Eyes like fire stared at me in the darkening jungle. Then he scowled and looked over at Charlie.

"Charlie this motherfucker with you on the float. I'll take fat boy with me in the jungle. We lay those cans and hit the hill, meet you with the bird. I want those cars down here, strapped and loaded by twenty two hundred hours. Equipment checks, inventory, then we roll."

Grabbing the bottle of whiskey, Reggie went to inspect the raft. Jumping nimbly on the bobbing wood, he kicked at some pegs, testing rope strength. Sunlight was fading, throwing the Marine in shadow while The Mekong whispered darkly.

Charlie pushed himself up with a grunt. "Gentlemen, you have your orders."

"I don't like it," I said. "Something's going to happen out there."

"Usually does," Charlie agreed.

He ambled off down the riverbank, trailing cigar smoke. Staring out through thick, hanging branches, the old man watched the river. Monteblan looked up from the maps, grinning wide.

"Told you this was good Chicken," he said. "When's the last time you did an armed invasion with a Vietnam vet?"

"Iraq," I said, walking with him through the trees back to Pablo Cruise.

"When were you in Iraq?"

"Not me, him." I swatted at more mosquitos, sweat running rivers down my back. "Reggie's an Iraq vet. A sniper. We're going into the jungle to set off hand grenade bombs with a sniper who doesn't like us and wears a bullet around his neck."

"I think he's cool with me." Monteblan stumbled and crashed through limbs, speaking up behind me. "Just you he doesn't really like."

"Great, thanks for pointing that out."

"Anyway, it's pretty damn…. *Chicken*." Monteblan said, finally finding the right word. "Kinda why I bought the body armor."

Finding the clearing he walked ahead to the car.

"Great," I muttered to myself with a grim feeling of dark foreboding. "Body armor, guns, hand grenades in gasoline and a sniper who doesn't like me. What could possibly go wrong?"

Walking to Pablo Cruise, I cleared some space near the tire, made a pillow with my suit jacket, and looked up at the stars. Watching them I felt the jungle pressing in, sensed the slow growth of roots and creeping vines tangling all around. Birds called out, animals answered and insects hummed in thick, stifling heat. I stared at dark shapes and melting shadows. Primal, tribal fears flickered within. Surely, this sinister thickness was another enemy to consider. I wondered if the jungle had been factored into Reggie's plans. The seething beast might trip us up in a million tangled ways. I thought of rising up, raising the question, but dark, narcotic heat trapped me like tar. Meaning only to rest, I slumped, then drifted, dropping swiftly into sleep.

**"Shhhh!"**

The sharply whispered command jolted me awake. I startled, drenched in sweat, pinned down by Reggie's knee. His hand covered my mouth. The car was gone. Crouching over me, the Marine stared intently into the brush.

Jungle sounds squawked and cawed all around. The world was one black wall. My eyes slowly adjusted. Through the trees, deep in distant grass, flashlight arcs were sweeping patrol. My heart froze. Voices floated through the steamy night; low chatter in Vietnamese. Reggie stared tensely at the roving lights, nine millimeter in hand. For a moment the patrol drifted closer, and I heard the soft click of Reggie releasing the safety. Heart hammering in my ears, I listened to voices growing louder, watched lights coming closer, until a distant commander called out from the road. The lights swept away, returning into the grass, then disappearing altogether. Reggie relaxed beside me, finally taking his hand off my mouth and standing up. Voice low, he started back towards the river.

"Let's move."

Pushing myself up from the dirt, I pulled at mosquito netting that Monteblan must have thrown over me. Stuffing it into my jacket pocket I followed Reggie. Floating shadow, the Marine moved fast through jungle trees. Moonlight flickered ahead, glowing on the Mekong. I reached it panting, heart hammering with nerves, nearly crashing into my friend.

Monteblan was barely visible. Slathered with greasepaint, black body armor and dark helmet obscured him further. His grin showed white teeth in the night. Behind him, the raft bobbed with both cars tightly bound. Darkness on the far bank was total and foreboding. Moonlight flickered on the rushing water. Charlie was pulling at ropes by the Camaro, fastening tires tighter. Reggie was dipping his hands into river mud, streaking his clothes, face, and legs. Tense excitement licked amidst us with strange electricity. Eyes wide, hushed instinctively, I whispered to my friend.

"Dude I fell asleep. Why didn't you wake me up?"

"Tried." Breathing heavily, dripping sweat, Monteblan whispered back. "You were out like a light. Reggie told me to forget you."

"Thanks," I replied. "He just had his gun out, by the way. Ready to shoot people."

Monteblan seemed nonplussed.

"Dead," I clarified. "Shoot people dead with the gun in his... what the hell is this?"

I tugged at the sticks of dynamite I just now noticed, sticking from the back of my friend's shorts.

"We got it," Monteblan shrugged. "Might as well use it. Chicken 65 and all."

"Yeah..." My eyes drifted over to Reggie, rifle raised to the moon, testing his scope. "Think maybe we should rethink our involvement in this level of Chicken?"

"Already hit some pretty heavy levels," Monteblan whispered, wiping sweat and streaking his paint. "Blew up a thermos, shit in jail, you thought you were Jesus, threw dynamite at a car, there was that sniper plus the la—"

"Right, the ladyboy, of course."

"Are you sure you only touched her boner?" Monteblan squinted through shadows, tightening his helmet strap. "Sounds a little... I don't know, light on details."

My face flushed. "Dude, it was a boner, I touched it, that's all!"

A smack hit the back of my head. I turned to see Reggie, whispering fiercely.

"Keep that ladyboy shit down, motherfucker. You want to suck a dick, we got to get through this shit first. On the raft. Move."

"I don't suck dick," I explained. "I touched a boner. It was an experience, very exotic, happened fast, I just, you know—"

"No. I don't know shit about that." Reggie said flatly. "Fat Boy, move."

Monteblan stepped away, dipping down and rising up with bamboo balanced on one shoulder.

"Are you just going to let him call you Fat Boy?"

Monteblan ignored me. Sloshing gas cans dangled heavily on both ends of the dipping pole. Struggling for balance, he saluted Reggie.

The Marine frowned. "Don't salute me Grimace. Makes my ass a target. I ain't trying to get shot out here. On me. Move."

Reggie hoisted a long canvas satchel onto his back. Clicking his gun, he checked bullets then slipped nimbly through brush, melting into darkness.

"Chicken 65," my friend whispered, hustling with tight steps through the brush after Reggie.

"Salute him!" I whispered after the dark space in the jungle where they disappeared.

*"Asser!"*

Charlie was standing on the raft, long pole in hand, a shadow in the moonlight.

*"Untie that rope! Get on this damn fool thing! Move!"*

I fumbled through branches toward the river, unlooping rope from a mud slicked tree trunk. The raft moved quickly, slipping into stream. Leaping for the drifting craft, I landed hard on the bobbing wooden deck. Arms spinning for balance while current pulled us faster, I dropped into an awkward squat. Charlie stood sure near the stern, pole in hand, touching the water lightly behind us. Bough thick banks shot past silently. Water whispered and swirled. Reaching for my pocket, I found the necktie and wrapped it fast around my forehead. Tense with adrenaline I grinned, wildness all around.

"Chicken 65," I whispered softly.

"Chicken 65," Charlie replied.

Floating silently under moonlight, we drifted down The Mekong towards the Chicken.

**We moved fast past shadowed banks draped with full, drooping branches.** Far away amidst scattered stars, the moon glowed softly silver. Free from jungle canopy, the night felt vast. Water rippled in shifting reflection. Current twirled us gently and Charlie prodded tensely with the pole, keeping us centered. For a while we drifted quickly, then gradually slowed. Charlie relaxed. I remembered something I had been meaning to ask.

"Charlie, what's a huckleberry friend?"

Mississippi laughed, surprised. "Where'd you pick that up?"

"Some old song I heard this morning," I said. "This guy was singing about the moon and his huckleberry friend. What's it mean?"

"Take the wheel a minute, will ya?"

"I don't know how to do that."

Pulling the pole from the water, walking barefoot, he moved in sure, balanced steps.

"Ain't gonna learn sitting there."

Charlie pushed the pole in my hand. Taking hold, I crouched nervously. The raft felt more balanced now; our pace steady on the water. Relieved, I walked in shuffle steps to the back of the raft. Dipping the pole nervously behind us, I poked around, trying to feel bottom. Charlie was at the Camaro, reaching through the front window, finding his whiskey bottle. Popping the cork, he took a large swallow then passed me the stuff. I shook my head.

Charlie frowned. "Son, how many times you gonna get a chance to drink whiskey under the moon while floating down the damn Mekong?"

Thinking of it that way, I took the bottle. The stuff went down like fire. I gasped. Charlie laughed. Swatting at some flies, he leaned against the car, looking up at the stars in the distant night.

"This right here," he drawled fondly. "Is what I'd bottle up and take with me if I could. Mmmm."

Tipping the bottle, he took another deep pull then plugged it with the cork. A bat or bird looped down from the sky. The water moved slowly. We pushed on towards Sabon Sai.

"You never told me what a—"

"A huckleberry friend..." Charlie interrupted, puffing deeply on his cigar. "Is your *real* friend. Back when I was a boy we'd go picking huckleberries. You only go out there with your best pal. Sure, you'd have lots of buddies, but only one huckleberry friend. Like Grimace there. He's your huckleberry. Somebody understands you. Knows what you're going through out there. Buddy to buy you a beer when you're down. Got one of them in this race, that's all a fella really needs."

Along the banks there were green rushes of bushes. The starlight twinkled and Mississippi Charlie's cigar was a red ember in the darkness. I touched the pole to the side, keeping us centered in the gently moving river.

"How many Chickens have you run?"

"This one here be twenty two," he drawled.

"Must have seen lots."

The red faced man laughed a little, flicking some ash off the side of the raft. "Yes sir."

"What's the wildest thing you've ever seen out here?"

Charlie squinted a moment, staring ahead into the darkness, thinking. Then his eyes opened and he nodded.

"Chicken Whisper."

"What's that?"

"Pass me the wheel." He reached for the pole, stepping towards me. "And reach for that bible there on the front seat."

Handing Charlie the bamboo I inched past him. The Camaro was lashed down tightly beside Pablo Cruise. Reggie had done stellar work securing the vehicles. Through the open window, I saw the old book in the passenger's seat. Taking it out, I heard Charlie's voice over my shoulder.

"Page hundred and eighty or somewheres, I do believe."

Leaning against the car on the slightly bobbing, dipping craft, I flipped through faded, poorly type set pages.

"Why do people hate the Chicken Bible?" I squinted at a grainy Xeroxed photo, too smudged to really see. "Is it true people can get arrested for what's in here?"

"Lordy." Charlie moved the cigar to the corner of his mouth. "That what they saying? Well, I guess that's what you get from a bunch a dummies never read the thing. Nah, nothing in there that would tarnish anyone's good name. Like they got one to start with."

He laughed.

"Real dope didn't make in them pages, anyways. Back in Biloxi I got boxes full. Deals. Magic. War stuff. Stories you wouldn't believe. Politics and money and things. Left all that out."

"But people still don't like it?"

"Nope, they don't."

"Why?"

Charlie didn't answer, just dug in deep with the pole, pushing us hard, the raft moving slow, spinning slightly as we moved with the stream. I hefted the Chicken Bible in my hand, all worn pages and crumbling cover.

"You didn't put the real dirt down," I pressed. "So what's to hate on?"

"Because that Bible makes this all mean something. Most people don't like that. You start telling them there's more to things then running in circles and dipping your dick, well, people get upset."

"Why?"

For a long moment we drifted in silence. Then Charlie spoke low, the glowing red ember of his cigar bobbing in the darkness.

"If Chicken 65 means something, a fella has a decision to make about the race. Some fellas just laugh it off and live it up. Another type of fella feels in his heart that there is something real important out there. But he pretends not to know that, so he can have his fun and win. Or he runs some of the race with it, but when the road gets rough, puts it down. Says it don't really count right there. That leaves just a few who are really out here for Chicken 65. Not many people race that way. Nobody likes us much. And we don't win much. But the race would be lost without us."

"Why?"

Mississippi Charlie stared ahead into darkness, sweating now, pushing the pole hard into the river bed below. Birds chirped in mournful calls across the river, strangely close, oddly human sounding.

"Well, that's difficult to properly say," Charlie finally said. "You see Asser, there's the Chicken, and there's Chicken 65. And people get confused between the two. They fight for the Chicken, and forget about Chicken 65. But folks like me, well, when it comes down to it? We'll always choose Chicken 65. That's how the race stays alive. All the races, all them years. Because just a few fellas out there are ready to let go of the Chicken, if it means holding onto Chicken 65."

I thought of this a moment. "How do you do that?"

"Different for everybody. You'll know when it happens. It won't be easy to do. Especially when you do it for folks who don't care about all that. Folks who don't particularly care for *you*. But son, if you do? The Bird will show you things. Powerful things, good and bad. Some them things best left in the dark. But with them are particular revelations which will light your night, bright as day. And you'll never be alone again. Because you'll be with it, then. You'll be out there with The Bird. Whole different road, son."

I thought a moment, drifting in the heated dark wilds.

He smiled. "Now pass me that bottle and open that bible. Find the page yet? Tell me about old Prasert. There's a rare man who got the Chicken *and* Chicken 65. Good one to go out with."

He nodded, satisfied, lips pursed around the cigar, and we moved downriver swifter now. Charlie tossed me his lighter. I lit the spark, peering through flickering light to read aloud.

## *PRASERT WIRAT*

## *Chicken 2012*

Prasert Wirat holds the unique distinction of being the only Thai aside from Somchai Kitapoon to win Chicken 65. The fact that this was done entirely on a moped is feat enough for the bible. But the real magic was, in fact, magic. Prasert had learned what was later termed 'The Chicken Whisper'. This powerful prayer was taught by jungle monks, deep in the Udon Thani region. Said with proper ritual, the incantation had the power to call the Chicken. Spoken miles away or mere inches, the Chicken Whisper sent the bird fl apping towards its master. Once in possession, The Chicken Whisper also calmed the bird. Through such magic Prasert claimed victory in Chicken 2012.

The bird rode the entire length of Chicken 65 perched peacefully on his moped handlebars. Along the way, rival racers at times stole, tricked, or cheated the Chicken away from him. Whenever that happened, Prasert's Chicken Whisper always called it back. Finally, racers realized there was nothing do but accept Prasert's powerful magic.

In spite of such slanted odds, the race has been claimed as one of the most enjoyable Chicken 65s ever run. All who raced say that peace and harmony prevailed in Chicken 2012. Former rivals became fast friends, building relationships that strengthened the bond of not just that Chicken, but every Chicken 65 to come. Following Prasert in cheerful procession into Bangkok, they showed Thailand a different face of Chicken 65. A pleasant, peaceful face that garnered much needed good will amidst the ever shifting seas of political and military favor.

It has been suggested by some that the race was on the verge of being eliminated when Prasert won. And that his Chicken 65, and the way he won, is the one that saved us all. But Prasert will never tell. Leaving Bangkok after his victory, the mystical moto taxi driver disappeared in the northern jungles of Thailand. His secret location is revealed only to high ranking politicians, army generals and titans of industry in Thailand. They present large payments for blessings and magical protection. This money is then distributed by Prasert to poor villages in the North, building schools, hospitals, and homes.

Winning the Chicken in such mystical fashion, then helping the land in such meaningful ways has made Prasert Wirat the most legendary of all Chicken 65 victors. Honored especially by moto taxi drivers throughout the land, his name is still invoked in prayer for protection on the road.

"Wow," was all I could say. "That sounds amazing."

"No," Charlie winked. "It sounds like this."

Closing his eyes, Charlie removed the cigar from his mouth. He turned his booze battered face towards the distant, glowing moon. Bathed in silver light, the old racer pursed his lips. The world melted away. Time seemed to tunnel around us. Then a strange sound emerged; a guttural, flickering whisper both haunting and hypnotic. It drifted in and out of jungle noises, more a part of nature than anything a human might make. Shocked, I stared at him until the sound softly trailed off. Charlie opened his eyes.

"Where'd you learn that?" I asked him, amazed. "You found him in the jungle? Did Prasert teach you that? Can *I* learn that?"

"'Fraid we don't have time for all of that."

Shaking his head, Mississippi Charlie smiled sadly. I felt the raft budge slightly, and looked up to see we had hit the bank. Charlie sighed, looking around at the jungle, taking it all in.

"Well, that was quite a trip."

"Yeah," I echoed faintly.

Stepping to me, Charlie shook my hand and looked me in the eye, voice soft.

"Glad it was you, son."

Transfixed by some strange power in his eyes, I stammered my response while the jungle buzzed all around.

"Y-yeah, me too, Charlie. Maybe Monteblan and you will party some, too. But that. Yeah. That was a good ride."

My voice trailed off. The old racer held my gaze, not letting go of my hand.

"Don't forget what I told you out here. Bird been talking to me about you, son. The Bird decided. That's all. Whatever happens, The Bird decides. Remember that."

I swallowed, my mouth dry. Charlie winked and lit up in a smile. Then Reggie was there.

"*Asser!*" The Marine's voice was a harsh, urgent whisper. "*Get off that damn boat, now!*"

**Charlie looked confused.**

"Where's the bird?"

Reggie scowled, reaching down and yanking the rope, throwing it in circles around a tree.

"Where's Monteblan?" I said.

There was a rustling commotion in the darkness. My friend came crashing through the jungle, stumbling and gasping. Kicking and pulling at limbs and branches, he fell face first into the mud.

"Half Vietnam hearing Grimace out there!" Reggie whispered harshly. "Can't keep up, neither."

Spread eagled, heaving in great breaths, my friend farted.

"*And* that," Reggie said angrily, waving his hand in front of his face.

"Sorry." Monteblan gasped, rolling over. "Ate a bag of bugs from Laos."

Reggie shot his piercing eyes at me.

"Out the boat. Now."

Instinctively obeying, I leapt off the raft into slippery mud. Passing Monteblan, I squatted down beside him.

"You OK?"

"I'm never saving a rainforest again." My friend gasped. "It tried to kill me."

"Grimace!"

Monteblan lifted his head at Reggie's urgent command. The Marine stood silhouette in the moonlight, pointing to the raft.

"Drive your damn car off the float. We are *not* doing this river with you."

Monteblan nodded, gasping for breath. "Yeah, OK."

"Wait," I protested. "How the hell are we going to get out of here?"

"There."

Reggie pointed down a dark tunnel of trees, running parallel to the river. Twin tire ruts showed the most primitive of roads.

"Where does that even go?" I asked.

"Find out later. Now get those glasses."

Monteblan was holding up a pair of binoculars with a weak, trembling hand. Grabbing them, slipping my head through the cord so they hung on my chest, I straightened up. Reggie didn't bother with orders. Just stepped into the jungle and melted.

For a moment I was stunned at how fast it was all happening. Then I followed, throwing myself into darkness. Heat strangled me. Jungle leaves and sticking nettles pulled at me. Just ahead, a shadow shot forward. Startled at Reggie's speed, I chased after him. Blindly through branches while lone, eerie calls of unseen creatures drifted down from the canopy, I ran with sweat blurring my eyes. Dodging ahead through unseen openings, Reggie was a flow of motion. Slipping artfully through branches and brush that tangled me in crashing falls, I struggled desperately to keep up with him. Breath burning, sweat stinging my eyes, I heard a fast rustling at my feet and jumped, astonished, as a huge snake slithered wickedly fast into brush. Then I banged into Reggie. He pointed through branches to an open path that looked like dry creek bed.

"There. Stay low."

Crouching down he shot into the dusty creek bed. I followed. Moonlight glowed down above. Loose ground slid underfoot as the terrain slanted, taking us sharply uphill. Climbing the last meters, pulling ourselves up and through rocks and wedged branches, we finally reached a flat plateau.

"Wow," I whispered, breathing deeply, looking down at the town we had seen in maps earlier that day.

*"Down!"*

Reggie whispered harshly, yanking on my belt loop. I collapsed in an awkward pile in the dust. The Marine was on one knee beside me. Pulling the pouch from his back, he unclasped fasteners and had it open before him. Moon shone down on rifle parts. His hands blurred like someone tying their shoe. Parts came together in memorized movements. Scope, stock, barrel, suppressor, all of it clicking, snapped into place, followed by bullets. Crossing himself quickly, he kissed the one hanging from his neck. Then he was prone, eye to scope, looking down at Chicken Town.

"Wait a second," I gasped, heart still pounding from our run. "Who are you shooting?"

"Nobody who gets out the way. Get those glasses live. Spot for me."

Heart pumping, I crouched kneeling beside him. Sweat poured from my skin. Bugs swirled, biting. I cursed but didn't dare stop to swat them. There was no question of disobeying Reggie's orders. The night felt like machinery moving. Preordained clicks of invisibly fit gears, silently grinding into inevitable events. I felt it. Sensed it. Couldn't stop it. Fumbling with the case, I pulled binoculars to my eyes and the darkness charged bright green with night vison.

"See them?"

Blurs moved through my lens and I adjusted dials. The world cleared. Bright green figures leapt into focus below.

"Yeah," I replied softly, excitement rising

The jeep was parked below a streetlight. Two soldiers were lounging in the front seats, AK-47s lying in their laps. Positioned to block
a driveway, the jeep served as barricade protecting a simple house at
jungle's edge. I followed the driveway path with my glasses, sweeping
the backyard area. Then I gasped.

"Chicken 65!"

"We have the bird," Reggie whispered. "Confirm."

"Bird confirmed," I whispered back, awestruck.

After wild, untold miles of dynamite, gun fights, whiskey, not-
quite-women and war, the Chicken of Chicken 65 was just a mere 500
meters away. Spellbound I watched the bird pecking and strutting in
a sparse, dusty patch behind the guarded house. Besides me, Reggie
shifted in the dirt, adjusting his position.

"Scope the area," he murmured. "Tell me what's happening. I am
locked on target."

"Target?" I lowered the glasses to look at him. "I thought the
Chicken comes back alive."

"No shit, Asser. 12 o'clock from the bird. Focus."

Raising the binoculars, I focused on the Chicken, then moved my
line of site to 12 o'clock.

"Oh."

"Yeah, oh," Reggie said sarcastically.

Leaning against the house wall, hidden in shadows, a lone guard
smoked his cigarette. Lanky and young, the large AK-47 rifle hung
awkwardly over his boney shoulder. Oblivious to our presence in the
darkness, he puffed calmly on his cigarette. Charged with tension, I
watched smoke materializing in weird, digital patterns of light green.

"You're not shooting him."

"If he's a good soldier I won't." Reggie replied.

"What does that mean?" I whispered, staring at the boy.

"A good soldier runs towards the cannon fire," Reggie murmured back. "If he's a good soldier I won't have to shoot him."

I frowned, not understanding. "What cannon fire?"

***BOOM!***

The blazing roar ripped through distant jungle, scorching the night with fire. Startled, I swept my glasses towards the chaos. Bright green blurs of heat blinded my view. I lowered the glasses. Deeper in the jungle, closer to our earlier camp, the night was on fire.

"Boom can one," Reggie said beside me, still staring through the scope.

I heard the smile of pleasure in his voice. Then from below I heard the sound of gunning engines. I grabbed the glasses in time to see the Jeep racing off around the corner, soldiers leaned forward and low.

I swept the glasses fast, back to the yard. The lone lanky soldier was standing in the yard now, head craned, staring up over the wall to see the distant flames. He looked at the Chicken. Then looked again towards the jungle flames. Reggie muttered beside me.

"Let's go my man, no chicken worth a bullet...."

Distant flames raged. Soldiers yelled. Frozen in place, staring at the young guard, the shrill sound of jungle insects pierced my ears. Blood pounded, shaking my vision. I wanted to yell. I tried. There was no sound. Frozen in shock, unable to move or make a sound, I heard the man with the rifle beside me, quietly laugh.

"Shit, this motherfucker here round me off. Twenty be a good number. Got nineteen hits confirmed, Asser. Mile away, most of them. Scoped up on some restaurant. Wouldn't tell me shit about the motherfucker. 'The target has a cigarette after lunch.' That's all. Mile away I'm watching. Then that motherfucker steps right outside and lights his cigarette. Stands there, smoking. I'm waiting for the order. Watching him. Thinking: yeah, enjoy that cigarette. Last thing you doing on this planet.' Nineteen of them motherfuckers. Most I knew about any one of them is they smoke a cigarette after lunch. How's that right?"

*BOOM!*

Fountains of flame shot up from another ripping blast in the jungle, a thundering roar louder than the first. This one was closer. The night danced with flames. Reggie laughed.

"Yeah, Grimace put the dynamite in that one. And look there, that's a good choice, son."

I swept the glasses from the flaming boom can and looked to see the Chicken guard run dashing down the driveway. Rushing around an unseen corner, he left the bird. Cold sweat and relief washed over me. I collapsed in rattled nerves. Reggie was already up, slinging the rifle case over his shoulder and dashing downhill through the night of licking flames. Fumbling to my feet, I followed him down the dry creek bed into a thick of trees, and then suddenly, magically, it was there.

In the simple yard of dirt and chicken wire, oil cans and beer bottles, the Chicken flapped nervously. While flames beyond the wall flickered wild, the bird jumped in circles. Unseen soldiers shouted as the first sprays of automatic fire started. Reggie was crouched, jungle fire dancing in his eyes. He took the first steps forward. The Chicken stopped. Cocking its head curiously, strangely calm with all the chaos around, it stared at the approaching Marine. Moving slowly in calm, measured strides, Reggie closed in. Flames flickered over the wall. The bird just watched. Closer now, Reggie paused, standing. His fast swooping move was instant. He turned to me grinning, bird pinned under his arm.

"See that?" Reggie said, pointing at me. "The Chicken didn't fight. That means The Bird is with me. The Bird decides. You saw that shit, Asser. This is my Chicken 65."

Then the soldier was there. Staring at Reggie, eyes wide, his mouth went open to yell. He never got the chance.

A blur in the night, Reggie hit low. Chicken pinned under one arm, he thrust up, flipping the young sentry. Grabbing a wrist, the Marine pulled down while the boy flew. His wild, pin wheeling spin was like a carpet had been yanked from underfoot. The rifle flew uselessly from his hands. Flipped flat in the dirt, I heard the *whoomp!* of breath knocked from his body. Reggie balled his fist, punched hard, and the body went limp. Then the Marine was moving past me, running towards the creek bed, pointing to the ground and snapping orders.

"Grab that AK."

While distant shouts and gunshots floated in the night, I reached down in the dirt for the weapon. Faraway firelight flickered on the dull barrel. Holding it heavy in my hands, I was taken with its ugly efficiency. The simple machine had one purpose: death. Realizing this I didn't want to hold it. But Reggie had told me and now Reggie was gone. Panicked to be left behind I clutched the weapon tight and threw myself into the jungle darkness.

Rushed with adrenaline, I ran racing up the creek bed. Sliding down the other side in a rain of rocks and dirt, I just barely saw Reggie reaching the trees. The Chicken looked back at me, tucked calmly under the Marine's arms. Then both were swallowed in jungle. Following the bird I plunged in after them, rushing towards the river. From behind I heard shouts and shots growing louder. I realized they were shouting and shooting at me. Smashing through branches I looked down at my hands. How did this happen? I was running through the jungle with a machine gun. Hefting it tightly, I grinned like a lunatic. This was good Chicken.

**BOOM!**

The third and final boom can went off in perfectly timed distraction. Shouts and shots behind me veered away, soldiers running towards the explosion. Slapping through leaves and pulling through brush I charged relentlessly forward, totally blind. Panic swirled. I almost shouted out, nearly called his name. Then moonlight on water danced through faraway branches. Smiling wide I raced towards the river. *We made it. We did it. We got the Chicken!*

Running distracted, the root caught me at full speed. I went sprawling, hands reflexively tensing, machine gun jumping alive. The startling spits lit white with muzzle flash. Circling as I tumbled, they blurred around me in evil halo. Finding my feet, sliding and scrambling, I burst through the last jungle leaves.

The raft had pushed off and was slowly drifting. The Chicken was flapping in the back of the Camaro. Reggie held the pole, staring at me in shock. Charlie sat leaning against the car tire, stunned in the moonlight. His hands clutched at his patterned shirt. A new shape was emerging in the design. He looked at it strangely, watching it slowly spread. Then Charlie took his hands away, slick with blood. Dripping to the raft, it glistened darkly in the moonlight. He looked to me while the boat slowly drifted away. Then Charlie's lips moved, hardly at all. His soft, southern drawl just a whisper.

"It was The Bird."

Pulled in swirling currents, the raft went spinning into swiftly moving darkness and was gone.

**Buzzing jungle insects screamed in my mind.** My knees weakened as the AK-47 fell numbly in the mud. Monteblan's arm wrapped around my shoulder, pulling me hard. Weaving unsteady on the muddy Mekong banks, I stared at the swirling river that had swallowed Charlie. Then I was shoved in Pablo Cruise. Sprawled numbly in the back seat I felt wheels spinning, spraying mud, and we were roaring through a tunnel of jungle trees. Shouts chased us, shots fired. Monteblan yanked us onto road.

*"You alright?!"*

I didn't answer my friend's shout, just held on, bucking in the back seat while he flipped off the lights in stealth mode. Road dark. Pablo Cruise a matte black phantom flying past shack houses and rice fields on perilous, narrow roads lit glowing in the moon light. Numbly watching tumbling landscape I felt the road open wider. Street lights appeared. Monteblan gunned us faster, harder, far from Sabon Sai where—

"I killed Charlie!"

The words erupted suddenly from my throat, as if had taken that long for my traumatized mind to realize what had happened.

"It was an accident!" Monteblan shouted back. "And you didn't kill him! You don't know that. You shot Mississippi Charlie! That's all!"

"That's all?!"

I yelled over the rushing wind as Monteblan took another turn, lights out, flying blind through Vietnam.

"I shot Mississippi Charlie and that's *all*!?"

Monteblan's tense eyes flicked back at me through the rearview. I wondered what I looked like now that I had killed a man.

"Sleep it off, bro!" He gunned around a turn, taking us farther into darkness. "We'll deal tomorrow. We'll hear it on the CB. I promise. Charlie's not dying."

I nodded vaguely, slumping down in the seat. My lowered view of passing roads flashed me back to youth. I remembered being little. Driving with my dad. Smelling his cologne and hearing ratatat chatter from AM news. Suburban green winding by. Then I blinked, back in Vietnam. There was a plastic bag of white powder by my feet. Warm beer rolled dumbly beside it. I yanked both up while Pablo Cruise raced through shadows. Popping the beer I drank half down. Ripping the plastic I poured in powder. Most missed. White dust flew wild in racing wind. The rest swirled in. Kicking my head back I drank the mix down.

"What the fuck did you just do?" Monteblan shouted back, eyes staring at the white powder. "Rich! That's opium! That's shit you don't fuck with!"

I smiled, sighing with pleasure, and saluted.

"Chicken...sixty....*five.*"

Things shifted. There's a strange plane stretched between dreams. Not really sleep. Not quite life. Charlie was there. Right beside me. He was sitting looking out the window. Wind ruffled his straw blonde hair and he smiled.

"The Bird decides."

**The door was thrown open and I had thrown up.** Blinking to focus, I stared down at the putrid mess pooled on the backseat floor. Puke blended with spilled beer and opium mush. Sticky sticks of dynamite lay half plastered with the maps and hundred dollar bills. I tried to remember how I had gotten here. Looking up, I tried to find out where 'here' was. Pablo Cruise was parked on the highway shoulder. The road was poorly paved with a rough dirt shoulder. Cars and trucks roared past. Monteblan was gone. I wiped my eyes. Felt heat flashes. My stomach clutched sporadically. Never had a hangover felt heavier. Frowning at the bitter taste in my mouth, I pushed on a pair of sunglasses and stepped outside.

Sun was rising. Trucks and scooters passed in fast, sporadic blasts. I looked around dumbly. The ocean shimmered through a low row of distant trees. I walked towards it down a hard packed dirt road. Pausing to dry heave, I felt cold sweat on my face. Blinking away the headache, I moved towards the beach. Sighing ocean sounds replaced the rough highway. Distant waves crashed majestically, foaming wild. Sitting alone on white sand, stripped of helmet and body armor, Monteblan watched. There were beers beside him. I kicked through sand and sat down with my friend.

"Hey."

Monteblan sipped a beer slowly, not looking at me, eyes squinting in the sun.

"What happened?" I said.

Waves crashed in, followed by more. I was going to ask again when Monteblan finally answered.

"You shot Mississippi Charlie and went into shock or something. I threw you in the car and half of Vietnam was chasing us. You poured half the opium in a warm beer and drank that. Now we're in Cambodia."

Charlie's shocked face floated in my mind. With it a wave of feelings too large to process. I didn't understand how to feel. I looked around at the beach, stretching empty in both directions.

"Cambodia, cool." I rubbed my itching face. "What it's been like?"

"You puked a bunch. I slapped you lots."

"No, I mean Cambodia?"

"Like Laos." He drank some beer. "With mud instead of dust."

Some waves crashed in.

"Sorry about the... uh..." Struggling for words that might capture what I had done in Vietnam, I rubbed my face.

"What, shooting someone with a machine gun then overdosing? No sweat. Chicken 65."

He didn't look at me and there was no humor in his voice.

"Just needed a little break, huh?"

"This isn't a little break." Monteblan sipped more of his beer, squinting at the crashing waves. "You lost me at manslaughter."

"You're the one who said it would be good Chicken back there in 'Nam!"

"Right, then friends are shot with machine guns and you're overdosing on motherfucking *opium*. You could have died, dude. There's a time to call shit. This is it."

Pushing himself up, he stretched and looked around. The morning beach glowed. Further up the sand, trees with low hanging branches swept down to incoming waves. Through the leaves I saw a wooden temple made of white wood with gold trim. Monteblan started walking towards it. I scrambled up from the sand, shaky on my legs, following.

"Wait. You didn't hear Charlie on the raft. What he said. *The Bird did it.* That's what he said then and he told me before it happened. He saw it. Said it was The Bird. There was all this stuff he was telling me on the raft like—like... The Forces? You know you have The Forces he's like that with the Chicken there's—"

"Stop." My friend cut me off. "No more Chicken Jesus."

"OK. You're right. Yes." I clasped my hands tightly together, staring at them as if they held some answer. "But we're really close, right? Bangkok is right there? We gotta finish. They'll bounce us if we don't. Then we can never come back."

"Not an issue." Monteblan pulled a smushed sandwich from his back pocket, took a bite, and slid it back. "Never coming back here."

"Please." I spun him round, staring at him desperately. "Just finish this thing. It's really bad to start things you don't finish."

My friend didn't speak. Just looked at me while waves crashed to the shore. I took the silence and ran with it.

"True." I straightened my filthy lapels, flicked dust off my suit. "I've read it on psych websites and the therapist I saw for three weeks told me the same thing. Starting things you don't finish is psychologically unhealthy."

I smiled triumphantly while Monteblan stared at me.

"Psychologically unhealthy?" he asked.

I nodded. "Yup."

"You just shot somebody with an AK-47, you're standing there with puke on your suit and smell like dynamite."

He walked away.

"*Wet* dynamite," Monteblan added, while pulling a candy bar out of his shirt pocket. "Which I never thought I would know the smell of."

"So what are you going to do?!" I called out after him.

Monteblan turned, chewing off a piece of candy bar and shoving the rest in his shirt pocket.

"What I should have done instead of Chicken 65. Play with monkeys on the beach."

"What? Really?" I looked around at the beach. "This is that monkey beach you wanted to see? That's great! Where are they?"

He jerked a thumb towards the temple, shrouded by low hanging branches.

"They're in there. And I'm having my life moment. I'm playing with monkeys on the beach and then I'm leaving. Don't fuck it up for me."

He turned and walked up the beach. I felt the anger rise and yelled after him in the sunlight.

"How am I going to fuck this up for you?!"

Monteblan stopped his forward march in the heavy sand. Turning around, he walked all the way back to me, stopping right in front of my face, sweating under the shining sun.

"Because that's what you do, Rich. You rip everything to pieces looking for shit that isn't there. Whatever's left you call disopium."

"Dystopian," I corrected.

"What*ever*." Monteblan hissed the word through clenched teeth, then raised a single finger. "Do *not* fuck with my monkeys on the beach."

Monteblan turned away. I didn't let him. Reaching out, I grabbed a fist full of shirt. He smacked my hand away, hard.

"Ow!" I shouted, stunned.

We stared at each other, glaring under the bright white sun.

"I don't rip things to pieces." I frowned. "I look for meaning."

"Then look, will you!" Monteblan stretched his arms, taking in sun, sand, and sea. "You know how many guys would kill to live a year here like you did? But that's not enough. No! Beaches and sex and the best bars in the world doesn't *mean* enough for Rich Archer. You have to pull me into some insane race of people blowing each other up. When you're shooting someone with a machine gun? That's when it means something? When friends die? When *you* die?"

Eyes flashing, he glared at me.

"It was an accident. I… I was running in the…" I blinked, staring at the sand, confused. "In—in the jungle. I hit a root. I didn't want the gun. Charlie knew. He said something really weird, like he was…"

I struggled to remember words from the swirl of jungle memories; stars, cigar smoke, twirling river currents. I looked up at my friend in the sharp sunlight.

"He said he was glad it was me. That's what he said. He knew. It was The Bird."

"You're insane." Monteblan shook his head. "I hate this race."

"No! Chicken 65 means something and *that's* what you hate." I thrust a finger at him. "You hate when things mean something."

Monteblan spun away, walking up the beach. I called out at him over the crashing waves.

"So you're walking away?"

"Yes, Rich!" He didn't bother looking back. "This is me walking away!"

I watched him trudge up the beach, kicking sand. Then the words just jumped out of me.

"That's what you did with driving."

He stopped in his tracks.

"Just walked away," I told him.

Monteblan turned around.

"Got fat," I added. "Put away this amazing talent you had? Because that's what your problem is! YES! Aha!"

He started towards me, head lowered, brow furious.

"You walked away from driving because it *meant* something! What you do out there on the road? It's unreal! Gears would kill to drive like you! A million guys would! But you don't want the responsibility! Because then you would have a purpose! Life would have *meaning* then. And that's the last thing you want in the world. You want to laugh everything off and watch titties on the internet and have a beer and say it's all bullshit but everybody has to do it and have a beer and—"

My friend lunged. Face red and furious Monteblan threw me to the beach. Sand flew as we rolled and fought. We had never hit each other before. Now we let loose with all we had. Punching, kicking, slapping, cursing we pummeled. My friend was heavier. He had me. Grunting with each punch I landed, he wrapped his hands around my throat, choking me while slamming my head into the sand.

"I *told* you not to fuck this up." Spit dripped with seething words. "*Not* monkeys on the beach."

"This isn't about me!" I gasped, red faced. "You haven't realized your potential! That's what you're mad about! That's what the Chicken is trying to show you!"

Reaching high, Monteblan came down with a blast of fist, hard into my face.

"OOWWWW!" I howled.

A stunned look lit my friend's features. He backed off me, eyes wide, then looked at his hand. Staggering back, he fell into the sand, shocked.

"I've never hit anyone in the face before," Monteblan whispered.

"Awgghhhhhhddddd!" was all I could say, holding my face.

"I've never hit *you* before."

"I deserved that." I blinked away tears from the impact, rocking in the sand while waves crashed. "I did."

Monteblan moaned, holding his head, then kicked out furiously into the sand.

"Damn it! Why can't you just be good with shit?!" My friend pleaded, pain in his eyes. "It's not like everybody else doesn't feel like crap about life and work and relationships but we... we *do* it man. We have to. It's life. That's all."

"I know." I blinked more tears from my eyes. "I just don't know how to do it. I want there to be more. I don't know why. I don't how to do it. Life. Every day, every year. Rigged, rotten bullshit. How do you do it?"

Monteblan looked up the beach towards the beautiful trees near the water.

"Me? How do I do it?"

I nodded, angry. Hesitating, he finally sighed.

"This is like The Forces. OK? I don't like talking about it. Just once, I'll tell you. And I'm really tripped out that I'm telling you here."

"Where?"

"Monkey Beach," he replied softly. "It's freaking me out we found this place without looking for it. I never told people about this."

"That's all you've been talking about this whole race."

"Yeah, but I never told you why. Dude, I've been dreaming about monkeys on the beach my whole *life*. That's how I do it."

"Do what?"

"Life. When things are bad it's what I have. When I was little I saw this nature show with monkeys on the beach. They were running around with the waves and it was the best thing I ever saw. I thought about it when bad shit happened. Like when my parents got divorced. I thought of those monkeys on the beach. I'd sit in my bed hearing my parents screaming and dream of monkeys on the beach. Not locked up in the zoo. Not in the jungle because the jungle is evil. Just monkeys running around on the beach. And what I decided is that it couldn't be a bad world. Because somewhere there were monkeys on the beach. It was like, a decision I made. That the world was OK. And I forgot about it for a long time."

He sighed, staring out at the ocean.

"But recently? I started thinking about it again. I'd find myself jammed in the subway some morning hating life. Or having some dumb fight with Rayne all pissed off. Wanting to leave. Wanting to drive. I don't know. But then I remembered monkeys on the beach. That decision I made when I was little. That the world was OK. Because there's monkeys on the beach somewhere. Maybe you'll find them, maybe you won't. But they're real. So it's not all bad. That's what I got. Something small and dumb. Because the big stuff? Like if you need The Forces and God talking to you and dynamite and ladyboys and—

"I was vulnerable."

"Not judging you, dude." Monteblan held up both hands. "It's just all pretty extreme. And if shit has to be extreme like that? It's not real life. And it's real hard to hold onto."

Tide was rising. A crash of waves rushed up the beach, reaching our feet. Water splashed to my face. I wiped it away, tears mixing with the sea salt.

"I don't like real life, man. I don't get it. Since day one I've been told to go after this, get that, and it didn't matter to me. I didn't get why people wanted all this stuff. Why they'd rip people apart to get it. And that always made me weird. Or a loser. And it won't change. I know who I have to be to win. I watch people change into that. And you either become one of them, or get used by them. That's it. I know what I have to crush inside me. The voice I have to shut up. The stuff to stop thinking. But I won't. So I'm fucked. I can shut my eyes and see the rest of my life. Shoved around until they shove me in the ground. But Chicken 65 is different. It's the first thing I want. That I can win. Where I belong. Where I'm safe."

"Dude, you just OD'd through Cambodia."

"OK, so sure, I might die." I threw a handful of sand into the wind. "That's how it is out there. That's chasing the bird. But I'm safe from *them*. Bastards won't bother with this. They won't have anything to do with this, those fucks, because there's nothing but a…but a… *chicken*, damn it. That's how The Bird wants it. To hide from them. So they don't find it and ruin this like they ruin everything else. That's what they do. They run shit and ruin shit. But not this. We get this. This is ours. And if you're leaving then it's mine. Because my whole life I've been nothing. Now I'm Chicken."

I looked out at the ocean, watching sun sparkle down and waves crash in. Sniffled back another tear. This one wasn't from being punched in the face. I felt Monteblan's hand come down on my shoulder and give a squeeze.

"I love that you found something. I'm psyched for you. But I miss Rayne. I want to have my moment with monkeys on the beach. Then get on a plane and go home. Can you be good with that? Can you just be my bro with that? Please?"

I had never seen my friend more serious. More earnest. More pleading and real. Sadly, I nodded.

"I just wish you could have heard Mississippi Charlie more."

"I'm not doubting that there's deep shit out here." Monteblan stood up, shaking sand out of his shorts. "I just don't want to push it. There's a time to step off. That's the most important thing I learned from driving. When to step off."

"So you believe me about Chicken 65?" I took off my glasses and looked up at him. "That it means something? That The Bird shows you things?"

He bit his lip a minute, looked up the beach towards the monkey temple, then back at me.

"Yeah, I do. Because the past few years? All I been thinking about is driving, and now I never want to drive again. And my whole life? All

I been thinking about is monkeys on the beach and now they're right here. So, yeah, The Bird showed me something. And it's freaking me out a little. Like The Forces. I don't want to play with that stuff. If you want to? Fine. But I don't. And that doesn't mean I don't want life to mean anything. It just means you want a chicken on the road and I'm good with monkeys on the beach."

I nodded, sighed, and he reached out his hand to pull me up. We bro hugged then let it go. Waves crashed higher on the beach. Monteblan turned to walk up the white sand in the bright sun towards the trees. As he reached the first hanging green boughs, the first little face poked out of the branches.

"HA!"

Pointing at the monkey, Monteblan laughed like a child. A few more animals clambered down, fast and agile. Fuzzy and bounding with energy, they lit upon the beach. Dodging waves with light dexterity, they scampered around Monteblan, chattering happily. My friend threw his arms wide.

"What's up little bros! Papa's here!"

I smiled, turning away to look at the sun rising higher over the ocean waves. Soft breeze blew in the clean scent of the sea. I breathed in deeply, closing my eyes, letting it melt the smells of burning rubber and gunfire, dynamite and blood, jungle mud, whiskey, and sweat; bizarre carnage churned up by Chicken 65. Cleaned deeply with each slow breath, I felt strangely happy that we had lost the bird, and fallen from the race. With warm sunshine on my face, I recalled Charlie's drawl. Sadness hit me like crashing waves from the sea when I thought of him gone. With a chill then, I suddenly understood what Charlie meant about losing. We had fallen out of the race on this beach. But this beach with Monteblan was what *my* Chicken had been driving towards. The Bird had brought me here. To talk, be heard, and get smacked upside the head by the one person in the world I would listen to.

Monteblan was right about the race. It *was* crazy. It was too much. But this beach was more than enough. And there were other things like it in our world. That's what The Bird had to show me. It had brought me under fire and sent me over the moon, bound me in chains and set me free in reckless speed. All to realize what I had when standing still. This was my Chicken. What The Bird wanted me to know. The world was enough. It had to be. If it wasn't, the problem wasn't the world. The problem was me. My heart held a beat. For a crystalline moment under dazzling sun on a spinning world, I marveled at how it had all come together through laws and forces I would never, ever understand.

Then Monteblan screamed.

**I opened my eyes and turned to see my friend surrounded by monkeys.** Moving in a tensely narrowing circle, 20 or more hostile animals were slowly closing in. More dropped down from the tree. Tails tense, eyes narrowed, they stared at my terrified friend. He took one slow, cautious step. The gang hissed as one. Monteblan froze. Then they were on him.

Leaping all over, pulling at his shirt, yanking at his shorts, monkeys jumped Monteblan in a furious chattering mass. Clothes ripped. Monkeys screeched. My friend screamed louder, swatting and pulling them, terrorized as they shredded his shorts and ripped off his shirt. I ran towards him to help. Two baby monkeys turned and hissed at me. I stumbled back in fear. Monteblan ran screaming in his underpants to the sea. Monkeys mauled the clothing he had left behind, pouncing madly, shrieking, ripping, pulling out sandwich pieces and candy bar crumbs in a frenzied mob while Monteblan stared traumatized from the waves.

"Food no good."

Dumbstruck, I looked up to see a guide in a *Monkey Beach* shirt. Barefoot in the sand, the old man walked towards tree branches at beach's edge. Pulling boughs aside, he revealed an ancient sign:

# DO NEVER FEED MONEY. FOOD NO GOOD. YOU WILL BE DANGER.

"How does anybody even understand that?!" I shouted.

The old man gazed at me.

"Your whole country should be copyedited! Border to border! My friend almost died out there!"

I turned towards Monteblan, shivering in the sea, floating in his underwear while waves crashed all around. Walking to water's edge, cautiously wide of the monkey gang still at work on his clothes, I yelled over the surf to my friend.

"Are you OK?!"

Wide eyed, struck dumb, my friend was staring at the sand where he had been attacked. Monkeys were slowly leaving the crime scene, casually climbing the tree, leaping into branches and disappearing.

"It was the food!" I called out over the sea. "That's all! You'll be fine now! Come on in! They won't hurt you!"

Monteblan either didn't hear or didn't believe me. Eyes wide, arms crossed tightly while waves bobbed him in the sea, my friend stared at the empty beach. By now the monkeys had vanished with his clothes, leaving nothing but a chaos of paw prints in the sand. For a long time, I stood waiting. Finally, he began paddling awkwardly through the waves up the beach, putting distance between himself and the tree. Then he came in. White briefs dripping, stripped of everything, my portly friend walked past me without a word.

"Did they bite you?"

Monteblan didn't reply. Soaking wet, staring at the sand, he moved like a man in trance.

"Should we go to the hospital?"

Ignoring me, he turned through the trees. I followed him up the dirt road under glaring sun. Cars shot by on the rough highway ahead.

Pablo Cruise was waiting. Monteblan walked to the rear tire, found the keys where he had stashed them, then walked to the trunk in his drooping underwear.

"You have more clothes, right?" I asked my friend. "Do you want my shirt?"

He answered neither question. Popping the trunk, he pulled out his body armor. Monteblan put on the vest, snapping the clasps, then reached for dynamite. Stick after stick were slid into the vest.

"What do you need all that for?"

He didn't answer. Just jammed his army helmet on, pulling the chin strap tight. Slamming the trunk, he walked to the driver's side where both his battered boater shoes were waiting. Stepping into them, wearing body armor and underpants, he opened his door and got inside. The engine gunned, thick clouds of exhaust bursting from the tail pipe. Coughing, waving it away, I found my door and got into the passenger's seat. Idling in neutral, still dripping wet, Monteblan revved the engine in long, loud roars.

"Are you OK?"

My friend stared vacantly out the windshield. He didn't answer.

"Look man," I began. "That was—"

"All I had." He interrupted softly, brown eyes empty. "That was it. There's nothing now."

We sat in the idling car. I tried to find words. None came. Then the engine roared. Monteblan shot us straight through two lanes of highway traffic. Horns blared and tires screamed as high speed pile ups were missed by bare inches. Monteblan didn't notice. Didn't care. Whipping the wheel in a shuddering turn he slid us skidding into lane, flooring forward. Acceleration screamed. We flew.

"Right on man! Punch it!" I shouted over the racing engine and wind. "Let's rock! Are we Chicken again?"

There was nothing in his eyes. A sign flashed past, pointing us towards Thailand. I dug for maps. Confirming our trajectory, I called out turns. Monteblan made them all in full speed rage.

"Eight hours!" I shouted out over the thundering engine. "Drive like this, maybe seven!"

Flashing past whooshing traffic, I was rocked to the door as Monteblan turned sharply, just dodging a bus. My eyes shot nervously to the trembling needles on the dash, pushed into red, quivering at maximum RPMs.

"Five perhaps," I corrected nervously. "Four and a half?"

Silent in dripping underwear, Monteblan floored. Pablo Cruise shook with the stresses of Cambodian macadam. Beers jumped in the back seat. A puke flecked hundred dollar bill flapped spinning out the window. Nervously clicking my harness in place, I tried to lighten the mood.

"OK, here's one. Why do women close their eyes during sex?"

Monteblan pressed faster, ignoring me.

"They hate to see a guy having a good time. *WHOA!*"

Swerving suddenly we barely missed a barreling truck, loaded high with bouncing metal construction plates. I shut my eyes. When I opened them we had passed that hazard to dance with others, leaping through lanes in high speed wheel flicks that just missed collisions. Swallowing nervously, I told another joke to keep from screaming.

"There's this guy. First night in Bangkok. Goes with a bar girl. Says to her: I never did this before. How much do I pay you? 'Up to you', she tells him. Guy has the night of his life. Falls in love with her. Pulls her out of the bar. Back home. Married and everything. Buys her a house. A car. Best years of his life. One night he's all romantic and says: honey I love you more than anything. I love you more than the whole world. How much do you love me? 'Up to you', she tells him."

Pouring on speed, wind a howling banshee, Monteblan pounded through pavement without laughing.

"OK," Nodding my head nervously, I braced both hands on the dashboard. "Not the time for jokes. Got that. I'm just going to let you have your space here at uh, 185 kilometers per hour. No problem."

From there my job was directions. Shouting them out, we hurtled through Cambodia. We crossed the country in wild, reckless miles. Sprawling poverty, mud roads, trees nowhere, sun screaming down hot. Distant construction sites where Chinese cranes swung huge pieces of metal. Roadside shacks selling sodas, cigarettes, and motorbike gas in whiskey bottles. Children playing naked with sticks in piles of dirt. Blasting through the border with mafia markings we thundered untouched into Thailand. Death narrowly missed for harrowing hours, we arrived alive at Bangkok's first highway signs. Our lanes into town were nearly empty. Steady traffic streamed from the city. Finally, I screamed.

*"Will you PLEASE slow down?!!"*

Monteblan didn't look at me. There was a strange emptiness in his eyes. Hammering over pavement under blazing, bright sun, Pablo Cruise didn't slow. I lowered my voice, breathing deeply, trying again.

"Can we maybe, slow down a little? Please?"

Blinking a few times, Monteblan eased off fifth and dropped us down into fourth. Slowing from there, engine falling, dash needles dropping, he settled Pablo Cruise into reasonable cruising pace. Heart slowing, finally relaxing, I let go of my tension with a long sigh.

"*Thank* you. Now, I understand what happened back there was really tough. When dreams we have cherished for long, long times are suddenly—"

The words were stopped in my throat by a cherry red flash of Camaro shooting past. I squinted at it, hardly believing, as two cars chased it. One a blur of modern angles, impossibly angled and low. The other a high floating Range Rover, house music pumping. In a blink they were past us, all three vehicles jumping towards dark, distant clouds on the horizon. Shocked, I turned to my friend.

"Reggie? The Koreans and Ladyboy Man. That's The Ch—"

Slamming gears, my friend hit gas. Roaring forward, Pablo Cruise joined the chase.

**Bangkok was burning.** We saw the smoke before we saw the city. Black patches clouded the horizon. Faintly at first, their intensity clarified into roiling black columns as we shot closer. Pablo Cruise hammered out empty expanses of thrumming pavement. Shining skyscrapers glittered through the haze. Barreling towards them down the barren, glaring highway, destruction choked the air. Burning rubber and melted plastic, scorched steel and melted pavement floated in sharply toxic cocktail. We alone drove towards it. Lanes escaping the chaos were crowded with fleeing Thais.

Jammed into cars that filled the road, crawling from the smoking city in jeeps and taxis, busses and sedans, their exodus inched along. Belongings had been jammed haphazard into trunks and tied to roofs. Pickups were piled with entire families. Some looked morosely towards their flaming home. Others cheered it on. Grinning laborers streaked with mud laughed and passed beers, toasting the revolution. Unseen vehicles blasted excited Thai political speeches. Pretty girls popped out from the procession at random, smiling to snap Burning Bangkok selfies before darting back into departing cars. Leaving them we lifted up, racing into the city on elevated lanes running high above local streets.

Neighborhood names shot past on signs: *Thonglor, Ekkamai, Ratchada*. Skyscrapers blazed with reflected midday sun. Windows thrown open revealed stranded office workers, shifting and craning for better views. Through flashing sightlines down rapidly passing avenues, I saw vignettes of urban war. Distant barricades of upended noodle carts, flaming cars scorching under the shining sun, the surreal glimpse of a lumbering military vehicle. Smoke choked thicker and Monteblan blasted us through.

*"Some Chicken, wouldn't you say?!"*

Enraptured with the disaster, I hadn't noticed Pablo Cruise overtaking Ladyboy Man. Shouting down at me from his Range Rover window, high speed winds whipped his blonde hair. The grin looked forced. He drove alone.

"Where are the girls?!" I shouted between the racing vehicles.

"On the beach!" His blue eyes flicked nervously towards the road ahead. "Coup d'états are no place for a lady!"

Monteblan accelerated, pulling us forward towards the futuristic sports car hurtling up ahead. Pulling parallel, I heard muffled opera music strike epic, triumphant crescendos. Then the driver side window slid down, soprano blasting. Moon grinned, shouting over the aria.

"Hi guys!"

Seoul Brother leaned forward, face a pale mask, hair flat in fear. Weakly waving, he slumped back in the passenger seat. Moon was oblivious, shouting happily over thundering opera and thrumming pavement.

"We've been chasing Reggie since Cambodia! Vietnam was insane! Everybody got arrested and the rest won't go into Bangkok! We're the only ones left! What a Chicken! Whoa!"

The racer swerved away suddenly, dodging a stranded pickup left burning in the center lane. Flicking the wheel, Monteblan pulled us just past it. Roaring heat thundered from licking flames. We swerved again, past a flaming hunk of army jeep. Black smoke billowed from an overturned sedan farther ahead. Fires lit all around. More abandoned, damaged vehicles dotted the horizon. I frowned, turning to Monteblan.

"How are all these cars getting—"

*Whoosh!*

The blast of rushing wind shot right overhead. Ducking instinctively, I felt Monteblan nearly lose control. Pablo Cruise whipped into a slipping, sliding skid, just straightening out as the bright, blooming explosion struck the highway rail. Staring at the flaming ball fade behind us, I heard soprano singing swoop in beside us. Moon was there, laughing out the window, face alight in wonder.

"RPGS!" He yelled. "They're shooting RPGS!"

Dumb with shock as the Korean roared with laughter, I caught a wild flutter of motion behind him. Their Karma Bird still hadn't been released. Jumping in the cage, dancing in panic, it reminded me what had lead us down this lunatic highway. I scanned the road ahead for Reggie. Over pavement glinting with shattered glass, through trailing smoke from burning vehicles I saw the Camaro. Parked recklessly at an angled tilt, the door was thrown open. Just beyond was a makeshift barricade of military vehicles, razor wire and sandbags. We rushed up towards it, Monteblan slowing with a long, drifting skid to a spot just behind the deserted, cherry red Camaro.

I was out before the car settled, running low over the scorching pavement while faint popping gunfire floated from far away. Through an opening in the coiled concertina wire, I ran into the midst of the military blockade.

"Chicken 65! Chicken 65!" Yelling it like a security clearance, I ploughed through the confusion. "I'm with The Bird!"

Soldiers rushed everywhere. Shouting in Thai, talking on phones, peering over barricades, piling up sandbags, Thai military dug in on the war torn highway. Plunging through the chaos, I rushed towards a familiar figure up ahead. Reggie was standing before a commanding Thai officer. The American Marine wore khaki shorts with his nine millimeter tucked in the back. One arm clasped a black, bulky package.

He shot tense, demanding words towards the impassive Thai soldier. The trim commander was signing orders with one hand, tapping a cell phone with the other, and shaking his head "no" as the angry Marine gestured furiously towards the burning city. Reggie spun away in frustration just as I arrived in a panicked rush. Breathless and desperate, I shouted the words:

"Where's Charlie?!"

I never saw what hit me. Just registered a blinding flash and then I was looking up from the pavement, holding my throbbing jaw.

"*That's* for Mississippi Charlie, motherfucker." Reggie growled at me. "And this is from him."

Pulling something from the side pocket of his cargo shorts, he threw it at me, hard. Fluttering pages smacked into my chest. I looked down to see the blood streaked Chicken Bible.

"You don't deserve that, Asser," Reggie said. "But that's what the old man wanted."

I blinked through tearing eyes, looking down to see the bloody Chicken Bible. The world dissolved in a tunnel of nothing around the uneven, blocky letters of the faded, dog eared cover. I looked up to see Reggie's contemptuous rage.

"Charlie's dead?"

He didn't answer, just whipped the nine millimeter out and leveled it. Eyes shut, my hands leapt up in absurd reflex to block the bullet while voices around me yelled.

"Easy now, old boy!"

"Reggie, it's cool!"

I waited but wasn't shot. Slowly opening my eyes, I saw that Ladyboy Man and Moon had found us. Reggie wasn't pointing the gun at me. He was sweeping it between all of us, slow and steady, speaking low and calm.

"My Bird. You all got that?"

We nodded, tensely silent. Reggie tightened his grip on the odd package under his arm. The shape finally registered. It was a flak jacket, wrapped tightly and bound with black tape. An arm hole was left open, and as I watched, the Chicken popped up through it. Head tilting, looking at us curiously, it ducked back down with a clucking fluff.

The bird. I stared at it a moment, realizing this creature was the cause of our chaos. One of us had died. A man I had shot dead. Charlie's cartoon drunk face, red and happy, floated ghostly a moment in my mind. Pulling myself to my feet, cold from the shock of what Reggie had told me, I heard myself asking it once more out loud.

"Charlie's dead?"

Looking at Ladyboy Man and Moon, both racers turned away, nervously avoiding my eyes. I faced Reggie then, saying it again in flat confirmation.

"Charlie's dead."

"What the hell you think?" Reggie looked bewildered I was even asking. "Shot him with a goddamn AK-47."

"He knew..." I said. "He—"

"Shut *up!*" The Marine hissed sharply, walking close. "Asser you will pack that shit up, you will lock it down until this race is finished. This is not the time to think about shit. This is the time to survive shit. We got rebels in the buildings, taking anybody out heading into the city. Captain here told me nobody is getting into Bangkok without a military escort. And he sure as shit isn't giving us one. So I need everybody focused. We have to work together, find our way around. Now—"

"This is too much."

Speaking softly to whomever heard, clutching the Chicken Bible, I weaved away. A distant explosion rocked the city. Reggie shouted after me.

"What, you shot Charlie and now you walking away? That old man died! Now Chicken 65 dies too?!"

I left him behind, leaving the shade of the base, into the blinding midday heat. Monteblan hadn't moved from Pablo Cruise. Sitting comatose in the driver's seat, he stared out the windshield. I staggered towards the car, strapped on the belt, and slammed the door. Distant flames danced from abandoned cars on the highway. Faint sirens and car alarms howled from the city.

"We can't get through without a military escort," I said. "Charlie's dead. It's done."

I stared down at the Bible in my hands. Cover worn and cracked, the book was dog eared and nearly falling apart. Blinking away tears, I flipped through pages of faded faces and poorly type set entries. A real world that would really end now. Chicken 65 was over. Not just for me, but for everyone. Taking a Chicken through that city was suicide. I didn't want to die for this thing. I realized in that moment that Charlie was right. I was just like the others. I really wasn't Chicken 65.

"You were right back on the beach," I said softly. "This is insane. We can—"

But the car was empty. Startled, I realized I hadn't even heard my friend leave. Monteblan had slipped out wordlessly. Now I saw his form glint past in the rearview mirror. I unbuckled and leapt from the car. My friend was walking toward the barricade camp. The battered briefcase from The VV Splits dangled from one hand. He still hadn't found pants. Wearing flak jacket and helmet, Monteblan crossed the highway in his underwear while smoke from the riots billowed on the horizon. He was halfway to the barricade when I caught up with him. Spinning my friend around I shouted.

"What are you doing?! This thing is over! It's all gone way, *way* too—"

*Whoosh!*

The rush of wind blasted overhead. I ducked and threw my hands up as the RPG smashed directly into Pablo Cruise. Flames exploded. Windows shattered. The blasted Datsun jumped in the air as debris shot scattering. My friend didn't flinch. Just stared at it. Mouth open, I was rising up to look at the rippling flames when another huge explosion ripped the air. What was left of the dynamite sent a roaring blast bellowing over the highway and a lone car part bounding, spinning, skidding to a stop directly at Monteblan's feet.

Blackened and charred, the Hideki 3000 smoked with unholy powers. My friend bent down and picked up the thermos. Standing in his underwear staring at it, Monteblan handed me the briefcase. I took it, watching him unscrew the Hideki. Placing his nose above the opening, he inhaled deeply. Then raising his thermos, he toasted the blackened, burning hull of our car and said the first words since we had driven madly into Thailand.

"For Pablo."

Monteblan threw back his head and chugged the cocktail of twice exploded drugs from Vang. Watching in horror as his Adam's apple bobbed and contents gulped down, I recalled the blasted brew inside. Weed shake, shromelet, ketamine, opium, whiskey, beer, all of it fermented then damn well shaken and stirred by two separate dynamite blasts. Finishing with a satisfied burp, wiping his mouth, Monteblan screwed the top on the Hideki. Hanging the indestructible thermos from his neck, he reached for the briefcase. I extended it numbly, then watched my friend in underwear walk calmly towards the sandbagged barricade.

Behind me, another part of Pablo Cruise exploded. I jumped, turning to see car flames roaring anew. Through a shattered front window, the melting face of the 60s crooner bubbled on 8 Track plastic. I looked down at the bloody Chicken Bible in my hand. Charlie's whispered voice came to me then, so clearly that I thought he was standing there.

*"The Bird decides."*

I jumped, seeing nothing but destruction all around. Blasted cars flamed. Sun shone down on a city burning. The battered, faded pages of the Chicken Bible fluttered in my hands. Even if I wanted to, I couldn't walk away. Pablo Cruise was gone. The Bird had decided. I was in. Slowly crossing the highway, I left the lost car behind, joining Chicken 65.

**Entering the outpost, Chicken Bible in hand, I saw that a fold out table had become Chicken command.** Surrounded by sand bags, the army Captain and Reggie bent over a map, talking in Thai. Reggie had found a tan flak jacket. It fit him naturally, tailored almost, compared to Monteblan's bulky vest. Nearby, my friend drifted aimlessly in his underwear. A lower ranking soldier counted out hundreds from the briefcase beside him. Watching from afar, Ladyboy Man leaned up against the back of a parked troop transport, slowly stroking his chin.

"Back for more?" The blonde Brit smiled as I joined him. "Well played, Asser. Quitting Chicken just isn't cricket."

"What's happening?"

Ladyboy Man tapped a cigarette from his silver case. Lighting in a flourish, he exhaled with studied *savoir faire*.

"Your friend rather gallantly purchased us a military escort into old Bangkok. Reggie and the Captain are discussing the most effective 'insert'. Rather interesting term. I've inserted parts of me in various places before but have yet to be fully inserted anywhere myself. Color me intrigued. There's talk of a convoy. Apparently if we piled into something as sensible as an armored transport we'd only create a single target. Which, I've learned, is to be avoided at all costs in urban combat."

Eyebrow arching, he smoked, puffed, tapped ash and continued.

"The outer ring is rather ferocious, but once we punch through, I'm told things calm considerably. Or, as much as they can when a third world country with 28 military *coups* to its credit has a bash at 29. Let's call it The Chicken Coup. Should be in good form with all that practice, shouldn't you say?"

Once more, the champagne flow of his bubbly patter outpaced me. Trying to sound witty, I struggled for words while Ladyboy Man carried on.

"From there, it's merely details. With luck, we'll avoid sporadic pockets of mortal combat, arrest by capricious armed forces, molestation by revolutionary upcountry yokels, detainment and/or torture by a fundamentally corrupt police force roving off the proverbial leash, find Phetchaburi Road—where mind you, anything goes—and bring the bird home. I do say it's all a bit much, even for Chicken 65. But you can't choose your race, and this is ours. Enjoy yourself with Ploy?"

The last question was added so casually I answered automatically.

"Yes. I mean, no. Wait. I don't know."

"Perfectly acceptable answer. Still mine, as well. I imagine I keep trying different positions *with* them trying to find my position *on* them." He grinned. "Welcome to Ladyboy Land, old boy."

I flooded scarlet with shame while he departed in a jaunty stride. Finally finding my voice, I shouted after him.

"I was just visiting!"

"Many do." Ladyboy Man spun deftly on his heel, raising an imaginary hat. "For many happy returns. You'll be back."

Spinning with a wink before I could reply, the dapper Brit disappeared around the jumbled wires of a communications outpost. Left simmering, I cursed to myself. Sexual confusion added to the urban chaos was little help. And that had been his point: throwing me off balance in these last, crucial moments of the race. That man was a viper.

Remembering Ladyboy Man's mannered performance in the jail, adding it to the ride he rigged with Ploy, weighing in the Fuck Chart he used to run his harem, I decided the man was rotten. But he didn't just bother me. This anger was too strong. Ladyboy Man was my nemesis. I realized this in crystal clarity, understanding that in some strange way, my hate for him was making this race complete. Every racer had a rival. That dashing sodomite was mine. While the acrid smoke of burning Bangkok scorched the air, I vowed to destroy him. The war zone we were entering would provide an arsenal of opportunities to blow his Chicken right off the road. While smiling to myself, inspired by this newly christened anger, I was suddenly struck by a piercing, gut wrenching cry of absolute human grief.

"No!"

My head snapped towards the source. Standing surrounded by sandbags, Moon stood frozen in shock. Face drained entirely, hands clutching at his custom jump suit, I was certain he had been shot. Pushing through soldiers, I scrambled frantically towards him. I found Seoul Brother and Monteblan standing near the stricken racer. My friend stood calmly, drifting on his feet like strange seaweed, hand held out in expectation. Seoul Brother backed away, sighing with visible relief, wiping sweat from his forehead.

"What's happening?" I asked.

"Remember that thermos we blew up?" Seoul Brother pointed at the Hideki on Monteblan's neck. "Grimace just collected his Chicken Promise: our car."

"No!" Moon shouted again, clutching at his stomach, twisting the satin fabric of his custom made racing suit. "Not now! Things are blowing up out there! *Please!*"

My friend didn't move, just stood with his hand out, drifting on his feet and mumbling. "A chicken promise..."

"Is a Chicken Promise," Reggie finished, joining the scene with the bird under his arm. "That's what this is about?"

Moon The Loon opened his mouth to protest. Reggie stared the racer down. The Chicken under his arm ruffled slightly, squawking softly in the body armor nest.

"You're not trying to break a Chicken Promise," Reggie said sharply. "Not with the damn bird right here. Tell me that, Loon."

The Korean clenched his teeth, breathing sharply. Hyperventilating, clutching his Moon suit in desperate, agonized twists, he stood rock still for an unbearably tense moment. Then it passed; entirely and suddenly. The tall, grief stricken Korean deflated in defeat, slowly lowering his head in wounded capitulation.

"Just let me get my Karma bird."

Trudging abjectly, Moon left the shaded barricade towards the futuristic sports car. Wiping a tear under the blazing sun, he pressed his key chain. Hydraulics sighed in soft lament. Glinting butterfly doors slowly raised. Sniffling slightly, the racer leaned into the back seat, pulling out the cage with the fluttering bird. Standing in the middle of the highway, surrounded by shattered glass while distant vehicles quietly burned, Moon opened the cage door. The tiny bird shot free, lofting in zig zag flight through distant riot smoke. Moon stood silently, face upturned, watching it disappear.

"Well, that's our Chicken," Seoul Brother said beside me. "At least we cleared our karma. Glad we're not driving into that mess. Thank Grimace for me, will you? I tried talking to him, but he's umm, not really *there* right now. What happened out there?"

"Ran into some monkeys. Hasn't been the same since."

"Is he alright to drive? Like, with bombs going off and people shooting and all?"

"I don't know." I shook my head, unable to make any sense of events anymore. "I guess The Bird decides."

We looked at the Chicken, clucking under Reggie's arm, flapping through an arm hole of the bullet proof vest.

"You know I never saw it before?" Seoul Brother said in soft awe. "I mean, this is Chicken 65, and that's the Chicken, right there. Wow. We really got close."

Seoul Brother shook his head sadly. I reached out and patted him on the back. Beyond the razor wire, Moon stood forlorn, watching the sky. Monteblan approached on the empty highway. Reluctantly, the custom suited racer handed his car keys to the man in underwear. Accepting them, Monteblan reached into his vest, tenderly pressing a stick of dynamite into Moon's hand. The Korean racer looked at it, wiping a tear from his cheek.

"Thanks man. It'll be nice to blow something up. Sure wish I was driving out there, but..." Managing a weak smile, he flipped the stick of dynamite and looked Monteblan in the eye. "A Chicken Promise is a Chicken Promise."

The racers shook hands.

Then Reggie's shouting voice boomed out in the shaded command post.

"Alright people, let's move! This is our Chicken and we are bringing it in!"

**Lead by a lumbering Thai troop transport, we spiraled down the off-ramp and rattled under the expressway.** Reggie's red Camaro roared up front, bird in back. Monteblan and I were just behind, cradled in hand-stitched leather seats, purring in the Korean's low riding Bertone. Ladyboy Man brought up the rear, a position assignment delivered with predictable jokes from Reggie. Together we wound through predetermined turns, blasting through intersections, shooting past flaming tires, and roaring down deserted avenues. Jeeps at our flanks with mounted machine guns drifted ahead or dropped back, covering neighboring streets. I glanced tensely through tinted windows, watching them pass. Shanties on the city's perimeter showed fans inside spinning, clothes outside drying, Thai eyes wide in surprise. The Chicken hitting Bangkok was hot news. Bookies were tipped in a ripple of frantic phone calls left in our wake. Before a minute had passed, the CB was crackling with chatter, most of it in Thai, all of it explained by Reggie in sharp, static bursts as we drove faster into the fallen city.

*"Whole city knows the Chicken is in town. That's good or bad depending on who we run into. We got lucky at the roadblock; that captain is from Udon Thani. My home village is out that way. Otherwise, just about all the military money is down on Grimace and Asser. Moist and Gears are mobbed up*

*with those motherfuckers, they all heard the shit fat boy pulled in The Splits. Police and taxi drivers, upcountry money, that shit's on me. So depending on who we run into we... hold up. What's happening back there, Grimace?"*

Reggie's CB rundown stopped abruptly. I glanced nervously at my driver. Things were definitely happening with Monteblan, but it was impossible to tell what. Helmet tilted down, laid back practically horizontal, the bulk of his blast jacket revealed dynamite sticks. The charred Hideki swayed from its NASA approved cord on his neck. Blinking erratically, muttering incoherently, Monteblan was rolling hard on whatever unholy ferment had been wrought by his twice blasted thermos. But some otherworldly level of instinct kept his driving tight.

Driving us through the fringes of riot blazing Bangkok, he pressed the new vehicle through an astonishing array of reflex tests. Surges of acceleration were stopped short in whiplash fishtails. Corners were taken in revving, artful drift. Lanes were inexplicably, suddenly changed. Whipping the wheel, kicking the clutch, tapping brakes and gassing, Monteblan melded his instincts with the precision tuned possibilities of the vehicle, finding out what he and this car could do. A particularly flourishing drift, blooming smoke in whining, maximum RPMs, had elicited Reggie's wary inquiry on the CB. In response, Monteblan reached out for the hand piece, ripping it off the console and throwing his head back to howl.

> *"Wellllllllllpulledintodetownaboutanhourago!*
> *Tookalookaroundseewhichwaythewindblow!*
> *Metalittlegirlinna—"*

I wrenched the mouthpiece away, pressing it close to my chest to block out my friend's singing.

*"The fuck was that?!"* Reggie shouted, alarmed.

*"L.A. Woman,"* I said quickly through the hand piece. "He does that

when he's... he's..."

'High' did not do justice to whatever astral planes Monteblan was hitting beside me.

"Driving," I decided to tell our leader. "He's fine. Really."

But I doubted this entirely. My underwear friend was out of his mind. Piloting us through the deserted streets, I watched him warily. Lead by military vehicles, rounding deserted street corners past sporadic, flaming blockades, new fears took hold. It wasn't just RPGs and machine gun fire that threatened us now. Whatever was in Monteblan was powerfully unpredictable, and my friend was utterly possessed by it.

"You OK there, buddy?" I said cautiously.

"100% money." Grooving and bobbing to some unseen, invisible orchestra, Monteblan shimmied in his seat. "Have some."

Thrusting one hand into his flak jacket, he yanked out a fistful of hundreds. Throwing them at me like confetti he laughed manically, shouting like a game show host.

"Kay-*razy* Thailand! You told the stories! Now you *are* the story! Congratulations Rich Archer! You've just won the cash prize for driving through a war zone with a man in his underpants!!!"

"Pull it together!" I shouted back, scrambling for the bills. "There's heavy weapons out there, dammit!"

Flipping into imitation army voice, Monteblan went instantly cool. "Roger that. Hostiles engaged, whiskey fox trot, break dance Campari."

Sinking back into the bucket seat, he went silent again. The suddenness of his manic switch unsettled me entirely. Monteblan was predictable. That was his beauty. Whatever had happened in his thermos was changing that. Monteblan was lost. Driving instinctively, eyes a barely visible flash from under his lowered helmet visor, he followed the vehicles ahead. Then brake lights on Reggie's Camaro went bright. Monteblan stopped just behind him. We were paused in the center of a deserted, central city intersection. Office towers and shopping malls towered on either side. An elevated train track curved overhead. Just beyond the intersection, past traffic lights, the wide avenue disappeared into a wall of black, roiling smoke. Burning rubber stench choked the air. I glanced in the rearview. Ladyboy man idled behind, his Range Rover shaded with a thin coating of black soot. His crisp, concerned voice cut through the CB.

*"Why did we stop here? Phetchaburi Road is still—wait what's this?!"*

The British racer's voice rose in dismay as our military escort lurched ahead. The boxy metal vehicle drove right towards the thick curtain of smoke shrouding the empty boulevard.

*"Hold tight."* Reggie said, calm and cool. *"We got intel it's hot round that corner and our boys are checking it out."*

Both Jeeps jumped ahead, leaving us behind as they darted in to flank the transport. Guns were mounted, barrels lowered parallel to the oil slicked, glass shattered road. Then all three were swallowed in the black smoke and disappeared. We idled in the empty intersection, waiting, watching, engines growling.

*"I do appreciate them testing the waters for us,"* Ladyboy Man joked nervously. *"But I dare say I don't fancy being left alone as a third world government violently changes hands."*

The ghostly silence of the revolutionary city was the only response. Monteblan revved the Bertone. Moments passed. Ladyboy Man tapped his horn impatiently. It rang echoing off the empty buildings. Then the jeep came bursting through the smoke. Roaring right in front of us, trailing fire, the army vehicle bounced and bounded on the empty avenue, fighting for control. Licking orange flames whipped behind like lashing tails. The gunner struggled with the bouncing barrel of the mounted weapon, slapping wildly at his burning clothes. Randomly squeezing off a hammering volley, the bullets kicked up pavement as a running mob of rioting Thais burst from the smoke screaming.

Faces red with fury, firing handguns, throwing Molotov cocktails, rebels chased the flaming Jeep. Wheeling wildly around a city block, the swinging turret poured a chattering volley of blind machine gun fire high into office buildings. Glass exploded, raining down on the streets and rioters cheered as the jeep disappeared down an unseen alley. Turning towards our three idling cars, they roared as one and flooded the intersection, running for us as the first Molotov cocktails arced up from the mob, two of them landing squarely on Reggie's Camaro. The front of the car burst into flames and The Marine was fast on the CB.

*"We are falling back people."* Reggie's voice was calm but quick. *"Falling back on the rear vehicle. Ladyboy Man, hold position. Wait my arrival."*

Reggie slipped out of the driver side. Gun in hand, flack jacketed Chicken tucked under his arm, the Marine ran bounding from his flaming red car as another bottle shattered on the roof. Just a few hundred meters away now, the mobbing Thais were swarming in. Wearing jeans, flip flops and T-shirts, many in cowboy hats and others with fluttering Thai flags, they surged into the intersection, yelling and throwing bottles.

Running ahead of them at full sprint, Chicken tucked under his arm like a football, Reggie suddenly stopped, shouting in fury.

*"Motherfucker!* Get back here!"

A high pitched squeal screamed from behind us. My panicked eyes shot to the side view mirror. Ladyboy Man was flooring straight backwards at high speed. Yelling furiously, Reggie raised his nine millimeter and fired. The first shot smashed an upper corner of the Brit's windshield. It didn't stop the man. Screeching around in a whipping 180, the Range Rover rocked heavily, sending a hubcap flying. Then Ladyboy Man jumped forward at full speed. The large car accelerated quickly and smoothly down the abandoned avenue, vanishing in the soot shrouded sun. Reggie chased after it in vain, firing his pistol and shouting furiously. Then spinning back towards us, he ran to the passenger side while I triggered the door to open. Scrambling into the back space behind the seats, I watched Reggie duck in under the sighing sports car's slowly raising door. Monteblan reached out to the control console, smacking the button to lower it just as the mob swallowed us whole.

The car rocked wildly. Our world went dark as a press of furious Thai faces blocked our view. Cheeks and foreheads smushed up against the glass, squeaking obscenely as others pressed in behind them. Screaming, chanting, frothing, they raged. The car rocked harder. The windshield cracked. A glimpse of Reggie's car just ahead showed the Camaro engulfed in flames, pushed by cheering rioters onto its side. The Chicken squawked wildly in Reggie's lap. The Marine smashed his pistol barrel through the shattered windshield corner and pulled the trigger. Shots fired. People tumbled back.

"Chicken 65!" Reggie bellowed through the broken glass. "Chicken 65!"

They didn't care. Waves of furious Thais surged in again, rocking the lightweight car easily, nearly flipping us. When wheels hit ground, Monteblan saved our lives. Yanking the parking brake tight he threw the car into gear and floored it. Screaming rubber from wildly spinning wheels sent plumes of smoke rising and crowds toppling over themselves in stunned surprise. Monteblan used the space instantly. Turning the wheel and gunning harder, the car started slowly spinning clockwise, tires screaming while smoke choked the air.

Revolutionaries jumped on the car and he upped the revolutions, sending them flying to the side as he opened up our radius, sliding in smoking, screaming, drifting circles that cleared the crowd. Bottles were hurled, smashing and shattering. Monteblan gunned harder, pulling the wheel, tires shrieking, engine bellowing, smoke billowing, and Reggie added fire. Jamming his gun through the glass again he pulled off shots aimed high. Yelling protestors ducked, falling back in fear, leaving just enough opening for Monteblan to straighten out and shoot us forward. We raced ahead, the only direction open, blasting full speed into the black wall of smoke that had swallowed Bangkok like a monster.

**The riot's heart of darkness was lit with burning tires.** Piles of them were stacked blocking entire roads, flames raging, billowing black smoke pouring horrifically wild. Shots popped at random from within the toxic fog. Driving blind, Monteblan didn't dare stop. Sensing things he weaved, darting through lanes missing deadly collisions with ethereal timing. Reggie yelled as the smoke suddenly parted to reveal the looming, flaming husk of an overturned bus. Monteblan flicked the wheel, missing it by inches. Jumping gears he cut right, just dodging a roving crowd of protestors, bandanas hiding faces, guns held high. Shots popped from all sides, missing wide, Monteblan untouchable in darting speed. Flames and smoke raged. The Bertone in this was blasphemy; fallen automotive angel flying through hell. My friend pressed us faster, skidding through oil slick streets, blurring us past gruesome tableaus of Bangkok gone Hieronymus Bosch.

Alley ways filled with soldiers, leveling weapons at shirtless rebels, hands raised. Fallen spirit houses. Flames swallowing an entire shopping mall, Buddha statue out front untouched, ringed with raging fire. Makeshift roadblocks of tires, TVs, and office desks crumbling suddenly, bulldozer pushing through. Bloody naked man pulled screaming by laughing mob. Military machine gun fire dancing on cement walls. Dog on fire darting through overturned cars. Dangling wires, smoking street craters, low running soldiers. Wide eyed children trapped in upstairs windows. Old women weeping. Shots fired. Our passenger window exploding in a million spraying shards...

"Down!" Reggie shoved me roughly down while shouting to Monteblan.

"Get us out of here, Grimace! Look for where the smoke thins out! Drive that way. *Fast!*"

The last part of his order wasn't necessary. Monteblan was handling all of this at speeds insane. Dressed appropriately in full battle regalia, piloting one of the world's most masterfully made machines, his inescapable Chicken destiny was fully realized in a crucible of flames. The bird which had authored this journey startled in panicking bursts. Reggie wrestled with the cawing, flapping creature, wings wildly fluttering, legs kicking hard, flat black eyes rolling wild. I stared at it, helpless, curled up in the small space where Moon had stashed his karma bird. Racing through bedlam my heart felt strangely cold. Essential questions floated like distant abstraction. Would we die here? What would The Bird decide? Then smoke dropped off as if blown by a fan and Monteblan floored us down an open avenue.

Sunlight shined. Reggie laughed in wild, whooping surprise, straightening up and slapping Monteblan on the shoulder. He grinned. Reggie pounded the dashboard in triumph. I saw the thing rumble around the corner ahead.

"Um, guys?"

The Thai military tank lumbered forward and lowered its cannon. Monteblan threw the car in reverse but a snarl of engine sounds screeched painfully. We didn't move. The Bertone shuddered, shot. The tank rolled closer. Reggie yelled.

"Out of the vehicle! Move!"

The Marine punched the door button and bolted. Ducked low I followed, running under burning sun. The Chicken looked back at me, head poked out from the flak jacket. Reggie dodged round a corner and sweating, panting, squinted back towards the car. Monteblan hadn't moved. Calmly working the gas, plying the clutch, he ignored the armored vehicle rolling towards him. Reggie whispered in wonder.

"What *the fuck* is fat boy doing?"

"That's a Bertone," I said. "He won't leave that car."

Running back for my friend, I looked down the narrow street. The first rumbling tank had been joined by two more. Rolling towards Monteblan, the three massive machines formed a moving, metal wall. I reached the car breathless. Monteblan looked up bewildered. Both eyes blared lunacy.

"Hey buddy, you OK?" I spoke softly, as if were a truant child. "We have to leave now."

"I'm not leaving this car."

Then Reggie was there, Chicken clucking under his arm. Tanks rumbled closer, shouting Thai language broadcast through sharp, echoing PA. I didn't understand the words, but the tone was unmistakable. Military warning. I told Reggie Monteblan wasn't moving. The Marine just nodded.

"Right, I seen this shit before. Hey, Grimace?"

Shoving the Chicken into my arms, Reggie slipped into the passenger seat, voice perfectly calm. "So you ain't going out there?"

"No."

"Alright, I understand. But I forgot my helmet. Mind if I borrow yours?"

Tanks thundered louder. Monteblan blinked, processing the request.

"Sure. But not my thermos."

"Oh, I wouldn't touch that thermos of yours. Just the helmet. That's right, there you go…"

The Marine spoke calmly, kindly, as Monteblan undid the chin strap and handed him the helmet. Reggie flipped it back in whipping backhand. Smashed in the temple, my friend dropped like a bag of rocks. Reggie hitched his fingers under Monteblan's flak jacket. He pulled with incredibly focused force. My fat friend flopped heavily through the car, tumbling out the open door, hauled roughly by Reggie.

"Pull back Asser, *now!*"

Reggie dragged Monteblan quickly away. I looked down and realized I was holding the Chicken. I looked up and saw the tanks ten meters out. I turned and ran then remembered Charlie's blood stained bible. Spinning fast I darted back to the car, just as the first crunching sound of pulverized metal swallowed the hood. The windshield burst, spraying glass. I turned to protect my face. When I looked back, the Korean's exquisite vehicle was flattened under rolling tank treads, Chicken history lost. For a stunned moment I was too shocked to move. Faces, tales, Chicken history and lore flashed through my mind on faded, poorly set type. Then sharply amplified military warnings blasted in Thai, sending me scrambling. Sprinting over burning pavement, I ran back to Reggie with the Chicken. The bird squawked sharply, flapping in the flak jacket, kicking wildly at my side. Breathless, I reached the racers behind a building corner. Monteblan was slumped on concrete steps, slowly coming around as Reggie shook him.

"I lost Chicken Bible!" I shouted.

Reggie spun. "You did *what?!*"

"It was in the car!"

"If that damn Bible gets in the hands of the military or police you know how many—"

A bottle smashed the wall, cutting Reggie's fury. Revolutionaries ran by shouting. Distant gun fire popped. The Marine frowned, wiping sweat from his eyes.

"Shit! We got other problems right now. Still in the goddamn hot zone."

A building door cracked open. Thai eyes looked out. First at us, then the bird.

"Chicken 65?"

"Chicken 65," Reggie replied.

The door opened wide.

**We followed a Thai man in grey slacks and dark blazer inside.**
He led us up marble stairs with maroon carpeting. Chandelier glass
tingled, shaking slightly from the distant boom of tank fire. Through
a draped velvet curtain we entered a vast, low lit room. Thick carpet
hushed the world. Distant fish tanks bubbled with swirling creatures.
All around were ornately carved circular wooden tables. Thai men sat
in burnished, cushioned wooden chairs, chatting in low tones while
smoking. Plates arrayed before them held all manner of food. Silver
side carts offered bottles of whiskey, ice buckets, and beer. The tables
were facing a glass wall. Beyond the glass were girls.

Set on rows of carpeted bleachers, draped in robes, bikinis beneath, each had numbers on circular badges. The wall behind showed
golden dragons, painted in flourishing mural. Some of the girls looked
almost as heavily painted. Rouged cheeks, red lipstick, and deep purple mascara lit glowing in the bright lights shining down from above.
Most looked bored. All looked blindly at the mirror side of one way
glass. Some men were discussing their various merits. Others ignored
them entirely, relaxing in the cool, hushed remove of the brothel while
outside, heated streets popped with the faint, faraway sound of gunfire or low, chandelier shaking blasts. Reggie took it all in, nodding in
satisfaction as we were ushered to the closest available table. Then he
frowned, listening to the doorman whispering Thai quietly in his ear.

He replied in fast words, then looked at me as I sat down, setting the Chicken on the table between us.

"What's up?" I said.

"They understand it's Chicken 65 and all," Reggie told me. "But your man without pants really ain't the Thai style."

"Hey Monteblan?" I turned to look at Monteblan, staring vacantly.

He replied with confusion. "What are all these people doing in my car?"

"Oh shit!" Reggie laughed, amazed. "I seen people fucked up before, but *what?*"

"He's somewhere beyond pants," I explained. "Maybe this will help?"

Standing behind my friend, I pushed him closer to the table and draped some tablecloth over his legs. Reaching into my pockets for money from The Splits, I folded a few hundreds and pressed them into the waiting maître d's hand. He nodded his thanks and turned to Reggie, satisfied. The Marine leaned back, gazing at the girls, absently rattling off a list of foods in Thai, followed with requests for whiskey and beer. Nodding in acceptance, our host whisked silently away, footsteps swallowed in the thick carpets.

"How did all these people get in my *car?*" Reggie was amazed, staring at my blasted friend while shaking his head. "What the hell did Grimace do?"

"Everything, I think."

"Well he can drive. Shit, wish I had him back in Iraq, never seen someone do a hot zone like that. How did he see half that shit?"

"He doesn't see. He just knows."

"OK." The Marine nodded slowly. "Grimace just knows."

Eyebrows raised, Reggie looked at me and Monteblan. Then he remembered something and scowled.

"Ladyboy Man."

"Broke the truce," I said with disgust.

"Truces never last." Reggie waved his hand. "Only promises hold on the road. Chicken Promises are everything. Would have made one but that's a motherfucker I don't want to owe."

I shifted uncomfortably in my chair, remembering Laos.

A silver cart rolled up quietly, laden with ice bucket, whiskey bottle, soda water and beers. I reached gratefully for the closest cool drink and gulped it down. Reggie watched as the waitress poured him a bubbling whiskey soda. The Marine raised his glass.

"To Charlie."

I frowned, closed my eyes, and felt all the regret and dread that had been burned away by the chaos of Bangkok's coup d'état return. Raising my bottle, I mumbled mournfully.

"To Mississippi Charlie."

Avoiding his eyes, I stared into the bottle of beer.

"Hey."

I looked up at Reggie.

"Don't trip. People die in Chicken 65. Charlie knew this was his last chicken. Told me that before we left Bangkok. He wouldn't have wanted to go out any other way. Last thing he told me on that raft was about The Bird. Said The Bird decided. Called him home."

"Well, you didn't pull the trigger," I mumbled.

"And you didn't bring that AK to Sabon Sai." He shrugged, leaning back. "Who told you to pick up and run with the thing? Who rode a damn raft into a firefight? Shit man, Iraq? Know how many people I seen in pieces for deciding to sit here instead of there? Don't trip. Not now. Race still needs you. That bird ain't home yet."

"So you're not mad about Charlie?"

"I really haven't decided to start thinking about all that yet." He frowned, swirling the ice in his glass. "But I will miss that old motherfucker, that's for sure. Shit. Charlie saved my life. Saw me chase that thing since I was a damn teenager. My first Chicken I wasn't even 17."

"You raced with Charlie for that long?"

"Nah, I didn't know Charlie back then."

"So, you did it with your dad? He's the one who brought you into the Chicken?"

Reggie shook his head sharply. "Never knew my daddy. He was a soldier. Came through Vietnam, met my moms, and you know, rotated out. That was that. Chicken 65 was some shit you just heard about in Thailand. If you were military, or had that background, it was just what you heard. So I jumped in real young, chased the bird a few times hoping to meet my daddy. Thinking maybe he'd show up since he'd been in country. That shit didn't happen. Forgot about it. Went to the States where some family was, did my university out in San Diego went into The Marines when the towers went down."

I raised my glass. "Thanks for your service."

"Damn." He laughed, disgusted. "Every rectangle glasses wearing motherfucker I meet says that. Don't know what email y'all got, but 'Thanks for your service' sounds like I tuned your car up or some shit."

He waved me away, shaking his head with derision.

"What am I supposed to say?"

"Pay for the drinks. That's what you do. Nothing you could say can cover what happened over there."

"Done." I poured some more beer over ice. "Drinks on me. Girl if you want."

"Pay for my own pussy." Reggie said sharply.

"Fine. Not trying to offend you. Just trying to be friendly. I don't know how it works out here. And I don't know what you did over there, but I appreciate it."

He narrowed his eyes. "Then how could you appreciate it?"

I blinked, sensing a drop in the mood.

He folded his arms, smiling without humor. "You don't know what happened over there, but you appreciate it?"

I had grown up with enough drunken Irish uncles to know when laughter and liquor took a fast left turn. Whiskey was kicking in. Reggie was laying his trap. I could step into it or kick it over. I chose the latter.

"Why don't you tell me, Reggie?" I pulled in closer to the table, tired of being pushed around by the man. "How about that? Why don't you tell the rectangle glasses wearing motherfucker something so I can try to understand? Then I'll let you know if I appreciate it. How's that?"

Reggie's eyes narrowed to near slits. I saw the muscle in his jaw twitch. The bird picked up the tension, clucking nervously and loudly. Reggie looked down at it, breathing deeply. Then he turned his face towards me, calm. Relaxed back in the ornate wooden seat, he swirled his whiskey.

"You want a war story? Here's your story." Reggie sipped his drink. "First day in Iraq. Brand new helmet. Plates without a ding. Ready to do some good. First patrol with this Chinese brother from Detroit. Had one of them milky eyes? You know? With a little scar right through it. Hard motherfucker. Kray. Called him Kray Kray, like crazy, right? He took me out, says to me: 'No matter what happens out here, you have my back. Got that?' This my first patrol, I'm 100%. 'Sir, yes sir! I'm your man out here.'"

Tapping his fingers on the table, Reggie drained his whiskey.

"So we drop out the Humvee for patrol. Door to door, look for insurgents. I got money on me to pay some family off they let us use their rooftop for recon. First house he knocks on the door saying 'US Military'. Old Iraqi man answers. Sixty or some shit. Kray just stabs the motherfucker. Out from nowhere. *Ya ya ya!* Like he's punching him and I see the old man's eyes all surprised, like shocked. Lady starts screaming inside. The wife. Comes running and Kray's into her same way. *Ya ya ya!* Stabs the shit out of that old lady and I'm just standing there watching till they dead on the floor. My commanding officer on patrol. I got his back, right? Standing there watch him murder those people, thinking: wait. No, it can't be like this. No. But..."

He shrugged, refilling his drink.

"It was. You go to war, you got motherfuckers off the leash. Saw lots of that. But just kept rotating in since I feel best when shit's crazy. Finally got the discharge, you know, decorated for all the hits but I had those faces coming out the wall at me. Nighttime, all those motherfuckers with their last cigarette, their last cup of coffee... Wife couldn't handle it. Got the girls, my house, restraining order. Watched it happen like a movie. Decided one last Chargers game and I'm out. Course those motherfuckers lost and I was checking the action on my piece about to eat the barrel when the phone rings. Charlie. From Chicken 65."

He laughed.

"You know how Charlie is, all 'hey there y'all!' I was like: who the hell this? He kept talking about running the Chicken back in the day and I remembered him like: Oh, right. *Charlie*. Chicken 65. Like coming out of some dream. Gun still in my hand. Charlie's all Charlie, telling me he was looking for a driver since his boy pulled out and someone lead to something, and he ended up with my number. I was like, yeah. Alright. Yeah, I'll do Chicken 65. Put the gun down. Got on the plane, met Charlie and chased that Bird. I swear to you he hadn't called that minute, that very minute? I'd be dead. Chicken 65 saved my life."

Reggie swigged down his drink, and before it was even placed down the maître d' had appeared. Pouring another, he spoke with Reggie in Thai for an extended, softly spoken exchange. Sharing information, talking, nodding, he eventually left us alone.

"What was that about?"

"Number 19 got good ass." Reggie raised his whiskey, gesturing to the girls behind glass. "48 does real fine massage and 28 not bad with the blowjob. That and he's working on helping us out of here. Still too hot, and we gotta hold tight, but he's a betting man and wants to see this Chicken through. Just about everybody in Bangkok does. We gonna be alright. Just got to wait it out a minute. Bet the bird can use a stretch while we do."

Reggie reached down, taking hold of the bulky flak jacket wrapped in tape. With fast flicks he undid snaps and the Chicken wriggled out. Fluffing its feathers, pecking at itself, the bird flapped its wings wide, strutted round, then peacefully settled in the center of the wooden table of the brothel. I noticed Thais at all tables murmuring, watching, some picking up phones, calling in bets, adjusting odds. Reggie noticed too, laughing out loud while looking at the Chicken.

"Shit, half these brothers in here got money on the bird. They all doubling it now."

Reggie waved like a celebrity, and smiling Thais raised their drinks in reply. The Chicken took no notice of the attention. Calmly turning, fluffing its feathers, it sat down quietly in the table's center.

"That's not natural." I stared at it. "I don't understand why it's so calm."

"That's The Bird, man. Nothing natural about it. Plus Charlie put The Whisper on it. Last thing he did on that raft."

I remembered the strange noise Mississippi Charlie had made, in that surreal drifting ride down the Mekong River. I stared hard at the Chicken, trying to imagine communicating with it. Ice clinked in glasses and I heard Reggie laugh.

"You don't want to look at that Bird like that, Asser."

Coming out of trance, I looked at the Marine. "Like what?"

"Like too close. Charlie did that. Know he used to be a handsome motherfucker? Real estate. Rotary club. All that. Started looking real deep at The Bird and just fell into it. Basically ended up with the bottle, that bible, and all them boxes in Biloxi. He was happy though. Lot of people out there, they're Chicken. Sure. They run every year, got it down, some of them even won. All them are Chicken. But Charlie? He was something more than that. He was…"

"Chicken 65?" I said.

"Yeah." Reggie smiled, laughing a little. "That about says it. But that old man did not learn his bird easy. And some shit you shouldn't look too hard at. The Bird being one of them. Chicken 65 goes deep. *Real* deep. Charlie got lost in that shit. I just run the damn thing. *Ya kit mak.*"

"Don't think too much," I replied.

Reggie was genuinely surprised. "Asser, I'm impressed. Where'd you learn that?"

"Ladyboy told me."

"Yeah, she would." He laughed. "She teach you *khao jai krap?*"

I shook my head. "What's it mean?"

"It means 'understand.'" He pointed to his heart, tapping his large chest. "'Into your heart' is the way Thais say understand. Not into your head. Into your heart. That's how you understand this part of the world. So stop tripping and let's hit some ass."

I shook my head. "Nah."

"Right, you into that ladyboy shit now. Got you. Motherfuckers hit that and never go back to pussy."

"No, it's not that. I just don't, you know, point at a girl and, I don't know, whatever. There's some things I have to keep…" I shrugged, not caring how stupid it sounded. "Special."

"What, like pussy?" He laughed. "Oh, you one of those. Go get married and divorced, watch your wife live in your house, fuck a stranger who raises your children. Then tell me pussy is special. Please."

"Not just pussy," I said.

"Then what?"

"Love? Relationships? Whatever happens between men and women? There are some things that—"

He opened his mouth to speak and I held up my hand.

"Dude. I understand you're the man and we're all just visiting, but do you ever listen? Since Viet damn Nam, it's do this, go there, do that. Can I talk to you Reggie? Does anyone? Or do you just walk around telling people what to do?"

Reggie's eyes flared. He smirked with a half smile, and sat back. Eyebrows up, he flourished his hand in an exaggerated gesture for me to continue.

"There are some things that I need to just keep believing in," I told him. "Even if they're not real. Even if I don't have it. Or never will. It's like…"

Looking at the girls, seeing them all sitting sexy in rows, I imagined how good it would be. Then I remembered every time they walked toward the door, and I handed them money, and how it ruined something inside me. I didn't understand how to explain it without sounding like a sap until I saw Monteblan, drifting and glassy eyed. He had picked up a dinner plate and was holding it like a steering wheel. I gently reached out and took it from him, laying it softly on the table between us and looked back at Reggie.

"It's like there's this beach," I told him. "Best beach in the world. You think about it all the time. Dream of going there. But you should never go to that beach. It just has to be there. To let you dream about it. Because if you tried to go, the whole thing would turn on you. Tear you to pieces. It's not a place to be. Just to believe in. That's all."

Reggie lowered his chin, looking at me long and deep.

"Shit Asser, you really do think too much. Charlie and you, I can see how you got along a minute."

The Chicken fluffed on the table. Reggie turned to Monteblan, who had picked up the plate again, holding it like a steering wheel.

"Grimace, I'ma get out up here at this next exit a minute, you mind pulling over?"

Monteblan nodded, rotating the plate. "Right on."

Reggie turned back to me. "Make sure he don't drive this damn soapy off the road while I'm getting some, will you?"

"Sure."

"*Ya kit mak*, Asser." Plucking up the whiskey bottle, he walked towards the girls and called out over his shoulder. "Watch my bird."

"*Ya kit mak*," I repeated.

Then my eyes turned to the bird, and I spoke much softer.

"But it's not your bird."

**Night fell.** Reggie returned. Wrapping the bird in body armor, we settled our whiskey bill and left the brothel. Three motorcycle taxis were idling in the darkness, taking the remainder of our winnings from The Splits for passage. Reggie rode point, head low, scanning the streets, one hand brandishing his pistol. I came second with the Chicken, wincing at every wing twitch, peck and kick. It's squawks and trapped flapping were especially frantic past flaming barricades. None of which, I hoped, would ignite Monteblan's dynamite. Riding behind us, my friend had insisted on holding a stick and sitting backwards, dedicated to foiling hostile pursuit. But we rode alone. None dared brave the blazing darkness, which only motorcyclists might manage. Ours were masters. Shifting past burning busses, tilting under spark spilling wires, they braved dismemberment, detainment and death to bring the Chicken home.

With Bangkok burning, our route was obscure. Slowing at empty intersections, the Thai drivers pulled parallel, debating different roads with urgent argument. Brother to the brothel owner's cousin, our lead driver had been personally summoned by our maître d' for the perilous mission. Protected with cheap Chinese helmets, shifting gears in flip flops, the darkly tan, weather beaten man employed shadows, smoke, and back alley detours to escape detection. Through fire choked avenues, down winding neighborhood roads, past shanty shacks and over dingy klong bridges, he led our mission to protect the bird. Holding back to dodge military patrols, jumping forward to outpace police trucks, we swerved wide to avoid rebel encampments where Thai militants shouted PA propaganda. Maneuvers were deft, our fleeting journey largely unseen. Only occasional neighborhood eyes flashed in recognition. Seeing our drivers debate directions near a dilapidated bridge, watching us wait in hiding near a temple, startled Thai citizens would run rushing to share the news: *Chicken 65!*

The bird hitting town was hot dope, even amidst the flames of *coup*. Bangkok was familiar with revolution. Tanks had rolled through town before, they would roll through town again. Hopeful handfuls fought while fatalistic masses let it pass like particularly damaging rain. For them, our race was welcome distraction. And with street business stalled, Chicken was the only money moving. Like every year, motor- cycle taxi drivers, cabbies, street vendors, river workers, bus drivers, bar owners, food cart hustlers, minor politicians, major criminals, and a large percentage of working girls all had coin on the bird. But with the explosion of political upheaval, betting took unprecedented turns. Odds had been split, doubled, and otherwise rocked. Anxiety from the riots was displaced into wild wagers. Brand new betting pools formed with absurdly lucrative potential: whether the Chicken would leave Vietnam, if the bird would breach Bangkok's military barriers, Miami arrival time over/unders, and whether Chicken 65 would even sur- vive. Fortunes were founded. Families were ruined. Savvy action split through rapidly developing streams. All fought to find the latest news. Nothing stopped the gambling. Tanks shot shells, rebels fell, and entire neighborhoods were evacuated. Chicken 65 remained.

Despite the military internet shut down and cell phone tower blocking, bookies deployed children throughout the city, collecting desperate bets as rumors blazed through the burning city. Political divisions on either side of these flames were transcended by the fran- tic trade. Rioters dispatched bookie runs between Molotov cocktails.

Army patrols swept for the bird, employing whatever means might favor their commanding officer's odds. This flurry of variables made reports of our passage vital and valuable news. Whoever managed to see the three of us—pistol, chicken, and dynamite—fly through the petrol streaked streets was privy to profitable information. Eluding them entirely was impossible, and a small, ever changing group had formed a persistent, shifting shadow in our final miles. Tapped into telegraphed understanding of our potential route, their faces popped up out of windows, peeked around corners, or gathered by shacks we flew past. Children mostly, with some old men amidst them, the gallery braved death or arrest, murmuring and whispering while shifting on their feet and watching. Huddling together now, whispering to one another, they watched us on the deserted, secluded street corner where our motorcycles had stopped. Reggie was annoyed, slipping off his bike and waving them away angrily. None moved. Raising his arm he fired a shot into the night sky. The blast made them scatter. I watched a young boy of nine fly away in flip flops, running scared around the corner.

"Was that really necessary?" I asked.

Reggie didn't reply. Turning to his driver, the two conferred in Thai. The back and forth between the men included pointing up and down the road, looking back the way we came, and ended with the driver's smiling, head shaking 'no.' Thoughtfully nodding, Reggie patted the man warmly on the back and walked towards me.

"Far as we go," Reggie said.

Clutching the clucking chicken, I swung my leg up over the bike. "This is Phetchaburi Road?"

I stared down at the abandoned avenue we overlooked. Pools of light illuminated the dark cement, and there were gloomy, foreboding shadows on either side. A soot stained pedestrian overpass spanned the divide. The city dipped into unseen territory beyond. Sporadic, far away machine gun fire drifted towards us through the hot, silent night.

Flashes of light bloomed deadly. Face grim, Reggie raised his pistol pointing towards the chaos.

"*That's* Phetchaburi Road."

My driver revved his engine, turning the bike around and stopping beside me. Pointing to the Chicken, he smiled.

"Prasert Wirat. Good."

"Yes!" My face lit up in surprise. "The Chicken Whisper!"

"Prasert Wirat good," He said again, giving me a thumbs up. "*Chok dee.*"

Turning the throttle, he jumped ahead to join the others. The three bikes melted into the night, engines fading, leaving us alone on the deserted city avenue.

"Why did he tell me Chuck D?" I asked Reggie. "Is Public Enemy big out here like Serpico?"

"*Chok Dee,*" Reggie corrected. "It means good luck. We need it."

Monteblan floated over holding dynamite. Somewhere in our journey through Bangkok, his hands had been stained with ash and grease. Accidentally or on purpose, streaks of the stuff had found its way to his face. The night cammo did little to offset his bright white underwear, but completed his battle ready appearance with a surreal flourish. Helmet wedged low, gazing out at distant fires and popping gunfire, he uttered cryptic words.

"The Forces fight for us." Turning to me slowly, he stared. "The Forces fight through us."

Chills ran through my body as I remembered those ancient stone faces from Laos. With flames raging all round, their possession of the city wasn't hard to imagine. What else explained such a colossal explosion of fury? Reggie walked close, looking at us both and frowned.

"The fuck is fat boy talking about?"

"Could we stop with the fat boy?!" I spun to Reggie with anxious anger. "First off, he's not a boy. He's a man."

"A man." Reggie smirked. "Standing there in his goddamn drawers,"

"Didn't hear you complaining about his underpants when he drove through a riot, saving your life *and* Chicken 65."

"Whatever." Reggie said, moving away. "Motherfucker like that shouldn't be walking around with dynamite. Shouldn't be walking around out here at all. Both you hardly even Chicken."

I watched him walk towards a distant telephone pole and seethed. Charlie might not have had a problem playing along with Reggie's Alpha game, but the Marine's endless commands and criticisms were wearing on me. I just wanted to get to The Miami. I just wanted to finish Chicken 65. I wanted to win. It wasn't his Chicken. The Bird decided. Reggie should know. I watched him now, studying a red piece of paper taped to the pole. Next predictable step was him shouting and pointing us across the highway.

I decided to cheat him of the chance to order us around. Pulling Monteblan towards the steps of crumbling stone, I started up them towards the pedestrian overpass. Reggie didn't notice. We went higher up the cracked, cement stairs, past a tangle of dangling wires. Climbing higher, pushing Monteblan ahead, my mind jumped back to Gears. The Israeli had taught a cruel but crucial lesson on that deadly road in The Splits.

Chicken 65 was a race. Races were about winning. That meant other people lost. Why should that be me? Why walk around letting Reggie tell me it was 'his Bird'? I looked down at the Chicken now, happily bobbing in its body armor basket. Right now, the bird was with *me*. Over the bridge and through the riot was The Miami. Events positioning me here had been impossible to author. Something had brought me this far. Wouldn't It bring me farther? Yes, I was sure of it. The Forces would steer us home. This was my Chicken Rubicon. Crossing it, the bird was mine. Sweating in the heat, heart beating fast, I hustled Monteblan ahead. Just when I reached the top step behind him, the first bullet slapped into stone, pinging with a wicked ring.

*Fzzzzzttt!*

I froze. Monteblan didn't. Lurched forward, running, tripping, he raced across the overpass as bullet after bullet kicked up dust all around. Hissing through the night they chased my friend as somewhere far away, I heard Reggie screaming.

*"Down! Down! Down!"*

I frowned, confused. If Reggie was shooting, why was he telling us to get down? Clutching the Chicken tightly, shock had me rooted. Bullets sang. The world blurred. Then magically fast the Marine was there, thick arm around my neck, yanking me down roughly and pulling me ferociously from the overpass. Down the stone stairs, bullets popping the night, he dragged me banging and bouncing into bushes by the landing. Pushing me out roughly, throwing me up against an empty building, Reggie roared.

"The *fuck* you do that for!"

"Why did you shoot at us?!" I screamed back.

"That wasn't me!" He shook a red piece of paper in my face. "Thai Military! You just got your boy killed!"

I groaned "No..."

Legs weak, head swirling, I stared out across the now silent avenue and shouted.

"Monteblan!"

Silence. Crickets from distant bushes purred.

"MONTEBLAN!!!" I bellowed.

Rushing towards the bridge I felt Reggie yank me back. Frantic, spinning off balance, I yelled.

"We have to get him!"

Reggie just shoved that red piece of paper in my face again. Thai letters blurred before my eyes.

"Thai military notice!" Reggie hissed. "Free fire zone! That whole road is lined with shooters. You cross, you die! Damn fliers are up to warn people!"

"How the hell was I supposed to know?"

"You *weren't!* That's why we stay close! Now you just got your boy killed!"

I dropped the Chicken to the ground. It squawked in confusion, frightened now, cawing and trying to flap folded wings bound by the flak jacket basket.

"We don't know he's dead," I heard myself say, words choking in my throat. "We have to get him. We go around. We circle back."

"There is no around," Reggie's voice was cold. "There is no back."

Sweat trickled down his face. Reggie flicked up his gun hand, wiping it away.

"The embassy," I uttered. "Police...?"

"US Embassy evacuated this morning. Police shoot you on sight for breaking curfew. This whole city will flip any minute."

"What...?" I held my head, world spinning. "Like it's not flipping now? Things are on fire, people are...shot. They're getting shot, Monteblan. Oh, no. I have to I have to—"

My words were throttled out of me as Reggie reached hard with both hands. Grabbing my lapels, yanking me close, I smelled sweat and cheap cologne from the brothel.

"*Listen to me!* That road there is how shit starts! Split the city, lock it down. If they dividing tonight, they're rolling tomorrow. Thai Military! Elite forces! Fuck if they care about some foreigners caught between tanks. We don't get this bird home tonight—*right now—*Chicken 65 is finished!"

"My friend might be dead!"

"My friend *is* dead!" Reggie yelled back at me. "Charlie gone and the Chicken done too? NO! This Bird saved my damn life! It does not shut down. We finish! I'd take anybody else in the whole damn world but it's you! And I need backup! Grimace is *gone.* Cross that bridge to find him, you're dead! Follow me, I'll get you out of here. Do you copy?"

I felt my stomach clench and thought I might vomit. Reggie shook me sharply, yelling now.

"DO YOU COPY?!"

Finally I nodded and he pushed me down to the ground. For a long, hard moment, the Marine glared at me.

"I was wrong about you hardly being Chicken." The large man turned away in disgust. "You ain't Chicken at all."

Reaching down, he scooped up the tape bound flak jacket. The bird popped up from the vest, staring at me with unforgiving eyes as Reggie carried it away. I saw flashing lights. I thought my brain was breaking. I squinted, watching the flash happen again. It wasn't my brain. It was a taxi parked nearby. The Thai boy who had been chased off earlier was beside it. While headlights flashed once more in signal, he waved excitedly. His faint young voice, urgent and eager, floated through the simmering night.

*"Chicken 65!"*

**I don't remember walking to the cab but I remember riding in the back.** Slumped down low I watched unknown turns and curves. Bangkok streets, spirit houses, shacks. I shivered cold while sweating. Reggie crouched beside me, speaking Thai to the driver. Incomprehensible words, dancing in tone. The bird beside me silently stared. I looked into its oval black eyes seeing nothing. I thought of my friend's eyes. I shut my own. The taxi stopped somewhere.

Water then. Reeking, grease streaked klong with shacks on the banks filled with faces. Hushed Thai voices. Money on the bird, all of them. I let go and let myself be handled like baggage. Pulled and pushed into place, clutching the bird, dropped down into a dilapidated boat. Covered in tarps. Choked by smells of grease and gasoline. The driver was barefoot, standing in filthy hull water that tilted when he kicked into gear. I didn't see Reggie. But I saw his gun. Clutched in hand, held low, his finger was extended down the barrel. The driver was telling him things and Reggie was responding repeatedly, absently, using the Thai word for 'OK'.

"*Dai... Dai... Dai,*" he said.

Die, Die, Die, I heard.

Death. That's where the Chicken was taking me. Like some final stinking, stygian journey, we were crossing over. Filthy water sloshed and splashed. Distant shots weren't distant anymore. Puttering upstream the rifles cracked sharper. Scattered shots became blasting tapestry. The boat driver didn't stop. Battle's babble grew louder. Explosions thundered. Tense and curled, I hugged the bird tightly. The Chicken was silent, strangely knowing what I was realizing too late. Chasing it blindly, stupidly, thinking it some liberating force, I had never asked where the flapping, feathered thing would lead.

Freedom. That's what I wanted. Sitting spellbound back home, powering faceless machines, I had dreamed of it. Collecting checks for sneakers ads I sold it. Airbrushed and positioned, freedom was fun. Tasted and experience, it was furious. Freedom didn't ring. It raged. Bangkok was burning with the stuff. Charlie had died from it. Monteblan lost to it. Now freedom was forcing me into war. Freedom didn't protect. Freedom didn't care. Freedom set life on fire and fools into the flames. Burning through them, it turned towards others who reached for freedom blindly. People like me. People who died. More were waiting. Everyone wanted to be free. Nobody would if they were.

The boat stopped, bobbing. Tarps tore back and the world exploded in cheers. Bewildered I stared up at Thai faces exultant, yelling, screaming wild.

*"Chicken 65! Chicken 65!"*

The chant rocked through rocket blasts. Raged over flames. *Chicken 65* roared in my ears as revolutionaries hauled me up like a puppet. Reggie yelled furiously then disappeared. Bodies pressed in on me. Thai eyes wild, some laughing, some raging, all pushing and pulling while the Chicken screamed. Then cracking gun shots thundered. Crowds melted away like receding waves. Reggie was there, eyes blazing, hand steady, nine millimeter sweeping.

Shouting in Thai he pressed them back. Cheers died down. Reggie pulled me towards him, gun held forward. Uneasy crowds, most of them armed, parted reluctantly.

"That's right motherfuckers," Reggie nodded. "Chicken 65 and all your family got money on this bird. Let us through. Let them get paid."

People parted and we moved further into the city. Storefronts were smashed. Flipped cars burned. Flames danced in Thai eyes, watching as we passed. Reggie didn't lower his gun. Rounding a corner he muttered.

"Show 'em the bird. Hold it high."

Following orders, I thrust the bird up overhead. Roars of approval rose from distant streets. Gun fire was falling off as more Thai fighters closed in on the Chicken. Some excited. Others exhausted. Streaked with blood, ash and grease, many were visibly injured. But all struggled to follow the bird. I pulled it tight while Thais pushed us along, pressing from all sides. Reggie swept his piece in even arcs, speaking calmly.

"Chicken 65. Chicken 65."

"Chicken 65," they answered all around. Gunfire had ceased now. Aside from flickering fires, the night was hushed. Voices volleyed all around; call and response through dark, flame licked streets. Listening to them, Reggie grinned.

"Got to love the Thais. Bunch a gambling motherfuckers. They giving us a cease fire till Phetchaburi Road. Too much money on the table. Even the military is standing down. Look."

Just ahead, army soldiers were grouped around an idling tank. The top popped up and a soldier appeared smiling, giving us a thumbs up.

"Chicken 65."

Bird, Marine and I moved forward through strange, uneasy peace. Narrow streets opened up into an empty intersection. Piled tires flamed. An avenue was just beyond. Large and lined with street lights, the debris of burning vehicles cluttered the road. Cement barriers lined the edges. Thais pressed in on them like an audience facing the road. Soldiers on one side, revolutionaries the other. Reaching the tangled asphalt between them, Reggie stopped and I finally realized where we were.

"Phetchaburi Road," I said in wonder, gazing at the glass strewn boulevard.

"Yup." Reggie nodded. "Anything goes."

Once more, I didn't see it. One moment I was standing beside the Marine. The next I was sitting on the cement, jaw blazing. The world blurred. Shaking my head sharply, I blinked for focus. Pain spread in pulsing waves through my head. Slowly, senses returned. The Chicken was gone. Leaning over the barriers, Thais jeered shouting, urging me up like boxing fans. Reggie had walked away with the bird. Past smoking, burned out vehicles, he headed towards a blinking neon sign. Pink letters wavered through riot smoke.

The Miami.

Staggering towards it, I shouted out.

"Hey! Wait!"

Reggie didn't bother turning around. He didn't run, either. Moving in calm, measured strides, the Marine moved forward with the Chicken. I walked after him. Then ran. Smoke from burning cars choked my lungs as Thais yelled at me. My eyes watered. My head pounded. Reaching Reggie, I grabbed his shoulder. Without breaking stride he pinned my hand and twisted. Hot, savage pain shot through my joints. Red haze clouded my vision. I let go screaming. Reggie didn't look. Reggie didn't stop. Reggie was winning Chicken 65. Reggie always did. Reggie was everyone. Everywhere. The whole world and every race in it. It didn't matter how fast I ran. How long I ran. Reggies hit first. Reggies hit hard. Reggies walked away with the bird. When would I learn? *Why* wouldn't I learn? Looking after him, I hated. Then something clattered down before me on the road.

The gun was mean and ugly looking. Silver with chipped handle, it glinted wickedly in the street light. A low, quiet voice murmured by the barrier. I looked and saw a Thai military officer. Face impassive, his hand flicked towards Reggie. Then melting into soldiers he disappeared. I blinked thinking I had hallucinated him. I hadn't. The gun was there, shining with dull menace. Grabbing it I stood, arm raised high, shooting straight up in the air.

*Bam!*

The single shot cracked like lighting. Up ahead, Reggie stopped. He turned around. Thais murmured on either side of Phetchaburi Road. The tone was dark and ugly. A chorus of clicks flickered through the night. I recognized the sound. Safety triggers slid off guns.

"The fuck you doing, Asser?" Flames flickered from a burning tire beside the Marine. "You know this whole place on a hair trigger, right?"

I didn't answer, just lowered the gun with trembling hands. Reggie seemed not to notice the weapon pointed directly at him. Bird in hand, he walked towards me through shattered glass and smoking cars.

"Won't take much to set shit off, Asser. Put down the gun."

"It's not your bird," I said.

He didn't answer. Just stopped right in front of me. Looking calm, inches from the pistol, the big man's voice was relaxed.

"What now, Asser?"

Thais watched from both sides. Sweat ran down my back. The bird popped its head from the flak jacket basket, staring at me. Fires flickered quietly all around.

"Anything." Sweating and shaking, I felt exhausted. "My friend is dead. I don't know where to go. This race is finished. I don't have anything so anything goes."

"Hey, man. I understand." Inching closer, his voice sounded almost kind. "Shit's wild this part of the world. People come out here and lose the plot. Happens all the time. Happened to you. No problem. Just put the gun down. Come on."

Murmurs from the barriers were now sharp discussions. Thai voices rose, calling out all around. Rival sides shouted across the road. Their foreign words confused me. Smoke choked my nose, blurring my eyes. Reggie laughed, relaxed and calm.

"Know what these motherfuckers yelling about, Asser?"

Shaking my head, I wiped sweat from my eyes, holding the trembling pistol.

"Trying to hold off the revolution and get another bet in."

"About which one of us wins?"

"Which one of us dies." Reggie smiled. "What you think? Where's the smart money go?"

He did it so fast I didn't see. But I had watched it before in Vietnam. Low and liquid fast, Reggie had flipped that backyard soldier in a blink. Now it was my turn. I hardly felt a thing until I felt myself slamming into cement. Then the Marine was over me, holding my pistol, pointing it at my face.

"Go home, Asser." He whispered with fierce, quiet words. "And don't you ever come back. Because you ain't Chicken. Not at all."

Rising up, Reggie spit to the cement.

From nowhere, Monteblan screamed.

Bounding the barrier, my friend rushed Reggie with a bellowing roar. Eyes flashed. Underpants gleamed. The thermos twirled like bolos above him. Reggie recoiled in reflex shock. The Chicken fell from his hands. Startled shots jumped from the cheap, ugly pistol.

*Bam! Bam! Bam!*

Hideki whirling, Monteblan never lost stride. Thoroughly gorgeous, flourishing swings of the thermos met three bullets in blinding response. I still see it in dreams: High left, low right, then a fanning, blurring arc passing just before his face, freezing time. Shots pinged harmlessly off the indestructible thermos while Reggie stood shocked. My friend stepped in spinning. Fully empowered by NASA approved interlock cord, the Hideki 3000 connected with resonant gong. The Marine dropped cold. Flowing with the motion of his circling thermos, Monteblan spun away like ballet, pirouetting absurdly in his underpants.

Then Phetchaburi Road exploded.

Like some surreal avatar sent to reignite chaos, my friend plunged us into war. Thais rushed the barriers, shooting across the road. Gunfire ripped the night. Ducking we scattered. Shots puffed up dust, pinged burning taxis and blurred the air. Cringing behind a bullet riddled bus stop, I pressed myself flat in roadside gravel. Reggie, dazed but conscious, found cover behind a half blasted taxi. Gun raised blindly over a smoking metal door, he fired off shots while shouting in rage. Monteblan was screaming. Across the road, I watched him slash at gravel frantically, trying to dig in. All around us gunfire thundered. Just ahead, The Miami glowed. Then fluttering white motion caught my eye in the road. Trapped within an overturned noodle cart, flapping wild, the Chicken danced in panic. Bracing to run for it, I heard Reggie scream at me through the melee.

"Hold position Asser! Hold!"

"No!" Lost to reason, I yelled at back at him. "I want to win! I'm Chicken!"

"That won't make you Chicken!" Reggie shouted through gunfire. "It'll make you *dead!* It's done! Chicken 65 is over! We are pulling out! Stay low! On my mark, right there!"

Jabbing his finger just up the road, I saw him point out a cement staircase leading down to the metro.

"What about Monteblan?!" I yelled.

He looked at me squinting, not understanding.

"Grimace!" I shouted. "Fat boy!"

Reggie jabbed his finger again, across from us. Another train entrance sank into the ground on Monteblan's side of the road. Flagging my friend, shouting wildly, I pointed it out. Understanding dawned on his face as Reggie joined in, mimicking a running motion with his arms. Monteblan nodded. The Marine shouted.

"Move!"

Springing from cover, he ran low up the road. Breathing fast, bracing myself, I was just ready to join him when I heard Charlie.

*"What about The Bird, son?"*

I turned and he was floating there, bright and smiling.

"Charlie?"

He looked different; not younger but restored. His face was fine. Handsome. Bullets passed right through him.

*"Can't leave The Bird. No sir."*

Confused, I squinted in the dark night. Halos of street light mixed with flickering gasoline flames. I blinked but Mississippi Charlie didn't leave. Floating just inches above Phetchaburi Road, he smiled in his bright Hawaiian shirt.

*"Bring the bird home. Come on now, I'm with you."*

He held out his hand to me.

"ASSER! PULL OUT! NOW!"

Confused, I turned away and looked up the chaotic road. Reggie was hunkered low in the metro stairway, screaming through the gunfire. Monteblan hunched in the entrance across from him, frantically waving.

*"Remember who decides,"* Charlie said softly.

I turned towards him.

*"The Bird."* He smiled. *"The Bird decides."*

I stood up. Things whisked past me and I felt them close, hissing like wicked insects. Ignoring them, I went for the bird.

"Asser! No!"

Reggie's voice was far away. I walked calmly towards the Chicken. Fires burned. Smoke billowed from scorched tires. Bullets screamed. Mississippi Charlie walked right beside me, holding my hand.

"How is it Charlie? I mean, where you are now. What's next?"

*"Oh, you won't believe what's waiting."* He laughed. *"Not like here much at all."*

I blinked in the smoke, taking measured steps towards the bird.

Gunfire sounded far away. I was frightened.

"I don't really like it here, Charlie. I'm lost."

*"Just stay close to The Bird, son."* He patted me on my back. *"Don't let it get away from you. That's the way through. We'll all be waiting for you. Go on now. See there?"*

The Chicken had jumped up out of the noodle car, right into my arms. I looked around me. Charlie was gone and the war had stopped. Thais with lowered weapons stared at me, dumbfounded. Flames flickered, softly crackling. The bird flapped happily. Chicken in arm, I walked towards The Miami.

All was silent. Past overturned vehicles and bullet casings, through smoke and shattered glass, I made my way with the Chicken. Reggie and Monteblan emerged from the metro steps. Both watched me pass, mouths open, struck dumb. Thais on either side stared. Up ahead was the neon sign. The General was waiting in the doorway. Hands on hips, pressed and sharp, it looked like he had ironed his socks. Reaching him I grinned, raising the bird.

"We brought Chicken."

His stern face broke into a smile. Then it stopped, falling to a frown. I didn't understand. Then I did.

"Good show!" The bright British voice piped up just behind. "Exceptional Chicken!"

The bird hissed, squirming in my arms. I looked behind me and saw Ladyboy Man.

The tailored suit was pressed and flawless. Bangkok blazed behind him, a landscape of overturned vehicles set through scattered fires. Somewhere in the carnage, Ladyboy Man had found a fresh boutonniere. He twirled it now.

"A Chicken Promise is a Chicken Promise." The Brit smiled. "Even on Phetchaburi Road."

Laos shot through my mind. Prison and briefcases, money and promises. Ladyboy Man extended a manicured hand.

"The bird."

Unbelieving, I blinked soot encrusted eyes. My dapper rival didn't disappear like Charlie had. For a moment I hesitated. The city was silent. All eyes watched. I stared down Phetchaburi Road. Thought of all the roads I had travelled to find it. All I had been through on them. Then I looked down at the bird. It looked up at me. Ladyboy Man cleared his throat.

"A Chicken Promise…"

"Is a Chicken Promise," I finished.

Letting go, I handed him the bird.

"Good show. *Oh!*"

The Brit winced in pain as the Chicken pecked his hand sharply. Rage flashed through blue eyes. Then smiling, Ladyboy Man recovered his panache. Nodding regards, struggling with a kicking Chicken, my rival walked smartly into The Miami. The General let him pass with a sigh. Shaking his head, he slowly closed the door.

Chicken 65 was finished.

**I turned to face Bangkok**. Phetchaburi Road was still. Smoke drifted from flickering fires. Across the barriers, warring Thais watched each other warily. Then tiredly, nodding their heads at some unspoken understanding, all just walked away. Weapons low, revolutionaries and military drifted away in different directions, dissolving into darkness. A flash of white glinted in their midst. Recognizing familiar underwear, I ran to the edge of the road.

"Hey! Where are you going?!" I shouted over the barriers. "What are you going to do?"

Monteblan stopped and faced me.

"Drive," he said.

Smoke blew up in shrouding swirls. When it passed, my friend was gone.

A hand clamped down on my shoulder. Reggie was there. The Marine squeezed tightly for a long moment, looking me in the eyes. Then he let go. We shook hands without a word. Then Reggie left. I watched him walk through the lamplights lining Phetchaburi Road.

"That was good Chicken, right?" I yelled when he was almost gone. "I'm Chicken now!"

"No Asser." Reggie didn't stop walking. "You ain't Chicken."

My heart fell. I blinked in the smoke. Reggie's footsteps echoed on the deserted, debris strewn road. Reaching the last light, he stopped and turned. Saluting with a smile, the Marine called out through darkness.

"You're Chicken 65."

**Leaving wasn't a choice.** More like directions I followed. The Bird decided. Through drifting smoke on Bangkok streets, I wandered home. Thais materialized amidst flames, picking me up without asking. "Asser", they whispered. "Chicken 65." Motorcycles and taxis passed me off, hands of karma, finding my condo, leaving me safe. The lobby was dark and the elevator was out. The job was waiting in my email. Brand inanity drafting an army of design drones, relocation included. I laughed when I read it. Then cried. Shuddering in the shower, tears ran streaming through steam. Didn't know why. When it finished I slept. Drifting dreamless, Thai TV chattering, nights and days a wave. Then one morning I shaved. Took the job and booked my plane.

Flying without baggage I boarded alone. The airport was strangely deserted. My flight practically empty. From the window of our rising plane, Bangkok sprawled, blackened by flames. But the higher we went, the more city I saw. Most was whole. The greater part was fine. Slow turns put the sun behind us. Rising higher, Thailand vanished. For a long time I looked out into clouds. I didn't know what to think. Then I remembered not to.

Portland hadn't changed. It rained. The industry was the same. All the wrong people made all the right moves. But sociopaths in rectangle glasses didn't trouble me anymore. Between meetings I looked more closely at them. Trapped in strategy, slick and friendless, they drove similar cars to semi-identical homes. The bird they chased had rules. It was all theirs. My bird had shown me things. Flaming anarchy put office politics in perspective. I didn't show up looking for meaning anymore. Just shut up and worked. Since I didn't give a damn, more jobs were thrown my way. Funny how that happens. Business has never been better. Monteblan was right.

I miss my friend. He vanished into those mists he had emerged from. I don't know when he'll return. But I'm used to that. One day a large man with a beard will appear, ready to party. That's Monteblan. My friend. He drives. He fought that or forgot it, but The Bird had something to show him. Some people are born for things. They're different. Riding with them changes you. My friend showed me places only seen when the world blurs past fast. We learned things only grasped at high speeds. I wonder what road he's on now. I think about him on weekends when I drive.

Found the Bertone in Arizona. Slim little coupe with a pop off roof. First car I ever owned. Flew down, paid cash and drove it home. There were tools in the trunk and I taught myself to tune the engine. Wired up the eight track myself. I'm still looking for that old song; the one about the moon we heard at dawn in Vietnam. On weekends I go to yard sales, digging through bins, searching for that smiling lizard guy in his V neck sweater. Probably I'd find it in two seconds on the internet. I'd rather drive around. It'll turn up one day. Or it won't. I don't think too much about it, either way.

*Ya kit mak.*

They say that at my Thai place. Not the bright, crowded downtown restaurant packed full of designers. My little spot is full on Isaan. Warm and worn down, the only place in Portland with Sangsom whiskey. They smile when I arrive and talk in Thai. While rain taps windows I listen to their patter amidst the clatter of dishes. Strange, sing song tones flash meaning in pieces: *khao jai krap. Dai, dai dai. Chok dee...*

Noises like code that trigger memories in droves. With passing gray days these fade. Part of me fights that while the rest sighs in relief.

Chicken had me bad.

But Chicken 65 was good to me. Etched things in my soul then let me walk away without a scratch. The Bird knew what I wanted then fooled me into getting what I needed. Chasing it I was wild amidst brothers and villains. Took turns too fast and lost the maps. Blew things up. There were times I trusted what was wrong and misjudged who was right. I touched strange things. Hit walls and felt the weight of chains. Fought through flames. Then for a moment I had it. But I was given a choice. The Bird showed me what winning takes and losing gives. So I let go. I wonder sometimes if that was right. The wrong ones all hold on. The race remains in their hands. This troubles me.

Mississippi Charlie wouldn't mind. He told me the damn fool thing is done before we start. Winning tricks people. Blinds them to what The Bird tries to show along the way. I understand that now. And I know what his Bible was all about. Not the history of the thing, but the mystery of it all. What happened out there can't be explained. Chicken 65 changed me. This was done against my will and I will never be the same. Living through such things is miraculous but who would listen? Around here people try to get their head around situations. Out there it's different. Like Reggie explained, into your heart is understand. That's tough for people to do. Forces are at work. Harder in some places, heavier on some people. Not much gets through. I don't like it. Not at all. Some nights are bad.

That's when I drive. Punch the Bertone and really open up. Passing traffic, we dash into hills. Travelling fast, my car feels happy, just like Pablo Cruise used to. Pressing through gears I try to remember how Monteblan moved. Then I get it. Hitting fifth the world melts. That abandoned airstrip in the jungle returns. Flying with my friend, I am recklessly, essentially alive. Shocked with power, laughing mad, existence blurs in brilliant, shining speed. Life is fast and I am free.

The guy who flew to Thailand wanted a world of that. The man who returned just needs a moment. Touching the clutch, I let it go. Shifting down, my car sighs regretfully. Roaring wind fades to pleasant breeze. Gears give in reluctantly. Freedom becomes peace. Moving reasonably, I wind through roads where fir trees tower and darkness shines with distant, silent stars. Drifting in memory, watching the signs, I press forward towards some place where that song will be.

## ABOUT THE AUTHOR

**Hugh O'Neil Gallagher** is both a U.S. and Irish citizen, and graduate of New York University. He is the author of the world famous *College Application Essay* and the novel *Teeth*. Hugh has written for *Rolling Stone, Wired, Newsweek*, and the Beastie Boy's *Grand Royal* magazine. His *Rolling Stone* feature "Seven Days and Seven Nights with MTV" was included in Douglas Rushkoff's *Gen X Reader*. Hugh is the creator of the 90's cult comedy hit *Hugh Brown Shu*, and artistic director for *Von Von Von*. He wrote the script for Daft Punk's video *Da Funk* with Spike Jonze, and the sequel *Fresh*. As a brand writer for Adidas, Microsoft, Nike, and Asian tech startups, Hugh has lived and worked in the U.S., Europe, and Asia. *Chicken 65* was inspired by five years living and travelling through Southeast Asia.

www.hughmuch.com
www.chicken65book.com

Made in the USA
Las Vegas, NV
10 February 2021